WHAT NEVER HAPPENS

ANNE
HOLT

GRAND CENTRAL
PUBLISHING

NEW YORK   BOSTON

Copyright © 2004 by Anne Holt
English translation copyright © 2008 by Kari Dickson
Originally published in Norwegian in 2004 as *Det som aldri skjer.*

Grand Central Publishing
Hachette Book Group USA
237 Park Avenue
New York, NY 10017

Visit our Web site at www.HachetteBookGroupUSA.com.

Printed in the United States of America

First American Edition: February 2008
10 9 8 7 6 5 4 3 2 1

Grand Central Publishing is a division of Hachette Book Group USA, Inc.
The Grand Central Publishing name and logo is a trademark of Hachette Book Group USA, Inc.

Library of Congress Cataloging-in-Publication Data

Holt, Anne
    [Det som aldri skjer. English]
    What never happens / Anne Holt ; [translated by Kari Dickson].—1st ed.
      p. cm.
    ISBN-13: 978-0-446-57803-5
    ISBN-10: 0-446-57803-7
    I. Dickson, Kari. II. Title.
    PT8951.18.O386D3513 2008
    839.82'38—dc22

                                                                    2007018774

Book design by Charles Sutherland

"For people today, only one radical shock remains—and it is always the same: death."

—Walter Benjamin, *Central Park*

She no longer knew how many people she had killed. It didn't really matter anyway. Quality was more important than quantity in most professions. And that was true of her business too, although the pleasure she once gained from an innovative twist had dwindled over the years. More than once, she'd considered what else she might do. Life was full of opportunities for people like her, she thought to herself every now and then. Bullshit. She was too old; she felt tired. This was the only thing she could really do. And it was a lucrative business. Her hourly rate was sky-high now, naturally, but so it should be. It took a while to recover afterwards.

The only thing she really enjoyed was doing nothing. And where she was now, there was nothing to do. But she still wasn't happy.

Perhaps it was a good thing that the others hadn't come, after all. She wasn't sure.

The wine was certainly overrated. It was expensive and left a sour taste in her mouth.

ONE

_____ ⚜ _____

To the east of Oslo, where the hills flatten out down toward Lørenskog, a station town by the Nita River, cars had frozen solid overnight. People on foot pulled their hats down over their ears and wrapped their scarves tighter around their necks as they trudged the few punishing miles to the bus stop on the main road. The houses in the small cul-de-sac fended off the frost with drawn curtains and snowdrifts that blocked the driveways. Huge icicles hung from the eaves of an old wooden villa at the end of the road down by the woods, disasters in waiting.

The house was white.

Inside the front door with its leaded glass and molded brass handle, at the end of the unusually spacious hall to the left, in a study that was dominated by minimalist art and lavish furniture, sitting behind an imposing desk between boxes of unopened letters, was a dead woman. Her head had fallen back, and her hands rested on the arms of her chair. A trickle of dried blood ran from her lower lip, down her bared neck, split around her breasts, and then joined again on her impressively flat stomach.

Her nose was also bloody. In the light from the ceiling fixture, it looked like an arrow pointing to the dark hole that had once been a mouth. Only a stump remained of her tongue, which had obviously been carefully removed. The cut was clean and sharp.

It was warm in the room, almost too hot.

Detective Inspector Sigmund Berli from the Norwegian National Criminal Investigation Service, the NCIS, finally closed his cell phone and looked over at a digital thermometer just inside the southeast-facing panorama window. Outside, it was seventeen degrees.

"Amazing that the windows don't break," he said, carefully tapping the windowpanes. "Nearly fifty-five degrees difference between inside and outside. Incredible."

No one seemed to pay him any attention.

Under her silk robe with its golden collar, the dead woman was naked. The belt lay on the floor. A youngish policeman from the Romerike police took a step back when he saw the yellow coil.

"Shit," he gasped, then ran his fingers through his hair in embarrassment. "I thought it was a snake or something."

The woman's missing body part lay beautifully wrapped in paper on the blotter on the desk in front of her, only the tip protruding from the middle of all the red. A plump, exotic plant; pale flesh with even paler taste buds and purple red-wine stains in the folds and cracks. A half-empty glass of wine was balanced on a pile of papers near the edge of the desk. The bottle was nowhere to be seen.

The detective sergeant cleared his throat. "Can't we at least cover her breasts? It just seems cruel that she has to . . ."

"We'll have to wait," Sigmund Berli replied as he put his phone back into his breast pocket. "I'm going to keep trying."

He went down on one knee to get a closer look at the dead woman.

"Adam would be interested in this," he muttered. "So would his wife, for that matter."

"What?"

"Nothing. Do we know anything about the timing yet?"

Berli stifled a sneeze. The silence in the room made his ears ring. He got up and needlessly brushed dust from his pants with stiff movements. A uniformed policeman was standing by the door to the hall. He had his hands behind his back and was shifting his weight from one foot to the other as he stared out the window, away from the body. Some Christmas lights still hung in one of the spruce trees. Here and there, you could see the bulbs glowing dimly under the branches and tightly packed snow, where it was dark.

"Does nobody know anything here?" Berli barked in irritation. "Don't you even have an estimated time of death?"

"Yesterday evening," the other man eventually replied. "But it's too early—"

"To say," Sigmund Berli finished his sentence. "Yesterday evening. Pretty vague, in other words. Where's—"

"They're away every Tuesday. The family, that is. Husband and daughter, who's six. If that's what you . . ." The sergeant smiled uncertainly.

"Yes," Berli said and walked halfway around the desk.

"The tongue," he started and peered at the package on the desk. "Was it cut off while she was still alive?"

"Don't know," the sergeant answered. "I've got all the papers for you here. As we've finished examining everything and everyone's back at the station, you might—"

"Yes," Berli said, but the sergeant wasn't sure what he was agreeing with. "Who discovered the body if the family was away?"

"The housekeeper. A Filipino man who comes every Wednesday morning at six. He starts down here, he said, so he doesn't wake anyone too early, and then works his way up. The bedrooms are upstairs, on the second floor."

"Yes," Berli repeated with no interest. "Away every Tuesday?"

"That's what she said," the sergeant answered. "In all the interviews and such. She sends her husband and daughter out every Tuesday. Then she goes through all her letters herself. It's a matter of principle—"

"Right," mumbled Berli cynically as he stuck a pen into one of the boxes of letters. "I can believe that. It'd be impossible for one person to go through all of this."

He pointed at the dead woman again. "*Sic transit gloria mundi*," he said and peered into her mouth. "Her celebrity status isn't much good to her now."

"We've already gathered lots of clips and press cuttings, and everything is ready—"

"Yeah, yeah."

Berli waved him away. The silence was overwhelming. No people could be heard on the street, no clocks ticked, the computer was turned off. The red cyclops eye of a radio stared at him mutely from the glass cabinet by the door. There was a Canada goose on the mantelpiece, frozen in flight. Its feet were faded, and it had hardly any feathers left in its tail. The ice-cold daylight painted a colorless rectangle on the carpet under the south-facing window. Sigmund Berli could hear his blood pounding in his ears. The uncomfortable feeling of being in a mausoleum made him run his finger down his nose. He couldn't decide whether he was irritated or at a loss. The woman still sat in the chair with her legs open, bare breasts and a tongueless, gaping hole. It was as if the horrendous crime had robbed her not only of an important body part but also of her humanity.

"You guys always get pissed off if you're called in too late," the sergeant said eventually, "so we just left everything as it was, even though we're done with most things—"

"We will never be done," Berli said. "But thank you. Smart thinking. Especially with this lady. Does the press—"

"Not yet. We hauled in the Filipino, and we'll hold him for questioning for as long as we can. We've been as careful as possible outside. Securing the evidence is important though, especially in snow like this, so I'm sure the neighbors are wondering what's going on. But no one could have tipped off the press yet. And in any case, they're all too busy with the new princess right now."

A fleeting smile became serious.

"But then again, obviously . . . Fiona from *On the Move with Fiona* murdered. In her own home and in this way, well—"

"In this way," Berli nodded. "Strangled?"

"The doctor thinks so. No stab wounds, no bullets. Marks on her throat, you can see—"

"Mmmm. But take a look at this!"

Berli studied the tongue on the desk. The paper was elaborately folded, like a low vase with an opening for the tip of the tongue and elegant, symmetrical wings.

"Almost looks like a petal," the younger policeman said as he wrinkled his nose. "With something horrible in the middle. Quite—"

"Striking," Berli muttered. "Whoever did it must have made this beforehand. I can't imagine you'd kill someone like this and then take time to do some origami."

"I don't think there's any suspicion of sexual abuse."

"Origami," Sigmund Berli repeated. "The Japanese art of paper folding. But . . ."

"What?"

Berli bent down even closer to the severed organ. The ser-

geant did the same. The two policemen stood like this for a
while, forehead to forehead, breathing in time with each other.

"It's not just been cut off," Berli said finally and straightened his back. "The tongue has been split. Someone has split
the tip in two."

For the first time since Sigmund Berli arrived at the scene of
the crime, the uniformed policeman at the door turned toward
them. He looked like a teenager, with an open face and acne.
He ran his tongue over his lips again and again while his Adam's apple jumped up and down above his tight collar.

"Can I go now?" he whimpered. "Can I go?"

"Throneowning," the young girl said and smiled.

The half-dressed man drew the razor slowly down his throat
before rinsing it and turning around. The child was sitting on
the floor, pulling her hair through the holes in an old swimming cap.

"You can't go like that, honey," he said. "Come on, let's take
it off. We can find the hat you got for Christmas instead. You
want to look beautiful when you meet your sister for the first
time, don't you?"

"Throneowning," Kristiane repeated and pulled the swimming cap on even further. "Hairgrowing. Throne hair."

"Do you mean heir to the throne?" asked Adam Stubo, rinsing off what was left of the shaving cream on his face. "That's
someone who's going to be a king or queen in the future."

"My sister's going to be a queen," Kristiane replied. "You're
the biggest man in the world, really."

"You think so?"

He lifted the girl up and held her on his hip. Her eyes roamed
uncertainly, as if eye contact and touch at the same time would
be too much. She was nearly ten and small for her age.

"Heir to the throne," Kristiane said to the ceiling.

"That's right. We're not the only ones who had a little girl today. So did—"

"Princess Mette-Marit is so pretty," the child interrupted and clapped her hands. "She is on TV. We had cheese on toast for breakfast. Leonard's mommy said a princess had been born. My sister!"

"Yes," Adam said and put her down again before carefully trying to remove the swimming cap without pulling her hair too much. "Our baby is a beautiful princess. But she's not heir to the throne. What do you think we should name her?"

The cap came off eventually. Her long hair clung to the inside, but Kristiane didn't seem to feel any pain as he loosened the rubber from her head.

"Abendgebet," she said.

"That means evening prayers," he explained. "That's not her name. The girl in the picture above your bed, I mean. It's German for what the girl is doing . . ."

"Abendgebet," Kristiane said.

"Let's see what Mommy says," Adam said, as he pulled on his pants and shirt. "Go and find the rest of your clothes. We have to get a move on."

"Move on," Kristiane repeated and went out into the hall. "Hoof on. Cows and horses and small pussy cats. Jack! King of America! Do you want to visit the baby too?"

A big mutt with yellowy brown fur and a tongue hanging out of his smiling mouth came tearing out of the girl's bedroom. He whined eagerly and scampered in circles around the girl.

"Jack will have to stay at home," Adam told her. "Now, where's your hat?"

"Jack's coming with us," Kristiane said cheerfully and tied a red scarf around the dog's neck. "The heir to the throne is his sister too. Leonard's mommy says we've got equality in Norway, so girls can do what they want. And you're not my daddy. Isak's my daddy. So there."

"All very true," Adam laughed. "But I love you lots. And now we have to go. Jack has to stay at home. Dogs aren't allowed in hospitals."

"Hospitals are for sick people," Kristiane said as Adam helped her with her coat. "The baby's not sick. Mommy's not sick. But they're still in the hospital. Spot the pill."

"You're a little rationalist, you are."

He kissed her and pulled her hat down over her ears. Suddenly she looked him straight in the eye. He stiffened, as he always did in these rare moments of openness, unexpected glimpses into a mind that no one could fully grasp.

"An heir to the throne has been born," she quoted ceremoniously from the morning's announcements on TV before taking a breath and continuing, "A great event for the nation, but most of all, for the parents. And we are delighted that it is a lovely little princess this time."

A muffled ringing interrupted from the coat rack.

"Cell phone," she said mechanically. "Dam-di-rum-ram."

Adam Stubo stood up and frantically felt all the pockets in the chaos of jackets and coats until he finally found what he was looking for.

"Hello," he said resignedly. "Stubo here."

Kristiane calmly started to take off her outdoor clothes again. First the hat, then the coat.

"Hold on a minute," Adam said into the phone. "Kristiane! Don't . . . Wait a minute."

The girl had already taken off most of her clothes and was standing in her pink underpants and undershirt. She pulled her tights over her head.

"No way," Adam Stubo said. "I've got fourteen days' paternity leave. I've been awake for over twenty-four hours, Sigmund. Jesus, my daughter was born less than five hours ago, and now . . ."

Kristiane arranged the legs of her tights like two long braids down her front. "Pippi Longstocking," she said, pleased with herself. "Diddle, diddle, tra la la la la."

"No," Adam said so brusquely that Kristiane was startled and began to cry. "I've got time off. We've just had a baby. I . . ."

Her crying morphed into a long howl. Adam never got used to this tiny child's howling.

"Kristiane," he said in desperation. "I'm not angry with you. I was talking to . . . Hello? I can't. No matter how spectacular the whole thing is, I can't leave my family right now. Goodbye. And good luck." He snapped the phone shut and sat down on the floor. They should have been at the hospital a long time ago.

"Kristiane," he said again. "My little Pippi. Can you show me Mr. Nelson?"

He knew better than to hug her. Instead, he started whistling. Jack lay down on his lap and fell asleep. A damp patch grew on his pants under the dog's open, snoring mouth. Adam whistled and hummed and sang all the children's songs he could think of. The girl stopped crying after forty minutes. Without looking at him, Kristiane pulled the tights off her head and slowly started to get dressed.

"Time to visit the heir to the throne," she said flatly.

The cell phone had rung seven times.

He hesitated before turning it off without listening to the messages.

———————— ✻ ————————

A week had passed, and the police were obviously no further along. It didn't surprise her.

"Internet reports are useless," the woman with the laptop said to herself.

As she hadn't bothered to subscribe to a local server, she was charged extortionate fees to surf the net. She got stressed when she thought of all that money being eaten up while she waited for a connection on the slow, analog line to Norway. She could, of course, go to Chez Net. They charged five euros for fifteen minutes and had broadband. But unfortunately the place was full of drunk Australians and braying Brits, even now in winter. So she didn't bother, not now anyway.

There had been remarkably little fuss in the first days after the murder. The little princess had the full attention of the media circus. The world truly wanted to be deceived.

But then it started to get more coverage.

The woman with the laptop simply could not stand Fiona Helle. It was an unbearably politically correct response, but there wasn't much to be done about that. She read phrases like "loved by the people" in the papers. Which was fair enough, given that the program had been watched by well over a million viewers every Saturday, for five seasons in a row. She had only seen a couple of shows, just before she went away. But that was more than enough to realize that for once she agreed with the cultural snobs' usual, unbearably arrogant condemnation of popular entertainment. In fact, it was just one such vitriolic criticism in *Aftenposten*, written by a professor of sociology, that made her sit down in front of the television one Saturday evening and waste one and a half hours watching *On the Move with Fiona*.

But it hadn't been a total waste of time. It was ages since she had felt so provoked. The participants were either idiots or deeply unhappy. But they could hardly be blamed for being either. Fiona Helle, on the other hand, was successful, calculating, and far from true to her love of the common people. She waltzed into the studio dressed in creations that had been bought worlds away from H&M. She smiled shamelessly at the camera while the poor creatures revealed their pathetic dreams, false hopes, and not least extremely limited intelligence. Prime time.

The woman, who now got up from the desk by the window and walked around the unfamiliar living room without knowing quite what she wanted, did not normally join in public debate. But after watching one episode of *On the Move with Fiona,* she'd been tempted. Halfway through writing a letter from an "outraged reader," she'd stopped and laughed at herself before deleting it. She had been in a good mood for the rest of the evening. As she couldn't sleep, she allowed herself to indulge in a couple of TV3's terrible late-night films and had even learned something from them, if she remembered correctly.

At least feeling angry was a form of emotion.

Readers' letters in newspapers were not her chosen form of expression.

Tomorrow she would go into Nice and see if she could find some Norwegian papers.

TWO

꙳

It was night in the two-family house in Tåsen. Three sad street-lights stood on the small stretch of road behind the picket fence at the bottom of the garden, the bulbs long since broken by excited children with snowballs in their mittens. It seemed that the neighborhood was taking the request to save electricity seriously. The sky was clear and dark. To the northeast, over Grefsenåsen, Johanne could make out a constellation she thought she recognized. It made her feel that she was totally alone in the world.

"You standing here again?" asked Adam with resignation.

He stood in the doorway, sleepily scratching his groin. His boxer shorts were stretched tight over his thighs. His naked shoulders were so broad that he almost touched both sides of the doorway.

"How much longer is this going to keep up, honey?"

"Don't know. Go back to bed."

Johanne turned back to the window. The transition from living in an apartment house to a house in this neighborhood had been harder than she'd expected. She was used to complaining water pipes, babies' cries that traveled through the walls, quarreling teenagers, and the drone of late-night programs from downstairs, where the woman on the first floor who was nearly stone-deaf often fell asleep in front of the TV. In an apartment, you could make coffee at midnight. Listen to the radio. Have a conversation, for that matter. Here, she barely dared open the fridge. The smell of Adam's nocturnal leaks lingered in the bathroom in the morning, as she had forbidden him to disturb the neighbors below by flushing before seven.

"Why do you creep around like this?" he said. "Can't you at least sit down?"

"Don't talk so loud," Johanne whispered.

"Give me a break. It's not that loud. And you're used to having neighbors, Johanne!"

"Yes, lots. But they're more anonymous. You're so close here. It's just them and us, so it's more . . . I don't know."

"But we get along so well with Gitta and Samuel! Not to mention little Leonard! If it wasn't for him, Kristiane would hardly have any—"

"I mean, look at these!" Johanne stuck out a foot and laughed quietly. "I've never had slippers before in my life. Hardly dare to get out of bed without putting them on now!"

"They're sweet. Remind me of little toadstools."

"They're supposed to look like toadstools, that's why! Couldn't you have gotten her to pick something else? Rabbits, bears? Or even better, completely normal brown slippers?"

The parquet creaked with every step he took toward her. She made a face before turning back to the window again.

"It's not exactly easy to get Kristiane to change her mind," he said. "Please stop being so anxious. Nothing is going to happen."

"That's what Isak said when Kristiane was a baby too."

"That was different. Kristiane—"

"No one knows what's wrong with her. So no one can know if there's anything wrong with Ragnhild."

"Oh, so we're agreed on Ragnhild, then?"

"Yes," Johanne said.

Adam put his arms around her. "Ragnhild is a perfectly healthy eight-day-old baby," he whispered. "She wakes up three times a night for milk and then goes straight back to sleep. Just like she should. Do you want some coffee?"

"Okay, but be quiet."

He was about to say something. He opened his mouth, but then imperceptibly shook his head instead, picked up a sweater from the floor, and pulled it on as he went into the kitchen.

"Come and sit down in here," he called. "If you absolutely must stay awake all night, let's at least do something useful."

Johanne pulled up a bar stool to the island in the middle of the kitchen and tightened her robe. She absentmindedly picked through a thick file that shouldn't have been lying around the kitchen.

"Sigmund doesn't give up, does he?" she said as she rubbed her eyes behind her glasses.

"No, but he's right. It's a fascinating case." He turned around so quickly that the water in the coffee pot spilled over the rim. "I was only at work for an hour," he said defensively. "From the time I left here until I got back was only—"

"Okay, okay, don't worry. That's fine. I understand that you have to go in every now and then. I have to admit . . ."

On the top of the pile was a photograph, a flattering portrait of a soon-to-be murder victim. The shoulder-length hair parted in the middle made her narrow face look even thinner. Not much else about Fiona Helle was old-fashioned. Her eyes were defiant, her full lips smiled confidently at the lens. She was wearing heavy eye makeup but somehow managed to avoid looking vulgar. In fact, there was actually something quite captivating about the picture, an obvious glamour that contrasted sharply with the down-to-earth, family-friendly program image she had so successfully constructed.

"What do you have to admit?" asked Adam.

"That—"

"That you think this case is damned interesting too," smirked Adam, banging around with the cups. "I'm just going to get a pair of pants."

Fiona Helle's background was no less fascinating than the portrait. She graduated with a degree in art history, Johanne noted as she read. Married Bernt Helle, a plumber, when she was only twenty-two; they took over her grandparents' house in Lørenskog and lived there without children for thirteen years. The arrival of little Fiorella in 1998 had obviously not put any brakes on either her ambition or her career. Quite the opposite, in fact. Having gained cult status as a presenter for the arty *Cool Culture* on NRK2, she was then snapped up by the entertainment department. After a couple of seasons on a late-night talk show on Thursdays, she finally made it. At least, that was the expression she used herself in the numerous interviews she had given over the past three years. *On the Move with Fiona* was one of national TV's greatest successes since the sixties, when there was little else for people to do other than gather around their TV screens to watch the one channel, doing the exact same thing as every other person in Norway.

"You liked those programs! A grown man sitting there crying!"

Johanne smiled at Adam, who had come back wearing a bright red fleece, gray sweatpants, and orange woolen socks.

"I did not cry," Adam protested, pouring the coffee into the cups. "I was touched, though, I admit that. But cry? Never!"

He moved a stool in closer to her. "It was that episode about the war baby whose father was a German soldier," he remembered quietly. "You'd have to have a heart of stone not to be moved by her story. Having been persecuted and bullied throughout her childhood, she goes to the United States and gets a job cleaning floors in the World Trade Center when it was first built. Then she took her first and only sick day on September eleventh. And she had always remembered the little Norwegian boy next door who—"

"Yeah, yeah," said Johanne, wetting her lips with the steaming hot coffee. "Shhh!"

She froze. "It's Ragnhild," she said tersely.

"It's not," he started, trying to catch her before she ran into the bedroom.

Too late. She rushed across the floor without a sound and disappeared. Only her anxiety remained. A bitterness gripped his stomach and made him pour more milk into his coffee.

His story was worse than hers. But to compare them was not only cruel, it was impossible. Pain cannot be measured, and loss cannot be weighed. All the same, he couldn't help it. When they first met one dramatic spring, nearly four years ago now, he had found himself getting irritated a little too often by Johanne's sorrow over Kristiane's strangeness.

She had a child, after all. A child who was alive and had a voracious appetite for life. Different from most, but in her own way Kristiane was a lovely and very alert young child.

"I know," Johanne said suddenly. She had come around the corner from the hall without him noticing. "You've had to deal with more than me. Your child is dead. I should be grateful. And I am."

A quiver in his lower lip, barely visible in the dim light, made her stop. His hand covered his eyes.

"Was Ragnhild okay?" Adam asked.

She nodded.

"I just get so frightened," she whispered. "When she's asleep,

I'm scared that she'll die. When she's awake, I think she's going to die. Or that something will happen."

"Johanne," he said helplessly, and patted the chair beside him. "Come here and sit down."

She sank down beside him. His hand rubbed her back, up and down, just a bit too roughly.

"Everything's fine," he said.

"You're angry," she whispered.

"No."

"You are."

His hand stopped, and he squeezed her gently on the neck.

"No, I said. But now—"

"Can't I just be—"

"Do you know what?" he interrupted with forced jolliness. "Let's just agree that the children are fine. Neither of us can sleep. So now we can take an hour or so to look at this"—he tapped Fiona Helle's face with his stubby fingers—"and then we can see whether we can get to sleep. Okay?"

"You're so good," she said and wiped her nose with the back of her hand. "And this case is worse than you fear."

"Right."

He finished his coffee and pushed the cup out of the way before spreading the papers across the large counter. The photograph lay between them. He ran his finger over Fiona Helle's nose, circled her mouth, and paused a moment before picking up the picture and looking at it closely.

"What exactly do you think we're worried about?"

"No clues whatsoever," she said lightly. "I skimmed through all the papers."

She was looking for a document without finding it.

"To begin with," she sniffed, "the footprints in the snow are as good as useless. Okay, there were three prints in the driveway that probably belong to the killer, but the combination of the temperature, wind, and snow makes their value limited. The only thing that's certain is that whoever did it had socks on over their shoes."

"Ever since the Orderud case, every damn petty thief has used that trick," he grumbled.

"Watch your language."

"They're asleep."

"The shoe size is between 10 and 13, in other words the same as around ninety percent of the male population."

"And a small share of the female population," he smiled.

Johanne tucked her feet in under the bar stool.

"In any case, wearing shoes that are too big for you is another well-known trick. And it's not possible to gauge the killer's weight from the footprints. He was simply very lucky with the weather."

"Or she."

"Could be a she. But to be honest, you'd need to use quite a lot of force to overpower Fiona Helle. A physically fit lady in her prime."

They looked at the picture again. The woman looked good for her age. Her forty-two years were apparent around the eyes, there were visible wrinkles around her mouth, and her lipstick had bled. But there was still something vibrant about her face, the direct look in her eyes, the firm skin on her neck and cheeks.

"Her tongue was cut out while she was still alive," Adam said. "The theory so far is that she lost consciousness from strangulation, and then her tongue was cut out. The bleeding was so heavy that she can't have been dead. Maybe the killer chose his method with care, or maybe—"

"It's almost impossible to say," Johanne said and frowned.

"Strangled her until she lost consciousness rather than died, I mean. He must have thought she was dead."

"Well, at least we know that the cause of death was strangulation. He must have finished her off with his hands. After he'd cut out the tongue."

Adam shuddered and added, "Have you seen these?"

He fished out a manila envelope and looked at it for a moment before obviously changing his mind and leaving it unopened.

"Just a peek," Johanne said. "Normally pictures of the scene of the crime don't bother me. But now, since Ragnhild was born, I"—tears welled up in her eyes, and she hid her face in her hands—"I cry for no reason," she said in a loud voice, nearly shouting, before pulling herself together and whispering, "Pictures like that really don't bother me. Normally. I've seen . . ."

She dried her eyes with abrupt, harsh movements and forced a smile. "The husband," she said, "he's got an airtight alibi."

"No alibi is airtight," answered Adam. Again, he put his hand on her back. The warmth spread through the thin silk.

"That's true," Johanne said. "But as good as. He was at his mother's with Fiorella. He had to sleep in the same room as his daughter, because his sister and her husband were also staying the night. And on top of that, his sister had a stomach bug and was up all night. And another thing . . ." She brushed her hand under her right eye once more. Adam smiled and ran his thumb under her nose and then dried it on his pant leg.

"And another thing. There's nothing to indicate anything other than the ordinary marital problems," she finished. "No relationship problems, and certainly no financial problems. They're fairly equal on that score. He earns more than she, she owns a bigger share of the house. His firm seems to be sound."

She took his free hand. The skin was coarse, and his nails were short. Their thumbs met and moved in circles.

"And what's more, eight days have passed," she continued, "without you finding anything. All you've done is rule out a couple of obvious suspects."

"It's a start," he said lamely and pulled back his hand.

"A very weak one."

"What are your thoughts then?"

"I've got lots."

"About what?"

"The tongue," she replied and got up to get more coffee.

A car crawled down the street. The slow throb of the engine made the glass in the corner cabinet rattle. The beam of light danced on the ceiling, a moving cloud of light in the big, dark room.

"The tongue," he repeated despondently, as if she had reminded him of an unpleasant fact that he would rather forget.

"Yes, the tongue. The method. Hate. It was deliberate. The 'vase' "—Johanne made quote marks with her fingers—"It was made beforehand. There was no red paper in the house. I saw in your papers that it takes about eight minutes to make something like that. And that's when you know what you're doing."

For the first time, she seemed to be really fired up. She opened a cupboard and took two sugar cubes from a silver bowl. The spoon scratched on the ceramic of the mug as she stirred.

"Drinking coffee when we can't sleep," she mumbled. "Smart move." She looked up. "Cutting someone's tongue out is such a loaded symbol, so aggressive and horrific that it's hard to imagine that it's motivated by anything other than hate. A pretty intense hate."

"And Fiona Helle was loved by all," Adam dryly retorted. "I think you've stirred the sugar enough now, dear."

She licked the spoon and sat down again.

"The problem is, Adam, that it's impossible to know who hated her. As long as her family, her friends, acquaintances, colleagues . . . everyone around her seemed to like the woman, you'll have to look out there for the murderer." She pointed out the window at a neighbor's home, where someone had turned on a bathroom light.

"I don't mean them, specifically," she smiled. "I mean the general public."

"Dear God," groaned Adam.

"Fiona Helle was one of the most high profile TV stars in the country. I doubt there are many people who *don't* have an opinion about what she did, and therefore also about who they thought she was, right or wrong."

"Over four million suspects, you mean."

"Yep."

She took a sip of coffee before putting down her mug.

"You can forget everyone under fifteen or over seventy, and the million or so who really adored her."

"And that leaves how many, do you reckon?"

"No idea. A couple of million, maybe?"

"A couple of million suspects—"

"Who possibly have never even spoken to her," she added. "There doesn't need to be any direct link between Fiona and the man who killed her."

"Or woman."

"Or woman," she agreed. "Good luck. And, looking at the tongue. . . . Shhh!"

A feeble cry could be heard from the newly decorated children's room. Adam got up before Johanne had time to react.

"She just wants food," he said and made her sit down. "I'll get her. Go and sit down on the sofa."

She tried to pull herself together. The fear was physical, like a shot of adrenaline. Her pulse quickened, her cheeks flushed hot. When she lifted her hand and studied her palm, she saw the light from the ceiling reflected in the sweat in her lifeline. She dried her hands on her robe and sat down heavily on the sofa.

"Is my little munchkin hungry?" she heard Adam murmuring into the baby's hair. "You'll get some food from Mommy. There, there."

The baby's half-open eyes and eager mouth made Johanne cry again, with relief.

"I think I've gone crazy," she whispered and adjusted her breast.

"You're not crazy," said Adam. "Just a bit tense and frightened, that's all."

"The tongue," mumbled Johanne.

"We don't need to talk about that now. Relax."

"The fact that it was split."

"Shhhh."

"Liar," she sniffed and looked up.

"Liar?"

"Not you, silly."

She whispered to the child before she met his eye again. "The split tongue can really only mean one thing. That someone thought that Fiona Helle was a liar."

"Well, we all tell a lie now and then," Adam said and gently stroked the baby's soft head with his finger. "Look, you can see the pulse in her fontanel!"

"Someone believed that Fiona Helle was lying," Johanne repeated. "That her lying was so blatant and brutal that she deserved to die."

Ragnhild let go of her mother's nipple. Something that could easily be mistaken for a smile flitted across her face, and Adam knelt down and put his cheek against her damp cheek. The blister on her upper lip from sucking was pink and full of fluid. Her tiny eyelashes were nearly black.

"It must have been some lie, in that case," Adam mumbled. "A bigger lie than I could ever make up."

Ragnhild burped and then fell asleep.

———————— ✿ ————————

She would never have chosen this place herself.

The others, notorious cheapskates, had suddenly decided to treat themselves to three weeks on the Riviera. What you were supposed to do on the Riviera in December was a mystery to her, but she said yes all the same. At least it would be a change.

Her father had become unbearable since her mother died. Whining and complaining and clinging to her all the time. He smelled like an old man, which was due to a combination of dirty clothes and poor bladder control. His fingers, which scraped her back when he gave the most unwanted good-bye hugs, were now disgustingly thin. Obligation forced her to visit him once a month or so. The apartment in Sandaker had never been palatial, but now that her father was living on his own, it had really gone downhill. She had finally managed, after many letters, furious phone calls, and a lot of bother, to get him a home aide, but it didn't help much. The underside of the toilet seat was still splattered with shit. The food in the fridge was still well past its sell-by date, and you couldn't open the door without gagging. It was unbelievable that the local council could offer an old, loyal taxpayer nothing more than an unreliable girl who could scarcely turn on a washing machine.

The idea of Christmas without her father tempted her, even though she was skeptical about traveling. Especially as the children were going too. It irritated her to no end that children today seemed to be allergic to any form of healthy food. "Don't like, don't like," they kept on whining. A mantra before every meal. Not surprising they were skinny when they were little and then ballooned out when they hit their amorphous puberty, ravaged by modern eating disorders. The youngest, a girl of three or four, still had some charm. But the woman with the laptop was not particularly fond of her siblings.

But the house was big, and the room they thought she should have was impressive. They had shown her the brochures with great enthusiasm. She suspected they were relying on her to pay more than her fair share of the rent. They knew that she had money, even though they had absolutely no idea how much.

Truth be told, she had chosen not to keep in touch with most of her acquaintances. They scurried around in their small lives, making mountains out of molehills, problems that in no way would interest anyone but themselves. The red figures in her social accounts, which she had eventually decided it was necessary to draw up, screamed out at her. Sometimes, when she thought about it, she realized that she had really only met a handful of people of any merit.

They wanted her to come with them, and she could not face another Christmas with her father.

So she was standing at Gardemoen Airport, with her tickets in her hand, when her cell phone rang. The little one, the girl, had suddenly been admitted to the hospital.

She was furious. Of course her friends couldn't leave their little girl, but did they have to wait until three quarters of an hour before the flight was due to depart to tell her? After all, the child had fallen ill four hours earlier. But she still had a choice.

She went.

The others would still have to pay their share of the rent, she made that absolutely clear to them on the phone. She had actually found herself looking forward to spending three weeks with the people who she had, after all, known since she was a child.

After nineteen days down there, the landlord had offered to let her stay until March. He hadn't managed to find any tenants for the winter and didn't want the house to be empty. Of course, it helped that the woman had straightened up and cleaned just before he came. He probably also noticed that only one of the beds had been used as he prowled from room to room, pretending to look at the electrical outlets.

It was as easy to write on her laptop here as at home. And she had free accommodation.

The Riviera was overrated.

Villefranche was a fake town, existing only for tourists. In her opinion, any reality that might have been there had disappeared a long time ago; even the several-hundred-year-old castle by the sea looked as if it had been built from cardboard and plastic. When French taxi drivers can speak half-decent English, there has to be something seriously wrong with the place.

It annoyed her immensely that the police had gotten nowhere.

But then, it was a difficult case. And the Norwegian police had never been anything to boast about, provincial, weaponless eunuchs that they were.

She, on the other hand, was an expert.

The nights had closed in.

THREE

Seventeen days had passed since Fiona Helle was murdered, and it was now February 6.

Adam Stubo sat in his office in the dreariest part of Oslo's east end, staring at the grains of sand running through an hourglass. The beautifully shaped object was unusually large. The stand was handmade. Adam had always thought it was made of oak, good old Norwegian woodwork that had darkened and aged over hundreds of years. But a visiting French criminologist, who had been there just before Christmas, had studied the antique with some interest. Mahogany, he declared, and shook his head when Adam told him that the instrument had been in his seafaring family for fourteen generations.

"This," the Frenchman said in perfect English, "this little curiosity was made sometime between 1880 and 1900. I doubt it has even been on board a ship. Many of them were made as ornaments for well-to-do people's homes."

Then he shrugged his shoulders.

"But by all means," he added, "a pretty little thing."

Adam chose to believe in the family story rather than some Frenchman he barely knew. The hourglass had stood on his grandparents' mantelpiece, out of reach of anyone under twenty-one. A treasured object that his father would turn over for his son every now and then, so he could watch the shiny grains of silver gray sand in the beautiful, hand-blown glass as they ran through a hole that his grandmother claimed was smaller than a strand of hair.

The files that were piled up along the walls and on the desk on both sides of the hourglass told another, more tangible story. The story of Fiona Helle's murder had a grotesque start but nothing that resembled an end. The hundreds of witness statements, the endless technical analyses, special reports, photographs, and tactical observations seemed to point in all directions but led nowhere.

Adam could not remember another case like it, where they had absolutely nothing to go on.

He was heading toward fifty. He had been on the police force since he was twenty-two. He had trudged the streets on the beat; hauled in down-and-outs and drunk drivers as a constable; considered joining the canine unit out of sheer curiosity; been extremely unhappy behind a desk in ØKOKRIM, the economic and environmental crime unit; and then finally ended up in the Criminal Investigation Service, by chance. It felt like a couple of lifetimes ago. Naturally, he couldn't remember all his cases. He had given up trying to keep a mental record a long time ago. The murders were too numerous, the rapes too callous. The figures were meaningless after a while. But one thing was certain and irrefutable: sometimes everything went wrong. That's just the way it was, and Adam Stubo didn't waste time dwelling on his defeats.

This was different.

This time he hadn't seen the victim. For once he hadn't been involved from the start. He had limped into the case, disoriented and behind. But in a way that made him more alert. He thought differently from the others and noticed it most clearly in meetings, gatherings of increasing collective frustration, in which he generally kept his mouth shut.

The others got bogged down in clues that weren't really there. With care and precision, they tried to piece together a puzzle that would never be solved, simply because the police only found clear blue skies wherever they looked for dark, murky shadows. They had found a total of twenty-four fingerprints in Fiona Helle's house, but there was nothing to indicate that any had been left by the murderer. An unexplained cigarette butt by the front door didn't lead to anything either; according to the latest analyses, it was at least several weeks old. They might as well cross out the footprints in the snow with a thick red pen, as they couldn't be linked to any other information about the killer. The blood at the scene of the crime gave no more clues either. The saliva traces on the table, hair on the carpet, and greasy, faint red lip marks on the wineglass told a very ordinary story of a woman sitting at her desk in peace and quiet, going through her weekly mail.

"A phantom killer," Sigmund Berli grinned from the doorway. "I can't believe I'm starting to believe the grumblings of the Romerike guys, that it's a suicide."

"Impressive," Adam smiled back. "First she half strangles herself, then she cuts out her tongue, before sitting down nicely to die from blood loss. But before she dies, she musters up enough energy to wrap the tongue up in a beautiful red paper package. If nothing else, it's original. How's it all going, by the way? Working with them, I mean?"

"The guys from Romerike are nice enough. Big district, you know. Of course they like to throw their weight around a bit. But they seem to be pretty happy that we're involved in the case."

Sigmund Berli sat down on the spare chair and pulled it closer to the desk.

"Snorre's been selected for a big ice-hockey tournament for ten-year-olds this weekend," he said and nodded meaningfully. "Only eight, and he's being selected for the top team with the ten-year-olds!"

"I didn't think they ranked teams for such young age groups."

"That's just some garbage the sports confederation has come up with. Can't think like that, can you? The boy lives for ice hockey, twenty-four/seven—he slept with his skates on the other night. If they don't learn the importance of competition now, they'll just get left behind."

"Fair enough. He's your child. I don't think I'd—"

"Where are we going?" Sigmund interrupted, casting his eye over all the files and piles of documents. "Where the hell are we going with this case?"

Adam didn't answer. Instead he picked up the hourglass, turned it over again, and tried to count the seconds. The sand took one minute and four seconds to run through the glass neck; he'd known that since he was a boy. A production flaw, he assumed, and said out loud, "Fifty-two. Fifty-three. Ahh, it's finished. I always get it wrong."

He turned the hourglass yet again. "One. Two. Three."

"Adam, stop it. Are the sleepless nights getting to you, or what?"

"No. Ragnhild's great. Nine. Ten."

"Where are we going, Adam?" Sigmund's voice was insistent now, and he leaned toward his colleague and continued, "There isn't a single fucking clue. Not technical at least. Nor tactical, as far as I can tell. I went through all the statements yesterday, then again today. Fiona Helle was well liked. By most people. Nice lady, they say. A character. Lots of people reckon it was her complexity that made her so interesting. Well-read and interested in marginal cultural expression. But she also liked cartoons and loved *Lord of the Rings*."

"People who are as successful as Fiona Helle always have . . ." Adam tried to find the right word.

"Enemies," Sigmund suggested.

"No. Not necessarily. But people who aren't friends. There's always someone who feels overshadowed by people like that. Outshone. And Fiona Helle shone brighter than most. But I still find it hard to believe that some NRK employee with ambitions of hosting a Saturday night show, who might feel that he or she has been wronged, would go to such drastic lengths as to . . ." He nodded at the board, where a poster-sized picture of a bare-breasted, open-legged Fiona Helle screamed at them.

"I think the answer is possibly somewhere in here," Adam said, pulling out a pile of letters that had been carefully placed in a red folder. "I picked out twenty letters. At random, basically. To get an impression of what kind of people wrote to Fiona Helle."

Sigmund furrowed his brow in response and picked up the letter that lay on top.

"Dear Fiona," he read out loud. "I am a 22-year-old girl from Hemnesberget. Three years ago I found out my dad was a sallor from Venezuela. My mom says he was a shit who just left never got in touch again . . ."

Sigmund scratched his ear. "She can't fucking write," he muttered before continuing to read:

"When he found out I was dew. But there is a lady here at the Coop says that Juan Maria was a nice man and it was my mom who wanted . . ."

Sigmund inspected his fingertip. A small dirty-yellow lump seemed to fascinate him. He paused for several seconds before wiping it off on his pants.

"Are they all as hopeless as this?" he asked.

"I wouldn't say it was hopeless," Adam said. "After all, she's shown some initiative. Just because she can't spell and has bad grammar doesn't mean that she can't do her own detective work. She actually knows where her father lives. The letter is a plea for *On the Move with Fiona* to take her quest one step further. The girl is terrified of being rejected and thinks there's a greater chance that her father will accept her if it's all on TV."

"Jesus," exclaimed Sigmund and picked up another letter.

"That one is of a completely different caliber," Adam said while his colleague glanced down the page. "An eloquent dentist who's approaching retirement. He was just a boy during the war and lived on the east side of Oslo. In 1945, he was sent to the country as a weedy, anemic orphan to be fattened up. There he met—"

"Fiona Helle was playing with fire," Sigmund interrupted, leafing through the other letters. "This is—"

"People's lives," Adam said lightly and shrugged his shoulders. "Every single letter that woman received—and believe me, it wasn't just a couple—told stories of loss and grief. Despair. But she's also been criticized for it. The usual debate in the end. On the one side, intellectual snobs who patronizingly argued against the exploitation of the ignorant masses. And on the other side, the People"—he drew a capital P with his finger—"who thought that the snobs could just shut up and turn off the TV if they didn't like what they saw."

"That's a fair point," Sigmund mumbled.

"Both camps had valid points, but as usual the debate didn't amount to much. Except shouting and screaming and of course even better ratings for the program. In Fiona Helle's defense, it must be said that the vetting of people who eventually made it onto the show was extremely rigorous. There were three psychologists on the production team, and every guest had to go through a kind of screening. Quite thorough preparations, as far as I'm aware."

"But what about the ones who didn't make it, then?"

"Exactly. There are people out there who poured their lives into a letter to Fiona Helle. Many of them had never told their story to anyone before. It must've been very painful, then, to be rejected, as most people were. Especially as the production team didn't have the capacity to answer them all. Some of the critics have also claimed"—Adam fished a matte aluminum cigar case out of his breast pocket. He opened it carefully, pulled out the cigar, and ran it under his nose—"that Fiona Helle became God," he sniffed. "A God who answered the prayers of desperate people with silence."

"Very dramatic."

"Or rather, melodramatic. Yes." He returned the cigar to its case with equal care. "But just a tiny little bit true, as Kristiane says when we catch her lying."

Sigmund burst out laughing.

"My boys just flatly deny it. Even if I catch them red-handed and the evidence is stacked against them. Tough little nuts. Especially Snorre."

He stroked the crown of his head in a shy gesture.

"The youngest one," he explained. "The one who looks like me."

"So there we have it," Adam said and sighed. "An unknown number of people who might have good grounds for being at least disappointed with Fiona Helle."

"Disappointed," Sigmund repeated. "That's hardly . . ."

They both looked up at the picture of the victim.

"No. That's why I've started a small investigation of my own. I want to find out what happened to the people who actually got help from Fiona. All of them had their fifteen minutes of fame and met their biological mother in South Korea, or their father who disappeared in Argentina, their daughter who was put up for adoption in Drøbak, and God knows what else—all of them had their lives turned upside down during prime time."

"Is there nothing like that already?"

"No, in fact, there isn't."

"But hasn't NRK followed up with all those who—"

"No."

Sigmund sank back in the chair. He stared at the cigar case that was back in place in Adam's breast pocket.

"Didn't you quit?" Sigmund asked in a tired voice.

"What? Oh, you mean this. I only sniff them. Old habit. Don't smoke anymore. If I want to, I have to go out onto the veranda. Especially if it's a cigar. It takes time to smoke one of these."

"But Adam . . ."

"Yes?"

"Do you think all the technical work is wasted?"

Adam gave a hoarse laugh and put his hand to his mouth as he coughed. "This is the result of all my damned smoking," he explained. He grimaced, swallowed, and then continued. "No, of course not. Technical investigations are never wasted. But as we don't seem to have come up with any results, not so far, I think we should start at the other end. Instead of working outward from the scene of the crime, we should start out there and work in. If we're lucky, we may find a motive or two. A sufficiently strong motive, I mean."

"Are you leaving? This early?"

Adam had stood up and was already over by his coat, which was hanging unwashed and creased on the coat stand by the window.

"Yes," he said seriously and pulled on his coat. "I'm a modern father. From now on, I have to leave work every day at three o'clock to spend quality time with my daughter. Every day."

"What?"

"Just joking, you idiot." Adam slapped his colleague on the shoulder and shouted as he disappeared down the corridor, "Have a good weekend, everyone!"

"What the hell am I doing here?" Sigmund muttered and looked at the door that had just slammed shut behind Adam. "It's not even my office."

Then he looked at his watch. It was already half past five. He couldn't understand where the day had gone.

The blonde woman in the Armani suit and sneakers felt good as she got out of the taxi. It was still a good half hour until midnight, and she was practically sober. In a portrait interview for tomorrow's VG newspaper, it said that Victoria Heinerback had realized that she was grown up when she started to leave parties and receptions early because she was thinking about her productivity the next day. Tomorrow's productivity. It was her own turn of phrase. It said something about her, both personally and politically.

Her sneakers didn't look quite right, given the rest of her outfit. But with a broken toe, her options were limited, and fortunately the TV producers hadn't cut the part in the talk show where she commented on her own klutziness, flirtatiously saying that she was, after all, only twenty-six. And that she'd broken her toe while playing with her nephew. Not quite true, but white lies were allowed every now and then, when it was nothing serious. The studio audience had laughed and warmed to her. Victoria Heinerback smiled to herself as she struggled to get her key in the front door.

It had been a good week.

Politically. Personally. In every way.

Despite the pain in her toe.

It was annoyingly dark. She looked up. The outside light was not working, and she could just make out that the bulb had been broken. That made her a bit anxious, and she looked over her shoulder. The light by the gate was broken as well. She tried to keep all her weight on her good foot as she held her keys up to see if she'd found the wrong one.

She never did manage to find out.

––––––––––– ❧ –––––––––––

The next morning, Victoria Heinerback was found by her boyfriend, who had wound his weary way home from his brother's bachelor party by bus and taxi.

She was sitting in bed. She was naked. Her hands were nailed to the wall above the head of the bed. Her legs were splayed, and it looked as if someone had tried to stuff something up her vagina.

Victoria Heinerback's boyfriend didn't see this detail at first. He tore her hands free, threw up violently all over the place, and then pulled the body out onto the floor, as if it was the bed itself that had attacked her so brutally. It wasn't until half an hour later that he came to his senses and called the police.

Then he discovered the green book that was still stuck between Victoria Heinerback's thighs.

The ensuing investigation would establish that it was a leather-bound copy of the Koran.

Four

———————— ❧ ————————

The woman in seat 16A seemed nice. She was reading the British papers and was obviously in need of a coffee. The flight attendant found it difficult to guess where she was from. Most of the passengers were Swedish, though everyone was being disturbed by a noisy Danish family with small children in the second to last row. He had also registered several Norwegians. It was by no means the high season, but lots of people were more than happy to get on a direct flight to Nice when the prices were so ridiculously low.

He should really stop working as a flight attendant. His weight had always been a problem, and now his colleagues had begun to make comments. No matter how hard he tried or how little he ate, the bathroom scales threatened to tip past 220 pounds at any moment.

It was good to have people like the lady in 16A on flights like this.

She was darker than most Scandinavians. Her eyes were brown and she had no reason to be happy about her weight either. She was big and heavy, but the first impression was one of strength. Powerful, he thought after a while. She was an Amazon.

And she certainly liked her coffee.

What's more, she didn't have any children, thank goodness, and didn't complain about anything.

The body was still warm.

The attendant at the Galleria multistory parking lot figured that it couldn't be more than a couple of hours since the prostitute had said her good-byes. Maybe he was wrong. He was no expert, he had to admit, though it was the second time in under three months that he'd had to call the police because some poor woman had chosen to inject what would be her last hit somewhere sheltered from the biting wind that whipped through the winter streets of Stockholm, forcing everyone to dress like polar explorers. As it was quite warm in the stairwell, it was difficult to say.

But she couldn't have been lying there long.

If you can't see forward and you can't look back—then look up in life.

The words of wisdom were written in red marker on the wall. The whore had obviously taken them literally. She was lying on her side with her head on her right arm, legs bent, as if someone had put her in the recovery position so that death would come gently. But she was looking up, with open eyes and an astonished, almost happy expression.

Peace, the attendant thought to himself, and took out his cell phone. The woman looked like she'd found peace. The man was tired of having to chase the prostitutes out of the huge parking lot, but deep down he felt for them. Their tiresome existence reminded him of the joys of his own life. His job was boring and monotonous, but he had a good wife, and the children seemed to be turning out okay. He could afford a beer or two on Friday night and prided himself on always paying his bills before they were due.

The reception for cell phones was terrible down here.

He recognized her. She was one of the regulars. She seemed to live down here, at the bottom of the stairwell, in a space that was barely fifty square feet. The blue and red stripes on the wall were no doubt meant to conjure up movement and light. A bag lay flung in the corner, and three papers and a magazine had been stuck underneath a rolled-up sleeping bag just under the stairs. A bottle of mineral water had fallen down behind her back.

The attendant trudged up the stairs. His asthma was bothering him, and he had to stop for a minute to draw a breath. Finally he got to the top and opened a drab door out onto Brunkebergs Torg.

The woman's colleagues were already at work. He spotted a couple of them, shivering and emaciated; one of them got into a BMW that immediately accelerated toward Sergels Torg.

He eventually got ahold of the police. They promised to be there within half an hour.

"Sure," he muttered and hung up. Last time he had been alone with the dead prostitute for over an hour.

He lit a cigarette. The other woman, in thin tights and faux fur coat, got an offer on the other side of the square.

The dead whore wasn't that thin. Quite the contrary, he thought as he took a long drag on his cigarette. She was the plumper type. There weren't many of those. Prostitutes normally shrank over the years. They got smaller and skinnier for every shot they took, every pill they swallowed. Maybe this woman remembered to eat, in between tricks and drugs.

He should go back down again to keep an eye on her.

Instead he lit another cigarette and stood out there in the cold until the police finally came. They took a few seconds to confirm what the attendant already knew, that the woman was dead. An ambulance was called, and the body was taken away.

Katinka Olsson was cremated three days later, and no one bothered to erect a stone to mark the remains of the late-thirty-something prostitute. The four children she had brought into the world before she was thirty would never know that their biological mother carried baby pictures of them in her otherwise empty wallet, faded photographs with worn, uneven edges; Katinka Olsson's only treasure.

She died of an overdose, and no one would ever ask about her. No one grieved for Katinka Olsson, and no one wondered why the dead prostitute smelled fresh and clean and had on newly washed, if worn, clothes.

No one.

———— ❧ ————

Victoria Heinerback's home surprised him.

Standing in the middle of the relatively large living room, he got the impression of a far more interesting person than the media had ever managed to portray.

When he thought about it, he couldn't remember having seen any features about Victoria Heinerback's house. Adam Stubo had used the early hours of the morning to go through a large pile of interviews and other press cuttings, sensational and glamorous tales of an apparently successful life.

When her boyfriend proposed to her, the couple traveled to Paris with *Hello!* The pictures of the two of them, embracing in front of the Eiffel Tower, under the Arc de Triomphe, outside well-known shops on the Champs d'Elysées, and on the streets of Montmartre reminded him of advertisements from the seventies. Victoria and Trond were both bottle blondes and inoffensively well groomed. They had an aura of self-confidence and matching psychedelic pastel shirts. Only the wineglasses that were raised in a couple of the photographs broke the illusion. They should have been Coca-Cola bottles.

When Victoria Heinerback was elected as Norway's youngest party leader, members of the press had been invited to follow her to her room when she retired after the national conference. The papers and magazines were waxing rhapsodic about her evening bath. Victoria raised a glass of champagne to the readers from a sea of pink bubbles, with her smooth, beautifully shaped left leg hanging over the edge of the bath. According to the picture captions, she was absolutely exhausted.

The setting for the photographs was a hotel room.

Victoria Heinerback was the ultimate example of young Scandinavian success. She only managed to complete a couple of years at the Norwegian School of Management before politics completely took over her life. She walked through the winter slush down Karl Johan in high heels, but also let herself be photographed wearing boots in the woods. She was always suitably dressed in the Storting, the Norwegian parliament. She adhered to a strict dress code when she participated in debates that were to be televised, but when she took part in programs that were less important, her style had earned her third place in a list of the country's best-dressed women. She has a real eye for sexy details, the jury said in admiration. Naturally, she was going to have children. But not yet, she smiled to the impertinent journalists, and kept on climbing up the ladder of a party that, on good days, gloried in being the country's leading party (barely) in the opinion polls.

As he looked around the living room for the third time, Adam felt a twinge of guilt at his own prejudices. His eyes fixed on a beautiful lamp shade in milky glass. The glass was held in place by three metal tubes, and the whole thing looked a bit like a fifties B-movie UFO. It was an impressive room. A cream corner sofa sat behind a steel and glass table. The chairs were upholstered in an intense orange fabric that was mirrored in small speckles on a huge abstract painting on the opposite wall. All the surfaces were clean. The only ornament in the room was an Alvar Aalto vase on the austere sideboard, where a colorful bunch of tulips was dying of thirst.

The woven steel magazine rack was overflowing with magazines and tabloids. Adam picked up a gossip magazine. Two divorces, a celebrity anniversary, and a singer's tragic decline into alcoholism graced the front cover.

To the extent that Adam had ever paid attention to Victoria Heinerback, he had admired, somewhat reluctantly, her instinctive understanding of people's need for easy solutions. On the other hand, he had never detected any real political understanding or overriding moral conviction in her. Victoria Heinerback believed that gasoline prices should be cut and that the country should be ashamed of its care of the elderly. She called for lower taxes and more police. She thought that shopping in Sweden was a justified protest by the Norwegian people; if the politicians chose to have the highest alcohol prices in Europe, it was all they could expect.

He had seen her as simple, superficial, and politically savvy. Not well read, he thought, and in one interview she seemed to think that Ayn Rand, whom she claimed was her favorite author, was a man.

It must have been the journalist who got it wrong, Adam thought, as he looked around the living room in more detail. Certainly not Victoria Heinerback.

He slowly ran his fingers over the book spines in the full shelves that lined two of the walls from floor to ceiling. A worn and well-read copy of *The Fountainhead* stood beside a paperback copy of *Atlas Shrugged*. An extensive biography of Frank Lloyd Wright, the eccentric architect and author, was in such a sorry state that several of the pages fell out when Adam tried to check the Ex Libris label.

Jens Bjørneboe and Hamsun, P. O. Enquist, Günter Grass and Don DeLillo, Lu Xun and Hannah Arendt. New and old side by side, in something that vaguely resembled a system. In order of love, Adam suddenly realized.

"Look," he said to Sigmund Berli, who had just come back in from the bedroom. "She's got all her favorite books between hip and head level! The books down toward the floor or above are almost untouched."

He stretched up and pointed to an anthology of Chinese authors he had never even heard of. Then he hunkered down, took out a book from the bottom shelf, and blew the dust off before he read out loud, "Mircea Eliade." He shook his head and put the book back. "That's the sort of thing Johanne's sister reads. But I would never have guessed that Miss Heinerback did."

"There's a lot of crime here too."

Sigmund Berli ran his fingers over the shelves closest to the kitchen door. Adam squinted at the titles. They were all there. The Grand Old Dames of British literature and the arrogant Americans from the eighties. And here and there a French-sounding name popped up. Judging by the covers, with big cars and lethal weapons in gray stylized strokes, they had to be from the fifties. She had such classics as Chandler and Hammett in American presentation copies, alongside an almost complete catalog of Norwegian crime novels published in the last ten years.

"Do you think they're her boyfriend's books?" Sigmund asked.

"He just moved in recently. These have been here for a while. I wonder why she . . . why she never mentioned this."

"What? That she read?"

"Yes. I mean, I've gone through a pile of interviews today that all gave the impression of a rather uninteresting person. A political animal, true enough, but someone who is more interested in banal individual issues than in putting things into context. Even in the"—Adam drew a square in the air before continuing—"boxes, is that what they're called? The frames with standard questions, she never said anything about . . . this. When they asked if she read, she said newspapers. Five newspapers a day, and not much time for anything else."

"Maybe she read more before. Before she became a politician, I mean. Just didn't have enough time anymore."

Sigmund had moved out into the kitchen. "Wow! Take a look at this."

The kitchen was a bizarre mix of old and new. The front-angled wall cabinets looked like they were made just after the war. But when Adam opened a door, it glided silently and easily on modern plastic and metal fittings. The sink was enormous, with faucets straight out of a thirties film. The porcelain buttons that indicated warm and cold in red and blue calligraphy had become unreadable with age. The countertops were dark and matte.

"Slate," Adam said and rapped the stone with his knuckles. "She's obviously restored a lot of the old features and mixed in some new ones."

"Classy," Sigmund hesitated. "It's pretty cool, isn't it?"

"Yes, and expensive."

"How much do they earn in the Storting, do you think?"

"Not enough," Adam said and pinched his nose. "When were the police here?"

"About seven o'clock this morning. Her boyfriend, his name is Trond Arnesen, had destroyed any evidence at the scene of the crime. Had thrown up everywhere and moved things around. He pulled her out of the bed and stuff like that. Have you seen the bedroom?"

"Mmm." Adam moved over to the kitchen window. Dusk was settling in the east, and heavy clouds hung over Lillestrøm in the distance, with the promise of snow during the night. He shifted a curved kitchen table with great care and put his face right up to the window, without touching the glass. He stood like that for a while, lost in his own thoughts, without responding to Sigmund's comments, which sounded more distant and muffled as his colleague moved around the house.

He looked at the compass on his sophisticated watch. He drew a map in his mind. Then he took a step back, closed one eye, and looked at the view again.

If you were to fell the three spruce trees at the bottom of the garden and demolish the small housing development a few hundred yards away, you could see the house where Fiona Helle was murdered only a week ago.

There couldn't be more than a mile between the two places.

"Is there any chance at all? I mean, that the cases are linked?"

Adam helped himself to a healthy portion of the fried potatoes before reaching for the Heinz bottle.

"Do you have to put ketchup on absolutely everything?"

"Do you think there is? A connection?"

"I'm going now," Kristiane shouted from the hall.

"Shit," Johanne exclaimed and ran to the stairs with Ragnhild in her arms, "she's not asleep."

Kristiane's nose was squashed up against the front door. Her red down jacket was zipped up. Her scarf was wound tightly around her neck, and her hat was hanging down over her eyes. She had her boots on the wrong feet. She was clutching a mitten in each hand. She leaned her whole body against the locked door and announced, "I'm going."

"Not now, you're not," Johanne called and handed the baby to Adam. "It's too late. It's past nine o'clock. You were in bed and . . . Do you want to hold Ragnhild for a while? Isn't she sweet and funny?"

"Horrible," hissed Kristiane. "Horrible child."

"Kristiane!" Adam Stubo's voice was so sharp that Ragnhild started to cry. He rocked her in frustration and murmured into the soft blanket that was wrapped around her. Kristiane started to howl. She rocked from foot to foot and banged her forehead against the wood. Her howling changed into desperate, rasping sobs.

"Daddy," she growled in between the sobs. "My daddy. I'm going to my daddy."

Johanne threw up her hands and turned around to face Adam, who was standing halfway up the stairs. "It might be best," she started. "I think maybe . . ."

"No way," Adam stopped her. "She's been with Isak for a week. So now she's going to stay with us. It's important for her to feel included. That she's part of the family. That . . ."

The baby had finally stopped crying. Some gunk from her eyes ran down her rosy cheek. Her soft hair stuck to her skull. Suddenly she blinked her eyes, reluctantly, as if she had just woken up from a long, deep sleep. She made a face that bared her gums.

". . . that this is her sister," he finished quietly, and his lips brushed the child's skin. "Kristiane must stay here. She can go to Isak's again in a few days."

"Daddy! I want to go to my daddy!"

Adam descended into the small porch they had on the first floor. He could feel the under-floor heating burning through his wool socks. He was worried that the electricians had done something wrong when they were building the house. God knows when he would have time to check it. He carefully gave the baby back to Johanne.

"Here comes Tiddly the Wriggling Tadpole," he said and

threw Kristiane over his shoulder in a fireman's carry, before marching back up the stairs.

"Don't," giggled Kristiane, against her will, as he pulled one of her boots off and planted it in a flowerpot. "Don't!"

"This will grow into a boot flower in a week or two. And this one . . ."

He threw the other boot into the wastepaper basket.

"Haven't got any use for this one," he said and maneuvered her into a firm hold. "Tadpoles don't need shoes."

He kicked open the door to her bedroom with a bang. Then he pulled off her clothes quick as a flash. Fortunately she still had her pajamas on underneath.

"Quick," he puffed. "Or the troll will sweat to death. I'm going to start counting now."

"Don't," shrieked Kristiane with delight as she buried herself under the duvet.

"One," he started. "Two, three. The magic is working now. Tiddly the Tadpole is fast asleep."

Then he pulled the door shut and shrugged his shoulders. "There!"

Johanne stood with a blank face and Ragnhild over her shoulder.

"That's what we usually do when you're not here," he excused himself. "Fast and effective. Do you think there's a connection? Between Fiona Helle's and Victoria Heinerback's murders?"

"That's how you put the girl to bed?" Johanne looked at him in disbelief.

"So what! Forget it! She's asleep now. Magic. Come on." He padded into the living room and started to clear the dinner table. Leftovers were thrown out, apart from the fried potatoes, which he ate as he cleared. The grease ran down his fingers, and when he tried to pour himself more wine, the bottle nearly slid out of his hand.

"Oops . . . do you want any? You don't need to worry anymore, you know. I'm sure a small glass won't hurt Ragnhild."

"No thanks. Actually . . ."

Gently, she lay Ragnhild down in her crib, which Adam had eventually agreed could be moved in and out of the living room, depending on where they were themselves. It was by the end of the sofa now.

"Maybe a small glass," she said and sat down at the empty table.

"Can you wipe the table with the cloth, please?"

With an everyday, almost casual expression on her face, she grabbed the papers that Adam had thrown down when he came home. It was a thin file. This time there were no pictures. A couple of police reports, two handwritten memorandums, and a map of Lørenskog with a red cross over Victoria Heinerback's address were stapled together. Johanne couldn't figure out any system to it.

"I see that you haven't much to go on here, either."

"The murder was only discovered this morning."

"And you've censored the file. Did you want to spare me the photographs?"

"No." He seemed to be sincere and sat down and scratched his head. "They haven't made enough copies yet," he added, yawning. "But you're not missing anything. Horrible sight. Especially the . . ."

"Enough, thank you." She shook her head and put up her hand. "You gave me enough details on the phone. And there are certainly similarities. Brutal murders. Both bodies have been mutilated."

Adam knitted his brow. He cocked his head and his mouth

moved, as if he wanted to say something but didn't know quite what.

"Mutilated," he repeated in the end. "Cutting out someone's tongue definitely qualifies as mutilation. But Victoria Heinerback . . ."

Again, his expression was one of doubt. He narrowed his eyes, blinked, and almost imperceptibly shook his head, as if the scenario of a killer on a deadly hunt for female celebrities was too much to take in. He glanced over at the crib.

"Do you think she can understand any of this?"

"She's only three weeks old."

"Yes, but the brain's like a sponge, you know. Maybe she's subconsciously taking it all in and storing it. And it will affect her, later I mean."

"Don't be a fool." She stretched her hand over the table and stroked his cheek. "You're scared that the press is right, aren't you?" she said. "Have you seen the special editions?"

He shook his head. She cupped his jaw with her hand.

"They're having a field day. It must be annoying for them that the murder wasn't discovered until this morning and only announced later on in the day. The special editions are botch jobs. Full of inaccuracies, incredible speculation, incorrect facts, from what I can see. They're calling him the celebrity killer."

"Or her," said Adam and grabbed her hand. He lifted it to his lips and kissed it.

"Or her. Okay. Don't be such a pedant. Fortunately they were more reserved on the TV news, but there's still speculation that there's a madman on the loose who's got it in for beautiful, successful women. VG even managed to get a well-known psychologist to outline a profile of a sexually frustrated woman-hater with a disability who was rejected by his mother." She laughed quietly and took a sip from her glass. "You know, it's only now that I realize how good this actually is. Having not tasted wine for ten months, that is."

"You are—"

"Lovely," she concluded for him and her smile broadened. "What do you think?"

"About you?"

"About there being a link. You must have given it some thought. You and Sigmund and several others are working on both cases. Both murders—"

"Took place in Lørenskog, both victims are women, both are well known, both are high-profile celebrities, both—"

"Are good looking. Were, at least." She swiveled the glass in her hand and continued, "And in both cases, the killer left a message, a highly symbolic violation of the body."

She was talking more slowly now, and her voice dropped, as if she was alarmed by her own reasoning.

"The press doesn't know about the book yet," he said. "About the Koran. It was actually taped between her legs. It would appear that the intention was to stuff it up her cunt, but . . ."

"Don't use that word!"

"Sorry, vagina. The book was taped to her thighs, right up by the vagina."

"Or anus."

"Or anus," he repeated, somewhat surprised. "Hmm, that's probably what he meant. Up yours, or something like that."

"Maybe. You want some more?"

He nodded, and she poured the rest of the bottle into his glass. She had only taken a sip from her own.

"If you were to look for similarities, apart from the obvious ones, which could be purely coincidental, I think the power of the symbolism is one of the most striking features," she said. "Cutting out someone's tongue and splitting it in two is such an unambiguous statement with such obvious symbolism that you could almost imagine that the killer read too many Red Indian books as a boy. The Muslim bible up her butt is hardly a divine message."

"I don't think our new compatriots would appreciate you calling the Koran a bible," said Adam, massaging his neck. "Would you mind?"

With an exasperated smile she got up and stood behind him. She leaned back against the kitchen island and took a firm grip of Adam's neck muscles.

He was so broad. So big. She could feel that his muscles were knotted under the surprisingly soft skin. It was his size that had first attracted her. She was captivated by this man, who must have weighed 250 pounds without actually appearing to be fat. Just after they moved in together, she had tried to put him on a diet. "Just thinking of your health," she said, but gave up after three weeks. Adam didn't get irritable when he ate less, he got desperate. She had stopped her project one afternoon when he wiped away something that could have been tears when faced with a plate of boiled cod with not a trace of fat, one potato, and a spoonful of steamed carrots. Then he disappeared into the bathroom and stayed there for the rest of the meal. He had butter with everything, sauces and gravy with most things, and believed that a proper meal should always be finished off with dessert.

"Obviously, it's too early to say," Johanne said and pressed her thumbs into the muscles between his shoulder blades and spine. "But I would advise against assuming it's the same killer."

"Of course we're not assuming anything," he groaned. "More. A bit further up. But the truth is, just the thought is enough to frighten the life out of me. I mean—Ow! There, right there."

"You mean if there really is only one murderer, you can expect more," Johanne said. "Victims, that is. More murders."

His muscles stiffened under her fingers. Adam straightened his back, pushed her gently away, and rearranged his shirt. Ragnhild's light breathing and snuffles could be heard from the living room. A cat was obviously courting outside somewhere. The yowling cut through the evening quiet, and Johanne was convinced she could smell cat spray all the way up to the second floor.

"I hate those semiferal beasts," she said and sat down.

"Can you help me?" Adam asked in an urgent voice, almost insistent. "Can you get anything at all out of the papers?"

"There's too little. You know that. I need to look through . . . I need to have . . ." She laughed feebly and shrugged her shoulders. "Good God, of course I can't help you. I've got a newborn to look after! I'm on maternity leave! Obviously we can talk about it—"

"There's no one as good as you in the country. There are no real profilers here, and we—"

"I am not a profiler," she said, agitated. "How many times do I have to tell you? I'm fed up with—"

"Okay," he interrupted and held up his hands in a gesture of peace. "But you damn well know enough about profiling to be one. And I don't know anyone other than you who has been taught by the FBI's best—"

"Adam!"

The evening before they got married, he had promised, with his hand on his heart, never to ask about Johanne's time with the FBI. They had argued in a way that was harsh and unfamiliar to both of them; she had used words he never imagined she could use, and he was positively furious that such an important period of her life was closed off to him.

But she would not share it. Never, not with anyone. As a naive young psychology student in Boston, she had been given the opportunity to participate in one of the FBI's profiler courses.

The head of the course was Warren Scifford, already a legend in his fifties, as much for his knowledge as for his relentless bedding of promising young female students. They called him the Chief, and Johanne had trusted the man who was nearly thirty years her senior. In the end she started to believe that she was something special. That she had been chosen, by him and the FBI, and that of course he would divorce his wife as soon as their children were old enough.

It all went wrong and nearly cost her her life. She got on the first possible flight back to Oslo, started to study law three weeks later, and graduated from the university in record time. Warren Scifford was a name she had tried to forget for the past thirteen years. Her time in the FBI, her months with Warren, the catastrophic event that resulted in the Chief having to work behind a desk for six months as punishment until it all blew over and he was one of the big boys again, was a chapter in her life that occasionally came to mind, but she only thought about it reluctantly. It made her feel sick and she never, no matter what, wanted to talk about it again.

The problem was that Adam knew Warren Scifford. In fact, they'd met up again only last summer, when Adam went to an international police conference in New Orleans. When he came home and mentioned Warren's name in passing over supper, Johanne smashed two plates in a sudden outburst of anger. Then she ran into the guest room, locked the door, and cried herself to sleep. For three days, he only managed to get monosyllabic replies out of her.

And now he was dangerously close to breaking his promise again.

"Adam," she repeated harshly. "Don't even go there."

"Take it easy. If you don't want to help, you don't want to help." He leaned back in the chair with an indifferent smile. "After all, it's not your problem, all this."

"Don't be like that," she said, dejected.

"Like what? I'm only stating the obvious. It's not your problem that a couple of famous women have been killed and mutilated just outside Oslo." He emptied his glass and put it down, a bit too hard.

"I've got children," Johanne said with feeling. "I've got a demanding nine year old and a two-week-old baby and more than enough to keep me busy without taking on a major role in a difficult murder investigation!"

"Okay, okay, I said it was all right." He stood up suddenly and got two dessert bowls out of the cabinet. "Fruit salad," he said. "Do you want some?"

"Adam, honestly. Sit down. We can . . . I am perfectly willing to discuss the cases. Like now, in the evening, when the girls have gone to bed. But both you and I know that profiling work is extremely demanding, and so far-reaching that—"

"You know what," he interrupted and banged a bowl of whipped cream down so hard on the table that the cream jumped. "Fiona Helle's death is one thing. A tragedy. She was a mother and a wife and far too young to die. Victoria Heinerback didn't have any children, but I still think that twenty-six is too young to die. But all that aside, people die. People get killed." He stroked his nose, his straight, beautifully shaped nose with nostrils that quivered when he, on rare occasions, got really angry.

"For God's sake, people are killed every second day in this country. But what upsets me, what really frightens me . . ."

Alarmed by his own choice of words, he hesitated before repeating himself. "Frightened. I'm frightened, Johanne. I don't understand these cases. There are so many similarities between them that I can't help wondering . . ."

"When the next victim will be killed," Johanne helped him, as he still couldn't finish the sentence.

"Exactly. And that's why I'm asking for your help. I know

that it's a lot to ask. I know that you've got more than enough on your plate with Kristiane and Ragnhild and your mother and the house and—"

"Okay."

"What?"

"Fine. I'll see how much I can manage."

"Do you mean that?"

"Yes. But then I need all the facts. About both cases. And I want it to be clear from the start that I can pull out at any point."

"Whenever," he nodded in confirmation. "Should I . . . I can catch a cab down to the office and—"

"It's nearly half past ten."

Her laughter was lame. But it was still laughter, Adam thought. He studied her face for signs of irritation, small twitches in her lower lips, a muscle that drew a shadow along her cheekbone. But all he could see was dimples and a long yawn.

"I'm just going to check the children," she said.

He loved the way she walked. She was slim without being thin. Even now, only a couple of weeks after giving birth, she moved with a boyish lightness that made him smile. She had narrow hips, straight shoulders. When she bent down over Ragnhild, her hair fell across her face, soft and tangled. She pushed it back behind her ear and said something. Ragnhild was snoring gently.

He followed her into Kristiane's room. She opened the door with great care. The little girl was asleep with her head at the foot of the bed, the duvet underneath her, and her down jacket over her like a duvet. Her breathing was steady and even. A faint smell of sleep and clean bed linens filled the room, and Adam put his arm around Johanne.

"Well, it certainly worked," she whispered. He could hear she was smiling. "The magic worked."

"Thank you," he whispered back.

"For what?" Johanne stood still. Adam didn't let go of her. A feeling of unease that she had tried to repress all afternoon overwhelmed her. She had first noticed it around one, when Adam called to explain why he would be so late, and she shrugged it off. She was always fretting. About the children, about her mother who had started to get confused after her father's third heart attack and didn't always remember what day it was, about whether she would ever get back to her research. About the mortgage and the bad brakes on the car. About Isak's easygoing attitude when it came to discipline, and about the war in the Middle East. There was always something to worry about. This afternoon she had tried to find out in one of her many medical books whether the white flecks on Kristiane's front teeth might be symptoms of too much milk or any other imbalance in her diet. Anxiety, bad conscience, and the feeling of never being good enough were all part of her normal frame of mind, and she had grown accustomed to living with it.

But this was different.

There in the dark, quiet room, with the heat from Adam's body against her back and the barely audible breathing of her sleeping daughter to remind her of everyday joys and security, she couldn't put her finger on what was making her uneasy, a feeling that she knew something she did not want to remember.

"What's the matter?" Adam whispered.

"Nothing," she said quietly and closed the bedroom door again gently.

It was years since she had dared to drink coffee on a plane.

But the tempting aroma of coffee had filled the cabin so quickly that she wondered if they had a barista on board.

The flight attendant responsible for her row must have weighed well over two hundred pounds. He was sweating like a pig. Normally she would have been disgusted by the unsightly rings of damp that were visible on the pale shirt fabric. She had nothing against male stewards. But she would prefer the more feminine type, thought the large lady who was now standing and staring southeast from her panorama windows on the hills above Villefranche. Pants-wearing stewards often had a slight gay twist of the wrist and chose aftershaves that were more like light spring perfumes than masculine musks. This red-haired boar was therefore an obvious exception. She would normally have ignored him. But the smell of coffee had undone her. She had asked for a refill three times and smiled.

And even the wine tasted good.

She had recently discovered that the prices the wine monopoly in Norway charged for goods that had been so carefully and expensively imported were in fact the same as in any old wine shop in the Old Town. Unbelievable, she thought, but true. That afternoon she had opened a twenty-five-euro bottle of wine and drunk a glass. She couldn't remember tasting a better wine. The man in the shop had assured her that the bottle could stand open for a day or two. She hoped he was right.

All these years, she thought, and stroked her hair. All the projects that had never given her more than money and a headache. All her knowledge that had never been used for anything other than entertaining other people.

This morning she had felt the edge of winter in the air. February was the coldest month on the Riviera. The sea was no longer azure blue. The dirty gray foam lapped tamely at her feet as she walked along the beaches and enjoyed the solitude. Most of the trees had finally lost their leaves. Only the odd

pine tree shone green along the roads. Even the path to St.
Jean, where noisy, well-dressed children with willowy mothers
and wealthy fathers usually shattered the idyll, was empty and
desolate. She stopped frequently. Sometimes she lit a cigarette,
even though she had stopped smoking years ago now. A slight
taste of tar stuck to her tongue. It tasted good.

She had started walking. The restlessness that had plagued
her for as long as she could remember felt different now. It was
as if she finally understood herself now, understood the feeling
of existing in a vacuum of waiting. She had wasted years of
her life waiting for something that would never happen, she
thought to herself as she stood at the window, holding her hand
up against the cool glass.

"For things just to happen," she whispered and saw a brief
gray hint of breath on the windowpane.

She still felt restless, a vague tension in her body. But the
unease that had previously gotten her down and pulled her
away had now been replaced by an invigorating fear.

"Fear," she whispered with satisfaction and caressed the glass
with slow hand movements.

She chose the word carefully. A good, exhilarating, bright
fear was what she felt. She imagined it was like being in love.

Whereas before she felt down but couldn't cry, tired but
couldn't sleep, she now accepted her existence so fully that she
often burst out laughing. She slept well, although she frequently
woke up with a feeling that could be mistaken for . . . happiness.

She chose the word happiness, even though it was perhaps a
bit too strong at present.

Some people would, no doubt, say she was lonely. She was
certain of that, but it didn't bother her. If only they knew what
she actually thought of the people who thought they knew her
or what she did. So many of them had allowed themselves to

be blinded by her success, despite living in a country where modesty was considered a virtue and superiority the deadliest of all deadly sins.

A nonspecific, unfamiliar anger flared up in her. Her skin crawled, and she ran her cold hand down her left arm and felt how firm she was, how compact her flesh was on her body, hard and dense, as if her skin was slightly too small.

It was a long time since she had bothered to think about the past. It wasn't worth it. But things had changed so much in recent weeks.

She was born on a rainy Sunday evening in November 1958. Her mother died within twenty minutes of giving birth, and the way the state had treated the tiny, half-dead child made it crystal-clear that Norway was not a country where you should believe you were worth something.

Her father was abroad. She didn't have any grandparents. One of the nurses had wanted to take her home to her family when she recovered a bit. She thought the baby needed more love and care than could be offered by a three-way shift at the hospital. But the egalitarian country of which the baby was now a citizen did not permit such special arrangements. So she was left in a corner of the children's ward, where she was fed and had her diaper changed at fixed times, but otherwise was given very little attention until her father came to take her home three months later, to a life where her new mother was already installed.

"Bitterness is not in my nature," the woman said out loud to her own diffuse reflection in the window. "Bitterness is not in my nature."

She would never have used the expression "burning rage." But that was the cliché that came to her all the same as she turned her back to the view and lay down on the far-too-soft sofa so she could breathe more easily. Her diaphragm was burning. She slowly raised her hands to her face. Big square hands with sweaty palms and short nails. She turned them around and noticed a scar on the back of one of them. Her thumb looked as though it had been broken. She tried to recall a story that she knew existed somewhere. She quickly pulled up the sleeves of her sweater, she pinched and touched her own skin. The heat was so extreme now that she could barely swallow. Suddenly she sat up and observed her body as if it belonged to someone else. She ran her fingers through her hair and felt the grease on her scalp against her fingertips. She scratched herself with small, sharp movements until her scalp started to bleed.

She sucked her fingers greedily. A vague taste of iron hung under the nails, and she tore them off, bit her skin, and swallowed. Everything was clearer now. It was important to reflect on the past; it was necessary to piece together her story, to make it whole.

She had tried once before.

She'd been thirty-five years old when she finally managed to argue her way into seeing a copy of the dry hospital report of her birth, full of terminology, and she couldn't face dealing with it then. She had leafed through the yellowing pages that smelled of dusty archives and found confirmation of what she had feared, hoped, and expected. Her mother had not given birth to her. The woman she knew as Mommy was a stranger. An intruder. Someone she didn't need to feel anything for.

She had felt neither anger nor sorrow. As she folded the handwritten pages, she simply felt flat. Or perhaps it was a sense of vague and almost indifferent irritation.

She had never challenged them about it.

She couldn't be bothered.

The false mother died soon after anyway.

That was ten years ago now.

Victoria Heinerback had always irritated her.

Victoria Heinerback was a racist.

Though naturally she wasn't open about it and wouldn't acknowledge it. The woman was, after all, politically savvy and had an almost impressive understanding of how the media worked. Her fellow party members, however, were constantly dropping stupid and completely ignorant comments about immigrants. For them, Somalians and Chinese were cut from the same cloth. Well-integrated Chinese people were lumped together with lazy Somalians. Victoria Heinerback's party believed that a conscientious Pakistani who ran his own corner shop was the same burden on society as a gold-digger from Morocco who had come to Norway thinking he could just help himself to the women and government money.

Victoria Heinerback was responsible for this.

The woman who was spending the winter alone on the Riviera got to her feet suddenly and stood up. She was a bit unsteady; a wave of dizziness forced her to hold on to something.

It was all so perfect, everything. Everything was working.

She laughed quietly to herself, astonished by the force of her mood swings.

Inspecting someone's house can tell you more than a thousand interviews, she thought as the nausea ebbed away.

Evening was falling, and she wanted to pour herself another glass of the good wine from the Old Town. The beam from the lighthouse at Cap Ferrat swept over her in a pulsing stroke when she turned to stare out over the bay. To the north, streetlights lit the roads that cut through the steep terrain.

She was a master of her art, and from now on, she would not be judged by anyone other than herself.

FIVE

The visit to Victoria Heinerback's apartment had not made Adam any less judgmental, but he now didn't know what to expect from the memorial service. He parked some distance from the house. The cars sat bumper-to-bumper along the narrow road, making it almost impassable.

The former party leader had generously offered his house for the occasion. His colossal villa by the water, only a few hundred yards from the old airport at Fornebu, was no longer plagued by pollution and noise following the long-awaited relocation of the main airport. The once beleaguered, uninhabitable timber house, with its scores of bay windows, large terraces, and two Ionic pillars framing the front door, had risen like a phoenix from the ashes, though the garden that sloped down to the fjord was still no more than clay and loose stones, ashen and snow white.

The number of mourners dressed in dark clothes was impressive.

Adam Stubo shook hands with a woman at the door and, just in case, mumbled his condolences. He had no idea who she

was. He almost stumbled on an umbrella stand further down
the hall. At least fifteen people were waiting to hang up their
coats. Then he felt someone tug his sleeve, and before he could
turn around, a young man with a thin neck and badly tied tie
had taken his coat from him and given him a gentle push toward one of several public rooms.

Before Adam knew it, he was standing with a half-full glass
in his hand. As he was walking, he looked around in desperation for somewhere to put it down.

"It's non-alcoholic," whispered a voice.

He recognized the woman immediately.

"Thank you," he said, bewildered, and squeezed in to the
side so he wouldn't block the door. "You're here too."

"Yes," said the woman in a friendly, quiet voice that could
be heard above the humming of the crowd. "Most of us are.
This is more than politics. It's a tragedy that's touched us all."

She was wearing a tight black suit that contrasted with her
short blonde hair and made her look paler than she did on TV.
Adam looked down self-consciously and noticed that the fu-
nereal mood had not prevented the Socialist Left leader from
choosing a skirt that was so short, it would have been more appropriate for someone ten years younger. But her legs were well
toned, and he realized he should look up.

"Were you a friend of Victoria's?" asked the woman.

"No." He cleared his throat and held out his hand. She took
it. "Adam Stubo," he said. "NCIS. Pleased to meet you."

Her eyes were blue and alert, and he registered a hint of curiosity in the way she tilted her head as she passed her glass from
one hand to the other. Then she stopped herself with a quick
nod.

"I just hope you get to the bottom of this," she said before
turning into the room, where the newly retired party leader,

Kristian Mundal, had positioned himself by a rostrum, presumably borrowed from a nearby hotel.

"Dear friends"—he coughed to get everyone's attention—"I would like to welcome you all warmly on behalf of Kari and myself. We felt that it was not only right but also very important to mark this sad occasion." He coughed again, but this time more. "Sorry," he apologized and continued. "It has been only two days since we heard the terrible news that Victoria had been so brutally taken from us. She . . ."

Adam could have sworn there were tears in the older man's eyes. Real tears, he thought, astonished. In public. Real, salt tears were wetting the weathered face of a man who for three decades had proved to be the toughest, most cunning, and most resilient politician in Norway.

"It is no secret that Victoria was"—the man stopped and took a deep breath before continuing—"I don't want say 'like a daughter to me.' I have four daughters, and Victoria was not one of them. But she was someone who meant a lot to me. Politically, of course, as we worked together for many years, despite her young age, but also personally. To the extent that it's possible in politics . . ."

He stopped again. The silence was intense. No one touched their glasses. No one scraped their feet or chair on the dark cherrywood floor. People hardly dared to breathe. Adam glanced around the room without moving his head. Over by one of the other rooms, squeezed between a couple of imposing armchairs and two men that Adam didn't recognize, was the chairman of the Standing Committee on Foreign Affairs, with his hands inappropriately deep in his pockets. His brow furrowed in expectation, he stared out the window, as if he hoped that Victoria Heinerback would surprise them all by waving from the deck of a small boat approaching the jetty just below the house. One of the Labor Party's youngest members of parliament was standing, weeping openly and silently, beside an arrangement of white lilies in a huge Chinese vase. She sat on the Standing Committee for Finance and Economic Affairs and therefore knew Victoria Heinerback better than most, Adam assumed. The minister of finance was standing next to the rostrum, with his head bent. He discreetly adjusted his glasses. The Storting's president was holding a woman by the hand. Adam looked down and concluded that the villa in Tveistveien must be one of Europe's least-guarded terrorist targets right now. He shuddered. On his way out here, he had only seen one marked police car, just outside the house.

". . . and to the extent that politics is a friendly place," concluded the elderly man. "And it can be. I am glad that . . ."

Adam nodded lightly to the blonde with the good legs, who gave a brief, sad smile back. He slowly withdrew from the room, while the man in front continued his speech.

"Excuse me," he whispered to irritated faces as he made his way toward his goal. "Excuse me, I just . . ."

At last he was out in the hall. It was empty. He carefully closed the double doors and sighed.

Perhaps it wasn't such a good idea to come. He had had a reason for coming, thinking that the memorial service would give him a better picture of Victoria Heinerback. She was obviously not the person he had taken her to be. She was more. Even though he never for a moment imagined that the pictures of public figures drawn with broad strokes in the press were in any way genuine, real, or exhaustive, his visit to the scene of the crime two days ago had made a deeper impression on him than he was prepared to admit. Earlier on, while he was rummaging around looking for a clean, white shirt, he had hoped that the people close to Victoria Heinerback might give more of themselves and say more about her at this impulsive memorial service, held so soon after the young woman's death. But even now, twenty minutes into the service, he realized that he should have known better. This was a day for praise. For good thoughts and happy memories, a shared grief across party lines.

Adam stood with his back to the reception rooms and wondered where he would find his coat. The former party leader's speech, with frequent pauses and a cough here and there, filtered through the wood of the solid doors as a muffled murmur.

Then he heard another voice to his left, through a door that was ajar to what might be the kitchen. It was the sibilant, urgent whisper of a woman who sounded like she actually wanted to shout but felt that it might be inappropriate, given the occasion. Adam was about to make his presence known when he heard a man's voice, deep and aggressive, say, "Don't you worry about that."

There was the sound of a glass being banged down on a table, followed by what was obviously a sniff from the woman. Then she said something. Adam could only make out a few individual words that meant nothing to him. He took a couple of cautious steps toward the half-open door.

"Be careful," he heard the woman say. "You had better watch it now, Rudolf."

She came out into the hall so suddenly that Adam had to step back.

"Jesus," he said and smiled. "You really scared me. Adam Stubo."

The woman let a man out after her, closed the door with care, took Adam's hand, and returned his smile. She was smaller than he'd imagined, almost strikingly petite. She had a slim waist, something she emphasized with a tight, fitted black skirt that stopped just below the knee. The gray silk blouse had ruffles at the neck and down the front. She reminded him of a miniature Margaret Thatcher. Her nose was big and hooked, and her chin was pointed. Her eyes were worthy of the iron lady. Icy blue and sharp, though her face was relaxed and welcoming.

"Kari Mundal," she said quietly. "Pleasure. You are very welcome here, despite the occasion. Perhaps you've already met Rudolf Fjord?"

The man was twice her height and half as old. He was obviously less practiced at hiding his feelings. His hand was sweaty when he held it out, and his eyes darted here and there for a few moments before he finally managed to pull himself together and smile. At the same time he nodded and nearly bowed, as if he realized that his handshake was not particularly impressive.

"Were you looking for something?" Kari Mundal asked. "The bathroom? Just down there." She pointed. "When the service is over," she added, "there will be a bite to eat. Of course, we hadn't expected so many people. But a little something is better than nothing. Victoria was such . . ." She smoothed her hair.

Kari Mundal was as close as you could get to the model of a good, old-fashioned housewife; she had stayed at home with her four daughters and three sons, and her husband was the first to admit that his stamina on the political front was entirely due to his loyal wife.

"Everyone should have a Kari at home," he often said in interviews, blissfully unaffected by the complaints of a younger generation of women. "A Kari at home is better than ten in the workplace."

Kari Mundal had looked after the house and children and ironed his shirts for more than forty years. She was happy to appear in magazines and on Saturday night TV, and since her husband had retired from politics, she had become a sort of national mascot, a politically incorrect, friendly, and sharp little granny.

"Were you looking for the bahroom?" she asked and pointed again.

"Yes," Adam replied. "Sorry to have to miss some of your husband's speech—"

"When you have to go, you have to go," interrupted Kari Mundal. "Rudolf, shall we go in?"

Rudolf Fjord bowed again, stiff and obviously ill at ease. He followed behind the older woman, who opened the door to the reception room. It closed silently behind them.

Adam was alone.

The voice on the other side of the door sounded as if it was conducting a church service now. Adam wondered whether the gathering would soon start to sing. Victoria Heinerback's body would not be released for a funeral for a long time, so in a sense there was nothing odd about holding a memorial service, but it struck him for the first time since he arrived that there was something vaguely distasteful about holding it here, in a private house. It was a sudden, but obviously well planned, event.

When he looked into the room where Rudolf Fjord and Kari Mundal had been having their whispered contretemps, his suspicion was confirmed. The kitchen was massive, as if it had been planned with occasions like this in mind. Silver platters of sandwiches, finger food, and elegant hors d'oeuvres stood lined up on the countertops and table, between bowls full of colorful salads. Cases of mineral water were stacked against the wall. On the windowsill, which was at least half a yard deep and two yards long, the hostess had lined up bottles of red and white wine. Some had already been opened.

Adam carefully lifted the plastic wrap on one of the trays and stuffed three bits of chicken into his mouth.

Then he left the kitchen again.

He noticed a wardrobe at the end of the hall. As he chewed

while trying to find his coat among all the other coats, jackets, hats, and scarves, it struck him that Mrs. Mundal had not even asked who he was and why he was there. It wasn't likely that she knew him from before. Adam had only ever had one interview in the national media. The following day, he had promised himself and his superiors that it would never happen again.

He eventually found his coat. He went out.

An argument, he mused as the raw sea air hit him.

Arguing on a day like today. Little Mrs. Mundal and Rudolf Fjord, second in charge of the party and, according to the papers, Victoria Heinerback's obvious successor as party leader. The disagreement was obviously important enough to make them miss Kristian Mundal's speech in the main room.

A gust of wind made his coattails flap against his legs. Adam looked up at the sky and then ran with heavy steps over the gravel.

Of course it didn't have to mean anything.

When he got to the car, he heard the helicopters. There were two of them, one over a hill to the east, the other low over the water a few hundred yards from the shore. He also now saw that the small boat down by the jetty was a police boat. He counted five uniformed men along the road, all armed.

The gathering indoors was safe.

To the extent that anyone was, he thought as he got into the car.

He spat out some parsley and had to drive in reverse for fifty yards before he was able to turn.

The physical pain was not the worst thing. She was used to it. Her body had been ravaged by multiple sclerosis for more than twenty years now. Even though she was only sixty-seven, she knew that she was nearing the end. Nothing worked anymore. Her bedsores leaked and were painful. Yvonne Knutsen's body was a shell around what could barely be called a life. She lay flat in a bed in a bland room in an institution that she had never liked. Grief drained what remained of her life force.

Bernt was wonderful. He came every day with little Fiorella and stayed with her for a long time, even though Yvonne was constantly falling asleep. Her medicine was stronger now.

She wanted to die. But God refused to come and get her.

The worst thing about just lying like this was time. Time multiplied when you weren't able to do anything. It went in circles, in loops, in great big arcs, before returning back to where it started. She didn't want this anymore. Her time on this earth should be over, it should have been over long ago, and her grief made the fact that her body was clinging onto life even more unbearable.

Fiona had been a good daughter. Naturally they had argued, like every mother and daughter. Their relationship had been cool now and then, but was it reasonable to expect anything else? It never took more than a few weeks before everything was the same as before. Fiona was kind. Yvonne's friends had always said so, in the days when she could still make and serve coffee, or even a meal on a good day.

"You're lucky, Yvonne."

Fiona had never let her down.

They shared a secret, the two of them.

Just as time warped beyond recognition when it had no meaning, so secrets could grow to be so enormous that they were invisible. At the beginning, it had been like a thorn between them. But since there was no turning back, they had managed to agree with surprising ease: *We'll forget this.*

Yvonne Knutsen could still hear her own voice back then, firm and maternal with an edge of determined protection: "We will forget this."

And they had forgotten.

Now Fiona was dead, and loneliness gave the secret new life. It haunted her, particularly at night, when she thought she could see a shadow by the window, a silent figure seeking revenge who had now found reason to plague her, now when she had no one to help her forget.

If only God would let her follow Fiona.

"Dear God," she whispered into the room.

But her heart went on beating stubbornly in her emaciated chest.

Daylight was disappearing fast. It was four o'clock in the afternoon on Monday, February 9. A thirty-seven-year-old man was about to climb a crane without permission. It was yellow and over twenty yards high, towering above a confusion of construction materials and machinery. He was only a few yards from the ground, and he could already feel the cold wind blasting through his clothes. His gloves were too thin. His friend had warned him. The metal felt like ice. But he had not dared to choose anything warmer. It was better, after all, to have more control over your fingers.

He wasn't going fast enough. His friend was already halfway up. But he was younger and well trained.

Vegard Krogh tried to be positive.

He didn't really have the energy for this sort of thing anymore. He was reluctantly approaching forty and had never received the recognition and publicity he deserved. He thought his writing was accessible, and his literary sarcasm was clever and good. The critics all agreed, but Vegard Krogh's work was seldom given more than a passing comment in the local paper from his hometown. Vegard Krogh had a distinct voice, a critic once said, an original and ironic pen. He was described as a talent. But since then he had not only gotten older, he had also become an author of some note. He knew it: he had important things to tell. His talent had blossomed, he should be established by now, a force to be reckoned with. A review of his third novel from a national newspaper hung on the corkboard at home. Not particularly impressive, just two columns, worn and yellow after several years in the kitchen, but the phrase "strong, vital and at times technically brilliant" was written there.

The readers, however, had totally let him down.

Don't think. Climb.

He should have worn overalls. There was a gap between the waistband of his pants and his sweater. The cold cut into his back like icicles. He tried to stuff his woolen vest into his pants with one hand. It helped for a few seconds.

He would just have to manage. He didn't know where he got the energy. Without thinking about the cold, without worrying about his increasing distance from the ground, without thinking about how dangerous the project was that he was now determined to carry through, he simply concentrated on lifting one leg after the other. Lifting one hand up a step while the other clung to the metal. Again and again. Keeping pace. Iron will.

He was up.

The wind was so strong that he could feel the crane swaying. He looked down. Closed his eyes.

"Don't look down," his friend shouted. "Don't look down yet, Vegard! Look at me!"

His eyelids were stuck to his irises.

He wanted to look but didn't dare. A violent wave of nausea washed over him.

"You've done this before," he heard his friend's voice saying, much closer now. "It'll be fine, just wait."

A hand gripped his lower arm. A firm grip.

"It's exactly the same as this summer," the voice said. "The only difference is the weather."

And the fact that it was illegal, thought Vegard Krogh as he tried not to look back.

His job at the left-leaning paper *Klassekampen* had been a dead end. He had stayed there too long. Maybe because he was, after all, allowed to write what he wanted. *Klassekampen* was important. It took sides. Papers should take sides, politically and on principle. And Vegard Krogh was allowed to rant as much as he liked. As long as his aggression was targeted in the right direction, as the editor put it. As *Klassekampen* and the young Vegard Krogh had more or less the same views on Norwegian cultural life, the paper fully supported his vitriolic, well-written reviews, angry analyses, and highly libelous remarks. He carried on for several years, until he was exhausted and finally had to admit that practically no one read *Klassekampen*.

He was never actually sued.

When he got the job working in the culture department of TV2, everything looked set to improve. For a brief year he achieved a sort of cult status among the angry young men who voiced their views about the state of the nation and what direction Norway should take. Vegard Krogh was one of them; even if he was a bit old, he was one of them. He had first gained notoriety as a stunt reporter for *Young and Urban* and was given his own irate ten-minute slot on *Absolute Entertainment* every Thursday.

Then after one too many lawsuits, which never made it to the courtroom thanks to the jolly and apologetic executive director, he lost the slot. TV2 was not as open as *Klassekampen* to what they ignorantly called "shit" in an internal review. Vegard Krogh was actually glad, when he thought about it. TV2 was a totally commercial channel, just like the worst American ones.

Finally he dared to look down.

"Can you see it?" his friend shouted. "On the orange target?"

Vegard Krogh looked down. The wind had blown his anorak up into a balloon, a great big bubble that made it difficult to see.

"Okay, let's go," he spluttered.

"We have to go further out on to the arm," his friend shouted and let go of him. "Can you do it?"

He finally managed to get to where he was supposed to be. He tried to relax. Ignore the cold. Forget the height. Fixed his eyes on the book down there, an almost invisible rectangle on a large orange target. Tears streamed down his face. He blamed the wind and tried to muster his own inner strength. The camera had been positioned to the left on a pile of foundation blocks. The photographer had pulled a hood over his head. Vegard Krogh raised his arm as a signal. A bright light blinded him, and it took him a few seconds to fix his eyes on the target.

The harness was properly buckled. His friend checked one last time.

"There," he said loudly. "You can jump."

"Are you sure the bungee rope will hold?" Vegard Krogh shouted back, even though he didn't need to.

"To the last ounce," shouted his friend. "I weighed you three times before choosing the bungee rope, for God's sake! And I measured this crane only yesterday! Jump! I'm fucking freezing!"

Vegard Krogh shot a glance at the photographer one last time. His hood, with its wolfskin trim, covered half the camera. The lens was focused on the two of them up there. He could hear sirens in the distance. They were getting closer.

Vegard Krogh took aim at the book. It was his latest collection of essays, an almost invisible speck on a round orange disk.

He jumped.

The fall was too slow.

He had time to think. He thought about the fact that he would soon be forty. He thought that his wife didn't appear to be very fertile. They had been trying to have children for three years now, without any results other than the monthly disappointment, which they didn't talk about anymore. He thought about the fact that they still lived in a one-bedroom apartment in Grønland and that they never managed to save anything more than a pittance.

When he was halfway through the fall, he stopped thinking.

It was happening too fast.

Far too fast, thought the photographer, his lens following the man's descent toward the ground.

The book grew in front of Vegard's eyes. He couldn't blink, couldn't see anything other than the white cover that just kept growing. He stretched his arms down and out, he was plummeting toward the ground and at last thought: this is happening too fast.

The wind pulled off his hat, and his fair hair, which was stuck to his sweaty forehead, brushed the orange target at the same moment that Vegard Krogh realized it was over. With great care, as if he had all the time in the world, he picked up his book and pressed it to his heart; his forehead brushed the ground, his bangs kissed the wood of the target.

The bungee rope recoiled. The movement rippled through his body, a powerful jolt from the soles of his feet, an oppressive pulse through his calves to his legs. It felt like his spine was being stretched by the tension.

He laughed.

He roared as he bounced up and down, from side to side. The laughter caught in his throat when the police car turned into the construction site and the photographer tried to pack away all his equipment as he ran toward the hole in the fence that protected the area.

Vegard Krogh had never felt so alive. As long as the film was okay, this would be perfect. The jump had been just as he had wanted, just like the book, just like Vegard Krogh believed he had always been: daring, dangerous, and provocative, bordering on what was permissible.

He didn't die that Monday in the middle of February. On the contrary, he felt immortal as he hung there, upside down below a bright yellow crane, above an orange target, in the sharp blue light of the police car that howled toward him on the ground. Vegard Krogh swung between two bright colors that gray, windy afternoon, clutching the first copy of his new book: *Bungee Jump*.

Vegard Krogh's death was postponed by one week and three days, but he didn't know that himself, of course.

No matter how hard she tried, Johanne could not get herself to like Sigmund Berli. The man was disgusting. He openly picked his nose, he farted constantly without even apologizing, he cleaned his ears and bit his nails in front of everyone. Right now he was sitting there tearing a dirty napkin to shreds without even thinking that the pieces would be caught on a draft and blown to the floor.

"He's a good guy," Adam usually said, exasperated by Johanne's cool attitude. "Just doesn't have many manners. Sigmund was the only one who actually spoke to me after Elisabeth and Trine died."

She couldn't argue with the last statement. The terrible death of his first wife and daughter had nearly finished him off. He was about to drop out of working life and disappear into a serious and destructive depression when Sigmund, with a combination of sudden authority and touching care, had managed to pull him back to a form of normalcy, but one that didn't truly take shape until he met Johanne two years later and started over again.

"You can't measure a bit of snot on someone's pants against true loyalty," Adam said. Consequently, the man was now sitting on a bar stool in Johanne's kitchen, having just enjoyed three helpings of Stange chicken and arugula salad.

"You make great food," he said and smiled broadly.

He was looking at Adam.

"Thank you," Johanne said.

"I made the dressing," laughed Adam. "The dressing is the most important part. But you're right. Johanne is the cook in this house. I'm just . . . a gourmet. I take care of the details. Everything that makes an ordinary meal more—"

He laughed when she hit him with the kitchen towel.

"Can't take being teased," he said and pulled her to him. "But good at heart." He kissed her and didn't want to let go.

"That argument in the kitchen," Sigmund started, self-consciously folding the napkin before pushing it away from him, not knowing what he should do with the torn remains. "It could've been about anything."

"Yes," Adam said and let go of Johanne. "But I still think we should make a note that there might be something to it. Not only were Kari Mundal and Rudolf Fjord at loggerheads, but the argument was so important that they also missed Kristian Mundal's well-prepared speech. It's not like Kari to miss an opportunity to praise and support her husband. And Rudolf Fjord was pretty worked up."

"Politics," Johanne said, "is no Sunday school, as you know. If all angry disagreements on the political sidelines were grounds for suspecting murder, you'd have your work cut out for you."

"Yes, but—" Adam pulled another bar stool up to the island

unit and made himself comfortable with his legs apart and his arms leaning on the counter—"there was just something about the whole situation," he said quietly. "Something . . ." Then he shook his head. "It has been noted," he said lightly. "But we'll leave it at that. We've got plenty else to do. At least at the moment."

"At the moment we've got next to nothing," Sigmund sulked. "In either of the cases. Nada."

"You're exaggerating a bit," Adam said. "We do have some leads."

"Some," muttered Sigmund.

"But nothing that fits together," Adam continued. "Nothing that leads anywhere. I agree with you there. We established almost immediately that there weren't any links between the two women, other than the obvious. And we've been over it a thousand times. The brutality of the murder. The gender of the victims. The fact that they were both in the public eye. Where they lived."

He gave a long yawn and continued, "But it's doubtful that we're looking for a killer who's got something against Lørenskog. Victoria and Fiona didn't know each other, had no mutual friends or acquaintances other than what is normal in such a small country. They weren't involved in any of the same work. They lived very different lives. One was single and loved parties, and the other had a family and a young child. To me, it seems—"

"That we're looking at two separate cases, all the same," Johanne said. She was holding the kettle under the faucet. "But both murderers must have been strong. Victoria was killed outside her house and lifted into the bedroom. Fiona was overpowered."

"Do you often talk like that?" Sigmund asked.

"Like what?"

"Finishing off each other's sentences. Like my sister's twins."

"We are of course spiritual twins," said Johanne, who smiled when Sigmund didn't pick up on the irony. "Think the same, feel the same. Coffee?"

"Yes please. But if"—he put his hand in front of his mouth and tried to muffle a deep burp—"if this really is two cases, is it possible that the second killer, the one who killed Victoria Heinerback, wanted to make it look like the work of a serial killer?"

"Hardly, when there's only been two murders," Adam said. "That's almost pathetic. But first we have to agree that it isn't the work of one killer."

"But that's obviously not possible," Johanne said. "Not yet. But I agree, even though there are many similarities, the type of similarities is not such that . . . well, the murders don't exactly look like a series."

"I wondered," Sigmund started and then blushed like a boy with his head full of sex. He scratched his thigh and cocked his head awkwardly. At that moment Johanne thought he was sweet. She poured the boiling water into the French press, filled a pitcher with milk, and put out a bowl of brown sugar.

"I just wondered"—Sigmund tried again—"about how the whole profiling . . ."

He couldn't decide whether to use the Norwegian or English pronunciation and pinched his nose between his thumb and forefinger.

"Just say it in Norwegian," Johanne said. "It sounds like some sort of detective film when you say it in English. Don't you think?"

He filled his cup with too much coffee and had to put his lips to the rim and sip the boiling hot liquid before he dared to lift it up.

"Ow. Ow." He rubbed his upper lip and snuffled on, "We

know quite a bit ourselves. A lot, in fact. But as you've actually trained with the FBI and all that, with that top guy, well, I thought—"

"Milk?" interrupted Adam and filled up Sigmund's cup with milk without waiting for an answer. "Sugar? Here."

"Profiling can mean many things," said Johanne and handed Sigmund a towel. "Any murder will generally involve elements that point to some of the killer's characteristics. In that sense, profiling is used in all investigations. It's just that you don't use that term."

As he aimlessly wiped the surface in front of him, the milky coffee going everywhere, Sigmund said, "You mean, when we find a man in his own filthy home with a knife in his groin and the guy who called the police is standing in the corner sloshed and sniveling, then we make a profile? A 'killer who's drunk and argued with a close relative and the knife just happened to be there but he didn't mean to kill him and is really sorry now and would have called for help later' type profile?"

Johanne burst out laughing and wiped away the remains of the coffee with paper towels. "I couldn't have put it better myself," she said. "And the profile you just gave is so usual and easily constructed that it takes no more than thirty seconds to establish that the drunk in the corner is guilty. But you and Adam don't deal with many cases like that. The NCIS deals with much worse cases."

"But Johanne," Sigmund said, eager now. "I assume that you analyze each case by picking it to pieces—"

"You analyze the modus operandi," Johanne said helpfully. "Take it to pieces, as you put it, look at all the elements of the crime. Then we make deductions based on the various factors and the overall impression. When we're analyzing, we give a lot of importance to the victim's background and behavior prior to the crime, both from his point of view and an external point of view, as well as the actual killing. It's a massive amount of work. And"—the steam from her cup clouded her glasses—"it would be hard to find a science that is more uncertain, more difficult, or less reliable than profiling."

"What you're describing is basically the same as tactical investigation," Sigmund said with a cynical frown.

"It's very similar." Johanne nodded and added, "The main difference is that tactical investigation, much more than profiling, deals with . . . how should I put it . . . undisputed fact. Profilers are often psychologists. A tactical investigator's purpose is to find the killer, whereas a profiler's job is to build up a psychological picture of the killer. So in a way, profiling is just a tool in the tactical investigation."

"So if you were going to say something about Fiona Helle's murder alone," said Sigmund, whose cheeks were flushed with excitement, "Forgetting Victoria Heinerback for the moment, what would you say?"

Johanne looked at Sigmund over the rim of her cup.

"I'm not quite sure," she said slowly. "The whole thing seems very . . . un-Norwegian. I don't like the expression, as it's no longer possible to protect ourselves from gruesome murders like these. But all the same"—she took a deep breath and then drank some coffee—"I would say," she started after a few moments, "that it's possible to see the outlines of two very different profiles. Starting with the similarities: Fiona Helle's murder was well planned. It was obviously premeditated, so we're looking for someone who's capable of planning someone else's death in detail. The little paper basket can have had no other function than to hold the severed tongue. It was a perfect fit. We can more or less dismiss the idea that someone might think about cutting their victim's tongue out without killing them. The time of the killing was also right. Tuesday evening. Everyone knew that Fiona Helle was on her own on Tuesday evenings. And in several interviews she boasted that Lørenskog was 'a peaceful oasis away from stresses of the city.' " With two fingers, she drew quote marks in the air.

"Quite a statement," Adam said.

"And it was very stupid of her to tell the whole world that she didn't need to lock her door in the little cul-de-sac where she lived, as everyone looked out for their neighbors, and no one was nasty."

Sigmund snorted and added, "The Romerike boys got in touch with her to warn her about saying things like that, afterwards. But she still left the door open. She said something about 'not giving in to evil.' Jesus . . ." He mumbled something incomprehensible into his cup of coffee.

"In any case," Johanne said and pulled over a pad of paper that Adam had found in Kristiane's red toy chest. "The murder was premeditated. So we've already come quite a long way." She leaned her elbows on the counter. "There are also grounds for drawing another relatively given conclusion. I would say that the killing shows signs of intense hatred. The fact that it was premeditated, the killer's determined, criminal intention, and the method . . ."

There was a short silence. Johanne wrinkled her brow slightly and turned her left ear toward the hall.

"It was nothing," Adam said. "Nothing."

"To strangle someone, tie her up, cut out her tongue . . ." Johanne was talking quietly now, tense, still listening. "Hate," she concluded. "But then the problems start. The drama of it, the split tongue, the origami . . . the whole thing, in fact . . ."

Her red pencil was drawing slow circles on the paper.

"It could be a cover. An act. Camouflage. The symbolism is so blatantly obvious, so—"

"Childish?" suggested Sigmund.

"Exactly. So simple, in any case, that it could almost appear to be a cover-up. The intention was possibly to confuse people. And then we're talking about an unusually cunning person who must have hated Fiona Helle intensely. And then we're no further forward than—"

"Back where we started," Adam said with resignation. "But what if the symbolism *was* sincere?"

"Goodness . . . Didn't the Native Americans use it literally? "White man speak with forked tongue"? If we assume that the killer mutilated her body to tell the world something, it must be that Fiona Helle was not what she pretended to be. She was a liar. A traitor. According to him, that is. The murderer. Which in this rather flimsy and therefore totally unusable profile would verge on . . . utter madness."

"Shame"—Sigmund said, yawning loudly—"that we can't find any problems in her life. No major conflicts. A bit of jealousy here and there; she was a successful lady. A dispute with the tax authorities a couple of years ago. And one with a neighbor about a spruce that blocked the light from Fiona's study. Of no consequence. The tree was chopped down, by the way. Without the case going to court."

"Strange that there isn't anything," Johanne started and then stopped. "Now?"

Her anxiety was obvious when she looked at Adam.

"It's nothing," he said again. "Relax. She's asleep."

Johanne had agreed that Ragnhild should sleep in her bedroom, at least when they had guests.

"It's strange," she repeated hesitantly, "that you can't find anything, nothing that even resembles dirt in Fiona Helle's life. Very strange indeed. After all, she was forty-two. You must've missed something."

"Look yourself, then," Sigmund said, obviously offended. "We've had fifteen men on the job for several weeks now and have come up with a big fat nothing. Maybe the woman really was a paragon of virtue."

"There is no paragon of virtue."

"But what about the profile then?"

"Which profile?"

"The one you were going to make," Sigmund said.

"I can't make a profile of the person who killed Fiona Helle," Johanne said and then drank the rest of her coffee in one gulp. "Not of any consequence, at least. No one can. But I can give you a tip. Look for the lies in her life. Find the lie. Then you may not even need a profile. You'll have the man."

"Or woman," said Adam with a faint smile.

Johanne didn't even bother to answer. Instead she tiptoed out to the bedroom.

"Is she always so stressed?" Sigmund whispered.

"Yes."

"That would drive me nuts."

"You hardly see your family."

"Shut up. I'm at home more than most people I know."

"Which doesn't say much."

"You're just whipped."

"You fool," Adam smiled. "More coffee?"

"No thanks. But some of that." He pointed toward the other end of the table, where a bottle glinted yellow and brown in the light of the candle on the windowsill.

"Aren't you driving?"

"The wife's got the car. Parents' night at school or something like that."

"See what I mean." Adam got down two oversized cognac glasses and poured some in. "Cheers," he said.

"Not a lot to raise our glasses to," said Sigmund and took a drink.

Jack's claws clacked over the parquet. The animal stopped

in the middle of the floor, where he stretched and gave a long yawn.

"Looks like he's laughing," mumbled Sigmund.

"I think he is," Adam replied. "At us, maybe. Our worries. All he thinks about is food."

The dog wagged his tail and padded out to the kitchen. He whined a bit by the garbage can. He sniffed around on the floor and greedily licked up the bits of grease and breadcrumbs.

"Your food's in the dish," Adam said. "Woof!"

Jack yapped and growled at the cabinet door.

"Don't wind him up. Stop it, Jack!" Johanne had come back with an awake Ragnhild in her arms.

"I knew I heard something," she said without trying to disguise the triumph in her voice. "She's wet. You can change her. Jack, go and lie down!"

"Daddy's little daisy," Adam babbled and gently took his daughter. "Baby daisy's wet."

"Completely ga-ga," Sigmund said.

"It's called being a good father."

Johanne smiled and followed Adam with her eyes as he disappeared into the bathroom. Jack followed with his tail between his legs. He stopped by the partition to the living room and sent Johanne another pleading look.

"Lie down," she said and the dog disappeared.

Muffled music could be heard from the first floor. Half the sound got lost in the floor insulation. The thumping of the bass was all that reached them, and Johanne wrinkled her nose before putting on the dishwasher.

"It's really noisy here," Sigmund observed without showing any sign of moving. "Do you mind?"

He pointed at the bottle of cognac.

"No, no. Not at all. Help yourself."

The music got steadily louder.

"Must be Selma," muttered Johanne. "Teenager. At home alone, I bet."

Sigmund smiled and poked his nose into the glass. He was relaxed here, he found himself thinking, to his surprise. There was something about the atmosphere here, the tone, the light, the furniture. There was something about Johanne. People at work whispered about her being so stern. They were wrong, Sigmund thought as he dipped his sore lip into the alcohol. The burn stung in a nice way, and he took a sip.

Johanne wasn't stern. She was strong, he thought, even though she was obviously overanxious about the baby. Not so surprising, really, when you thought about her strange older daughter, odd little thing who looked like she was three years younger than she actually was. Adam had taken her to work a few times, and she could frighten the life out of anyone. One minute she behaved like a three-year-old, and then the next minute she said something that could have come out of a college student's mouth. Evidently there was something wrong with her brain. They just didn't know what.

Sigmund had always liked Adam. He enjoyed the older man's company. But they seldom spent time together outside of work. Sigmund had, of course, done as much as he could after the accident, when Adam's daughter fell down on top of her mother while trying to clean the gutters, killing them both. He remembered the low sun through the trees and the two bodies in the garden. Adam hadn't said anything, hadn't cried, hadn't spoken. He just stood there with his crying grandson in his arms, as if he was holding onto life itself and was in danger of crushing it.

"Do you still have Amund over here on the weekends?" he asked suddenly.

"In principle, we have him every other weekend," Johanne

said, taken aback by the question. "But now, with the baby and all that, well . . . originally the arrangement was to help give Adam's son-in-law a break."

"No," said Sigmund.

"Sorry?" She turned toward him.

"That wasn't why it started," he said calmly. "I talked to Bjarne a lot at the time, I did. The son-in-law, that is."

"I know Adam's son-in-law's name."

"Of course. But . . . well, that arrangement was really to help Adam. To give him something to live for. We were really worried, you know. Extremely worried, Bjarne and I. It's good to see . . ." He downed the rest of the cognac in one go and cheerfully looked around. "You've got a good home," he said with unexpected formality in his voice; his eyes were moist.

Johanne shook her head and chuckled. She stood with her hands on her hips, cocked her head, and followed his hands with her eyes. He poured a generous amount into his glass before putting back the cork with a dramatic thump.

"There, that's enough for today. Here's to you, Johanne. I have to say you're a great lady. I wish I could come home every day to the wife and know that she was interested in what I did at work. Knew something about it. Like you. You're a great girl. Cheers."

"And you're a strange one, Sigmund."

"No, just a bit tipsy. Hi!" He raised his glass to Adam, who lifted his arms in triumph and clapped his hands above his head.

"One baby, one nine-year-old, and one canine sleeping like logs. Dry and happy, all of them."

He plopped down on the bar stool.

"Are you celebrating, Sigmund? On a Monday?"

"Yes, there hasn't been much of that recently," Sigmund answered. He had started to hiccup. "But Johanne . . ."

"Yes?"

"If you were going to imagine the worst possible . . . the most difficult serial killer . . . To catch, I mean. If you were to draw a profile of the perfect serial killer, what would it be?"

"Don't you two have enough with the criminals who actually exist?" she said and leaned over the counter.

"Go on," Adam smiled. "Tell us. Tell what he'd be like."

The candle on the windowsill was about to burn out. There was a violent hissing. Bits of soot floated around in front of the reflection in the dark glass. Johanne got out a new candle, pushed it down into the candlestick, and lit the wick. She stood for a few seconds, studying the flame.

"It would be a woman," she said slowly. "Simply because we always imagine it to be a man. We find it difficult to imagine evil incarnate in the shape of a woman, strangely enough. History has definitively shown that women can be evil."

"A woman," Adam said and nodded. "What else?"

Johanne turned toward them and counted quickly on her fingers, "Knowledgeable, of course, and insightful, intelligent, cunning, and unscrupulous. At least, that's what they normally are. But the worst, the worst thing would be . . ."

Suddenly she looked like she was thinking about something else, as if trying to catch a thought that had just passed through her head. The two men sipped their cognac. A gang of boys could be heard shouting out on the street. A light was turned off in the neighbors' house. The darkness outside the kitchen window became denser, the reflections sharper.

"It's just as if"—she started and straightened her glasses with her forefinger—"it's as if . . . this case gives me a feeling of . . . déjà vu. But I just can't think . . ." She studied the candle flame again. It danced in the draft from the window they couldn't afford to replace. A fleeting smile passed over her face. "Forget it. Probably just nothing."

"Go on," Sigmund said. "So far you've just given us the obvious list. What else would make it impossible for us to catch this lady of yours? Aren't they always basically insane?"

"Not insane." Johanne gave a convinced shake of the head. "Disturbed, perhaps. Twisted. I would guess that she suffers from some kind of personality disorder. But she's definitely not insane. Murderers are rarely not accountable, or insane, in a legal sense. But what would make it really difficult . . . what would make it almost impossible to catch her, if she wasn't caught the first time, that is—"

"Which this superwoman wouldn't allow to happen," Adam interjected and rubbed his neck.

"Precisely," said Johanne and fell silent.

The boys out on the street had moved on. Lights were being turned off all the way down Haugesvei. It was finally quiet in the apartment downstairs. One of the damned cats was howling in the garden again, but then it disappeared. Johanne realized that she was enjoying the peace, the safety of the house. For the first time since they had moved in, she really felt at home. She stroked the surface of the counter in surprise. Her finger ran over a dent. Kristiane had played with a knife in an unobserved moment. Johanne's eyes traveled over the living room to the west. The baseboards were covered in Jack's eager claw marks, the parquet was damaged by the runners on Ragnhild's crib. A red felt-tip drawing of a skyscraper rose up crookedly from the floor to the windowsill.

She sniffed. It smelled a bit stuffy, of food, clean babies, and dirty dogs. She bent down to pick up a colorful baby's toy from the corner by the dishwasher and noticed that Kristiane had written her name along the bottom in strange, crooked letters.

The house was well lived in now, Johanne thought. It was home.

"The worst thing," she said as she played with a smiling lion with teething rings and multicolored ribbons around its head, "the worst thing would be a murderer with no motive."

She took a deep breath, put down the toy, and took off her glasses. She tried to wipe away the grease from food and children's fingers with a corner of her shirt. Then she turned her short-sighted gaze on Sigmund and repeated, "the most difficult murderer to catch would be one who killed without a motive. A qualified, intelligent killer who isn't out to get even with his victim at all. All modern tactical investigations are based on the assumption that there is a motive for the crime. Even the most seriously mentally disturbed serial killer can be caught, as the most absurd and apparently random selection of victims will have some kind of hidden pattern, connections. When there is nothing, no reason, no connection, no logic— no matter how twisted that sounds—we're just stuck. A murderer like that could keep playing with us . . . forever."

The candle on the windowsill flickered violently and then went out. Johanne put her glasses on and closed the window properly.

"But I've never heard of any monsters like that," she added lightly. "I have to go to bed. Any more questions before I go?"

There were no questions.

Rudolf Fjord was cleaning the bathroom.

It was three o'clock on Tuesday morning. The lanky man was down on all fours, scrubbing the grout between the floor tiles with a toothbrush and ammonia. The smell ripped at his nose. He coughed, scrubbed, swore, and rinsed it with water that was too hot for his bare hands. He was almost there. The tiles from the sink to the toilet bowl were now framed by light, pale gray grouting against steel blue ceramic. Strange that a bathroom could get so dirty in less than six months. He wanted to do the walls as well, he thought, and wiped his nose on his sleeve. He should empty the cabinets, wash the drawers. And give the inside of the toilet tank a going over. It was still hours until he had to go to work.

He couldn't sleep.

Maybe he could empty the bookshelves, vacuum the books, one by one. That would certainly get the time to pass.

The relief he had felt when Victoria died, the physical, jubilant relief on Saturday morning, had lasted for exactly twelve minutes. Then he had realized that, paradoxically, Victoria Heinerback was better insurance in life than in death, and he was literally overwhelmed. He had tried to get up from the sofa, but his legs had given way. Sweat poured off him, but it felt cold. His thoughts were racing. Eventually he managed to get into the shower and then put together a suitable outfit for the emergency meeting of the Steering Committee.

They had looked at him.

Scowled.

Rudolf Fjord picked up the toothbrush.

The brush was flat and gray. Unusable. He staggered to his feet and rummaged around at random in the garbage can, looking for another one. Couldn't find one. The lump in his throat grew. He pulled open a drawer in the bathroom cabinet, cut himself badly as he tried to get a new brush out of the stiff plastic packaging. The stench of ammonia was unbearable now. He couldn't find a bandage.

They had really scowled.

"Good party comrades," Victoria had smiled, somewhat stiff, when inquisitive journalists had tried to delve deeper into their relationship. "We work very well together, Rudolf and I."

He tried to breathe deeply.

Straightened his back. Lifted his chest, tightened his stomach, as he had on the beach, last summer, that fantastic summer when the weather was great and nothing had been settled. When he was still certain he would be the next party leader as soon as the old man decided it was time for a change.

He simply couldn't breathe.

Red stars danced in front of his eyes. He was about to faint. With his hands against the wall, he stumbled out of the bathroom. It was better in the hall. He gagged without throwing up, staggered into the living room, toward the doors to the balcony. They were locked. He tried to stay calm; there was something wrong with the hinges, he just had to lift it, like this. The blood drew funny patterns on the door frame. The door opened.

The ice-cold air brought him around.

He opened his mouth and breathed in.

They had looked at him in an odd way.

Strange, they had no doubt thought. Strange that Rudolf Fjord was the one who was most obviously affected by Victoria Heinerback's brutal murder.

Kari Mundal was the worst.

People really had no idea what she was like. Everyone thought she was a funny, tiny, sharp housewife.

She was certainly sharp.

At best, nothing will happen, Rudolf Fjord thought to himself and gulped in the clean air. He was calmer now and buttoned his shirt with shaking hands. The blood had already started to clot. He carefully sucked his finger.

He realized that he had to dilute the ammonia.

At best, absolutely nothing would happen.

SIX

The house at the edge of the woods was typical of its day. A boxy wooden house with vertical paneling and a bay window in the middle of a symmetrical façade. It was about the size of a cottage. The porch was small, with a bench on either side. The steps were concrete, and the middle step was in need of repair. Otherwise the building was well maintained. Adam Stubo stood on the road by the fence. He noticed that the roof was new and the exterior red paint so oily that the moon was reflected in it.

The light on one of the gateposts was broken. As any evidence had long since been secured, he leaned over the broken light and lifted the wrought-iron casing to get a better look at the bulb. Smashed to smithereens. Only a small, jagged piece of glass was left in the socket. He ran his finger over the base of the light. Minute shards of fine, matte glass stuck to his skin. In the beam of his flashlight, he could see that the filament was untouched. He turned off the flashlight, pulled on his glove, and stood there for a few moments while his eyes adjusted to the dark.

There was another light just below the porch roof, above the front door. It was broken too. The evening was clear and cold. The moon hung above the bare trees at the bottom of the garden, a perfect half, as if someone had sliced it in two. It made it possible to see the details of the house, the gravel path and overgrown garden, although there was no other light nearby, except for a streetlight some fifty yards up the road.

"It's pretty dark here," Trond Arnesen said unnecessarily.

"Yes," Adam said. "But it was darker a week ago, as there wasn't even any moonlight."

Trond Arnesen sniffed. Adam put a hand on his shoulder.

"Listen," he said in a quiet voice. His breath hung in blue white clouds between them. "I know that this is incredibly difficult. I just want you to know, Trond . . . Is it alright if I call you Trond?"

The man nodded and wet his lips with his tongue.

"You're not a suspect in this case. Okay?"

Another nod, and this time he bit his lip.

"We know that you were at a bachelor party the night she was killed. We know that you and Victoria had a good relationship. I understand you were going to get married this summer. In fact, I could go so far as to say"—he looked around, very furtively—"we never let things like this out," he whispered, not letting go of the other man's shoulder. "No one in Victoria's family is a suspect. Her parents, her brother. You. You were actually the first person we struck from the list. The very first. Do you hear?"

"Yes," mumbled Trond Arnesen as he brushed his eyes with his gloved hand. "But I'm inheriting . . . I get the house and everything. We had a . . ."

His words were stopped by his crying, a strange, soft crying. Adam let his hand slide down his back. He held him tight. The boy was a head shorter than Adam, and he leaned in toward him as he raised his hands to his face.

"The fact that you had a cohabitation agreement only shows that you were sensible young people," Adam said quietly. "You have to stop being so frightened, Trond. You have nothing to fear from the police. Nothing, do you understand?"

Victoria Heinerback's fiancé had been so terrified during the hearings that the officer present found it difficult not to laugh, despite the tragic circumstances. The fair man in the pink Lacoste shirt, good-looking and well groomed, had gripped the edge of the table and drunk quarts of water, as if he still had an almighty hangover, three days after the bachelor party. He was barely able to give the police his date of birth and address.

"Relax," Adam said again. "We'll go calmly into the bedroom now. It's been cleaned up. The blood is gone. Okay? Everything is more or less as it was before. Do you hear what I'm saying?"

Trond Arnesen pulled himself together and straightened up. He coughed lightly into his hand and then smoothed back his hair. A couple of deep breaths later, he gave a faint smile and said, "I'm ready."

The gravel, mixed with ice and snow, crunched under their feet. Trond stopped again by the steps, as if he needed to steel himself. He stood there for a moment, rocking on the balls of his feet. Then he stroked back his hair again, a helpless, vulnerable gesture. He straightened his scarf and pulled down his jacket before mounting the steps. A uniformed policeman guided him into the bedroom. Adam followed. Nothing was said.

The bed was empty, apart from two pillows. The room was neat. A huge reproduction of Munch's *History* hung above the head of the bed. Three neatly folded duvet covers, some towels, and a couple of colorful cushions were stored in a shelving unit along one wall.

The mattress was clean, without a trace of blood. The floor was newly washed, and there was still a faint smell of floor cleaner in the air. Adam took some photographs out of a manila envelope. He stroked his nose thoughtfully while he studied the photographs for a few minutes in silence. Then he turned to Trond Arnesen, who looked deathly pale in the bright light from the ceiling, and asked in a friendly voice, "Are you ready, Trond?"

He swallowed, nodded, and stepped forward.

"What do you want me to do?"

Bernt Helle had been a widower for twenty-four days. He kept careful track of time. Every morning he drew a red cross over the previous day's date on the calendar Fiona had hung up in the kitchen to help Fiorella understand the concept of days, weeks, and months. There was a Moomin character above each date. This morning he had crossed off Snufkin, who had the number twelve on a silver chain around his neck. Bernt Helle didn't know why he did it. Every morning another cross. They said that time heals all wounds, and every hour was a step closer.

Every night an empty double bed.

"Today is Friday the thirteenth," he thought and stroked his mother-in-law's hair.

Fiona was always so superstitious. Frightened of black cats. Gave ladders a wide berth. Had lucky numbers and believed that the color red made you restless.

"Are you still here?" Yvonne Knutsen said and opened her eyes. "You should go now, really you should."

"Don't need to. Fiorella is at Mom's tonight. It's Friday, you know."

"No," she said confused.

"Yes, it's Fri—"

"I didn't realize. One day is like the next, lying here. Could you get me some water?"

She drank greedily through a straw.

"Have you ever thought that Fiona had something . . ." he asked suddenly, without having really thought about it, "that it was as if she . . ."

Yvonne had fallen asleep again. Or at least her eyes were closed, and she was breathing regularly.

Bernt had never understood Fiona's leaning toward religion. It might have been different if it was the church, the normal Norwegian state church, which he had grown up with and where he felt comfortable attending weddings, funerals, and the odd service. But Fiona had no church. No sect, either, thankfully. No parish, no spiritual home other than herself. She slipped in and out of something she would never share with him. When they were young, he thought it was fascinating that she read so much about other religions, Eastern philosophy, the great thinkers, and great thoughts. For a while, probably at the start of the nineties, maybe even earlier, she had flirted with New Age philosophy. Luckily that didn't last very long. But then, at the end of what seemed to be a search for a theological anchor that had lasted more than a decade, she was even more distant. Not always, and certainly not in every area of her life. When Fiorella was born, their feeling of togetherness was so strong that they arranged a second wedding, fifteen years after the first.

"An incurable loneliness of the soul" is how she explained her need on the rare occasions when he asked. She would close down, smile without warmth in her eyes, and her face would become inscrutable.

Sometimes he wondered if she had a secret. But that was hard to imagine. They had always known each other; their childhood homes were barely a couple hundred steps apart.

They didn't see much of each other when they were teenagers; they were too different. So he couldn't believe his luck when they accidentally met in a café in Oslo when they were twenty. He had just finished his apprenticeship and started to work in his father's plumbing business. Fiona had long blonde hair and was studying at the University of Oslo. He had hoisted his pants up at the bar so she wouldn't realize that he was starting to get a plumber's crack. They got together that evening, and Bernt Helle had never been with another woman since.

She was strangely restless and yet she clung on to anything and everything that was fixed and lasting.

"I shouldn't have done it," Yvonne said suddenly and opened her eyes. "We shouldn't have done it."

"Yvonne," he said and leaned over her.

"Oh," she exclaimed weakly. "I was dreaming. Water, please."

"She's starting to lose it," he thought flatly.

She fell asleep again.

It was no longer possible to have a normal conversation with Yvonne, he realized. But it didn't matter. They shared a great sorrow. That was enough.

He got up and looked at the clock. It was nearly midnight. He quietly put on his jacket and pulled the duvet over Yvonne. She obviously didn't want to carry on. They were each dealing with the loss in their own way; she was using what little strength she had left to shrug off this life while he, on the other hand, hoped that he would be able fight his way back into it one day.

The reconstruction was over. Most people had gone. Only Adam Stubo and Trond Arnesen were left in the bedroom. The young man couldn't pull himself away. He looked around the room, again and again; he walked about stroking things, as if he needed reassurance that they still existed.

"Do you think it's strange that I want to move back?" he asked without looking at Adam.

"Not at all. It's perfectly natural, if you ask me. This was your house. It's still your home, even if Victoria is dead. I understand that you helped her fix it up."

"Yes. This room too."

"Is this how you remember it?"

"No."

"You should try. This is what the bedroom looks like."

Adam opened his arms and then hesitated before he continued, "Our people have done nothing except . . . clean. Unfortunately, the duvet and the bedclothes were beyond saving. Otherwise, everything is as it was, as far as I know. And this is how you should remember it. You're going to live here, Trond. You may live here for many years. In some way or another, you have to let go of that evening just over a week ago. I know just what you're going through. And I can assure you, it gets easier. I've been there, Trond. It passes."

The younger man looked directly at him. His eyes were blue with specks of green. Only now did Adam notice the hint of red in Trond Arnesen's thick blond hair and a shadow of freckles over his nose, despite his winter pallor.

"What do you mean?" he said indistinctly.

"I found my family dead in the garden," Adam replied slowly, looking at Trond squarely. "An accident. I was convinced that I would never be able to go near the place again. I wanted to move, but didn't have the energy. Then one day, it must've been a couple of months later, I opened the terrace door and went out. I didn't dare open my eyes, but I started to listen."

Trond sat down on the bed. His body was stiff and tense, as

if he didn't believe that the bed would hold him. He put both his hands on the mattress to support himself.

"What did you hear?" he asked.

Adam fumbled around in his breast pocket and found the cigar case. He let it slide between his thumb and forefinger, backwards and forwards, again and again.

"So much," he said in a hushed voice. "I heard so much. The birds were still there. Just as they had been long ago when we first moved in, right after we got married. We were only twenty. We rented it at first, then bought it later. They were singing."

Suddenly he gasped for breath.

"They were singing," he repeated, louder this time. "The birds were singing as always. And through the birdsong, and in amongst all that damned chirping, I heard . . . Trine. My daughter. I heard her shouting for me when she was only three, bawling her eyes out because she'd fallen off the swing. I heard the clinking of ice cubes in glasses when my wife came out with juice. Trine's laughter as she played with the neighbor's dog was suddenly so clear. I swear I could hear the hissing of evening barbecues. Suddenly I could smell them both. My wife. My daughter. I opened my eyes, and there was the garden. A garden full of the best memories I have. Of course I couldn't move."

"Do you still live there?" Trond was more relaxed now. His back was bent, and he was leaning on his elbows.

"No, but that's another story." Adam gave a short laugh and dropped the cigar case back into his pocket.

"You'll get new stories," he said. "New stories happen all the time, Trond. That's life. But in the meantime, you have to take ownership of this room again. The house. The whole place. This is your home. And it's full of happy memories. Remember them, and forget that terrible evening."

Trond got up, stretched his body, rolled his head from side to side, and straightened his pants. Then he gave a weak smile.

"You're a nice policeman."

"Most policemen are nice."

The young man went on smiling. He looked around one last time and then walked toward the door.

Trond Arnesen was at last ready to leave.

Halfway across the floor, he stopped, hesitated, and took another step forward before turning and walking back to the bedside table on the left of the bed. He opened the small drawer with a slow, cautious hand, as if he expected to find something nasty in it.

"Did you say that nothing else had been done here?" Trond asked. "That you'd just cleaned the place? Nothing was removed?"

"Yes. Not in here. We took some papers and the computer, obviously, but we told you we were going to do that and—"

"But nothing from here?"

"No."

"My watch. It was lying on the bedside table. And my book."

"Okay?"

"I've got a diving watch. A great lump of a thing. Can't sleep with it on, so I always leave it here in the evening." He tapped the bedside table with his fingers. Then he pressed them to his lips in concentration.

"But you didn't go to bed. You were at your brother's . . ."

"Exactly," Trond interrupted. "I was dressed up. We were all wearing tuxedos, and a great big black plastic watch doesn't exactly match. So I left it here . . ."

"Are you sure?" Adam inquired with an edge to his voice.

Trond Arnesen turned toward him, and Adam could hear the irritation in his voice when he answered, "My book and

watch were lying here. On the bedside table. Victoria was"—
when he mentioned her name, the aggression in his voice disappeared—"Victoria had a slight allergy," he muttered. "She
didn't want books in the bedroom. I was only allowed to have
the one I was reading at the time. Berger's latest. I was halfway
through. It was lying here."

"Okay . . . I'll ask you once more, are you certain about it?"

"Yes! My watch . . . I mean, I really liked that watch. Got it
from Victoria. I would never have—"

He stopped himself. A faint blush was visible along his hair-
line. He tugged his ear in discomfort. "Of course, I could be
wrong," he said feebly. "I don't know, I—"

"But you remember—"

"As I remember . . . Maybe I did leave the book somewhere
else. But I only read in bed, I . . ."

He stared at Adam, obviously upset. This had nothing to do
with the book, Adam thought to himself. Trond Arnesen had
for a moment allowed himself to believe that everything could
be as it was. Adam had, for a moment or two, convinced him
that the image of the crucified Victoria in bed could be erased
and disappear.

"I wouldn't have . . . Not the book. The watch perhaps, that
might have been left somewhere else, but I—"

"Come on," Adam said. "I'll find out what's happened. They've
probably just been put somewhere else. Come on, let's go."

Trond Arnesen opened the drawer again. It was empty. Then
he went over to the other side of the bed. But he didn't find
anything there either. He had a slightly crazed look in his eyes
as he stormed into the bathroom. Adam stayed where he was.
He heard the sound of drawers and cabinets being opened and
shut, the banging of what could be the lid of the trash can.

Then the boy was there again, in the doorway, holding out
his empty hands.

"I must've made a mistake," he said in a hoarse voice.

His eyes were downcast as he followed Adam out of the bedroom.

"Victoria was always saying that, that I was an airhead."

———————— ❧ ————————

Evil is an illusion, she thought.

She was standing by the bronze bust of Jean Cocteau. In her opinion it looked slapdash, with the features running into each other as if a child had been playing with melted wax and suddenly decided to make a bust and dedicate it to someone. The sculpture stood on the edge of the quay, a short distance from the small chapel that Cocteau himself had decorated. You had to pay to get in, so she only caught a glimpse of the frescos. It was Christmas, and she had been overwhelmed by a nostalgic desire to visit a church. St. Michel, the church on the hill behind her, had been unbearable with all its Catholic kitsch and the monotonous mumblings of the priest. She had backed her way out.

But paying to meet a God she had never believed in was even worse. She had the urge to remind the fat old woman inside the chapel door of Christ's rampage in the temple. The sour-faced old witch sat behind a table of simple but outrageously overpriced souvenirs and demanded an entrance fee of two euros. It was irritating that her French didn't stretch to anything more than mild swearing under her breath.

It was late in the day on Friday, February 13. The spring tides that afternoon had caused considerable damage. The panorama windows of restaurants along the promenade had been broken by the high seas. Shivering young men in white shirts ran backwards and forwards with plywood that they nailed up without much skill, temporary protection against the wind and weather. Chairs had been smashed to kindling. A table was floating some distance from the quay. Most of the boats in the bay were loosely moored and had survived the storm, but four or five dinghies that had been moored by the jetty had fared worse, and now only driftwood and the remains of some rope could be seen in the turbulent, murky waters.

She leaned toward Jean Cocteau and once again thought to herself, "Evil is an illusion."

The dark side of humanity was her bread and butter. She was never sloppy. To the contrary. She knew more about betrayal, malice, and spiritual bankruptcy than most.

She had once felt some pride in that.

To begin with, nineteen years ago, when she was still in her twenties and had newly discovered how easy it was for her to use this hidden and surprising talent, she had been excited by it. Enthusiastic. Even happy. At least, that is how she remembered it. She wasn't even bitter about all the years of education she would never use, all the conscientious effort in college that had only helped to pass the time. It was all a waste. But that didn't matter anymore, once she found her niche in life at the age of twenty-six.

The cliché made her smile.

One March evening in 1985, she sat with a copy of her bank statement in front of her, a beer in her hand, and tried to imagine what her niche was, her special place on the imaginary bookcase of life. This niche would make her special and valuable, completely unique. She had laughed at the well-worn metaphor and imagined everyone creeping around, searching for their niche on some vacant corner.

The sea was calmer now. The temperature was no more than a few degrees above freezing, and what little warmth there was was cut through by the gusts of wind that continued to blow from the south. The boys in shirts had managed to patch up the worst holes and obviously couldn't be bothered to do any more.

A young couple in dark clothes walked toward her. They giggled and whispered something she didn't understand as they passed. She turned around and followed them with her eyes as they slipped on the wet cobbles and then disappeared into the dark.

They looked Norwegian. He had a backpack on.

Fortunately, the last photograph of her had been taken twelve years ago. Almost exactly. She was slimmer then. Much slimmer, and she had long hair. The picture, which she sometimes looked at by mistake, looked like someone else. That was what she had to think. She wore glasses now. Long hair didn't look good on her anymore. When she looked in the mirror, she saw that life had shown no mercy in leaving its mark on what was once a very ordinary face. Her nose, which was as small back then as it was now, looked like a button. Her eyes had never been big, but they were brown and therefore not like everyone else's. They were now almost entirely hidden by her glasses and bangs that were far too long.

The idea that anyone was unique was an illusion.

People were so damned alike.

She didn't know when the truth had dawned on her. She figured it must have been a gradual realization. She became impatient with the repetitiveness of her work without really knowing what she wanted to change. Of course, every plan was special, every crime had its own value. The circumstances varied, the victims were never the same. She put in tremendous effort. She was never sloppy in her work. But she still couldn't think of it as anything other than an enervating, endless repetition.

She could no longer make time pass.

It just happened, of its own accord.

"Until now," she thought and drew breath.

Everyone was the same.

Time, which everyone was so keen on "filling," was a meaningless concept, created to give false meaning to what was meaningless: simply being alive.

The woman pulled her hat down over her head and slowly climbed the steps that were squeezed in between the old stone houses. The narrow alleys were unusually dark. Maybe the storm had knocked out the electricity.

By studying people's behavior, she had at some point understood that consideration, solidarity, and goodness were no more than empty expressions. Virtues of model behavior, as given by God and set in stone, extolled by aged monks and in the prophecies of an Arab warrior, in the musings of philosophers and tales from the mouths of persecuted Jews.

Evil was the true human nature, she thought.

Evil was not the work of the devil or the result of original sin, nor was it a dialectical consequence of material need and injustice. If a lioness abandoned a sick cub to a painful, loveless death, no one would say she was evil. The male alligator was not judged in zoological terms because he sired more children than he instinctively knew the environment could support.

She stopped in the alley by the insignificant door into St. Michel's church. She hesitated for a moment. She was breathing heavily after climbing all the stairs. She gently put her hand on the door handle but then pulled back and kept going. It was time to get home. It had started to rain again, a fine, light rain that covered her skin in a moist film.

There was no point in stigmatizing natural behavior, she thought. That was why animals were free. Humans were likely to exterminate themselves if there was no culture, no order, bans, or threats of corrective punishment, so it might possibly be expedient to brand anyone who deviated from the norm and followed their true nature with the mark of Cain.

"It's still not evil," she whispered and gasped for breath in the Place de la Paix.

The pharmacy's bright green cross winked at the deserted, closed café over the street. She stopped in front of a real estate office.

Her thighs ached, a dull pain, even though she had not climbed more than a couple hundred steps. She could taste the sweat on her upper lip. A blister was stinging on her left heel. It was a long time since she'd known the pleasure of physical exercise. The dull pain gave her a sense of being alive. She lifted her face to the sky and felt the rain run down the inside of her collar, over her skin and down her shoulder; she felt her nipples harden.

Everything had changed. Life had taken on a palpable, tangible intensity that she had never experienced before.

At last, she was unique.

SEVEN

It was too big a job.

Johanne Vik wrinkled her nose at her tea. It had steeped for too long and was dark and bitter. She spat the yellowish brown liquid back into the cup.

"Ugh," she muttered. She felt glad to be alone as she put down the cup and opened the fridge.

She should have refused. The two murder cases were hard enough to crack for professional policemen working in a team, with access to modern technology, advanced data programs, progress reports, breaking news, and all the time in the world.

Johanne had none of that. She had bitten off more than she could chew. The children ruled her days. Sometimes she felt she moved on autopilot, from the washing machine to helping Kristiane with her homework, making food and trying to snatch a few moments' peace on the sofa while feeding the baby. Even when Kristiane wasn't at home, there was plenty to do.

But the nights were long.

They passed slowly, the hours she spent poring over the copies of documents that Adam took home with him every afternoon, which was highly irregular for him. It was as if the clock also felt it deserved a rest after a tiring day.

She grabbed a mineral water, opened it, and drank straight from the bottle.

"Perineal rupture," she said to herself as she sat down at the table again and looked through the final postmortem report in the Fiona Helle case.

A rupture was some kind of tear or another.

"Periscope," she mumbled, chewing her pencil. "Periphery. Peri . . ."

She slapped her forehead lightly. A good thing she hadn't asked anyone. It was embarrassing for a grown woman not to know what it meant immediately. Even though both her children had been born by cesarean, Johanne had plenty of friends who had described the problem to her in great detail.

Little Fiorella had left her mark.

Okay.

She lay the document to one side and focused on the reconstruction report. It told her nothing that she didn't know already. She kept on leafing through the papers impatiently. As the case had already generated several hundred, if not more than a thousand, documents, she obviously didn't have access to them all.

Adam selected and prioritized. She read.

Without finding anything.

The papers contained nothing but endless repetitions, a round dance of the obvious. No secrets were uncovered. There were no contradictions, nothing surprising, nothing to spend more time on in the hope of seeing things from another angle.

Exasperated, she slapped the covers together.

She had to learn to say no more often.

Like when her mother called earlier in the day and invited the whole family to lunch next Sunday. With Isak, of course.

It had been nearly six years since their divorce. Although she often worried and was irritated by Isak's lenience with regard to Kristiane, with no set bedtimes and fast food and candy on weekdays, it made her genuinely happy to see them together. Kristiane and Isak had the same physical build and were on the same wavelength, even though the girl suffered from an inexplicable handicap that had never been diagnosed. She found it harder to accept that her ex-husband still spent time with her parents. More time than she did, if she was honest.

That hurt, and she blamed him for her shame.

"Get a grip!"

Without knowing why, she pulled out the post-mortem report again.

Strangulation, it stated.

She already knew the cause of death.

The tongue was described in clinical terms.

Nothing new there.

Abrasions on both wrists. No sign of sexual trauma. Blood type A. A tumor in her mouth, on the left cheek, about the size of a pea and benign. Scars, in several places. All old. From an operation on the shoulder, the removal of four moles, and a cesarean. And a five-pointed, relatively big but almost invisible mark on her right upper arm. Probably a cut from way back. One earlobe was inflamed. The nail on her left index finger was blue and had been about to come off at the time of death.

The report, for all its precise details, still told her nothing. She was just left with the vague feeling that there was something important there, something that had caught her eye, the impression that something didn't add up.

Her concentration was failing. She was annoyed with Isak, with her mother, by their friendship.

A waste of energy. Isak was Isak. Her mother was the same

as she had always been: scared of conflict, hard to understand, and extremely loyal to those she cared for.

"Stop letting it bother you," Johanne thought, exhausted, but couldn't stop all the same.

"Focus," she said out loud to herself. "You have to fo—"

There.

Her finger stopped at the bottom of the page.

It didn't make sense.

She swallowed, then lifted her hand to go through the report, furiously looking for something that she had just read in passing. She noticed that her hand was shaking. Her pulse was racing, and she was breathing through her mouth.

There.

She was right. It couldn't be right. She grabbed the phone and discovered that her hand was sweaty.

On the other side of Oslo, Adam Stubo was babysitting his grandson, who was nearly six. The boy was asleep on his grandfather's lap. Adam buried his nose in the boy's dark hair. The smell of baby soap was soft and warm. The boy should really be in bed. His father was an easygoing, flexible sort of guy, but he was adamant that the boy should sleep on his own. But Adam couldn't resist his round, dark eyes. He had smuggled one of Ragnhild's bottles from home. The look on Amund's face when he realized that he was going to be allowed to sit on his grandfather's knee with a bottle was priceless.

Strangely enough, the boy had never been jealous of Kristiane. Quite the contrary, he was fascinated by the strange girl who was four years older than he was. But it was very different when he was told that his grandfather was going to be a daddy again. He had clearly decided to ignore Ragnhild's arrival three weeks ago.

The telephone rang.

Amund didn't wake up. His grip on the baby bottle loosened when Adam carefully leaned over to the table to answer the phone.

"Hello," he said quietly, holding the telephone between his chin and shoulder as he reached for the remote control.

"Hello, my dear. Are you boys having a good time?"

He smiled. The eagerness in her voice gave her away.

"Yep. We've had a great time. Played a silly card game and made some Lego houses. But that's not why you called."

"I won't keep you long if you're—"

"Amund's asleep. I've got all the time in the world."

"Could you . . . tomorrow, or as soon as possible, could you check a couple of things for me?"

"Of course."

He pressed the wrong button on the remote control. The newscaster shouted out that four American soldiers had been killed in Basra before Adam managed to find the right button. Amund grunted and buried his head in his grandfather's arm.

"I've been sitting a while . . . hang on a second."

"I'll be quick," she insisted. "You have to get me Fiona Helle's medical records, about Fiorella's birth. From when her daughter was born."

"Okay," he said. "Why exactly?"

"I don't like talking about this kind of thing on the phone," Johanne said with some hesitation. "You either have to come home from Bjarne and Randi's first thing tomorrow morning so we can talk, or—"

"I won't have time. I promised Amund I'd take him to day care."

"Trust me then. It might be important."

"I always trust you."

"And with good reason." Her laughter rattled down the phone line.

"What about the other thing?" he said. "You wanted me to do two things?"

"You have to let me . . . from the papers it's clear that Fiona's mother is very ill, and—"

"Yes, I questioned her myself. MS. Sharp as a tack upstairs, but wasting away otherwise."

"So she was all there?"

"As far as I know, the brain is not affected by multiple sclerosis," he said.

"Don't be like that!"

Amund stuck his thumb in his mouth and turned in toward Adam again.

"I'm not like that," he said and smiled. "I'm just teasing you."

"I need to talk to her."

"You?"

"I'm working for you, Adam."

"Very unofficially and without any form of recognition. It's bad enough that I have to sneak around with the documents. The boss has given a kind of silent consent to that. But I can't really give you—"

"But surely no one can prevent me from visiting an old lady in a nursing home as a private individual?" she said.

"Why are you asking me then?"

"Ragnhild. I don't think it would be a good idea to take her with me. Is there any chance of you coming home early tomorrow?"

"Early," he repeated. "What's that?"

"One, two?"

"I might be able to tear myself away around half past two. Would that be okay?"

"It'll have to be. Thank you."

"Are you sure you can't tell me anything? I have to admit I'm dying of curiosity now."

"And I'm dying to tell you," she said and took a drink of something. Her voice almost vanished. "But it was you who taught me to be careful on the phone."

"I'll have to contain myself then. Until tomorrow."

"Now put Amund to bed," she said.

"He is in bed," he said, crestfallen.

"He's not, he's sleeping in your lap with Ragnhild's baby bottle."

"That's a lie."

"Put the boy to bed, Adam. And sleep well. You're the best in the world."

"You are—"

"Wait. If you get time, could you check one more thing? Could you try to find out whether Fiona was away from school for any long periods of time while she was in high school?"

"What?"

"If she went on an exchange or something like that. Language course, or a long-lasting illness, or if she visited an aunt in Australia, for that matter. It should be easy enough to find out."

"You can ask her mother," he sighed, "as you're going to see her anyway. She's probably the best one to ask."

"I'm not sure that she'd answer. Ask the husband. Or an old friend or someone. Will you do it?"

"Yes, yes. Go to bed."

"Good night, darling."

"I mean it. Go to bed. Don't sit up reading those documents. They're not going to run away. Good night."

He put down the receiver and got up as carefully as he could from the overly soft sofa. He struggled to get his balance and hugged Amund too tight. The boy whimpered but continued to lie in his arms like a rag doll.

"I don't know why everyone assumes that I spoil you," Adam whispered. "I just don't understand it."

He carried the boy into the guest room, put him down in the middle of the bed, undressed quietly, put on his own pajamas, and lay down with his back to the child.

"Gramps," the boy murmured in his sleep. A hand stroked Adam's neck.

They slept soundly for nine hours, and Adam got to work nearly an hour late.

Trond Arnesen had made sure that the lights by the gate and in the porch were both working before he moved back into the small house that he would now inherit. His brother had offered to stay with him for the first few days. Trond said no. He didn't want to make the transition to a life alone in stages. It was his home, even if he'd only moved in a couple of months ago. Victoria was quite old-fashioned and had not agreed to living together until a date had been set for the wedding.

He tried to avoid the windows. He drew the curtains before it got really dark. The gaps were threatening, black strips of emptiness.

The TV flickered but there was no sound. Victoria had bought him a forty-two-inch plasma screen for his birthday. She was far too generous, and they couldn't afford it after all the work they'd done on the house. "So you can watch football," she had smiled, opening an expensive bottle of champagne. He turned thirty that day, and they had decided to make babies in the fall.

He didn't feel like watching TV, he was far too restless, but the silent people on the screen were a friendly presence. He had wandered from room to room for several hours now, sat down, touched some object or other, got up, moved on, anxious about what he might find behind the next door. He felt safe in the bathroom. It had no windows and was warm, and at around six o'clock, he had locked the door and stayed in there for about an hour. In desperation, he had taken a bath, as if he had to legitimize his need to feel secure in a house that he, at that precise moment, half past ten on Monday, February 16, did not think he would be able to live in.

He heard a noise from outside.

It came from the back of the house, he thought, from the slope going down to the small stream, fifty yards behind the garden, where a picket fence marked the boundary to an abandoned scrap yard.

He froze, listening.

The silence was overwhelming. He couldn't even hear the usual clicking of the thermostat on the heater under the window.

Just his imagination, no doubt.

"You're a grown man," he thought to himself in irritation and took down a random book from the shelf.

He looked at the title page. An author he'd never heard of. Must be new. He put it back, horizontally across the top of the other books. It struck him that that kind of thing always annoyed Victoria, so he took it out again to put it back properly between two books.

The noise had sounded like something breaking; now he heard it again.

His brother had always called him a coward. That wasn't true. Trond Arnesen wasn't a coward, he was just cautious. If his brother (younger than him by fifteen months) had climbed past him on trees, it was simply because common sense told him that to climb any further was stupid. When his brother was seven and jumped from the roof of a twelve-foot-high garage with a parachute made from a sheet and four bits of rope, Trond stood on the ground and advised him not to do it. His brother broke his leg.

Trond was not a coward. He always assessed the consequences.

The fear that gripped him now had nothing to do with the future. The unfamiliar taste of iron clung to his tongue, which immediately felt dry and too big. When the fear reached his eardrums, he had to shake his head if he wanted to hear anything other than the blood pumping through his body.

He looked quickly around the room.

Victoria's furniture.

Victoria's things here and there. A copy of *Her* magazine with a Post-it to mark an article about young families struggling to find enough time to get everything done. A steel and plastic lighter he had given her for Christmas to show that she didn't need to hide her cigarettes from him anymore.

Victoria's things.

His home.

He was no coward. Although the sound had come from behind the house, he now ran toward the front door without even looking out the living room window to check if it was an animal, a confused elk or one of the many skinny feral cats.

Without a moment's hesitation, he pulled open the front door.

"Hello," said an obviously startled Rudolf Fjord. "Hello, Trond."

He was standing with his foot on the first step up to the porch.

"Hi," he said again, pathetically.

"You idiot," hissed Trond. "What the hell do you think

you're doing sneaking around in the garden like that? What the fuck are you—"

"I just wanted to see if anyone was home," Rudolf Fjord said. His voice was louder now but still feeble, as if he was trying to pull himself together without succeeding. "May I offer my condolences."

Trond Arnesen threw out his hands and went forward onto the steps.

"Condolences? You've come here at"—with a swift movement he pulled up his left sleeve. His diving watch had still not reappeared—"It's pretty late on a Monday night," he continued furiously, "to give your condolences. Again! You've already done it! What the hell . . . You frightened . . . Just go!"

"Okay, okay, calm down."

Rudolf Fjord had managed to pull himself together. He put out his hand in a conciliatory gesture, but Trond showed no signs of taking it.

"I was just checking whether you were at home," Rudolf tried again. "I didn't want to disturb you if you were already asleep. That's why I went around the house. But you've blacked out all the windows, so it was only when I saw a sliver of light from the living room that I knew you were at home. I was just about to ring the bell when—"

"What do you want? What the hell do you want, Rudolf?"

Trond had never really liked Victoria's colleague. Nor had she. The few times he'd asked her about the man, she got a stern look on her face and said that he wasn't to be trusted. She wouldn't say anymore. Trond didn't know whether Rudolf Fjord was trustworthy or not, but he didn't like the way the guy treated women. Trond thought he was good-looking, tall, well-built with a prominent chin and rather intense blue eyes, but Rudolf used women. Exploited them.

"Like I said, I just wanted—"

"I'll give you one more chance." Trond was shouting now. "People don't turn up to give their condolences in the middle of the night. You're not fooling me. What do you want?"

"I'd also thought," Rudolf Fjord started and then looked as if he was literally trying to catch a word on the tip of his tongue. His eyes darted aimlessly around the garden. "I just thought I would ask you if I could look for some important papers Victoria took home with her from the office. She was going to bring them back on that Monday, the one after she was murdered, that is. I think—"

"For God's sake!"

Trond Arnesen was laughing now, a loud, joyless laughter.

"Are you completely . . . stupid? Are you soft in the head or what?"

He laughed again in desperation.

"The police have taken all the papers. Are you . . . Don't you understand anything? Do you have no idea about what happens when someone is murdered? Hmm?"

He took a step forward and remained standing at the top of the steps. He covered his ears with his hands, as if trying to block out a catastrophe. Then he lowered his arms, took a deep breath, and said, "Talk to the police. Good night."

He went back into the house and was just about to shut the door when Rudolf Fjord leaped up the steps. He put his foot in the door to stop it from closing, his lower leg caught between the door and the frame. Trond stared at it. He was surprised by his own outburst of rage when he slammed the door shut with all his might.

"Ow, shit, Trond! Ow. Listen . . . listen . . . ow!"

"Move your foot," Trond said and let go of the door for a moment.

"My laptop," Rudolf said and stuck his leg in the door a bit further. "And . . . and . . ."

Trond didn't back down. He had both his hands on the door handle.

"Your leg will break soon," he said, very calmly. "Move."

"I need those papers. And the laptop."

"You're lying. The laptop was hers. She got it from me."

"But the other one, then—"

"There wasn't another one."

"But—"

Trond gathered all his strength and pushed hard.

"Ow! Oooowww! She'd also borrowed a book from me."

His leg was badly twisted now. Trond stared at the black boot with fascination. The door was cutting into the leather just by the ankle.

"Which book?" he asked without looking up.

"The latest one by Berger," Rudolf groaned.

That at least was true. Trond had noticed the Ex Libris label and had been surprised that the two of them borrowed books from each other.

"It's disappeared," he said.

"Disappeared?"

"Jesus, Rudolf! The book's not here, and right now that's the least of my worries. And yours for that matter! Buy a paperback."

"Let me go."

Trond gave him a few inches of slack. Rudolf Fjord edged his leg out. He let out a pathetic whimper as he carefully tried to massage the blood back into his lower leg.

"Good night," he said weakly.

He limped down the steps. Trond stood in the doorway and watched him. The man nearly collapsed on the gravel driveway. Rudolf Fjord looked pathetic as he limped out to the road, despite his broad shoulders and his expensive camel-hair coat. His car was parked some distance away. Trond could just see the roof, a silver disk under the streetlight, at the top of the hill. For a moment he felt sorry for him. But he didn't know why.

"Pathetic man," he said to himself and realized that he was no longer scared of being alone.

Rudolf Fjord sat in the car until the windows steamed up. Everything was quiet. His foot ached intensely. He didn't dare take off his boot to see if there was any real damage, in case he couldn't get it back on again. He tried to push down the clutch. Luckily the pain was bearable. He'd been afraid he wouldn't be able to drive.

At best, nothing would happen.

The police had the papers. They wouldn't find anything. It wasn't what they were looking for.

Rudolf Fjord wasn't even sure that there was anything to find. Victoria had never told him what she had seen. Her hints were subtle, her threats vague. But she must have found something.

Rudolf Fjord had hoped he would find the house empty. He couldn't understand why, because now the whole venture seemed absurd. Breaking in was out of the question. He was neither dressed nor equipped to break into a house. Maybe he had hoped that they could have a rational conversation. That Trond would give him what he asked for, without asking any questions. That it would be possible to draw a line through the whole thing; the whole depressing, aggravating affair would be over for good.

He could feel the tiredness behind his eyes, which were dry from lack of sleep.

He had never known that it was physically painful to be frightened.

Maybe she just made it up.

Of course she hadn't, he argued with himself.

His foot was getting steadily worse. He had a cramp in his calf. Frustrated, he wiped the condensation from the windshield and started the car.

At best, nothing would happen.

Three dull meetings were finally over. Adam Stubo sank into his chair and looked despondently at the pile of mail. He quickly flicked through the letters and memorandums. Nothing urgent. His hourglass was standing perilously close to the edge of the desk. He carefully pushed it to a safer place. The grains of sand formed a silver peak in the bottom glass. He set the sand in motion, and more and more grains moved faster and faster.

Time was running out.

That was becoming increasingly apparent with each day that passed. No one said much. They all still had a false confidence, and people still accepted overtime without any protest, but with waning enthusiasm. There were still moments of optimism among the investigators. After all, new discoveries were made every day, even though they proved to be insignificant later.

It couldn't go on like this much longer.

Three weeks or so, Adam reckoned. Dissatisfaction would spread fast once it took hold. He knew the score from earlier cases when no tangible evidence was forthcoming. Today was exactly four weeks since Fiona Helle was murdered. After twenty-eight days of intense investigation, they should at least have an idea of a possible suspect, an indication of a possible killer, a hint, a direction to follow.

But there was nothing in the folders that lay on Adam Stubo's desk. And soon people would get fed up. Despondency was seeping into the most recent case too, as if they all, despite

repeated warnings not to, just assumed that Victoria Heinerback had been killed by the same person as Fiona Helle and
that the man had quite simply gotten away with it.

The cases would not be shelved. Of course not. But grumblings about resources, insufficient results, and too much overtime would gradually turn into sharp protest. Everyone knew
what no one dared to say: for every hour that passed, the solution to the murders was slipping away.

The NCIS probably had the most motivated staff in the
country. There was no doubt that it was the most competent.
All of the investigators involved were therefore painfully aware
of the depressing time-to-solution ratio.

Adam was dying for a cigar.

He picked up his phone and dialed a number that was written on a scrap of paper at the bottom of the corkboard.

The craving for a cigar was stronger than it had been for a
long time.

"Bernt Helle? This is Adam Stubo from the NCIS."

"Hi," said the voice at the other end of the line.

Then it was quiet.

"I hope that everything's going well, given the circumstances."

"Yep."

More silence.

"I called because there's something I want to ask you, but I
won't keep you long," Adam explained, and pressed the conference call button before putting the receiver down and patting
his breast pocket. "Just a minor detail, really."

"Okay," Bernt Helle said and coughed. "I was actually just
on my way out . . ."

Scraping. A loud cough.

"Fire away," he said eventually. "What's it about?"

His cigar tube had dents in it.

"I don't really know whether it's of any significance or not," Adam said and tried to remember how long he'd been carrying the same tube around. "But could you tell me . . . Was Fiona ever an exchange student?"

"Exchange student?"

"Yes, you know, programs where—"

"Yes, I know what an exchange student is," Bernt Helle said indignantly and coughed again. "Fiona didn't go abroad in high school. I'm fairly sure of that. Even though I didn't know her particularly well at the time. She was in high school, and I was at polytechnic. But, you know . . ."

Adam knew.

And he felt like an idiot. If he had waited until the next day, he would know why he was phoning him. But Johanne had insisted.

With great care, he pulled the cigar out of its aluminum tube.

"Yes," Adam said. "If she had spent any time studying abroad, she would of course have talked about it later."

"Yeah, I'm sure she would have."

There were some silver scissors on the shelf behind Adam, a miniature guillotine. When he cut the end off the cigar, the noise made his mouth water. He took his lighter and rotated the cigar slowly over the flame.

"Not abroad at all," he summed up. "No language schools in England? Summer vacations? Long stays with friends or family abroad?"

"No . . . listen"—a terrible coughing fit rattled in the receiver—"Sorry," Bernt Helle sniffed.

The cigar tasted better than Adam had ever dreamed it could. The smoke was blue and dry on his tongue and not too hot. The smell stung his nose.

Bernt Helle continued, "Obviously I can't know everything

Fiona did when she was in school, in detail that is. Like I said, we didn't hang around together then. We only really met later, after"—a loud sneeze—"Sorry."

"No problem. You should get to bed," Adam said.

"I run a business. And I've got a little girl who has just lost her mother. I don't really have time to go to bed."

"Now it's my turn to say sorry," Adam apologized. "I won't keep you any longer. Hope you feel better soon."

Adam hung up. A delicate, light gray fog was starting to fill the room. He smoked slowly. A drag every half-minute or so allowed the taste to settle and stopped the cigar from getting too hot.

He would never manage to quit. He took breaks, long periods when he didn't enjoy a good cigar, the taste of pepper and leather, with perhaps an undertone of sweet cocoa. He often wondered whether the masculine aroma on the odd Friday night would really do the children any harm. Cuban cigars were best, of course, but he could also enjoy a mild Sumatra after dinner on a Friday evening, with his cognac or preferably a good calvados.

But those days were over.

He ran his finger over his lower lip. The cigar was a bit dry after lying in his breast pocket for weeks. It didn't matter. He already felt lighter and leaned back in his chair and blew out three perfect smoke rings. They floated slowly up to the ceiling and then vanished.

"Weren't you going to go home early?"

Adam's feet, which had been crossed on his desk, now slammed to the floor.

"What time is it?" he asked, putting out the cigar carefully in a mug with some coffee still in it.

"Half past two."

"Shit."

"It smells all the way down the corridor," Sigmund Berli

remarked and sniffed the air disapprovingly. "The boss'll be pissed off, Adam. Didn't you read the last newsletter about—"

"Yeah. Have to run."

He knocked over the coat stand as he tried to get his coat off the hook.

"I should've been home by now," he said and rushed past Sigmund without bothering to pick the coat stand back up. "I'm really late."

"Wait," shouted Sigmund.

Adam slowed down and stopped as he tried to get his arm into a twisted sleeve.

"This just came in," Sigmund said and handed him an envelope.

"Oh, for Christ's sake," hissed Adam between clenched teeth, his coat half on while he fumbled with the rest. "Has this stupid thing gone to pieces?"

Sigmund laughed. He patiently straightened the sleeve, as if he was helping an overgrown schoolboy. Then he held the coat by the collar and helped Adam put in his arm.

"There," Sigmund chuckled and thrust the envelope under Adam's nose.

"You said it was urgent."

"You can say that. Express delivery."

Adam gave a fleeting smile, stuffed the envelope in his pocket, and dashed out. Sigmund could feel the floor heaving under his heavy steps.

"One day you'll get into trouble for all these papers you keep dragging backwards and forwards," Sigmund said to himself. "It's not right."

The smell of Adam's cigar hung heavy in the air, sour and unpleasant.

Vegard Krogh drank the flat beer and felt happy.

There must be something wrong with the taps at Coma, the only decent lunch place in Grünerløkka. He held the glass up toward the window. The head was thin and pathetic. The afternoon light barely managed to filter through the tepid beer. Golden brown reflections played on the table in front of him, and he grinned before taking another drink.

The bungee jump stunt had been a disaster.

The film was fine until about halfway through the jump. Then Vegard Krogh disappeared from the picture. The lens wavered around, up to the sky. Slipped past a crane. Tipped back toward the ground. Suddenly, for a split second, it caught Vegard Krogh on the rebound. Straight up. With the background music of sirens and the photographer's desperate attempt to get away from the place. The rest of the film showed only earth, stones and building materials.

But it didn't matter now.

The invitation arrived yesterday.

Vegard Krogh had hoped and waited. At times he was absolutely certain. It would come. He thought about the invitation in the evenings. His last conscious image before he fell asleep was of a beautiful card with a monogram and his name, written in neat calligraphy.

Then it came.

His hands were shaking as he opened the envelope, thick, stiff, eggshell-colored paper. The card was just as he'd imagined it. A dream card waiting for him in his mailbox, just when he needed it most.

Vegard Krogh had finally arrived.

He was now someone who mattered. From now on he would be one of them. One of the chosen few who answered "no comment" when the tabloids called as they did relentlessly on the couple's friends.

"I'm going to be hounded," he mumbled to himself, drowning his euphoric grin in the pint glass.

The young royals in Sweden surrounded themselves with the upper classes, aristocracy, and decadence. It was completely different in Norway. In Norway, it was culture that mattered. Music. Literature. Art.

It was six years now since he had first bought wine for a dandy young man with doe eyes and feminine clothes. The boy was sitting in a corner, surrounded by girls. Vegard was shitfaced but had always had a nose for where the girls were. The man thanked him politely and chatted away until Vegard picked up a brunette and left.

They bumped into each other every now and then. Had a drink. Shared stories. Until the young man's circle of friends was purged a couple of years ago, for obvious reasons, and Vegard was dropped.

Bungee Jump must have made an impression.

He had sent a signed copy. Not one review of the book had been written yet, eight days after publication. But it had had an impact on the most important critic of all.

From one bungee jumper to another. To dare! From your friend, Vegard.

It had taken him an hour to find the right words. It was important not to be too pushy.

Vegard Krogh downed the rest of his beer in one gulp, a great, satisfied draft.

The glass of cheap merlot was finally starting to kick in.

Dress: casual & sharp, it said on the invite.

He would have to swallow his pride and borrow money from his mother.

She wouldn't be angry this time.

———— ❧ ————

"You say this Stubo guy's okay."

Bård Arnesen leaned over the table and gave his brother an encouraging slap on the shoulder. Then he scratched his head before saving a lettuce leaf from drowning in dressing at the bottom of the glass bowl.

"Lying to the cops isn't very smart, Trond."

Trond didn't answer. He just stared straight ahead without looking at anything. His plate was half empty. He moved the leftovers from side to side, meat and fried potatoes. He listlessly picked up a piece of asparagus and put it in his mouth, then chewed it slowly without swallowing.

"Hello, planet earth calling. You look like a cow."

Bård waved a hand in front of his brother's face.

"It'll be much worse if they find out themselves," he said earnestly. "In fact, it's pretty strange that they haven't—"

"Don't you understand?" Trond exclaimed. "I can't say anything to Stubo. For a start, I'd blow a hole in my alibi. And then I'm in shit up to here"—his hand made an aggressive cut across his forehead—"just for having lied. They'd pull me in immediately, Bård. Immediately."

"Yeah, but you said that they knew you were innocent. That Stubo guy said you were the first one they crossed off from the list. You said that—"

"Said! What the fuck does it matter what I said!"

His fist hit the table. He was struggling to hold it together, his lower lip trembled, his nostrils flared, and his eyes had nearly receded into his skull. He pushed the plate away, then pulled it back, balanced his knife on the fork, and folded his napkin so many times that he couldn't fold it anymore.

Bård kept quiet. The smell of his brother's fear added a sweet edge to the greasy, heavy fried potato scent that filled the kitchen. Bård had never seen his brother like this before. He had been a scaredy cat for as long as Bård could remember.

Wary of everything. A real mama's boy. Cried whenever he got hurt, which he seldom did.

But now he wasn't worried or nervous.

His brother was terrified, and he couldn't swallow the piece of asparagus.

"Hey," Bård said in a friendly voice and gave him another gentle push. "There's no one who would seriously believe you murdered Victoria. For Christ's sake, she was a real catch. Good-looking, fun, with money and a house and things like that. Can't you just . . . hello, Trond!" He clicked his fingers in resignation. "Listen to me at least!"

"I'm listening."

"Spit out that damned stuff."

Trond spat it out. A gray green lump of mulch dropped onto the leftovers on his plate.

"You trust me, don't you, Trond?"

The question got no reaction.

"You're my brother, Trond."

Still no reaction.

"Oh, god damn it!"

Bård got up suddenly, and the chair fell back. It slammed into the fridge door and scraped off some of the paint. Perplexed, he put his finger on the green patch in the middle of all the white.

"I'll fix that," he said in a flat voice. "I'll paint it later, sometime."

His brother still didn't react. He just brushed his hand over his eyes quickly.

"What did you do during those hours?" Bård asked. "Can't you at least tell me? Eh? I'm your brother, for fuck's sake!"

"It was an hour and a half."

"Whatever."

"You said hours. It wasn't several hours. It was an hour and a half. Barely one and a half hours."

Trond Arnesen had managed to forget that tiny bit of secret time. It had been easier than he'd expected. Surprisingly easy. He left the whole episode behind on the way home. When the taxi that picked him up from the bus stop at twenty past six in the morning on Saturday, February 7, stopped so he could throw up by the roadside, he'd tried to focus on the vomit in the snow. Bent double, with his hands on his knees, he recognized an undigested peanut in all the red-wine redness. When he saw the shreds of meat, he threw up again. The taxi driver shouted impatiently. Trond stood there. That was the last time, he thought to himself in a haze. He studied his own spew, fascinated, the revolting remains of everything he had consumed in the past twenty-four hours. And it was out now. Gone. Done with.

Never again.

He scraped the snow with the tip of his boots, wanting to cover the puke, but he lost his balance. The taxi driver helped him into the car. Took him home. Everything was forgotten, and it was the last time ever.

Since then, no one had asked.

The bachelor party, from which he eventually crawled home, had grown during the course of the night. At six o'clock on Friday evening, nineteen men dressed immaculately in tuxedos had headed into town. Then they met Bård's football team, with dirty red shirts and a victory to celebrate. The party grew in size. Things started to warm up. Ten or twelve of Bård's colleagues appeared at around eight o'clock, when the bridegroom was selling French kisses from a stall on Karl Johan for fifty krone a shot. By the time his brother slurred that Trond had to help him to the bathroom to release the pressure at around half past ten, the party had turned into a blind drunk, random, rowdy bunch of men: the Skeid team, some economists from Telenor, a gang of cricket players from Hokksund that had tagged along since about nine, and the odd drunk whom they didn't know from Adam.

At least fifty people, Trond thought.

And no one had noticed.

No one had told the police anything other than that Trond was at his brother's bachelor party from six o'clock on Friday evening until someone put him on the first bus to Lørenskog the next morning.

Everyone had said that. Everything was forgotten.

"What makes you say that?" he finally asked.

"Can't you just tell me where you were?"

His voice was no longer impatient. His brother was pleading with him now, a whining, demanding little brother voice that Trond recognized from childhood and that still annoyed him.

"What makes you say that, and why are you asking me now?"

After all, he was the oldest.

Bård shrugged his shoulders.

"What with everything that's happened . . . I've had other things to think about. But now, now that . . . You just disappeared! I looked for you everywhere. After I'd taken a leak. You helped me. Do you remember?"

Trond nodded but said nothing.

"You were the only who wasn't absolutely trashed. I wanted to borrow some money. Spent over three thousand krone. Think I bought rounds for everyone. You weren't there. Couldn't find you anywhere."

"Did you ask anyone where I was?"

"Everyone was asking where everyone was all the time! Don't you remember? We just about had the run of the place.

It was crazy." He grinned, then pulled himself together. "The next time I saw you, it was three minutes past twelve. And I'm sure about that, because you made such a big thing about your watch, the one you got from—"

"My watch? I didn't have my watch on."

"Yeah you did, cut the crap. When we had that beer-drinking competition, you stood on the bar and took the time with that monstrosity on your arm."

Trond flushed. And then got hotter. He could smell his own body odor, sharp and bitter. His bladder was bursting. He wanted to get up. He wanted to go to the bathroom, but his knees refused to help him.

"Why did I admit it?" he thought. "Why didn't I just deny it? Bård was shitfaced. He might have made a mistake. Confused the times. There were so many people there. Everyone said that I was just mingling and drinking. Showing off. I should have denied it. I had every chance to deny it. I'll deny it."

"You're getting it all confused," he said and clutched the table with both hands. "I didn't go anywhere. You fell asleep on the toilet. Don't know how long you—"

"What the hell are you saying? I know I didn't fall asleep! I didn't get to bed until eight the next morning. I was pretty drunk that night, but not enough not to notice . . ."

Trond forced himself out of the chair. He took a deep breath. Pushed out his chest and held his shoulders back. He was the big brother. Bigger, too, several inches taller than his brother.

"I need to piss," he barked.

"Right?"

"You're my brother. We're brothers."

"Right," Bård repeated with a puzzled, slightly irritated look, as if Trond was wasting his energy trying to convince him that the world was around and circled the sun. "And?"

"You're wrong. I was there all the time."

"Do you think I'm a complete idiot, or what?"

He slipped around the table and stood in front of Trond, his fists balled. Bård was shorter than his brother but much stronger. Their faces were barely a hand apart.

"You admitted it ten minutes ago," he hissed, his eyes narrowed. Trond felt a fine shower of spit on his skin.

"I admitted nothing."

"You said that you couldn't say anything to Stubo. You said that you'd lied. Isn't that admitting, or what?"

"I really need to piss."

"Admit it."

Bård punched his brother on the shoulder. Hard, with his fist.

"Admit."

Suddenly, without warning, Trond grabbed him around the waist. Bård struggled to keep his balance, holding onto his brother's shirt with his left hand as he tried to find something solid to hold onto with his right. A bit too late, he noticed that Trond's foot was in the way as he tried to take a step sideways. They fell over. As they went down, Bård got caught on the electric cord of the mixer. A survival instinct made him move his head when he saw the heavy Kenwood. The steel edge caught his ear. He howled and tried to lift his hand to feel the wound. His arms were pinned down. Only his head was free, and he threw it from side to side as he shouted.

Trond punched him.

Trond sat with a knee on each of his brother's arms and let rip.

He closed his eyes and laid into his brother.

When he was exhausted, he got up quickly. He smoothed down his hair, as if he couldn't quite believe what had just happened and wanted to pretend that nothing had. His brother groaned. Blood was pouring from his ear. One eye had already started to swell up. His upper lip was split. His shirt was torn.

His upper groin was soaking, a dark butterfly-shaped patch on the khaki material of his pants.

"You've pissed yourself," Bård slurred, holding his ear. "You've fucking pissed on me."

He sat up, stiff and unsure if anything was broken. He studied his damned hand and then put it over his ear again.

"Is the lobe still there?" he asked. His voice was hoarse, and he spat out some blood. "Did I lose my earlobe, Trond?"

His big brother crouched down and looked at the wound.

"No. Nasty cut. The ear's all there."

Bård started to laugh. At first Trond thought he was crying. But his brother was laughing, he laughed until he coughed, holding his knees, roaring with laughter and spitting blood.

"What the hell's wrong with you?" he groaned. "You've never beaten me up before. You've never even managed to tackle me to the ground. Have you ever been in a fight before?"

"Here," Trond said and gave him a hand.

"Wait. Hurts everywhere. Have to do it myself."

It took him a few minutes to get to his feet. Trond stood helplessly by, watching him, hands hanging by his side. He scratched his thigh uncertainly.

"Worst thing is the piss," Bård said, and carefully shook a leg. "In any case, you've still got an alibi."

"What?"

"An hour and a half," Bård said and gently tested one of his front teeth.

"What?"

"I can swear on the Bible that you were in the center of Oslo at half past ten and around midnight. You wouldn't make it out here and back. Not without anyone seeing you, anyway."

"I could've taken a taxi."

"The driver would've told the police ages ago."

"I could've driven."

"Your car was at Mom and Dad's. All the boys know that; they picked us up there."

"I might've stolen one."

"Aw shit, this ear," Bård said and closed his eyes as he tried to move one of his shoulders. "It's really hurting. Do I need stitches?"

Trond bent down closer.

"Maybe. I'll drive you down to the emergency room."

"You still have an alibi, Trond."

"Yes, I was at Smuget. All evening."

Bård bit himself gently on his split lip.

"Okay," he said and nodded.

They looked at each other. It's like looking into my own eyes, thought Trond, even though his brother was beaten and damned. The same slightly slanting left eye. Green specks in the blue iris. The epicanthic fold in the corner of the eye, which his mother always said was so unusual in this country. Even their eyebrows, which were so fair that their foreheads almost looked naked, were the same. He had beaten up his brother. He couldn't understand why. And he found it even harder to believe that he'd managed to do it—Bård was stronger, faster, and much bolder.

"Okay," Bård said and wiped his nose on the back of his hand. "You were at Smuget. All night. Fine."

He limped toward the living room door.

"I won't say anymore," he said and stopped. "But—"

He turned around and took a breath.

"No one is going to think you killed Victoria, Trond. I think you should tell the police everything. I can come with you, if you want."

"I was at Smuget all night," Trond repeated. "So it's not necessary."

Bård shrugged and limped on.

He was on his way to the bedroom to lay claim to Trond's most expensive pants. He could have Theresa, his fiancée, hem them. He had a right to take at least his best pants.

"You gave me a good beating," he muttered, impressed.

———————— ✺ ————————

The visit to Yvonne Knutsen was not a success. Johanne had already been warned in the corridor. The nurse whispered that she was suffering from severe MS and refused to see most people. Only her son-in-law and granddaughter were always welcome.

The woman in white was right. Yvonne Knutsen clammed up the minute Johanne walked into the room. She lay rigid in her bed, which stood in the center of the room. Otherwise the room was more or less empty. A faded lithograph hung askew in a broken frame on one wall, and there was a wooden chair by the bed. Through the dirty, streaked windowpanes, the sharp light of the low sun that had blinded Johanne as she drove the last stretch to the nursing home had been reduced to a dull disk above the horizon. Johanne got nothing out of Yvonne Knutsen other than "Please go away" before the sick woman turned her head and pretended to fall asleep.

"I'm so sorry," the nurse had said while resting a comforting hand on her shoulder when she came out, as if it was Johanne's mother who lay there motionless, waiting to die.

The journey home was awful. One of her tires went flat on the E18 on the way back to Oslo. It took a while to find a rest stop where she could pull over, and when she finally inspected the tire, she could see that it was frayed to shreds. It was raining buckets and was stormy, and by the time she got the jack out, she was soaked to the skin.

She finally got home, an hour late.

"MS is a horrible disease," she muttered and rearranged the

cushions to get more comfortable. She was sitting on the sofa in her sweats, with Ragnhild half asleep at her breast.

"You think all illnesses are horrible," replied Adam.

"No, I don't."

"Oh, yes you do."

He put a large spoon of honey in her tea and stirred it.

"Drink up. I've put some ginger in, so that should help."

"It's too hot. What if Ragnhild moved suddenly and I spill—"

"Here," he said with determination and took the baby. "She's full. Drink up so you don't catch anything. Do you want a shot of something?"

"No thank you. It was so awful to see."

"I agree. I had to talk to her just after the murder."

Johanne lifted the cup to her mouth.

"Tell me about it," Adam said, and sat down on the sofa facing her.

She pulled up her feet and tucked the cushions behind her back.

"Fiona has two children," she said.

"Fiona, she's . . . she's got a daughter."

"Yes, but she definitely gave birth to two children."

Ragnhild burped. Adam put her over his shoulder and stroked her tiny back.

"I don't get it," he said.

"Nor do I, in fact," she retorted.

She reached out for the papers he had given her when she got home, soaking wet and grumpy. The bottom page was still damp and soft.

"In the medical records from Fiona's pregnancy and birth, she is constantly referred to as a first-time mother. And I can assure you"—she dropped the papers back onto the table and made herself more comfortable—"a doctor or a midwife can easily identify whether a woman has had a child before or not. It's routine. But nothing like that is written in the records. Fiorella was delivered by cesarean, and it was planned. As far as I can tell from Fiona's records, she suffered from anxiety in connection with giving birth, which they obviously took seriously. A cesarean on a set date, for no reason other than the psychological."

"Yes, but . . ."

Adam put Ragnhild down in the crib, which had been moved back into the living room. He was rocking it gently with his feet.

"I don't understand."

"Not so strange. Everyone thinks that Fiorella was Fiona's first child. The doctors too, even though they must have known it wasn't the case."

"But you"—Adam's brow was wrinkled with skepticism—"you know better than everyone else."

"Not me, the pathologist."

She went into the kitchen and came back with the teapot in one hand and the autopsy report in the other.

"Perineal rupture," she read out loud.

"Which means?"

"Think about it."

"I'm thinking. What does it mean?"

"Listen to the words," she said impatiently and helped herself to more tea and honey. "I'm coming down with a cold."

"Oh give it up," Adam said. "Tell me what you're getting at. How can you—"

"Perineum," she interrupted, "is the medical term for the area between the vagina and the anus. A perineal rupture can occur during childbirth, when you get torn from—"

"Enough," he said and made a face. "I understand. But

why the hell haven't we seen that? If it's there in black and white . . ."

He was put out and leaned over the coffee table, grabbed the autopsy report from her, and started to read.

"You just didn't get what it meant," Johanne said. "You simply ignored it. You were blinded by looking for some sort of sexual motive, so—"

"Ignored it," Adam asked, raising his voice. "Ignored it?"

"You're in good company. It's been revealed that in the Knutby case, the Swedish police shelved a possible murder because they didn't know what 'toxic mass' meant. Don't you read the papers?"

"Preferably not," he retorted, leafing frantically through the report trying to find something. "But these new . . . What about that medical report there?"

He tapped the other papers with his finger. "Why would the doctors lie? Are the records fake?"

"Probably not. I called my cousin, Evan—the doctor you met—"

"I remember Evan. What did he say?"

Adam sat down in the sofa opposite her again.

"There can be only one reason why the records don't include details that are so relevant for doctors and midwives, and so easy to verify," Johanne explained.

"And that is?"

"If it would cause considerable distress to the patient to include it. Considerable distress, Evan said. And as far as I understood, doctors attach great importance to that."

They sat in silence. Adam scratched his neck. The craving for a cigar had returned. He swallowed and stared out the window, distracted. The rain was drumming on the windowpane. A car had stopped. "Kids," he thought. The engine revved up again and again. Someone shouted something, the others laughed. A door slammed, and the car jangled down the road and vanished.

Ragnhild was fast asleep. Jack trotted in from the hall. He stood for a moment with his head to one side, ears pricked, as if he couldn't quite believe how quiet it was. Then he buried his snout in Adam's lap and pawed his thighs.

"Not the sofa," Adam mumbled. "Lie down on the floor. Down, boy."

The dog appeared to shrug his shoulders and then crept lithely under the table and jumped up onto the other sofa, beside Johanne.

"Can you get that kind of injury from rape or something like that?" Adam eventually asked, without commenting on how badly trained the shit brown dog was.

"Adam, really."

"But—"

"Imagine a birth. A child's head. Why do you think women get torn?"

Adam stuck his fingers in his ears.

"The answer is no," Johanne said. "Not from rape."

"But"—Adam tried again and swallowed—"wouldn't a man . . . Wouldn't Bernt have noticed if—"

"No," Johanne replied. "At least, that's what Evan said. Not necessarily. Not during intercourse or . . . other such pleasure."

He smiled. "Strange."

She smiled back. "But it's the truth."

Jack growled in his sleep.

"So, to sum up," Adam said and stood up again. He stroked his chin with his thumb and index finger. "We can confirm the following: Fiona Helle was pregnant twice. The first child was born under circumstances in which she tore badly. It must have been a long time ago, as there is nothing to indicate that Bernt Helle knows anything about the child. And nor does anyone else. Fiona publicly expressed her delight at being a late first-time mother. She would hardly have dared to say something like that if there was anyone out there who knew . . ."

He went over to the window. He could feel the draft. He ran his finger around the window frame.

"Damn me if it's not blowing straight through the wall," he muttered. "We'll have to get that fixed soon. Can't be good for the kids."

"A bit of draft just makes it cooler and fresher indoors," Johanne said and waved her hand. "Go on."

"No . . ." He pulled and fiddled with the old-fashioned insulation tape that was about to fall off.

"I just can't believe that Bernt is a liar," he said slowly and turned to face her again. "The guy's behavior has been fine throughout the investigation. Even though he's no doubt sick and tired of our constant questions that never seem to come to anything, he always answers and does what we want him to. He answers the phone, he comes in when we ask him to, he seems to be well-adjusted and intelligent. So I'm sure he would have understood that information like that would be relevant for us. Wouldn't he?"

Johanne wrinkled her nose.

"Um, yes," she said. "He probably would. I think we can at least assume that the child wasn't born after they became a couple. Gossip is rife in small towns. They married quite quickly too, and I can't imagine that a normal, if very young, couple would have any reason to hide a pregnancy. In fact, I think the answer to this mystery is simple. It must have been a very unwanted pregnancy, when she was very young."

"Please don't say it was incest," Adam warned. "That's all this case needs now."

"Well, it certainly couldn't have been Fiona's father. He died when she was nine. And I think we can safely say that she wasn't that young. But she must have been young enough to disappear or be sent away for a while without it causing a stir. Fiona was a teenager in"—she mouthed the numbers as she calculated—"at the end of the seventies," she finished. "She was sixteen in seventy-eight."

"That late," Adam said, disappointed. "It wasn't exactly a catastrophe to be a teenage mom then."

"Huh," exclaimed Johanne and rolled her eyes. "Typical man! I was terrified of getting pregnant before I was sixteen, and that was in the mid-eighties."

"Sixteen," Adam said. "Were you only sixteen—"

"Forget it," Johanne swiftly interrupted. "Can we just concentrate on the case?"

"Yes, but sixteen . . ." He sat down and scratched Jack behind the ear. "Fiona didn't go abroad," he said. "Not for any length of time, anyway. I checked with Bernt. And I guess he would have known that. Even though not everyone I know likes to talk on and on about time spent studying abroad, I doubt that Fiona would have kept her mouth shut about—"

"Stop it," Johanne said and leaned over to him.

She kissed him lightly.

"So, a child was born," she continued. "It isn't necessarily relevant to the investigation, but, on the other hand, it does bear an uncanny resemblance to her show—"

"That she hosted so successfully for several years, and that gave her such a high profile."

"Adopted children and grieving mothers. Reunited or rejected. That sort of thing."

Jack lifted his head and pricked one ear. The house groaned in the strong wind. The rain was hurled against the window from the south. Johanne bent down over Ragnhild and tucked the blanket more snugly around the child, who slept on undisturbed. The stereo clicked on and off by itself several times, and the main light above the table flickered.

Then everything went dark.

"Damn," said Adam.

"Ragnhild," said Johanne.

"Take it easy."

"That's why I went to see Yvonne Knutsen," Johanne said in the dark. "She knows what happened. You can be sure of that."

"Presumably," Adam replied. His face was covered in great flickering shadows as he struck a match.

"Maybe that's why she didn't want to speak to me," Johanne mused. "Maybe the child has turned up, maybe—"

"A lot of maybes there now," Adam pointed out. "Hold on a minute."

He finally managed to find a candle.

She followed him with her eyes. He was so lithe, despite his size. When he walked, he stepped heavily, as if he wanted to make a point of being so big. But as he crouched in front of the fireplace, tearing newspaper into strips, then reaching out for wood from the metal basket and building a fire, there was something light and easy about his movements, a fascinating softness in his solid body.

The flames licked the paper.

She clapped quietly and smiled.

"I'll cheat a bit, just to be on the safe side," he said and pushed in a couple of fire starters between the wood. "I'll just go down to the cellar for some more wood. Power outages can last a while in weather like this. Where's the flashlight?"

She pointed to the hall. He went out.

The flames crackled warmly and threw a golden red light into the living room. Johanne could already feel the heat on her face. Once again she tucked the blanket in around her daughter and was grateful that Kristiane was at Isak's. She took the woolen blanket that was lying over the back of the sofa and wrapped it around her legs, then leaned back and shut her eyes.

Adam should talk to the doctor who was there at the birth. Or the midwife. They would both cite patient confidentiality but would give in in the end. They always did in cases like this.

It would take time though, Johanne realized.

If there was actually a living adult descendant of Fiona Helle, they might be getting close to something that resembled a clue. A pretty flimsy one, to be sure, and it might lead to nothing. He or she wouldn't be the first child in history born out of wedlock and adopted into a loving family. Probably a perfectly normal twentysomething person—maybe a student, or a carpenter with a Volvo and two snotty children. Not a cold-blooded murderer with a need to avenge the rejection a quarter of a century earlier.

But when she died, Fiona's tongue had been split and cut out.

The child was Fiona's great lie.

Victoria Heinerback had been nailed to the wall.

Two women. Two cases.

An illegitimate child.

Johanne sat up suddenly. She was just about to nod off when a feeling of déjà vu ran through her again, the uncomfortable feeling that there was something important she couldn't grasp. She lifted Jack closer and laid her face on the dog's fur.

"Can we talk about something else?" she asked when Adam came back with his arms full of wood.

He put down the wood.

"Of course we can," he said and kissed her on the head. "We

can talk about whatever you want to. The fact that I want a new horse, for example."

"New horse? I've said it a thousand times: no new horse."

"We'll see," Adam laughed as he went into the kitchen. "Kristiane's on my side. And I'm sure Ragnhild is too. And Jack. That's four against one."

Johanne wanted to respond to his laughter, but the feeling of unease still clung to her body, the remnants of a fleeting premonition of danger.

"Forget it," she said. "You can just forget the horse."

EIGHT

―――――――― ※ ――――――――

The storm had died down. The wind was still blowing strong, but the clouds had opened to reveal light blue stripes to the south. Old, dirty snow lay compacted and rotting in gardens and by the roadside after the rain. Johanne tried to avoid the worst puddles as she maneuvered the carriage on the narrow pavement along Maridalsveien. Heavy traffic and buses thundered past. She didn't like it, so she crossed the road at Badebakken to cut down to the Aker River. Jack was pulling at the leash and wanted to sniff at everything.

The temperature was dropping, and snow was forecast for the evening. Johanne stopped and tightened her scarf, then kept going. Her nose was freezing. She sniffed. She should have put a hat on. At least Ragnhild was warm enough, snug in her Baby Grobag with a sheep fleece under her and extra woolen blankets on top. When Johanne gently pulled back the edge of the bag, she could only just see her little face tightly tucked in. Her pacifier was pulsing, and Johanne could tell from the movements behind the thin, fine eyelids that Ragnhild was dreaming.

She sat down on a bench just by the day care at Heftyeløkka and let Jack off the leash. He shot off down to the river and barked at the ducks, which paid no attention to him. They just swam around in the open channels in the ice. The King of America whimpered and barked and stuck an adventurous paw into the water.

"Stop it," she muttered, scared of waking Ragnhild.

The cold wind ripped through her duffel coat, but she liked sitting here, on her own, rocking the carriage, back and forth, back and forth with one hand. It was Tuesday, February 17. She could make the call at midday. In eight minutes, she discovered when she looked at her cell phone. Fiona Helle's best friend had said that she would be back in the office by then. She seemed puzzled but happy to talk. Johanne had not introduced herself as a policewoman, but her choice of words may have given Sara Brubakk the impression that her inquiry was of an official nature.

Not good.

It wasn't like her. In fact, she wanted to pull out of the case, or at least not get in any deeper, and certainly not use methods that verged on the unethical.

Johanne blew her nose. She was getting a cold, as expected.

There were no people around. Then a jogger came puffing by in a cloud of condensation. He nodded and smiled, but then jumped when Jack came tearing out of some bushes and snapped at his heels.

"Keep your dog on a leash," he shouted and raced on.

"Come here, Jack."

He wagged his tail as she tied him to the carriage. Then he lay down.

It was twelve o'clock. She dialed the number.

"Hi, this is Johanne Vik," she started. "We spoke earlier this morning and . . ."

"Oh yes, hello again. Just a minute while I sit down. I've just got in the door and—"

Scraping. Scratching. A bang.

"Hello?"

"I'm still here," Johanne confirmed.

"There. I'm ready. Now, how can I help you?"

"I've just got a couple of questions about Fiona Helle's time in high school. You were in her class, weren't you?"

"Yes. As I said when I was questioned, Fiona and I were at school together from elementary school on. We were inseparable. Always friends. It's just been so awful since . . . I couldn't face coming back to work until a week ago, in fact. I got bereavement leave. My boss is so—"

"I understand," Johanne assured her. "And I definitely won't keep you long. I just wanted to find out if Fiona was ever . . . away from school? For a long period of time, I mean."

"Away from school—"

"Yes. Not just for a few days because she had a cold, I mean, something longer."

"She was away at Modum Bad in our first year. For quite a while."

"Sorry?" Johanne wasn't cold anymore. She switched the phone to her right hand and asked again. "Excuse me, what did you just say?"

"Fiona had some kind of nervous breakdown, I think. It was never really talked about. We were about to go back to school after the summer break. I remember I'd been in France all summer with my family, so I was really looking forward to seeing Fiona again. We . . . She didn't come. She was in the hospital."

"At Modum Bad?"

"Well . . . to tell the truth, I'm not sure. I've always just presumed it was Modum Bad because I didn't know of anywhere else you could go for that sort of thing. Breakdowns, I mean."

"How do you know it was a breakdown?"

Silence.

More scraping, not as loud this time.

"Now that you ask," Sara Brubakk said slowly, "I'm actually not sure about any of it. Except that she wasn't there. For a long time. I seem to remember that she wasn't back until after Christmas. Or no . . . she came back just before. We always had a school show and started rehearsals at the beginning of December."

"School show? Right after a nervous breakdown?"

Jack growled at an overconfident drake. It puffed out its feathers and tried to take a piece of bread that was only a couple of yards from the dog's snout.

"Quiet," Johanne said.

"Excuse me?"

"Sorry. I'm talking to the dog. So, did Fiona take part? Did she tell you why she'd been away?"

"Yes. Well, not . . . Oh, it was all so long ago."

Her voice sounded slightly apologetic. But it also sounded as if she really wanted to help.

"Like I said, we were best friends. Talked about everything and anything, like best friends do. But I remember that I was a bit put out, hurt, that Fiona didn't really want to tell me where she'd been and what was actually wrong with her. That I'm sure about. I remember my mother said I should just let it lie. That kind of . . . sickness was never easy."

"But Modum Bad and the nervous breakdown could easily be your own conclusions, not necessarily something you know or are certain about," Johanne summarized.

"Yes, I'm afraid so."

"Could you just give me an idea of what she was like when she came back?"

"No . . . what she was like? Just normal, really. Like before.

I hadn't seen her for, well . . . five months, it must have been. From midsummer until the end of November. And at that age you grow up so fast. But we were best friends. Still, I should say."

A group from the day care walked by, two by two, hand in hand, waddling down the path in their oversized winter clothes. A little boy with his hat down over his eyes and a snotty nose was crying. A woman took him by the arm and called, "Not far to go now, children. Come along!"

"Do you think she might have been pregnant?" asked Johanne.

"Pregnant? Pregnant?" Sara Brubakk laughed lightly. "No, you can forget that. Goodness, time showed that it was extremely difficult for her to get pregnant at all. You know that Fiorella was a test-tube baby?"

Johanne didn't know. In fact, there was a bit too much about Fiona Helle's life that hadn't found its way into the NCIS investigation files.

"In any case," Sara Brubakk added, "I'm a hundred percent certain that Fiona would've told me if it was anything like that. We were like two peas in a pod. Pregnant? No, never."

"But you didn't see her for five months," Johanne argued.

"No. But pregnant? Absolutely not."

"Okay. Well, thank you very much for your time."

"Was that all?"

"For the moment, yes. Thank you."

"Are you getting anywhere with the case?"

"We generally manage to solve them," Johanne said evasively. "It just takes time. I realize that it must be very difficult for you all. Family and friends."

"Yes. Just give me a call if there's anything else I can do. I am more than willing to help."

"Thank you, I understand. Good-bye."

The line of children had turned into Mor Go'hjertasvei and disappeared between the apartment buildings. The ducks had settled down. They were sitting in groups on the ice, their legs underneath them and their beaks tucked into the heat of their breast feathers.

Johanne started to wander up the path along the river.

"For a long time there were no secrets in this case," she thought to herself. Jack lollopped obediently along beside her. "It was remarkably free of hate and secrets. But then they popped up. As they always do, in all cases, after all murders. Lies. Half-truths. Veiled facts and forgotten, hidden stories."

Ragnhild started to cry. Johanne looked into the carriage. Her toothless gums were bared in a furious howl. Her mother filled the gaping hole with the pacifier. All was quiet.

She had pondered it for a long time. Why both cases, Fiona's and Victoria's, were so strangely free of contradictions and underlying conflicts.

She picked up speed. The wind was bitter and biting. Ragnhild would fully wake up soon. They had to get home.

"Maternal rejection has ended in murder before this," she mused as she struggled with the curb in Bergensgate. "But why nearly twenty-six years later? Had the child, now an adult, only just found out the truth? Could the revelation of a past betrayal have stirred such hate? Could it be the driving force behind a murder like this, a gruesome, symbolic execution? Or . . ."

She stopped. Jack looked at her in surprise, with his tongue hanging out of his slavering mouth. A bus drove past. The exhaust made Johanne cough and turn away.

Maybe the rejection wasn't that long ago.

The thought had struck her the night before, when Adam warned her against unfounded speculation. Maybe Fiona Helle's secret child had only recently traced his or her biological mother. Ironic, she thought to herself, if Fiona herself had become an object of desire, like those she had exploited for entertainment, on which she had built her career. "Don't speculate. Adam was right. This is too vague. And if the child really does exist, what the hell would that person have to do with Victoria Heiner-back?" she asked herself aloud and then shook her head.

It had to be two murderers.

Or maybe not.

Yes, two. Or one.

"I've got to stop," she thought. "This is crazy. Unprofessional. A profiler uses sophisticated data programs. Works in a team. Has access to archives and know-how. I am not a profiler. I'm an ordinary woman out walking with her baby and dog. But there's something, there's something that . . ."

She started to run. Ragnhild was screaming in the carriage, which rattled and shook and nearly turned over when Johanne slid on some ice as she turned the corner into Haugesvei.

When she finally got home, she locked the door and put on the security chain before taking off her coat and boots.

Trond Arnesen couldn't sleep. It was two o'clock on Wednesday morning. He had been up a couple of times to get water. His mouth felt like sandpaper, but he didn't know why. There was nothing on TV. At least nothing that caught his interest, or stopped him from worrying, or gave him a few minutes' respite from his brain that was churning things over and over and keeping sleep at bay.

He gave up. Got up for the fourth time. Got dressed.

He thought he would take a walk, get some air.

The snow had started to fall at around eight. It lay like a clean, light blanket over the ground, over the rotting leaves and winter remains, dirty gray snow banks and sludgy roads. The gravel crunched under his feet, and the gate squealed when he opened it. He walked aimlessly up the hill, as if lured by the streetlight.

There was no way he could tell the truth.

He couldn't even have told the truth right away, at the time, when he still had a chance, in that sweaty room with the policeman who looked like he was about to burst out laughing.

It had definitely been the last time that Friday, and it had been so easy to forget.

Then Bård came.

Idiot.

Trond thrust his hands deep into the pockets of his down jacket. He walked fast. There was no else around at this time of night, and people had gone to bed hours ago in the dark houses along the road. A cat darted across the road, stopped for a moment, and stared at him with yellow, luminescent eyes before disappearing between the trees on the other side.

He missed Victoria. There was a vacuum behind his ribs, a longing that he couldn't remember ever having felt before, but it was like missing his mom when he went to camp as a boy.

Victoria was so strong. She would have figured things out.

The tears left frozen tracks on his cheeks.

He sniffed, blew his nose in his fingers, and then stood still. This was where the taxi had stopped for him to throw up. He prodded the snowdrift with the toes of his boots. It was lighter up here, with streetlights every five yards or so. The snow shimmered like blue white diamonds when he kicked it.

His watch suddenly appeared.

Puzzled, he bent down.

It was his watch. He blew on it and shook off the snow, held it up to his eyes. Ten past three. The second hand ticked loyally on, and the date showed the 18th.

When he put the watch on, the plastic burned ice-cold against his skin.

He was glad and smiled. The watch reminded him of Victoria, and he put his hand around the black watchband and squeezed it.

He should tell them.

He'd made such a fuss about the diving watch that he should let Adam Stubo know that he'd found it. Trond had simply been mistaken. He hadn't left it at home but had worn it to the party, and it'd fallen off when he was bent double, puking up his guts.

The policeman might have moved heaven and earth to try and find the watch. And Trond didn't want heaven and earth to be moved. He wanted peace and quiet, and to have as little as possible to do with the police.

He could send a text message. That was the solution. Stubo had given him his number and assured him that he could call whenever he wanted. Texting would be safest. It was ordinary and undramatic, the modern way to communicate trivial messages and minor events.

Found my watch. Had dropped it in the snow. Sorry about the fuss! Trond Arnesen.

There, it was done. He turned around. Couldn't wander the streets all night. Maybe he could find a DVD to kill time. He could take one of Victoria's sleeping pills. He'd never tried one before. It would probably knock him out completely. The idea was very appealing.

He didn't care about the book that had disappeared. Rudolf Fjord could buy a new copy.

"Adam."

She prodded him.

"Hmmm."

"I'm scared."

"Don't be scared. Go to sleep."

"I can't."

He gave a demonstrative sigh and pulled the pillow down over his face.

"We have to sleep sometime," was Adam's muffled response. "Every now and then."

He peeped out from behind the pillow and yawned.

"What are you frightened of now?"

"I woke up because your phone was beeping and then—"

"Did my phone ring? Crap, I should've . . ."

His hands fumbled around trying to find the light switch on the bedside table. He knocked over a glass of water.

"Shit," he groaned. "Where . . . ?"

The light exploded in his face. He squinted and sat up in bed.

"It didn't ring," Johanne explained quickly. "Just beeped. And then—"

"Jesus," he mumbled. "Great time to send a text. Poor boy. Guess he can't sleep either. Seems a bit pathetic, to tell the truth."

"Who?"

"Trond Arnesen. Forget it. Nothing important."

He got out of bed and pulled on his boxer shorts.

"It's good that you've finally agreed to let Ragnhild sleep in her own bed. Otherwise we'd all be going around like zombies. As if we don't already."

"Don't be angry. Where are you going?"

"Water," he grumbled and pointed. "Have to get a towel."

"Just leave it. It's only water."

He hesitated for a moment. Then he shrugged his shoulders and crept back under the duvet. He turned down the light and held out an arm toward Johanne. She snuggled up to him.

"What are you frightened of?" he asked again. "Ragnhild's just fine."

"It's not that. It's these cases—"

"I knew it," he sighed and made himself more comfortable. The light still hurt his eyes.

"Should never have gotten you involved in this mess. I'm an idiot. Can I turn off the light?"

"Mmm. I just don't think you've got much time."

"What do you mean?"

"What I said."

"We all know that time is our worst enemy," he said and gave a long yawn. "But then again, as we haven't even found one hot lead, it's better to be painstaking. Turn over stone after stone."

"But what if—"

He suddenly pulled himself away and sat up.

"It's nearly three in the morning," he groaned. "I want to sleep! Can't we leave this until the morning?"

"What if the murderer was only out to get one of the victims?" she said slowly. "If, for example, it was Fiona he wanted to get, and then Victoria was killed to camouflage his real motive."

"Hello," Adam exclaimed and filled his cheeks with air. "We're living in Norway. Camouflage killings! Have you ever even heard about that sort of thing?"

"Yes, lots of times."

"But not here!"

His hands hit the duvet with a dull thud.

"Not in the tiny kingdom of Norway, where people generally kill each other with knives in drunken brawls! And in any case, one more murder is a pretty pathetic camouflage, I must say! But now we have to go to sleep!"

"Shhh," she whispered.

"I will talk as loud as I like."

"I agree that one killing is a poor camouflage. But that's why you don't have much time."

He stood up abruptly. The floorboards creaked under his weight. The water spilled even more, and he swore under his breath. The glass rolled slowly under the bed. He pulled off the duvet and walked toward the door.

"You seem to get by on remarkably little sleep," he snapped. She could have sworn that his voice trembled, as if he was holding back tears. "But I can't. If you're frightened . . ."

His shoulders sank. He struggled with the bedclothes. Then he took a deep breath and continued, "You can wake me, of course. But then you have to be really frightened. Absolutely terrified. Since Kristiane is at her father's, I'm going to sleep in her bed. Good night."

The door slammed, and Ragnhild started to cry.

"No," she heard a groan from the hall. "Dear God, noooooo!"

------------ ꙮ ------------

Vegard Krogh had never liked the woods that he had to go through to get to his mother's house. When he was little, he never dared to take the path unless it was broad daylight, and then preferably with someone else. There was a story that a ghost lived there. Supposedly the place had once been a graveyard. It had been leveled in the eighteenth century, with no respect for the dead. The poltergeists were taking their revenge—that was what the children in the neighborhood said—and would hound anyone who dared to go into the woods after dark.

Total crap, of course, and Vegard Krogh couldn't be bothered to walk all the way around. It was late in the evening on Thursday, February 19. The snow that had fallen over the past couple of days still lay on the bare branches and covered the ground in a thin blanket between the trees, and thankfully gave off some light. He could at least see his feet in front of him.

He was carrying two desirable designer bags. His mother had lent him fifteen thousand krone without any hesitation and without the usual complaints that he was grown up now and a married man, so he had to figure out his own finances. Quite the opposite—she had handed him the money with a twinkle in her eye. In return, he had promised to spend a couple of evenings with her. Which was easy enough, with good food on the table and free wine in his glass.

Fifteen thousand didn't go far. But he was happy. When he was writing his daily blog entry, he was tempted to say something about the invitation. But he didn't. Discretion, he thought to himself, and stuck to giving an account of his shopping trip. It was an ironic epistle about shops where there were only five garments and two assistants who seemed so bored with life that they might at any moment put guns to their heads.

The most important readers would perhaps understand why he, who normally only wore jeans and hooded sweatshirts, had suddenly spent a fortune at Kamikaze and Ferner Jacobsen, the shops where he had eventually found something that he believed was both casual and sharp.

He had released three of the essays from *Bungee Jump* on his Web site. He hadn't asked the publishers about it. They didn't make any effort to get the material distributed anyway, so what did it matter? He'd release another two tomorrow morning. People had devoured them. It was only a couple of hours before the first discussions started. The piece about established popular culture, in particular, had generated debate. He used the milk carton as a metaphor for the welfare state's excessive mass production. They tasted of nothing, were of no benefit to anyone, were to be found everywhere in easily recognizable branded packaging, and were politically correctly recycled ad nauseam. The essay was called "Skimmed Culture," and once he added a link on *Dagbladet's* literature pages, things really took off.

Vegard Krogh walked with a light step. His new boots fit him like a glove. The solid soles meant that it was no problem to walk on the muddy path.

Maybe he should do a bit more to get a freelance contract with NRK television. *Big Studio* was not exactly his thing. Too fluffy, obviously, and far too superficial. But the show was fast and at times could be quite hard-hitting and urban, and Anne Lindmo was a babe.

He would push harder for the job.

Soon he would be out of the woods. He just needed to go around the corner, over the crest of the hill where he had once built a tree house in an old oak tree, and then he would be at his old childhood home by the edge of the woods. His mother had promised to make him food, even if he was late.

Someone was walking behind him. Fear constricted his throat; he recognized the terror he had felt as a boy, when he ran through the woods, out of breath, with ghosts at his heels.

He turned around slowly. He noticed he was gripping his bags even harder, as if the worst thing that could happen to him was to be robbed of his new clothes.

He realized now that the person wasn't behind him. The person emerged from the woods, from between the trees, where there was no path, leaving a necklace of black, uneven footsteps in the new snow. It was difficult to see anything other than the outline of the body. Vegard Krogh was nearly blinded by the beam from a powerful flashlight.

Unusual outfit, he noticed.

A white coverall.

It rustled quietly.

His fear receded somewhat.

"God damn it," Vegard Krogh said, holding up his arm to shield his eyes from the bright light. "You'll scare people sneaking around like that."

The flashlight was lowered and turned; now it lit up the other person's face—from below, like the big boys had done when they tried to frighten the younger kids on those dusky summer nights, when they dared each other to make a terrifying dash over the living dead.

"You?" Vegard Krogh said in surprise and irritation; he squinted and looked at the face more closely. "You? Is this . . . ?"

He leaned forward, furious now.

"What are you . . . you've got a damned . . ."

He didn't die when the four-pound flashlight hit him with great force on the temple. He simply collapsed and sank to his knees.

The flashlight struck him again, this time on the back of the head, with a cracking, fleshy sound that would possibly have fascinated him had he been able to hear. But Vegard Krogh was deaf to it. He died before his body hit the freezing, muddy ground.

NINE

⚜

The first thing that struck Adam Stubo as he followed Sigmund Berli and Bernt Helle in through the glass doors of the yellow nursing home just outside Oslo, on the morning of February 20, was the institutional smell. He could not fathom why people in need of nursing care should be forced to live with the reek of overcooked fish and strong detergents. The public sector might well be struggling, but fresh air was free, after all. When he came into the room where Yvonne Knutsen lay immobile in bed for the third year running, he could hardly resist the urge to open the window.

"Yvonne," Bernt Helle said. "It's me. I've got the police with me today. Are you asleep?"

"No."

She turned her face toward her son-in-law. Her smile was reserved. Bernt Helle laid his hand on her lower arm and gave her a quick peck on the cheek. Then he pulled the only chair in the room over to the bed and sat down. Adam and Sigmund stayed standing just inside the door.

"I know that you don't like talking to anyone," Bernt Helle

said and wrapped his great hand around Yvonne Knutsen's emaciated hand, with blood vessels that traced blue just under the skin. "Apart from me and Fiorella, that is. But this is very important. You see . . ." He ran his hand over his hair and gave an audible sigh.

"What is it?" Yvonne asked.

"You see, something has happened . . ." Again he faltered. He fiddled with a tape measure that was poking out of one of the pockets in his khaki pants.

Adam approached the bed.

"Adam Stubo," he said, raising his hand in greeting. "I've been here before. Just after—"

"Yes, I remember that," Yvonne Knutsen said. "Unfortunately I'm not senile yet. As far as I can remember, you promised not to bother me again."

"Yes, that's true," Adam nodded. "But I'm afraid the situation has changed."

"Not for me," Yvonne replied.

"There's been another murder," Adam told her.

"I see," said the paralyzed woman.

"And once again, the victim is a celebrity."

"Who?"

"Vegard Krogh," Adam said.

"Never heard of the man."

"Well, there's famous and there's famous. It's all relative. The point is that we—"

"The point is that I'm lying here waiting to die," Yvonne Knutsen said in a very calm voice, without a trace of hysteria or self-pity. "The sooner the better. And while I'm waiting, I don't want to be disturbed. Or talk to anyone. A modest request, if you ask me, given my condition."

Adam glanced swiftly up and down the quilt. There was not even the slightest movement to indicate that the person lying there was alive; not even her chest rose visibly beneath the covers. Only her face showed the traces of what had once been a beautiful woman, high forehead and big almond eyes. Her mouth was reduced to a slit between sunken cheeks. But there was still enough information in the pale death mask for Adam to catch a glimpse of Yvonne Knutsen as she must once have been, straight-backed, confident, and attractive.

"I understand," he said. "Really I do. The problem is that I unfortunately can't comply with your wish. The situation is now so serious that we have to follow what leads we have."

"As I said, I don't know anyone named Vegard Krag and can—"

"Krogh," Sigmund corrected from where he was standing in the middle of the floor. "Vegard Krogh."

"Krogh," she repeated weakly without even looking in Sigmund's direction. "I don't know anyone by that name. So, I don't see how I can help you."

"I've got some questions about Fiona's children," Adam said quietly.

"Fiorella?" asked the woman in the bed, surprised, looking from Adam to Bernt and back. "What about her?"

"Not Fiorella," Adam explained. "Her first child. I'd like to know a bit more about the baby Fiona had when she was a teenager."

Yvonne Knutsen suddenly changed. Her nose reddened. Color spread quickly, like butterfly wings, over her gray skin. Her breathing was faster and deeper, and she made a vain attempt to sit up in bed. Her mouth grew. She licked her lips, and they became redder and plumper. Her eyes, which only a moment ago had looked like they'd died already, now sparked with great distress.

Bernt carefully laid his hand on her chest.

"Take it easy," he said.

"Bernt," she gasped.

"It's alright."

"But—"

"Relax."

Adam Stubo moved even closer. He leaned against the high bed frame and bent down over the sick woman.

"I realize that this must be very distressing . . ."

Bernt Helle pushed him away. For the first time during the long, fruitless investigation into Fiona's murder, his behavior was aggressive. He didn't relent until Adam was standing a few feet from the bed. Then he stroked Yvonne's hair.

"Actually, hearing this has been a relief for me," he said in a quiet voice, as if the police were no longer there. "Fiona was so . . . always searching, you know. I often wondered why. I don't understand why it would've been so hard to tell me, though, after all these years, so many . . ."

There was an edge of repressed anger in his voice, which he heard himself and swallowed. Adam noticed that the grip on his mother-in-law's hand was firmer when he continued, "I accept that there's a lot of this I don't understand. We have to talk. Properly, I mean. But right now you have to answer Stubo's questions. It's important, Yvonne. Please."

She was crying silently. Her tears were as big as raindrops. They gathered in the corners of her eyes for a moment before overflowing and running down her temples into her hair.

"I didn't want . . . We thought . . . It was . . ."

"Shhh," Bernt comforted. "Take it easy."

"Her life would have been ruined," Yvonne whispered. "She wasn't even sixteen. The baby's father . . ."

Speech failed her. A fine stream of transparent fluid escaped from her left nostril, and she wiped the back of her hand over her face.

"He was a good-for-nothing," she said loudly. "And Fiona

was just about to start high school. The boy ran away, and it was too late to . . . I should have noticed, of course, but who would . . . Teenagers have a right to a private life too. And a bit of baby fat . . . I—"

"Yvonne," Bernt Helle said firmly, trying to look her in the eyes. "Listen to me. Just listen to me for a minute!"

She had turned away from her son-in-law. She was trying to pull her hand from his firm grip.

"Listen to me," he repeated, as if he was talking to a rebellious daughter. "The two of us can take all the time we need to talk about this later. But what is important right now is that the police get some answers."

No one said anything. Yvonne had given up the fight with her reluctant muscles. She lay there helpless once again, bereft of energy. Even her hair looked lifeless, spread out gray and thin across the pillow.

"His name is Mats Bohus," she said suddenly, the same old voice, dismissive and indifferent at the same time.

"Sorry?"

"Mats Bohus. He was born on October 13, 1978. I don't know anymore."

"How can you . . ." Bernt Helle started but couldn't finish the question.

Once again, Adam approached the bed.

"And this Mats got in touch with Fiona recently," he stated, as if he didn't need confirmation from Yvonne.

She mumbled in agreement all the same, without looking at Adam.

"Before or after New Year?" he asked.

"Before Christmas," Yvonne whispered. "He was . . . he is . . ."

Her nose would not stop running. Bernt Helle fished out a handkerchief from a drawer in the bedside table and gave it to her. She had just enough energy to lift her left hand and put the hanky to her nose.

"I sent her away," she said. "I sent Fiona to my sister in Dokka. Far enough away. Secluded enough to prevent any questions."

Adam shuddered when the woman laughed. She sounded like a wounded crow; her laugher was hoarse, grating, and joyless.

"Then she gave birth prematurely," Yvonne continued. "I wasn't there. No one was there. They just about died, both of them. Then . . ."

She gulped as she breathed in and then coughed so much that Bernt sat her up in bed. When the coughing eventually subsided, he carefully wiped around her mouth and lowered her back down.

"There was something wrong with the boy," she said, her voice hard, "but it was no longer our problem."

"Something wrong with the boy," Adam repeated. "What exactly?"

"He was too big. Slow, heavy, and unbelievably . . . ugly."

For a split second, Adam envisaged Ragnihld just after she had been taken from her mother's womb, red, slimy, and helplessly un-beautiful. He put his hand to his mouth and coughed. His eyes narrowed. Yvonne Knutsen didn't appear to notice his disapproval.

"What happened then?" Bernt Helle asked, almost inaudibly.

"We forgot," Yvonne replied. "We had to forget."

"Forget . . ."

Adam took a silent step away from the bed.

"The boy was given away," said the woman. "Adopted. Obviously I don't know by whom. It was best that way. For him and for Fiona. She had her whole life in front of her. If only we managed to forget."

"And did you manage? Did you manage to forget, Yvonne?"

Bernt Helle had let go of her hand now and was sitting on the edge of the chair, as if he was about to make a break for it. His left leg was twitching, and the heel of his boot was tapping on the linoleum.

"I forgot," Yvonne said. "Fiona forgot. It was best. Don't you understand that, Bernt?"

Her fingers clawed the sheets, where his hand no longer was. His gaze was fixed on the crooked, faded lithograph. He leaned back in the chair and cocked his head. His eyes did not leave the picture. He stared, blinked, and squinted at the abstract composition of discolored cubes and cylinders.

"Please try to understand," Yvonne pleaded. "Fiona was too young. It was the best thing to do, to send her away, put the child up for adoption once it was born, and then forget the whole thing. Carry on as if nothing had happened. It was absolutely necessary, Bernt. I had to think about Fiona. And her alone. She was my responsibility. I was her mother. The boy would have a better life with mature parents, with people who could—"

"We're not exactly talking about the thirties," Bernt exclaimed and pulled away from the bed even more. "It was the late seventies! The age of feminism, Yvonne! Gro Harlem Brundtland and eco-activism, abortion and positive discrimination for women in the workplace, for Christ's sake, it was . . ."

He got up suddenly. He stood over her with his balled hands raised in a manner that was at once threatening and desperate. Then he lifted his face to the ceiling and ran his open hands over his head.

"For years and years we struggled to have children! We went abroad, to all kinds of clinics, we tried and tried and—"

"I think," Adam interrupted tersely, "that we should stick to your own wise words, Helle. These are obviously issues you need to talk about, but that can wait until later."

The big man looked at him in surprise, as if he had just registered that the policemen were there.

"Yes," he said in a feeble voice. "But then I think I'll . . ."

He moved slowly over to the other side of the bed. The air in the room was stale. Adam could feel the sweat dripping from his armpits, cold trickles down to the waist of his pants. He wiped his finger under his nose.

"What are you going to do?" he asked cautiously.

Bernt Helle didn't answer. Instead he straightened the picture. Gently pushed it to one side, then a fraction to the other.

"I understand that you need answers," he said, still facing the wall. "And I really want to help. But right now there's actually not a lot I can do. I shouldn't be here. So I'll go."

Sigmund blocked the door.

"I'm not under arrest," Bernt Helle said. He was at least a head taller than the compact policeman. "Out of the way."

"Let him go," Adam instructed. "Of course he's got the right to do exactly as he pleases. Thank you for your help, Mr. Helle."

The widower didn't answer. The door closed slowly behind him, and they could hear his steps, hard rubber on polished linoleum, fading down the corridor. Adam took Bernt Helle's place on the chair.

"So now it's just us."

The sick woman seemed to be even sicker now. Her flush had died down. Her face was not as gray as when they arrived, but it now had a frightening bluish white tint. Her eyelids slid shut. Her lower lip was trembling, the only indication that Yvonne Knutsen was still alive.

"I understand that this is difficult," Adam tried. "And I won't bother you for much longer. I just want to know what happened—"

"Go away."

"Yes, I just want—"

"Go away." Her voice broke.

"What did he want?" Adam asked. "Mats Bohus. What happened when he turned up?"

"Go away."

"Does he live in—"

"Please, leave me alone."

Her hand fumbled for the alarm button that was taped to the side of the bed. He got up.

"I do apologize for all this," he said. "Good-bye."

"But," Sigmund Berli protested when Adam grabbed him by the arm and led him out into the corridor. "We have to—"

"The man's name is Mats Bohus, and we know his date of birth," Adam said and looked over his shoulder.

Yvonne Knutsen was gasping for breath and pushing the alarm button again and again.

"How difficult can it be to find him when we already know that much?" Adam whispered and remained standing in the doorway.

When a coated man in his thirties appeared in response to the frantic alarm, Adam took Sigmund's arm again and started to walk away.

"It can't be that difficult," he said again, as if he was trying to convince himself.

He glanced at his watch.

"Quarter past twelve already. We don't have much time."

The air outside was cold and sharp, with a scent of spruce and burnt wood coming from a nearby house. Adam stood still for several minutes before sitting down with heavy movements in the passenger seat.

"You drive," he said to Sigmund, who took his place behind the wheel in surprise and put the key in the ignition. "We don't have much time."

He didn't find it hard being on his own anymore. In fact, he did whatever he could to stop people from coming. They were lining up. His parents, especially his mother, called several times a day. He hadn't seen hide nor hair of his brother since the fight, but friends, colleagues, and acquaintances all seemed to think that Trond Arnesen had none of the skills required for living alone. Yesterday, two old friends from school had turned up on his doorstep with homemade lasagna. They were put out when he wouldn't let them in.

He had read that normally it was the opposite.

He had read in the glossy women's magazines that he hadn't gotten rid of yet that normally the nearest and dearest were left in peace and quiet following a tragic death in the family. He had read how the death of a child often left behind an emptiness that the parents' friends and acquaintances avoided in silent embarrassment.

It wasn't like that for him. People were elbowing their way in. His boss at work had said that he should take it easy. Take the time he needed to grieve, was the expression he'd used on the morning he laid his arm around Trond's shoulders and offered to drive him home. As Trond accepted, it was difficult not to invite him in. The man was in his fifties, balding with a comb-over and a snub nose in the middle of his round face. His boss had sent stealthy glances in every direction, as if storing impressions that he could expand on when he got back to work. Finally he was satisfied and left.

Another celebrity had been murdered.

Trond put the newspaper down and went into the kitchen. He had everything he needed for the weekend in the fridge. His mother had insisted on shopping for him. He opened a beer. It wasn't even one o'clock yet, but he had locked the doors, taken the battery out of his home phone, and turned off his cell phone. He wanted to be alone, right until Monday. The very thought gave him a boost. For the first time since Victoria had been killed, he felt something that resembled peace.

The unaccounted-for one and a half hours were nearly forgotten. He drank half the can in one gulp before sitting down in an armchair with the day's newspapers.

Even *Aftenposten* was making a big deal about it. The greater part of the front page and two whole inside pages were dedicated to the murderer who, according to the paper's grim comments, was a killing machine the likes of which Norway had never seen. Six columns were taken up drawing a speculative profile. They imagined that it was a man, obviously, with heavy features and unruly hair. The news desk had superimposed pictures of Fiona Helle, Victoria Heinerback, and Vegard Krogh across his chest. There was no more talk of a woman-hater who had been rejected by his mother. Rather, they veered toward the idea of an unsuccessful wannabe. The underlying implication of a major opinionated interview with three well-known psychologists and a retired policeman from Bergen was that the murderer was probably to be found among the ranks of people voted out of the *Big Brother* house, unsuccessful *Pop Idol* contestants, or Eurovision Song Contest finalists who hadn't won. The brutal killer had probably experienced his fifteen minutes of fame and couldn't cope with the withdrawal symptoms when the spotlight was suddenly turned off. That's what the experts believed.

Vegard Krogh was described as a rising talent, an uncompromising artist.

He was found with a pen stuck in his eye.

Trond laughed so much that the beer sprayed out of his mouth.

Vegard Krogh was the world's biggest creep.

The guy had hated Victoria and everything she stood for.

Lots of people did, but Vegard Krogh had not been satisfied with mere discontent. After one of Victoria's harangues about culture's inability to adjust to market forces, Vegard had approached them at Kunstnernes Hus. It was late on a Friday night, and everyone was there. In a loud voice, he'd picked an argument with her. Then, when Victoria turned her back on him with her little finger bent like a pathetic penis for all the others around the table to see, he had poured his beer on her head. Quite a scuffle followed. Trond wanted to report him to the police.

"That'll just make him feel more important than he is," Victoria said at the time. "He wants attention, and I can't be bothered to give it to him."

Since then, they had neither seen nor heard from Vegard Krogh, except for the odd barbed comment in articles that the *Observer* sent to Victoria. She didn't care, but Trond got rattled every time he came across one of Krogh's rotten pieces. When the guy was given a short guest appearance on *Absolute Entertainment*, Trond stopped watching that channel.

A prick of the highest order, he thought.

Vegard Krogh wanted to be a celebrity at any cost and had now finally succeeded.

Trond drank the rest of the beer and went to get another can.

He was going to be alone all weekend and decided to get drunk. Maybe he would take a bath. Watch a movie. Take a couple of the pills in Victoria's medicine cabinet and sleep for twelve hours.

Those one and a half hours were nearly forgotten.

"A pen," Sigmund Berli said lamely.

"Mont Blanc," replied the pathologist. "Type, Bohème. Appropriate, according to what I've read in the papers. I didn't want to remove it till you'd had a look."

"How is it . . ."

Adam broke off and bent down over the body. He studied the exposed face. The mouth was half open. The nose was covered in scratches. The unscathed eye stared at a point on the ceiling. Poking out of the other eye was a stubby pen. When Adam walked around the metal table, he could see that the writing instrument had been thrust into the corner of the eye. It went deep, he assumed, as only about two inches of the black pen could be seen, perfectly positioned at a right angle to the cheekbone. A small jewel in the clip shone ruby red in the harsh light.

"Has the eyeball itself been perforated?" Adam asked and leaned even closer.

The deceased's right pupil looked alarmingly alive as it squinted toward the alien body in the corner of the eye. It looked like Vegard Krogh had realized that his favorite pen was on its way into his brain.

"Well," the pathologist said. "The eyeball has in all likelihood been destroyed, naturally. But he . . . the killer didn't stab the pen into the eye itself."

"But he may have tried to," Adam suggested.

"Yes. The pen may have slipped on the eyeball and then penetrated here"—he used a laser pointer and made the red dot dance around the corner of the eye—"where it is of course easier to get in."

"Interesting," Adam mumbled.

Sigmund Berli said nothing. Unnoticed, he had retreated a couple of steps from the metal table.

"So he was actually dead before this was done?" Adam asked.

"Yes," the pathologist replied. "Possibly. What killed him

was the blow to the neck. As I said, I haven't done a detailed investigation yet, because I understood that you wanted to see him first. However, it seems to be reasonably clear that he was hit here."

The red dot vibrated just above Vegard Krogh's left temple. His hair was matted and dark.

"Knocked out, more than likely. Then this blow to the neck"—the pathologist scratched his cheek and then hunkered down so that his face was at the same level as the head of the victim—"killed him. It's a bit difficult to show you without turning him over and I don't want to do that before I've taken out the pen and—"

"That's fine," Adam said. "I'll wait for the final report. So it was a blow to the neck. Having been knocked out first by a blow to the left temple. With what?"

"Something heavy. Probably something metal. My initial guess would be a solid bar. When we have a closer look, we'll no doubt find particles in the wounds, which will give us more precise information."

"Then we can assume that the murderer is right-handed," Adam said. "Not that that's much help."

"Right-handed?"

"Left temple," Adam explained, distracted. "Hit with the right hand."

"Only if they were facing each other," Sigmund said. He had gone over to the door and was sucking on a piece of candy. "If the murderer came from behind, he might—"

"They were facing each other," Adam interrupted. "At least, that's what the team who examined the scene have concluded. From the footprints. Thanks for your help."

He held his hand out to the pathologist, who took it and then sat down at a desk in the corner.

"What's the matter with you?" Adam teased Sigmund once

the door to the postmortem room had closed behind them. "You usually cope with worse things than that!"

"God damn it. A pen in your eye, come on!"

"Don't know what's worse," Adam said and groped for his notebook in his coat pocket. "Pen in the eye, tongue in a nice bag, or the Koran stuffed up your fanny."

"Pen in the eye," muttered Sigmund. "A damned fancy pen shoved into your brain is the worst thing I've seen."

A passer-by stopped for a moment outside the impressive building down toward the central station. He was in a hurry. If he didn't make the bus, he would have to wait a whole hour until the next one. But he still stopped. He heard clapping coming from inside. The applause was so loud that he imagined he could feel vibrations in the ground, as if the enthusiasm contained by the solid brick walls was so great that it set the whole of Oslo in motion. The man looked up. He had passed this place, on his way to and from work, five days a week for five years. He had passed the building, which had been abandoned for some time as the neighbors called for it to be pulled down, nearly two and a half thousand times.

He had watched new life being breathed into the building over the past four seasons. Last winter, it had been wrapped in scaffolding and plastic, which shivered and flapped in the gusts of wind from the fjord. During the spring, the building had been reduced to a façade with nothing behind it, like a Hollywood stage set. And before the summer was over, the empty space once again became a four-story building, with grand stairways and hardwood floors, beautiful doors and carefully restored leaded windows on the first floor. Throughout the fall, Polish and Danish curse words could be heard from the scaffolding and the openings that still gaped in the walls, twenty-four/seven. The papers wrote about budget overruns, delays, and open conflicts about money.

The new party headquarters was finally unwrapped just before Christmas. Right on time. The building was officially opened with a new Christmas play for children, performed in the beautiful, elegant auditorium.

The man looked at the façade.

Passing this building gave him inexplicable pleasure. The colors were an exact replica of what had been chosen at the end of the eighteen hundreds, when the building was built as a residence and office for the town's richest entrepreneur. When his grandchild died in 1998, ancient and childless, the property was gifted to the party. As they barely had the means to pay the taxes, it had stood empty until yet another new liberal capital- ist, appreciative of the party's high-profile tax policy, gave them an astonishing donation that allowed them to create the grand- est party headquarters in the whole of Scandinavia.

The clapping seemed to be unstoppable.

The man smiled. He pulled his coat tighter and ran for the bus.

If, however, he had instead gone up the stone steps to the huge, heavy oak door, he would have discovered that it was open. And if he had gone into the hall, he would no doubt have admired the floor. Pieces of hand-turned solid wood spiraled out from a case in the middle of the floor, where the party's motto was engraved in pure gold, behind glass: *Mankind • mar- ket • moral*.

The man who was now getting onto the bus three blocks further west was a loyal social democrat, so he would probably have been antagonized by the banal message. But the beauty of the entrance hall, with its hand-painted dome and crystal and silver chandeliers, might possibly have drawn him up the stairs. The thick carpets would have felt like summer pastures under his feet. Perhaps he would have let the endless clapping lure him into the auditorium. Behind the double doors at the end of the wide corridor, on the opposite side of the room, he would have seen Rudolf Fjord behind a lectern, with his hands raised above his head in victory.

The man who was sitting on the bus, dreading admitting to his partner that he had forgotten to buy wine, might possibly have been astonished by the overwhelming display of jubilation at the emergency meeting of the national congress such a short time after their young leader had been murdered.

A new party chairman had just been elected.

If the passer-by, who was leaning his forehead against the bus window, trying to decide which of his friends might have three bottles of red wine he could borrow, had instead slipped into the back rows of the auditorium, he would have seen something that only Rudolf Fjord had noticed until now.

In amongst all the whooping, clapping, and whistling delegates, there was one person who neither smiled nor laughed. Her hands moved slowly toward each other, in a demonstrative silent protest.

The woman was Kari Mundal. The man on the bus would have seen her turn her back to the stage and leave the auditorium, quietly and calmly, before Rudolf Fjord had had a chance to thank the delegates for their overwhelming confidence in him.

A sharp observer would have seen all of this.

But the passer-by had a bus to catch. And now he was fast asleep, his head on a stranger's shoulder.

———————— ✿ ————————

It was one o'clock on Saturday morning. Kristiane was back. She was always over-excited when she'd been away from her mother and hadn't fallen asleep until around midnight. Adam had gone to bed about the same time. He didn't even try to convince Johanne to come with him. They had barely managed to talk in all the commotion. Isak had stayed until very late.

Johanne knew that she shouldn't let herself be irritated by Isak. And yet she felt that she would never succeed. It was his naturalness that annoyed her most, the nonchalant assumption that it was always fine for him just to sit down, that they had nothing better to do than serve up food and make small talk every time he took Kristiane home. Even now, only a month after Ragnhild was born, he ran boisterously around the house playing Superman with Kristiane on his back, with not a thought for Ragnhild, who was sleeping.

"Just be glad," Adam had said before he went to bed, with some exasperation in his voice. "Kristiane has a good dad. He may be a bit . . . He takes liberties, but he does love that girl. Give him some credit."

Maybe it was actually Adam's fault that she had no patience with Isak. He was the one who should protest. It was Adam, her husband, who should put his foot down, take the intruder to task, her skinny ex-husband who always cheerfully slapped his successor on his twice-as-broad back and offered him a luke-warm beer from the six-pack he usually brought every other Friday, along with a bag of Kristiane's dirty clothes. Always dirty clothes. He never remembered her toiletries.

"I've got some cold beer," Adam always smiled.

Johanne refused to see it as a sign of weakness.

Compliancy.

She got up from the sofa abruptly.

"What's wrong now?" Adam asked.

She stopped and shrugged her shoulders.

"Nothing. Go back to bed."

He was dressed. The sloppy fleece and gray sweatpants irri-tated her. She had given him a dark blue Nike set for Christmas to wear around the house. It still lay unused in the dresser.

"Go to bed," she snapped and went into the kitchen.

"This has to stop," he said. "You can't be angry with me every other Friday. It's not going to work."

"I'm not angry with you," Johanne retorted and let the faucet run. "If I'm pissed off with anyone, it's Isak. But we'll just let it lie."

"No, we can't—"

"Let it lie, Adam."

And they let it lie. He wandered into the living room. He heard her filling a glass with water. She took great gulps. The thump of the glass on the counter was harder than necessary. Then it was quiet.

"What about doing some work?"

His smile was timid. He grabbed her hand as she passed to go and sit on the other sofa. She let him hold it for a moment before pulling her arm into her body.

"A pen in the eye," she said slowly as she relaxed into the cushions. It was as if she had to concentrate on showing any interest at all. "Certainly very symbolic."

"You can say that," Adam nodded, still not sure where he had her. "And for the first time we can safely say that the victim had enemies. Victoria Heinerback had people who objected to her, and she had fallen out with some politicians. There were people who were jealous of Fiona Helle and who talked behind her back. Vegard Krogh, on the other hand, had fallen out with everyone. Because of his behavior and what he wrote. But mainly the latter, perhaps."

"People like that are awful," Johanne burst out. "All cocky and hard when they're sitting at home behind their computer, but pathetic and cowardly when standing face-to-face with the person they're ripping to shreds. Unless they've drunk themselves stupid, that is."

"Quite an outburst," Adam mumbled under his breath. "Is there any more wine left?"

She nodded and pulled the blanket more tightly around her.

"I think hotheads like that are okay," he said and put his generously filled glass down on the coffee table. "Do you want some?"

She shook her head.

"Honestly," she said with unusual passion. "People like that ruin any kind of public debate. It's impossible in this country to . . ."

Her voice shocked her, and she was quieter when she continued, "There's no point in discussing anything anymore. Certainly not in the papers. People are more interested in making extreme statements and elegantly crucifying their opponent to make themselves look good, rather than discussing an issue properly. Elucidating the matter. Being nonjudgmental. Gaining insight. Sharing knowledge."

Adam picked up the glass and leaned back. He looked at her. Her hair was tousled, and she had bags under her eyes. She was pale, like everyone else at this time of year, but he thought there was also something transparent about her skin, a vulnerability that she was trying to hide behind the unfamiliar anger.

"Come over here," he said softly. "Don't take it all so seriously. People can be outspoken if they like. They generally don't mean to hurt people. Exaggerating things, arguing, a bit of passion, it's just entertaining. You shouldn't take it too seriously."

Johanne pulled in her legs and ran her fingers through her hair. Her lower lip trembled.

"Come here," Adam said. "Come here, honey."

"I just get so angry," she said quietly. "I'd rather sit here by myself."

"Okay. That's fine."

"Mats Bohus," she started.

"That's his name."

"Have you found him?"

"No."

"Why not?"

Adam ran his hands through his fair hair, which was getting too long. He knew it looked stupid, thinning on top with a bit of a mullet at the neck and by the ears. He normally kept it shorter, which made it look thick and youthful.

"His home address is in Oslo," he explained. "In Bislett. Louisesgate. But he's not there. The neighbors have described him as being slightly odd. The woman across the corridor said he was away a lot. Never any trouble with the boy, but he's often away for long periods. Doesn't talk to anyone, apart from saying hello on the stairs. And we get the impression that he looks a bit strange. Can you cut my hair tomorrow?"

"I can cut it now, if you like."

He laughed and drank some more wine.

"Now?"

"Yes, this is when we have time."

Jack wagged his tail joyfully when Adam shrugged his shoulders and got up to get the clippers.

"No walk," he said sternly. "Lie down."

The dog padded over to a corner, turned around a few times and then lay down on the parquet with a thump.

"Not too short," Adam warned and tied a towel around his neck. "Not a buzz cut, that is. I want some hair."

"Okay, okay. Sit down."

He felt like a sheep as the clippers cut their way through the hair on his neck. The vibrations resounded in his skull.

"It tickles my ears," he smiled and brushed the hair off his chest.

"Sit still."

"The killer really has had so much luck," he said thoughtfully. "If it really is one and the same man who is making his way through a list of Norwegian celebrities, he's either planned it meticulously or been very lucky."

"Not necessarily," Johanne said and moved the clippers steadily over Adam's left temple.

"Yes," he said, stubbornly. "Yet again, he has managed to get to and from the scene of the crime without being seen. As things stand now—and we've got thirty men from Asker and Bærum doing a major door-to-door canvas. There's plenty of evidence at the scene, and a lot of it is good enough to get a fairly detailed picture of what happened in the minutes before the murder. The murderer was waiting in the woods, let Vegard Krogh walk past on the path, then followed him, got him to turn around, and then knocked him down. But there's nothing—"

The clippers cut into his skin.

"Ow! Be careful! And I said I didn't want a buzz cut!"

"You'll look great. What were you going to say?"

"We're still pretty blank. No organic evidence. Difficult to conclude anything from the weight and size of the foot, except that the killer isn't the lightest of people. He's been lucky."

She turned off the clippers. She stood behind him for a moment, thoughtful, without really focusing on anything.

"You don't necessarily need to have luck. If you're smart and careful, that might be enough. All the victims are public figures, more or less, and it is surprising . . ."

There was silence. The children were fast asleep. The neighbors had gone to bed. There wasn't a sound from the garden or the street. No cats. No cars or drunk youths on the way to another party. The house was silent; the new extension had finally settled and no longer creaked at night. Even the King of America was sleeping soundly and silently.

"I was at Lina's today," she said eventually. "Our computer is hopeless, and Lina's got broadband. It only took me a few minutes to find out that these victims, these"—she put down the clippers and squatted down in front of him—"these public figures really are public," she said and put her elbows on his knees. "Truly. Victoria Heinerback's homepages have remained unchanged since her murder, it's—"

"Her family has no doubt had other things to think about."

"I don't mean to criticize," she interposed. "The point is that her brother-in-law's bachelor party—"

"Brother-in-law to be."

"Don't interrupt. There was a bit about the bachelor party with a link to Trond's homepages, where the reader had access to a detailed itinerary! Anyone who wanted to could have found out that Victoria was likely to be at home alone that evening. Most people knew that she went to bed early, as she made such a fuss about it in all her interviews."

"I'm not quite sure what you're getting at. My hair must look pretty strange."

"It'll be fine."

She stood behind him again and turned on the clippers.

"Fiona Helle was also pretty generous with her private life. She had told the whole world that she was alone every Tuesday. Vegard Krogh kept a blog, one of those incredibly self-centered things that the author thinks are interesting for the rest of the world. Yesterday he told his readers that he had to have supper with his mother because he owed her money. The revolting man really was a great—"

"What are you doing?" Adam turned around with a subdued cry. "I said not a buzz cut!"

"Oops," Johanne said. "A bit short, maybe. Hang on a minute."

She quickly made a few strokes with the machine from his neck up and over to his forehead.

"There," she said with some doubt. "Now it's even, at least. Can't we just say it's a summer cut?"

"In February? Let me see."

She reluctantly passed him the mirror. His expression changed from disbelief to desperation.

"I look like a loaf of bread," he wailed. "My head looks like a big loaf of white bread! I said not to cut it all off!"

"I didn't cut it all off," she said. "You look great. And now we have to concentrate."

"I look like Kojak!"

"Do you think they lie a lot?" she asked, trying to sweep all the hair into a dustpan.

"Who?" he muttered.

"Celebrities."

"Lie?"

"Yes. When they're interviewed."

"Well . . ."

"I've heard some people admit it. Or boast about it, depending on how you look at it. I fully understand if that's the case. They create a pretend life that we can all be part of and then keep the real one to themselves."

"You just said that they write everything about their lives on the Internet."

"Bits of it. The safe things. It makes the lie more effective, I presume. Don't know. Maybe I'm talking trash."

She emptied the hair into a plastic bag, tied it up, and put it in the garbage can. Adam stayed sitting on the stool with the towel around his neck. The mirror was lying on the floor, facedown. There was a thin trickle of blood on his neck from a cut just behind his ear. Johanne moistened one of Ragnhild's bibs and pressed it to the wound.

"Sorry," she whispered. "I should have concentrated more."

"What do you mean when you say you don't necessarily need to be lucky?" Adam asked. "That this killer hasn't just been lucky as hell?"

"A murder in itself doesn't need much planning," she said. "Unless you're someone who will immediately be suspected, that is. If I want to kill someone who everyone knows I have a grudge against, I would have to think about it. Make sure I have an alibi, for example. That's the biggest challenge."

"A enormous one," Adam nodded in agreement. "That's why so few succeed."

"Exactly. But bank robbery . . . then we're talking about planning! Money is far better protected than people. A successful armed robbery depends on prior knowledge and meticulously planned logistics. Expertise. Modern weapons and other cutting-edge equipment. But humans, we're so"—she put her hand on his head. The cropped hair felt terrific against her palm—"so vulnerable. A thin layer of skin. And inside we're vulnerable too. A blow to the head, a knife in the right place. A push down the stairs. In fact, it's strange that it doesn't happen more often."

"For a woman who I know has a good heart and who's just had a baby, you're painting a pretty grim picture," he said and got up. "Do you really think that?"

"Yes. I said it just the other day. When Sigmund was here. The worst thing would be a murder without a motive. If we can't catch him red-handed or he doesn't slip up, he gets away with it."

"I completely disagree with you," Adam said, spitting out some hair while trying to scratch his back. "A murder also needs to be planned. Prior knowledge."

She looked over at the bottle of wine. About a third full. She got a glass and poured herself some.

"Of course," she agreed. "You're right. It takes some skill. But that's all. You don't need much equipment, for example. None of the three victims has been killed with a gun, which you would have to get hold of and also leaves interesting traces. The most important thing is that you can pull out. Right up until the last second. If something goes wrong, something un-expected happens or disturbs you, you can calmly walk away without killing the person. Especially as you don't need any-one else with you to commit murder. That's a huge advantage. What one person knows, no one knows; what two people know, everyone knows."

"Your mother," Adam laughed and plopped down on the sofa.

"Mmm. Not everything she says is stupid."

She followed suit and this time she sat next to him.

"It frightens me to think about the possibility that this per-son knows what they're doing. A . . . professional."

"Do they actually exist?" Adam asked. "Professional killers? I mean here, in Norway, in this part of the world?"

She tilted her head and sent him a look as if he had asked whether it was ever winter in Norway.

"Okay," he muttered. "They exist. But would they not have a motive? A cause to fight for? Or some distorted reason, be it money or God's will?"

For a moment, their eyes met. Then she leaned against him. He held her tight.

"What do you think about Mats Bohus?" she asked in a quiet voice.

"We have to find him."

"But do you think he has anything to do with the mur-ders?"

Adam sighed loudly. Johanne made herself more comfortable, pulled her legs up onto the sofa, and took a sip of her wine. He ran his fingers up her under arm.

"It's easy to imagine that he might have been involved in Fiona Helle's murder," he said. "At least he has a motive. Possibly. We don't really know enough about what happened when he contacted her. But what the hell would the guy have against Victoria Heinerback and Vegard Krogh?"

"Nemo," said the nine year old in the doorway. "Me and Sulamit want to watch Nemo."

"Kristiane," Johanne smiled. "Come here. It's night time, dear. We don't watch movies in the middle of the night."

"Yes we do," Kristiane said and climbed up onto the sofa, forcing herself in between them. "Leonard says that Sulamit isn't a cat."

She hugged the fire engine to her body and kissed the ladder, which was broken.

"It's up to you whether Sulamit is a cat or not," Adam told her.

"Only me," Kristiane nodded.

"But I do think that Leonard will think Sulamit is a fire engine. Is that okay with you?"

"No, cat."

"Cat for you, fire engine for Leonard."

"And cat for you," Kristiane said and held the sad, wheelless toy up to Adam's face. He kissed the hood.

"Now you have to go back to bed," Johanne said.

"With you," Kristiane replied.

"In your own bed," Adam said. "Come along now."

He lifted up the child, and the fire engine and disappeared. Johanne stayed on the sofa. Her joints ached with fatigue. She felt weaker than she had for ages. It was as if all the energy had drained out of her; the greedy baby's mouth sucked out what little she had left after the birth, every four hours, all day and all night; the little bundle made her anxious and weak. Of course she should spend more time with Kristiane. But there wasn't more time to be had.

Not even the nights were her own anymore.

Mats Bohus could feasibly have killed his biological mother.

But could he have killed the other two?

She should really get some sleep.

She drank some more wine. She held it in her mouth, let it run over her tongue, tasted it, then swallowed.

If Mats Bohus wanted to camouflage his mother's murder, he had made a big mistake. He killed Fiona Helle first. The actual murder in a series of camouflage killings should never come first.

Elementary, she thought to herself. A beginner's mistake. No skill.

The murderer was professional. Had insight.

Maybe not.

She had to sleep.

There was another case. Something similar. Somewhere in her brain's hard disk was a story that she couldn't locate.

All was quiet. She was missing something without knowing quite what.

Johanne fell asleep and was not disturbed by dreams.

Sigmund Berli emptied his fourth cup of bitter coffee in three hours. Not only was it bitter, it was also cold. He wrinkled his nose. A bag of gummy bears lay on the desk beside his screen. He popped three into his mouth and chewed slowly. The missus wasn't happy that he was putting on weight. She should try sitting here at four in the morning, in front of a damned computer that didn't want to tell him anything. The woman should try staying awake for twenty-four hours and then try to find some meaning in the columns, names, numbers, and flickering letters on a bright square screen that made his eyes water.

It was sometimes hard to find a wanted person. Even in a small country like Norway, there were plenty of places to hide. The Schengen Agreement meant that they now worked with police forces all over Europe, which helped when they were looking for someone. But then the Agreement also made it easier to cross borders, and thus the number of hiding places had mushroomed. A wanted person could escape. But an ordinary Norwegian, a Mats Bohus, a pure-blooded Norwegian with no criminal record, with a permanent address and personal identity number—they should be able to trace him in a couple of hours.

They'd been looking for nearly twenty-four hours.

Gone. The man had simply vanished.

When they finally managed to confirm that he had been last seen at his apartment in Louisesgate on January 20, the whole NCIS went into action. Adam was probably the only person who was allowed to go home. New baby and all that.

A stab of envy. A wisp of desire; Sigmund saw Johanne's face reflected on the screen. He filled his mouth with three red gummy bears. The sugar hurt his teeth. His tongue stuck to the roof of his mouth. He grabbed his cup, even though he knew it was empty.

Foreigners, all these damned foreigners, they just came and went, in and out of Norway, as they pleased, as if they just came here to take a dump. They played with the police. If only people knew. Some people were starting to realize. Luckily. Foreigners.

But Mats Bohus?

Fiona Helle had been murdered on January 20. And since then, no one had seen him. Where the hell was he?

"Hallelujah, Sigmund!"

Lars Kirkeland was standing in the doorway with his shirt tails out and eyes red. He had a stupid grin on his face and thumped the door frame with his fist.

"We found the guy!"

Sigmund burst out laughing and clapped his hands a couple of times before stuffing the rest of the gummy bears in his mouth.

"Mmmm," he said and chewed furiously. "We have to call Adam."

She should have chosen another hotel. The SAS Hotel, for example, with its Arne Jacobsen design and discreet, cosmopolitan staff. Almost everything you needed was there under one roof, so she wouldn't have needed to go out. Copenhagen was a Norwegian town, far too Norwegian, haunted by beer-drinking men in stupid hats and women with shopping bags and cheap sunglasses. Like shoals of fish, they streamed backwards and forwards over Rådhusplassen, driven by instinct, between Tivoli and Strøget, always Tivoli and Strøget, as if Copenhagen consisted entirely of a big park with a bar at one end and a dirty shopping street at the other.

She stayed in her room. Even now in February, with an ice-cold wind blowing in from Øresund, Copenhagen was full of Norwegians. They shopped and drank and flocked together in the brown cafés, ate frikadeller, and couldn't wait for their next visit, in spring, when they could enjoy their beer outside, and Tivoli would be open for the season once again.

She wanted to go home.

Home. To her astonishment, she realized that Villefranche was home. She had never liked the Riviera. Never. But that was before.

Everything was new now.

She had been reborn, she thought to herself, and smiled at the cliché. Her fingers stroked her stomach. It was more toned now, certainly flatter. She was lying naked on the bed, on top of the duvet. The heavy velvet curtains were open and only the thin, semitransparent curtain hung between her and anyone who might be outside. If anyone wanted to look in, if someone on the second or third floor on the other side of the street was looking in, if someone really wanted to see her, she was visible. There was a draft from the window. She stretched. She could feel the goosebumps under her fingertips when she ran her hands up her arms. Braille, the woman thought. Her new life was written in Braille on her skin.

She knew that she was taking chances now. No one knew that better than she did, and she could have chosen a safer path.

The first one was perfect. Flawless.

But safety soon became too safe. She had realized that as soon as she was back in the villa at the Baie des Anges.

The constraints of boredom, the numbness of a life without risk were something she had never thought about before and therefore had never been able to do anything about. Not until now, when she had finally woken up, broken out of an existence that was protected and padded by routines and passive obligations, where she never did more than she was paid for. Never more, never less. The days slowly accumulated. Became weeks and years. She got older. And better and better at her work. She was forty-five years old and about to die of boredom.

Danger gave her a new lease on life. Terror kept her awake now. Fear made her pulse leap. The days waltzed by, enticing her to give chase, happy but scared, like a child running after an elephant that has escaped from the circus.

"And you're dying so slowly that you think you're alive,"

the woman thought to herself and tried to remember a poem. "It's about me. It was me he was writing about, the poet."

The Chief claimed that Vik was the best. He was wrong.

"I am the BASE jumper, testing equipment that no one else dares to try. And she is the one standing on the ground, not knowing whether it will hold or break. I dive down where no one has been before, while she sits up in the boat and calculates how long it will take for my lungs to explode. She is a theoretician, as I once was. Now I take action. I am the practitioner, and finally I exist."

She slid her fingers down between her legs. She looked over at the windows on the other side of the road. There was a light on, and a shadow was moving around in one of the rooms. Then it disappeared. She was cold. She turned her body toward the window. With open legs. The person who was casting a shadow didn't come back.

She could lead Johanne Vik in a merry dance forever.

But there was no fun in that.

No tension.

Ragnhild burped. A pale white liquid ran down her chin into the deep folds on her neck. Johanne wiped it off carefully and laid the baby over her shoulder.

"Are you asleep?" she whispered.

"Mmm."

Adam turned over heavily and pulled the pillow down over his head.

"I just thought of something," she said quietly.

"In the morning," he groaned and turned over again.

"Even though all the victims had strong links with Oslo," she continued showing no consideration, "they were all murdered outside Oslo. Have you thought about that?"

"Tomorrow. Please!"

"Vegard Krogh lived in Oslo. He just happened to be out in Asker that night. Fiona and Victoria both worked in Oslo. And they worked long hours. They spent most of their time in the capital. But they were killed outside of town. Strange, isn't it?"

"No."

He hauled himself up onto one elbow.

"You've got to stop," he said, earnestly.

"Has it ever struck you that there might be a reason for that?" she asked, unaffected. "Have you ever asked yourself what happens when a murder takes place outside town?"

"No, I've never asked myself that."

"The Criminal Investigation Service," she stated and put Ragnhild down gently in her crib. She was asleep.

"The NCIS?" he repeated in a daze.

"You never help the Oslo police with murders.

"Yes, we do."

"But not with tactical investigations."

"Well, I—"

"Listen to me, then!"

He lay back down on the bed and stared at the ceiling.

"I'm listening."

"Maybe the killer wants to take on more? A stronger opponent?"

"Jesus, Johanne! Your speculation knows no bounds! And we still don't know that there's only one murderer. And another thing, we are so close to a possible suspect. And, and . . . Oslo police are good enough. I would've thought that the most infamous villains would find them challenging enough."

"After that Wilhelmsen woman stepped down, there's been rumors that everything's going to pieces and—"

"Don't listen to rumors."

"You just don't want to even consider it."

"Not at ten past four in the morning, no," he said and hid his face in his hands.

"You're the best," she murmured.

"No."

"Yes. They write about you. In the papers. Even though you never give interviews after that fiasco—"

"Don't remind me about it," he said in a strangled voice.

"You are portrayed as a great tactician. The big, wise, strange outsider who didn't want to move up the ladder, but who—"

"Oh, come on."

"We need to get an alarm installed."

"Please stop being so frightened, honey."

His arm was lying heavy on her stomach. She was still half sitting up in bed. She wrapped her fingers around his. The telephone rang.

"Fuck!"

Adam fumbled around on the bedside table in the dark.

"Hello," he barked.

"It's me, Sigmund. We've found him. Are you coming?"

Adam sat up straight. His feet hit the ice-cold floor. He rubbed his eyes and felt Johanne's warm hand on his lower back.

"I'm coming," he said and hung up.

He turned around and stroked his unfamiliar, naked head.

"Mats Bohus," he said quietly. "They've found him."

TEN

⚜

The medical director of the psychiatric department greeted them in a friendly but rather restrained manner. He too had been pulled out of bed at an ungodly hour. It was still pitch black outside the windows of his office when he asked Adam Stubo and Sigmund Berli to sit down on the gray sofa. A woman with red lips and green hospital scrubs brought them some coffee. When she went out, she left behind a smell of spring that made Sigmund smile at the door, which closed silently behind her. The office was neat and quite cosy. On a shelf behind the doctor's chair was a sculpture that reminded Adam of Africa, masks and fat, headless goddesses. A framed child's drawing in vibrant colors brightened the room.

"I understand," said the doctor when Adam had explained why they needed to talk to him. "Just fire away. I'll answer as best I can. Now that all the formalities are in place."

Adam sipped his coffee. It was scalding hot. He looked at Dr. Bonheur over the rim of his mug. The man was probably around forty and in good shape. His hair was even shorter than Adam's. He had dark skin and brown eyes. His name might have indicated that he was foreign, but he spoke Norwegian without an accent. He was slim and moved gracefully when he went over to a small fridge, poured some milk into a pitcher, and offered it to them. They both declined.

"Need the kick," Adam said and chuckled. "At this time in the morning."

Sigmund yawned without putting a hand over his mouth. Tears sprang to his eyes, and he shook his head vigorously.

"Been up all night," he explained.

"I see," the doctor nodded, his close-set eyes sparkling. Adam had the uncomfortable but distinct feeling that he was sizing them up.

"Mats Bohus," Adam started. "What's wrong with him?"

"Right now?"

"Well . . . I get the impression that he's in and out of here quite often. I'm not too sure about psychiatric terminology, so I don't know whether these illnesses . . . does he have a diagnosis?"

"Yes. He suffers from bipolar disorder. He's a manic-depressive. And yes, he's been coming here for quite a while. Mats Bohus has never been scared of asking for help. In that sense, he's a model patient. It's just a shame that he often comes here a bit too late."

"Born October 13, 1978," Adam read from his notebook, and then leafed on. "Is that correct?"

"Yes. He came here for the first time when he was eighteen. He had been referred to us by his GP, who had been struggling to help him for some months. Since then, well . . . he's been here relatively frequently."

"Does he come when he's manic or depressed?" Sigmund asked.

"When he's down," Dr. Bonheur smiled. "It's unusual for people to feel the need for help when they're in a manic phase.

Then they generally feel like they can take on the world. You should be aware that he . . ."

Once again, Adam felt the doctor looking at him, watching him, sizing him up.

"Mats is a very intelligent boy," Dr. Bonheur said. "But as a child, he was not very good in school. His parents were wise enough to move him to a smaller school. A private school. Not that I want to push an opinion . . ."

He raised his hands with a smile. Adam noticed that the pinkie on his right hand was missing. There was only a stump, pink against his otherwise dark skin.

"But the Steiner school was perfect for Mats. He's a . . ."

Again, there was some hesitation. It seemed as though he was weighing every word.

"He is an exceptional young man. Very knowledgeable. Plays chess like a professional. And he's good with his hands too."

Adam had noticed the chessboard just by the door. It was freestanding, and the squares looked as if they were made from ebony and ivory, in a hardwood frame. The pieces had been left in the middle of a game. Adam got up and went over to the table. The white knight on c3 was foaming at the mouth, its hooves rearing above the pawn beside it, a hunchbacked man in a cloak with a staff.

"The opening move at Reykjavik," Adam said and smiled. "When they finally started to play after all the setbacks. Spassky played white."

"You play chess?" asked Dr. Bonheur in a friendly voice and came over to the table.

"Played. Don't have the time anymore. You know . . . But the world championships in Iceland were something else. Great moves. Followed it all the way. Then."

Adam picked up the queen.

"Beautiful," he murmured, and admired the cloak of blue stones and the crown with a band of crystals.

"But totally unpractical to play with," the doctor said and laughed. "I prefer a classic wooden board. I got this for my fortieth birthday. I don't really use it. But it's decorative."

"I thought one of the symptoms of bipolar disorder was the inability to concentrate," Adam said and put the queen carefully back in place. "Doesn't really work with chess."

"You're right." The doctor nodded. "I repeat: Mats Bohus is an exceptional and special young man. He can't always play. But in his good periods, he enjoys a game. He's better than me. He sometimes just drops by for a game, even when he's not committed. Perhaps he gets particular pleasure from beating me."

They laughed a little. Sigmund Berli yawned and yawned.

"What is this actually about?" asked Dr. Bonheur, his tone suddenly very different. Adam straightened up.

"I would rather not say yet."

"Mats Bohus is in a very vulnerable position."

"I fully understand and respect that. But we're also in a . . . vulnerable situation. A completely different one, of course."

"Does this have anything to do with the death of Fiona Helle?"

Sigmund suddenly woke up.

"Why do you ask?" he said.

"I'm sure that you know that Mats was adopted."

"Yes . . ."

Adam drew it out.

"He loved her program," Dr. Bonheur continued and gave a fleeting smile. "Taped them all. Watched them over and over again. He didn't know he was adopted until he was eighteen. His mother decided to tell him the truth when his adoptive father died. He could at times be quite obsessed with stories similar to those on *On the Move with Fiona*. His mother died as well, about a year ago now. Mats talked constantly about trying to find out where he came from. Who he was, as he put it."

"Did he manage?" Adam asked.

"To find out who he was?"

"Yes."

A brief smile swept over Dr. Bonheur's face as he said, "I tried to get him to realize that the key to understanding himself lay in his life with his adoptive parents. Not in looking for someone who accidentally brought him into the world."

"But did he find his biological parents?"

"Not that I know of. Evidently one of the social workers gave him some guidelines on how to trace his parents. But I don't think he ever got any further."

"Why did you ask if our visit had anything to do with Fiona Helle, then?" asked Sigmund as he rubbed one of his eyes with his knuckles.

The doctor held Adam's eyes when he answered.

"I see I've hit the nail on the head."

He picked up a pawn, thought for a moment, and then put it back where it was before. Adam picked up the same piece.

"How does his illness manifest itself?" he asked as he gently fingered the staff.

"Over the past twelve months, the intervals between phases have been shorter," Dr. Bonheur explained. "Which is, of course, exhausting for him. He was very manic for a period before Christmas. Then he had a relatively good period. On . . ."

He crossed the floor and leaned over his desk. Looked through a pile of papers. He ran his finger down a page and then stopped.

"He came here in the morning on January 21," he finished.

"Early?"

The doctor turned the page.

"Yes. Very early. He got here around seven, in fact. In a very bad way."

"Do you think he's"—Adam put the pawn down again and looked at his watch—"awake yet?"

"I know that he is," the doctor replied. "He normally wakes up about five o'clock. Sits alone in the common room until the others turn up. Likes to be on his own. Especially when he's as down as he is now."

"Could we . . . ?" asked Adam and raised an arm toward to the shut door.

Dr. Bonheur nodded and led the way. He locked the door behind them and went over to the elevator. No one said anything. They went in.

"I should let you know . . ."

The elevator stopped. Halfway down the corridor, the doctor turned and finished his sentence: "I should let you know that Mats Bohus has a . . . very special appearance."

"I see," said Adam, perplexed.

"He has problems with his metabolism, so he's very large. Heavy. And he was born with a harelip, which was operated on, though obviously not very successfully. We have offered him another operation several times, but he has refused."

Without waiting for a response, he walked on. He opened a door and went in.

"Hi, Mats. You've got visitors."

Mats Bohus was sitting on a wooden chair by a Formica table in the middle of the room. His buttocks oozed over the edge of the seat, and it looked like he had trouble getting his thighs under the table. He was dressed in a shapeless sweatsuit. In front of him was a row of beautiful animals. Adam could make out a swan as he got closer. A giraffe. Two lions with glorious manes and open mouths. The elephant was shiny and golden, with a raised trunk and big, see-through ears.

"What are you making?" Adam asked quietly. He was right up by the table; the other two men were still by the door.

Mats Bohus didn't answer. His fingers were nimble, working fast with something that looked like tissue paper. Adam stood beside him and watched a horse being created, with great anatomical detail, down to the hooves and raised tail.

"Adam Stubo," he finally said. "I'm with the police."

Mats Bohus got up. Adam was astonished by the ease with which he pushed back the chair, put the horse with the lions and the giraffe, took a step to one side and turned toward him.

"I knew you would come," he said without smiling. "But you took your time."

The scar on his upper lip was angry and red. It pulled. You could see one of his front teeth, even though his mouth was shut. He had a small nose, and his chin was invisible in the folds of skin that ran down his neck.

But his eyes were like Fiona Helle's. Slightly slanting and clear blue, with long, dark lashes.

"I don't regret it," Mats Bohus said. "Don't for a moment think that I'm sorry."

"I understand," Adam Stubo said.

"No," Mats Bohus retorted. "I don't think you do. Shall we go?"

He was already halfway to the door.

ELEVEN

Lina Skytter padded into her study. Her slippers were too big. The robe must have been bought for someone else. The cuff on the sleeves was at least eight inches wide.

"Even though you're my best friend," she said as she sat down on the guest bed, "I hope you're not going to get into the habit of showing up at half past seven on a Saturday morning to borrow my computer. Don't you have Kristiane right now? What've you done with her?"

"With the neighbors," mumbled Johanne. "At Leonard's."

A battered notebook lay by the keyboard. She hadn't opened it for years, but she had always known where it was. Thirteen years, she calculated. She had moved three times since then. Three times she had found the notebook in a shoebox of small secrets: a brass ring from when she was a child—she had been engaged to the best-looking boy on the street when she was five. The plastic name tag that Kristiane had around her arm in the maternity ward. Johanne Vik's girl. A love letter from Isak. Her grandmother's brown cameo.

The notebook.

Three times she had decided to throw it away. Each time she had changed her mind. The yellow notebook, with a spiral binding and a tiny heart on the next to last page, continued to accompany her through life. Once upon a time she had written W inside the heart. Childish. But she was a child then, she argued with herself. A girl of twenty-three.

"What are you looking for?" Lina asked.

"You don't want to know. But thanks for letting me come again. Our computer is just hopeless. Virus-ridden and slow."

"My pleasure. I hardly see you these days."

"It's only been a month since I gave birth, Lina! For the sixteen weeks before that, I was waddling around like a duck, with pelvic dysfunction and insomnia."

"You've always had problems sleeping," replied Lina cheerfully. "Can't you just stay here today? We could go into town when you're finished. Do a little shopping. Go to a café. It's nonsmoking almost everywhere now, so it wouldn't be a problem with Ragnhild."

She looked out the window. The carriage was just below.

"They just sleep all the time at that age, anyway."

"In fact they don't," Johanne told her friend. "Thank you for asking, but I have to go home."

"Where's Adam? How are you getting along at the moment? Is he completely crazy about Ragnhild? I bet—"

Johanne groaned loudly and looked at Lina over her glasses.

"I'm very grateful that I could come here," she said slowly. "But when I actually dare to disturb my childless, party-going friend early on a Saturday morning, it's because I actually have something really important to do. Do you think you could leave me alone to work uninterrupted for a while, then we can talk afterwards?"

"Of course," muttered Lina and got up. "Jesus, you are—"

"Lina!"

"Fine. I'll make some coffee. If you want any, you'll have to tell me."

The door slammed a bit too hard. Johanne looked over at the carriage. Not a movement. Not a sound. She sat back in her chair with relief.

In the old days, she still would have been confined to bed after the birth. She needed peace and quiet, she thought every time Lina called or her sister pestered her or Adam made cautious noises about how nice it would be if people came to visit. Just a light dinner, maybe, or Sunday tea? As soon as he mentioned it, he could see her shoulders tense up, so he let it drop. Talked about something else. Then she forgot. Until the next time the phone rang and someone went on and on about seeing Ragnhild, about coming to see them all.

She had to find a way to normalize her sleep schedule.

She had to sleep.

Her fingers danced on the keyboard.

www.fbi.gov

She clicked her way to the History page, mainly because she didn't really know what she wanted. Under a picture of a fluttering American flag, J. Edgar Hoover was portrayed as an excellent and democratic boss: a model of neutrality, in political terms, for nearly half a century. Even now, well into a new century, over thirty years after the perverted director had died, he was still patriotically hailed as the responsible and visionary innovator of the modern FBI, the world's most powerful police organization.

She smiled. Then she burst out laughing.

Enthusiasm. Self-confidence. The indomitable American superiority that was so infectious. She was young, in love, and she nearly became one of them.

The notebook was still closed.

She clicked on the link to the academy. The picture of the

building, surrounded by a beautiful park full of autumn colors, made her stomach turn. Johanne didn't want to remember Quantico, Virginia. She refused to remember Warren striding around the classroom; she didn't want to see the thick gray bangs that fell over his eyes whenever he leaned over one of the students' shoulders, usually hers, as he recited Longfellow and winked his right eye with the last line. Johanne heard him laugh, coarse, vigorous, and infectious. Even his laughter was American.

The notebook was still unopened.

Opening the notebook with all those addresses loaded with memories would turn back the clock. For thirteen years she had banished the thoughts of her months in Washington, weeks in Quantico, nights with Warren, picnics with wine and skinny-dipping in the river, and the catastrophic, unspeakable turn of events that had ruined everything and nearly broken her.

She didn't want to do this.

She picked up the yellow book. It smelled of nothing. She touched the spiral binding with the tip of her tongue. Cold, sweet metal.

The picture of the academy covered half the screen.

The auditorium. The chapel. Hogan's Alley. Demanding days, beers in the evening. Dinner with friends. Warren, always late, unfocused as he poured a pint of beer down his throat. They always left the others separately, with some minutes in between, as if no one knew.

The notebook would remain unopened. It wasn't necessary.

Because she remembered.

Now she knew what she had been looking for since Adam had come home on the evening of January 21, exactly one month ago, and told her about the body without a tongue in Lørenskog. The story had touched something in her, light and diffuse, like a cobweb in a dark attic. The feeling had bothered her again when Victoria Heinerback was killed and had been frighteningly intense when Vegard Krogh had been found a day and a half ago, dead, with a fancy pen stuck deep in his eye.

But now she knew.

A glimpse of the secret, forgotten chamber was enough.

Ragnhild was crying. Johanne dropped the notebook into her bag, speedily exited the Web sites she had visited, logged off, and pulled on her jacket as she was leaving.

"Oh," Lina said, now fully dressed. "Are you leaving already?"

"Thanks for your help," Johanne kissed her on the cheek. "Have to run. Ragnhild's crying!"

"But you can—"

The door shut.

"Jesus," Lina Skytter muttered and wandered back into the living room.

She had never seen her friend in such a state.

Calm, kind, predictable Johanne.

Boring Johanne Vik.

———————— ✤ ————————

Mats Bohus had been in the hospital for a month now. Exactly a month. He liked numbers. Numbers didn't argue. Dates followed one after the other, neat and orderly, without any discussion. He had come here four weeks and three days ago. It was five to seven in the morning by the time he finally made it to the entrance. He had walked and walked around Oslo all night. A cat had accompanied him the last part of the way, from Bislett, where he had stood looking at his own apartment for a while. There was no one there. It was completely dark. Of course there was no one there; it was his apartment, and he lived alone. He was completely alone, and the cat was gray. It meowed. He hated cats.

Of course they would come.

He didn't read the papers.

Not the way things had turned out. It seemed as if the snow was never-ending. At night, when everyone else was asleep, he often sat watching the snowflakes dance in the night light. They weren't really white. More gray, or luminescent blue. Every now and then someone popped in to check up on him. They said it wasn't snowing. They just couldn't see it.

"Mats Bohus," the large man said to him. "This is your lawyer, Kristoffer Nilsen. You know Dr. Bonheur. This is my colleague, Sigmund Berli. Do you need anything?"

"Yes," he replied. "I need a whole lot."

"I mean, would you like a coffee or something like that? Tea?"

"No, thank you."

"Water, perhaps?"

"Yes, please."

Stubo poured him a glass of water from the carafe. It was a big glass, and Mats Bohus gulped it down in one sip.

"This is not an ordinary hearing," the policeman said. "Okay? You haven't been charged with anything for the moment."

"Right, I see."

"If we do find it necessary to charge you later, we'll certainly take your . . . illness into account. You'll be taken care of. I just want to talk to you now. Get some answers."

"Understand."

"That's why your doctor is here and, just in case, we asked Mr. Nilsen to attend. If you don't like him"—Adam Stubo smiled—"you can have someone else. Later. If necessary."

Mats Bohus nodded.

"As far as I understand, you were quite old when you discovered that you were adopted."

Mats Bohus nodded again. The man who called himself Stubo was sitting opposite him, in the doctor's chair. Behind the doctor's desk. He thought it was impertinent. It was a personal desk, with a picture of Dr. Bonheur's wife and three children in a silver frame. Alex Bonheur was sitting on the windowsill. It looked uncomfortable. Behind him, through the window, Mats Bohus could see the day dawning, a gray, dull light.

"Can you tell us a little bit about it?"

"Why d'you ask?"

"Because I'm interested."

"I don't actually believe that."

Mats Bohus had picked up the rook from the chessboard on the way in. He was hiding it in his right hand.

"Well, I am, in fact."

"Okay. I'm adopted. Didn't know anything about it until I was eighteen. Then my father died. On that day. My birthday. There's isn't much more to tell."

"Were you . . . shocked? Surprised? Sad?"

"Don't really know."

"Try."

"Try what?"

"Try to remember. How you felt."

Mats got up. The men's eyes were burning into his body, the same look that branded him wherever he went. They were all staring, except Alex, who gave a slight smile and nodded. Mats pulled at his sweater.

"I don't know how much you know about my illness," he said as he crossed the floor. "But for your information, it's hard enough for me to deal with the feelings I have already, now.

More than enough. I have to say that I'm not very impressed with you."

"Okay, fine. Is there anything in particular that you're upset by?"

"Don't know that I can be bothered to stay here any longer."

He had reached the door now. He put one hand on the handle and slowly opened the other. He studied the black rook.

"Tactics are nothing new to me," he said. "Your tactics suck."

Stubo smiled and asked, "Any suggestions as to how I can improve?"

"Stop treating me like an idiot."

"That was certainly not the intention. If I've treated you like an idiot, I apologize."

"You're doing it again."

"What?"

"That attitude. That 'poor monster' attitude. Cut it out."

Stubo got up. Came over to the chessboard. The policeman was as tall as him. He moved the bishop.

"That's wrong," Mats said.

"Wrong? I'll decide that."

"No, it's a set game. The opening of the—"

"Nothing is set in stone, Mats Bohus. That's what's so fascinating about all games."

Mats let go of the door handle. His head hurt. He tended to get headaches about this time of day. When the place came alive, and there were too many people. The room was overcrowded. The lawyer was standing in a corner with his hands behind his back. He rose up on his toes and then down again. Up. Down. He reminded Mats more of a stressed policeman than a person who was there to help him.

"I know what you're trying to do," Mats said to Adam Stubo.

"I'm trying to have a conversation."

"Bullshit. You're trying to build up trust. Talking about harmless things to begin with. You want to create a relaxed atmosphere. Make me feel safe. Make me think that you're actually trying to help me."

"I am trying to help you."

"Really? You're going to arrest me. You think this pandering helps. Eventually you'll get to the point. That guy there"—he pointed a stubby, fat finger in Sigmund Berli's direction. Sigmund was sitting on a chair, repressing yawn after yawn—"he'll probably turn out to be the bad guy. If your good-cop tactics don't work. Pretty obvious, really."

The policeman had a small cut just behind his ear. The scab looked like an A, as if someone has started to carve his name on his scalp, but then changed their mind.

"This is just a waste of time," Mats Bohus said.

The rook's embrasures were framed with silver. A miniature figure with a crossbow was kneeling down, aiming, in one of them. Mats poked the tiny soldier carefully.

"Don't you remember what I said when you came?"

"Yes."

"What? What did I say?"

Adam Stubo looked long and hard at the young man. It didn't look as if he was thinking of leaving anymore. The door was still closed, and Mats Bohus was standing with his back to the others.

"You said that you didn't regret it."

"Exactly. And how do you interpret that?"

"As a confession."

"Of what?"

"I'm not quite sure yet."

"I killed her. That's what I was talking about."

The lawyer opened his mouth and took a step into the room as he raised his arm in warning. Then he stopped suddenly, his jaw shutting with an audible snap. Dr. Bonheur was sitting with his arms crossed, his face devoid of expression. Sigmund Berli looked as if he was about to get up but changed his mind and sank back into the chair with a grunt.

No one said anything.

Mats Bohus crossed the floor and sat down in the deep visitor's chair. Adam followed him with his eyes. There was a strange aesthetic in the way the young man moved. He rolled. His flesh rolled forward, streamlined in waves, like a whale in the depths of the sea.

"I killed my mother."

His voice was different now. His whole appearance was of a man who had just expended a huge amount of energy. The scar on his upper lip looked redder, tighter; he licked it with his tongue. His arms hung heavy on either side of the chair.

Everyone was still silent.

Adam sat down as well. He leaned over the desk.

Mats Bohus seemed younger than his twenty-six years. There was hardly any sign of stubble. His skin was smooth. No pimples, nor scars apart from the broad red stripe above his mouth. His eyes filled with tears.

"She didn't want me," he said. "She didn't want me when I was born, and she didn't want me now. In her programs . . . In interviews, she always said that nothing bad could come of families being reunited. Everyone else got Fiona Helle's help. She only turned her back on me, her own son. She lied. She didn't want me. No one wants me. I don't want myself either."

"Your mother wanted you," Adam said. "Your real mother and father. They wanted you."

"But they weren't real, as it turned out."

"You're too intelligent to actually believe that."

"They're dead."

"Yes, that's true."

Adam hesitated for a second before continuing, "The others, what about them?"

Mats Bohus was crying. Big, round tears hung on his lashes before breaking and running down his nose. He leaned forward slowly, brushed the papers and family photos from the desk, and buried his face in his arms. The glass of water fell on the floor without breaking.

"The others," Adam Stubo repeated. "Victoria Heinerback and Vegard Krogh. What had they done?"

"I don't want myself," cried Mats. "I . . . don't . . . want . . ."

"I don't understand," said Alex Bonheur, his voice sharp. "First of all, I must insist that this . . . hearing ends immediately. Continuing is not advisable. And"—he put his hand gently on Mats Bohus's back. The young man responded with some loud sobs—"I don't see how there can be any connection between—"

"I'm sure you understand," Adam said calmly. "Even though Mats doesn't read the papers, I'm sure you do. As you know, there have been several murders with similar features and—"

"There's no question," Dr. Bonheur said and sent a reproachful look to the lawyer, who was still standing there with his mouth open, not knowing what to say. "Mats Bohus has been here since January 21."

Sigmund Berli was trying to think. His brain cells were asleep. He was so tired that he barely managed to get up, but he had to think and he burst out, "But the man's here voluntarily. So he must be allowed to come and go as he pleases. Sometimes—"

"No," Dr. Bonheur said. "He's been here the whole time."

An uncomfortable silence followed. The lawyer had finally

managed to close his mouth for good. Sigmund held his hand up as if to protest but didn't manage to say anything. Adam closed his eyes. Even Mats Bohus had stopped crying. Earlier they had heard footsteps going up and down the corridor, people talking, a very loud scream on the other side of the closed door. Now there wasn't a sound.

It was Sigmund who finally ventured to ask the question, "Are you absolutely sure? One hundred percent sure?"

"Yes. Mats Bohus came to the hospital on January 21, at seven in the morning. And he has not been out since. I can vouch for that."

Sigmund Berli had never felt so awake.

The TV was appalling on Saturday night, which worked out well for Johanne. Every now and then she drifted off but was woken abruptly by her own thoughts that mutated into strange dreams as she dozed.

Kristiane was staying with the neighbors. It was the first time she had stayed the night with a friend. Leonard had turned up with a written invitation on a piece of red construction paper, with big, bold letters. Kristiane's bed-wetting and the fact that Sulamit had to be a cat before she could fall asleep went through Johanne's mind. She hesitated.

"The fire engine can be a cat for tonight if that's what matters," Leonard said.

Gitta Jensen, who was standing halfway up the stairs, smiled.

"That's true," she said. "Leonard would really love Kristiane to stay. And what with Ragnhild and having to get up every night, we thought it might be nice for you too."

"I want to," Kristiane decided. "I'm going to sleep in the bunkbeds. On the top one."

Kristiane was allowed to go, and now Johanne regretted it.

The girl could get so frightened. She was so wary of change. It had taken her months to get used to the new house. For a long time, she had woken up every night and looked for the grown-ups' room where it had been in the old apartment, only to be confronted with a wall. Her disconsolate cries did not stop until she was allowed to sleep on a small mattress beside Adam's bed.

Kristiane would wet the bed. Then she would be ashamed and sad. She had started to register what was going on around her recently and was more aware of her differentness. It was a step forward, but also incredibly painful.

For Johanne, at least.

Adam had called. He was brief. Said that he would be home late.

Johanne turned off the TV. But then it was too quiet, so she turned it on again. She strained to hear sounds from the apartment below. They must have gone to bed already. More than anything, she wanted to go down and get Kristiane. To have her on her lap, chatting about strange, harmless things. Put a night diaper on the nine-year-old, which was invisible and no one apart from Mommy knew. They could play chess, according to Kristiane's rules, which meant that the knight was allowed to charge wherever it liked, and it was the only one that was allowed to eat pawns for dinner. They could watch a movie. Stay awake together.

Johanne was shivering. It didn't help to snuggle up in a blanket. That morning, in a home that wasn't her own, she had finally dared to peek into a room that had been closed for so long. She had been forced to do it. She didn't want to. She felt humiliated and pathetic, and she was cold.

If only Adam would come home soon!

She held Ragnhild to her chest. She weighed nearly eleven

pounds now, and her skin lay in small folds over her plump hands. Time passed so quickly. Her first dark baby down had almost disappeared, and it looked like she would have fair hair. She could hold her gaze now, and even though everyone said it was too early to tell, Johanne was sure that she would have green eyes. There was a shadow of Adam's cleft in her chin.

If only he would come home. It was eleven o'clock already.

They were going to her parents' house for a family meal tomorrow. Johanne didn't know whether she'd be able to leave the house.

The noise of a door downstairs made Johanne instinctively hug Ragnhild closer. Her mouth slipped from the nipple, and she howled.

The rattling of keys. Heavy steps on the stairs.

At last she could tell Adam what they were up against.

One murderer.

A murderer who had killed and mutilated Fiona Helle, Victoria Heinerback, and Vegard Krogh. There was a monster out there. The incomprehensible outlines of a plan that for the moment told her little other than that the murders were carried out by one and the same man.

Adam stood in the doorway, his shoulders sloping under his coat.

"It was him. Mats Bohus. He's confessed."

"What?"

Johanne got up from the sofa. She was shaking and nearly dropped her daughter. Slowly, she sank back into the sofa.

"So . . . but . . . What a great relief, Adam!"

"He killed his mother."

"And?"

"Fiona Helle, that is."

"And . . ."

"There is no 'and.' No more."

Adam pulled off his coat and dropped it on the floor. He went into the kitchen. Johanne heard the fridge door opening and closing. A can of beer being opened.

Adam was wrong, and she knew it.

"He killed the others as well, didn't he? He—"

"No."

Adam crossed the floor and stood behind the sofa, with one hand on her shoulders and the other around the beer can. He drank. His swallowing was audible, almost demonstrative.

"There is no serial killer," he said and dried his mouth with the back of his hand before finishing the can. "Just a series of bloody killings. Must be contagious. I'm going to bed, honey. Exhausted."

"But," she started.

He stopped in the door and turned around.

"Do you want a hand with Ragnhild?"

"No, it's okay. I'll . . . But, Adam . . ."

"What?"

"Maybe he's lying? Maybe he's—"

"He's not lying. So far, everything he's told us matches the evidence we found at Fiona's house. We managed to question him again this evening. Probably not advisable, in terms of his health, but . . . he knows details that haven't been released. He had a clear motive. Fiona didn't want to have anything to do with him. Like you said. She simply rejected him. Mats Bohus said she was repulsed by him. Repulsed, he repeated it again and again. He even"—Adam rubbed his face with his left hand and let out a great sigh—"kept the knife. The one he used to cut out her tongue. He killed her, Johanne."

"But he might be lying about the others! He might have confessed about murdering his mother but lied about—"

Adam was still clutching the empty beer can.

"No," he said. "I've never heard a better alibi. He hasn't left the hospital building since January 21."

He stared at the beer can in exasperation, as if he had forgotten that he'd crushed it. Distracted, he looked up and asked, "Were you going to say something?"

"What?"

Johanne put Ragnhild over her shoulder and pulled the blanket tighter around them both.

"You looked like you wanted to tell me something when I came in," Adam said and gave a great yawn. "What was it?"

She had waited for him for hours, watched for him from the window, stared at the phone, looked at the clock. She had been impatient and anxious, longing to share the burden of what she had seen and remembered. But now it was only a coincidence, everything.

It couldn't be a coincidence.

"Nothing," she said. "It was nothing."

"Okay, I'm off to bed then," he said and left the room.

Sunday, February 22 had barely dawned. The streets were unusually quiet. Scarcely a pedestrian was to be seen on the main drag of Karl Johan, even though the clubs and the odd pub would be open for a few more hours. A snowstorm was blowing in from the fjord, thick and furious, discouraging people from looking for a new watering hole. Even the taxi line by the National Theater, which normally generated its fair share of fights and arguments, was almost empty. Just one young woman wearing far too short a skirt and bad shoes was leaning into the wind. She was stamping her feet and talking angrily into her cell phone.

"It's easiest to drive down Dronning Maudsgate," said one of the policemen as he put a piece of paper in his pocket.

"Isn't it better to—"

"Dronning Maudsgate," he repeated crossly. "Have I been driving these streets for years, or what?"

The younger one backed down. It was his first shift with the big man in the passenger seat. He had learned long ago that it was best just to keep your mouth shut and do as you were told. There was silence for the rest of the journey.

"Here we are," said the younger policeman, and he parked the car in a snowdrift on Huitfeldtsgate. "Can't find anywhere better to park."

"Fucking hell," muttered the other man as he unfolded himself out of the tightly parked car. "If we have problems getting out again, you can deal with it. I'll get a taxi. Just so that's clear. I'm damned if I'm . . ."

The rest of what he said was lost in a mumble and the wind.

The young man followed behind his colleague.

"That's a bit of luck," said the older man, having managed to pick the lock on the door in a matter of seconds, sheltered by his broad back. "The door was open. Don't need a fucking blessing from any crappy lawyer. C'mon, Constable Kalvø."

Petter Kalvø was twenty-nine and still clung to some of his childhood beliefs. He had thick, short hair and was well dressed. Compared with the unkempt man in jeans and worn-out Doc Martens who marched over to the elevator in front of him, Petter Kalvø looked as if he had just been accepted to West Point. By the stairs, he took on a stern posture and put his hands behind his back.

"This is highly irregular," he said, his voice breaking. "I can't—"

"Shut up."

The elevator doors opened. His colleague walked in, and Petter Kalvø followed with some hesitation.

"Trust me," laughed the older man. "Can't survive in this job without taking shortcuts here and there. We have to take them by surprise, you know. Otherwise . . ."

He winked at him. His eyes were frightening, one blue and one brown, like those of an ice-cold husky.

They came to the fourth floor. The bald policeman pounded on a green door with his fist before even looking at the name, which was written in clumsy letters and attached with a thumbtack.

"Ulrik Gustavsen," he read. "Right place then."

Suddenly he took two steps back. With considerable force he rammed his shoulder against the door. There was a shout from inside. The policeman aimed and ran at the door again. The door gave way, torn from its frame and hinges. It fell into the hallway in slow motion.

"That's the way we do it," the policeman said, grinning, and went in. "Ulrik! Ulrik Gustavsen!"

Petter Kalvø stayed out in the corridor. He was sweating under his Burberry coat. "He's crazy," he thought to himself, dazed. "The man is a raving lunatic. The others said I should just do what he says. They said just to obey and keep my mouth shut. No one can stand working with the guy after his suspension. A loner, they said. Someone who's got nothing to lose anymore. But I do have something to lose. I don't want—"

"PC Kalvø," his colleague yelled from somewhere inside the apartment, "Come here! Get your ass in here, god damn it!"

Reluctantly, he went in. He could see a TV in what was probably the living room. He crept closer.

"Get a look at this whippersnapper," his colleague said.

A man in his early twenties was standing in the furthest corner, beside a sound system, under a shelf of books that ran right around the room, just below the ceiling. He was naked and clutching his penis. His back and shoulders were hunched, and his shoulder-length hair was standing out in all directions.

"Got 'im under control there," the older man said to Kalvø. "Now you stay here and keep an eye on our boy while I have a look around. He's got such a grip on his dick, you'd think he was scared of losing it. But we ain't going to steal it. Relax."

He directed these words at the young man who lived in the apartment, who was still cowering in the corner.

"Take what you want," he stammered. "Take what . . . I've got money in my wallet. You can just take—"

"Relax," Petter Kalvø said.

He took a step toward the naked man, who raised his arm to protect his face.

"Didn't you say?" Kalvø asked, surprised at the force of his anger. "God damn it, didn't you tell him we're with the police?"

The boy sobbed.

His colleague hissed, "Take it easy. Of course I did. The guy must be fucking deaf. Don't let him go anywhere."

PC Petter Kalvø tried to think clearly. He straightened his collar, tightened his tie, as if it was more important than ever, during this alarmingly unlawful search, to be correctly dressed. He should do something. Stop it. He should stand up to his much older colleague. Call someone. Raise the alarm. Protest. He could, for example, go out to the car and call a patrol.

"Just relax," he whispered instead and tried to force a smile. "His bark's worse than his bite."

His voice was weedy and lacked any conviction. He could hear it himself. He took another step toward the boy, who had at last let his arm drop.

"Fucking amateur," his colleague complained by the door. "Ulrik Gustavsen is obviously a novice!"

In his hand he had a small plastic bag of white powder.

"In the toilet tank," he said, smacking his lips. "That's the first place we look, Ulrik. The very first place. Take me to an apartment where I think there's drugs, and I walk straight to the toilet, lift the tank lid, and take a look. God, that's boring."

He stroked his rust red, peppered mustache. He shook his head from side to side as he opened the plastic bag, stuck his pinkie into the white powder, and then tasted it.

"Cocaine," he said and pretended to look surprised. "And here's me thinking it was corn starch. Or heroin or something like that. But instead it's a nice amount of fancy shit. Dear oh dear. Stand fucking still!"

The boy in the corner straightened up, terrified. He had been about to sink down to a sitting position, with his hands still holding his balls. He was crying without shame now.

"Take it easy, little boy. Just stay there. Don't you go anywhere."

The policeman opened cabinets and drawers. He ran his hands under all the shelves and behind all the books. Around all the picture frames and under all the cushions. He stopped by a computer desk in the kitchen. Four IKEA storage boxes were stacked on the printer. He opened the top one and emptied the contents onto the floor.

"Now, what have we here?" he said contentedly. "Let me see. Five condoms . . ."

He tore open one of the packets and held it up to his nose.

"Banana," he sniffed. "If that's what turns you on."

He picked through the pile on the floor and pulled out a trumpet-shaped cigarette.

"Seek and ye shall find," he said. "A secret little joint."

He smelled the contents.

"Shitty quality," he wrinkled his nose. "You obviously don't know much about weed. Shame on you."

Another box was emptied.

"Nothing of interest here," said the policeman and flicked through a pack of cards before he emptied the third box.

It was empty, apart from an envelope.

"Trond Arnesen," he read out loud. "That's a familiar name."

The boy in the corner forgot himself. He took four steps out onto the floor, stopped abruptly, and put his hands to his face.

"Please don't," he wept. "Please don't touch it. It's not drugs. It's . . . nothing. Nothing . . ."

"Interesting," said the policeman and tore open the envelope. "You've made me curious."

There were five smaller envelopes inside, held together with an old elastic hairband. They were all addressed to Ulrik Gustavsen, in neutral capital letters that sloped slightly to the left. No return address. The policeman pulled a letter out of the top one and started to read.

"You don't say," he murmured and put the letter carefully back in the envelope. "Trond Arnesen. Trond Arnesen . . . Where do I know that name from?"

"I beg you," the young boy pleaded; he wasn't crying anymore. "Please just leave them. They're private, okay? You've got no damned right to just burst in here and . . ."

The policeman was astonishingly fast and nimble. Before Petter Kalvø even realized what was happening, his colleague had crossed the floor in four strides and lifted the naked man with a firm clasp around his waist and dumped him back in the corner. His index finger was thrust deep into Ulrik Gustavsen's left cheek.

"Now you listen to me," he said in a low voice and pressed his finger in even harder. He was about a head and a half taller than the boy. "It's me who decides what's interesting around here. All you have to do is stay put and do as I tell you. I've been wading through the shit that you and your kind make for nearly thirty years. And that's a long time. A fucking long time. And I'm fucking bored of fancy . . ."

It looked like his finger was about to go through the boy's cheek and into his mouth.

"I think we should . . . now . . ." Petter Kalvø started. "I think perhaps—"

"You shut the fuck up," hissed his colleague. "Trond Arnesen is the prick who was engaged to Victoria Heinerback. I'm pretty sure that the boys at Romerike and the NCIS will want to have a look at these letters."

He let go. Ulrik Gustavsen sank to the floor. The rank smell of feces filled the room.

"You've shat yourself now," said the policeman with some resignation. "Go and wash yourself. Find some clothes. You're coming with us."

"Should I go with him?" Petter Kalvø asked. "So that he—"

"He won't jump out from the fourth floor. He'd die. He's not that stupid."

Ulrik Gustavsen kept his legs apart as he left the room. He left a trail behind him, and Petter Kalvo stepped to one side as the boy passed on his way to the bathroom. They heard the sound of muffled sobs and running water.

"Now let me just make one thing clear, Petter."

The older policeman put his hand on his partner's shoulder, a gesture that was in part threatening and in part friendly.

"The door downstairs was open," he said quietly. "Okay? And as to why it was necessary for us to break in here"—he nodded at the hallway—"well, we heard shouting and screaming, as if someone was being attacked. Raped, maybe. Okay?"

"But he . . . he was alone!"

"We didn't know that beforehand. The shouting was really alarming, don't you remember? You do, don't you? In fact, the guy was sitting here jerking off and screaming, but how were we to know that?"

"I don't know how—"

"You don't need to know anything, Petter. We found what we were looking for, didn't we? We've got a good bag of cocaine, a pathetic joint, and a pile of letters that might be worth their weight in gold."

Ulrik Gustavsen came out of the bathroom with a towel around his waist.

"My clothes are in the bedroom."

"Well, we'd better go in there then, right?"

"But listen! Trond had nothing to do with . . . Trond doesn't do drugs. I swear. He doesn't know that—"

"Come on now. Get dressed."

They followed Ulrik into a chaotic bedroom and waited while he put on some underpants, a T-shirt, a red wool sweater, jeans, and socks. The older policeman found a pair of boots on the shoe rack and flung them across the floor.

"Here," he said. "Put these on."

"I need to go to the bathroom again," said Ulrik and clutched his stomach.

"Well go then, kid."

The boy shot past them.

It was quiet. The policemen studied the destruction in the hallway. The hinges on one side of the door had been torn away from the door frame. It would be pointless to try screwing the door back in place.

"We can't leave the apartment open," Petter Kalvø said.

The other man shrugged.

"We'll take any valuables with us," he said. "We can put the door back in place and then leave it like that."

"But—"

"Only joking," chuckled the older man. "Call a patrol car.

Ask them to get a locksmith or carpenter or whatever the fuck they need to repair this."

The toilet flushed. They heard the sound of a cabinet being opened and shut.

"Go on, tell me," Petter Kalvø whispered, looking over at the bathroom. "What were the letters about?"

His colleague slapped his breast pocket.

"Love letters," he whispered back with a grin. "Judging by what's written here, these two were at it like rabbits. And Trond, who was about to get married this summer. Tut tut."

"What are you going to do with the door?" Ulrik complained when he came out of the bathroom with his boots on. "We can't just—"

"Come on," said the policeman and grabbed him by the arm. "You've got more to worry about than a broken door. And don't think I don't know what you did just now. In the bathroom. You don't open a cabinet when you're taking a shit, you know."

"I—"

"Shut up. You deserve a few pills to calm you down. And it'll be a while before the next ones."

He gave a loud laugh and pushed the detainee out toward the elevator.

They had survived the meal, and Johanne had to admit somewhat reluctantly that it had even been a success. Her mother had been on her best behavior, warm, happy and utterly wrapped up in the children. Her father seemed to be healthier than he had been for a long time. He ate well and for once didn't touch the wine. It irritated her that Isak was so familiar with everyone and everything, but Kristiane was, as always, delighted to have them all together.

"My family," she said and lay down on the floor with her arms in the air in the middle of the meal. "Fy mamily. Dam-di-rum-ram. I didn't pee in Leonard's bed."

Even Marie, Johanne's three-years-younger, childless sister, had managed not to pass comment on Johanne's homemade sweater and worn velvet pants. She came to the table in a deep green suit that didn't look like it had been bought in Norway, and her hair must have taken at least an hour to style and curl. However, Johanne's glasses had not escaped her sister's insulting remarks.

"I'm sure smaller glasses would really look good on you," Marie had smiled as she tucked a loose lock of hair back in place. "Have you tried them?"

"I think her glasses are fine," Adam said as he helped himself to a third serving of beef. "And in any case, it's a waste of money buying designer glasses when Ragnhild will soon be pulling them off. Solid frames, just what she needs."

Isak had played with Ragnhild and claimed that she laughed. Adam didn't say much but patted Johanne's knee every now and then. Her father shed a couple of tears when he said a few words after the meal. Things were just as they had always been. Not one of them had noticed that Johanne checked the driveway outside the house several times during the meal and that she jumped when the telephone rang.

It was nearly midnight.

It was as if the mere thought that it was close to bedtime made her wake up. She had yawned and dozed the whole day, but as soon as it was dark, it was impossible for her to get any rest. Her anxiety had been justified in the first couple of weeks after she'd given birth; she thought of Kristiane every time she saw the baby. She remembered the strange baby with eyes that never looked at anything or anyone. When Ragnhild was feeding, Johanne was reminded of the listless little bundle that didn't want to eat, with fists that were always balled and lips that turned blue when she had one of her breathless, alien crying fits.

But Ragnhild was healthy. She screamed and was a glutton, she waved her arms and legs around and slept as she should. There was nothing wrong with her.

But healthy children could also die. Suddenly, without reason or explanation.

"I need help," Johanne thought to herself and picked up a binder. "You can go crazy if you don't get enough sleep. I don't smoke, I barely drink. I have to pull myself together. She's not going to die. I won't find her lifeless and limp in bed. She uses a pacifier and sleeps on her back. Like they said she should."

Adam had given up. When he went to bed, he didn't ask anymore if she was coming. Sometimes he got up at night, sat with her for a while on the sofa, yawning, and then went back to bed.

"Something's wrong," Johanne thought. "Not with Ragnhild. There's nothing wrong with her. But there's something that isn't right. Someone is playing with us. Coincidences like that don't happen. It's too close to be a coincidence."

She turned the pages in the binder about the three murders, but without any real interest. The dividers were red. She resolutely ripped out the pages about Fiona Helle. Then she regretted it and tried to put them back in. And didn't manage. The holes were torn. She went to grab some tape from a drawer in the kitchen. With dogged determination, she set about repairing the damage she'd done, but then she threw the tape on the floor and put her face in her hands.

"I can't take anymore. There's someone out there."

Aloud, she hissed with clenched teeth, "Pull yourself together. Get a grip, Johanne."

"I agree," Adam said.

He was up again. Without saying another word, he went into the kitchen. The smell of coffee spread through the apartment, and Johanne closed her eyes. Adam could stay awake and be on guard. If only she could keep Ragnhild in bed beside her, she was sure she would sleep then. But the baby might die if she let her sleep with them. That's what the latest research had shown. She'd read about it in all the publications on her bedside table, medical periodicals and magazines for concerned parents. Ragnhild had to sleep on her own, and Johanne had to stay awake and watch over her, because there was someone out there, someone who wanted to harm them.

She fell asleep.

"I fell asleep!"

She got a fright when he tried to put a blanket over her.

"Just go back to sleep," he whispered.

"No. Awake now."

"You need help."

"No."

"The risk of crib death is not—"

"Don't say that word!"

"Strictly speaking, the risk isn't over until Ragnhild is two," Adam said dryly.

He sat down heavily beside her. There was only one cup of coffee on the table, and he pushed it away when she reached for it.

"And you damn well can't stay awake every night for two years!"

"I've discovered something," she said.

"Well, I would be very happy to hear about it in the morning," he said and ran a hand over his hair, still unused to the short cut. "When the children have gone to bed and there is still a decent amount of time left in the day."

She pulled the mug over. He shook his head and lay back in the sofa in resignation. She drank. He closed his eyes.

"This series of killings has absurd similarities to something else," she started, hesitant, tentative, "Something that I . . ."

The sofa was full of Adam. His arms were resting along the back of the sofa, and his legs were wide apart. His head fell back with his mouth open, as if he was fast asleep.

"Stop it," she said. "I know you're awake."

He opened his eyes. He squinted at the ceiling. But didn't say a word.

"A lecture," Johanne said quickly and drank some more coffee.

"What?"

"I heard about these murders in a lecture. Thirteen years ago."

He struggled to sit up properly.

"You heard about these murders thirteen years ago," he repeated, his voice expressionless. "Right."

"Not the actual murders, obviously."

"I guessed that."

His voice was alert now.

"But ones that were very similar," she finished.

"Could I get my coffee back, honey?"

He smiled reassuringly, as if she wasn't all there and needed to be grounded in reality by a normal, simple act. She got up, keeping the cup firmly in her hands.

"I was at Lina's yesterday," she said. "That computer of ours is—"

"I know," he interrupted. "I promised I'd get it fixed. One of the boys at work . . . It's just that . . ."

"I went on a kind of sentimental journey, if you like. Only it wasn't that sentimental."

Three defined furrows appeared in his brow as he leaned forward.

"What d'you mean?"

"For a long time, I've had a nagging feeling that there's something familiar about the cases. The murders of Fiona Helle, Victoria Heinerback, and Vegard Krogh. I just wasn't able to grasp it. The feeling, that is. The memory. But it had to be something that . . ."

She took a sip of coffee. The steam clung to her face.

"Something what?"

"It had to be something that I'd come across in Washington. Or Quantico. It was very distant. So . . . forgotten and long ago. And I was right. I didn't need to look very far. When I saw . . . Just a picture of . . . Forget it."

She tucked her hair behind her ear and didn't want to let go of the warmth from the mug of coffee. She clutched the cup in both hands and turned her back on Adam.

"My darling."

"Sit down."

"Okay," he said reluctantly.

"All I needed to see was the picture of the academy," she said so quietly that he had trouble hearing. "Then I remembered. I remembered the class. I remembered the long days, the tiring, demanding, fun . . ."

She approached her reflection in the window, as if it was easier to talk to herself.

"Now I even know which lecture series it was, Behavioral Science. Warren amused us with a lecture he called 'Proportional Retribution.'"

For a moment, Adam thought he saw the reflection smile.

"Amused us," she repeated. "That was actually what he did. We laughed. Everyone laughed when Warren wanted us to laugh. It was toward the end of June. Almost summer break. It was warm. Very humid and warm. The air-conditioning in the auditorium was broken. We were sweating. But not Warren. He always seemed so cool—in every sense."

Slowly she turned around. She lowered her cup. It was empty and hung from her finger by the handle.

"I expend so much effort trying to forget," she said without looking at him. "Maybe it isn't that strange that I found it so hard to remember. Although . . ."

Her eyes filled up. She leaned her head back to prevent the tears from running down her face. Adam started to get up again.

"Don't," she said harshly.

She smiled suddenly through the tears and wiped her left eye lightly with the back of her hand.

"The lecture was about revenge, people with a strong sense of 'eye for an eye, tooth for a tooth,'" she said. "About criminals with an exaggerated need for the punishment to fit the crime. At least symbolically. Warren loved things like that. He loved anything that was violent. Clear. Exaggerated."

"Sit down, Johanne."

He patted the cushion next to him on the sofa.

"No, I'd rather stand. I have to tell you this. While I still have the energy to do it. Or rather"—another fleeting, thin smile—"when I don't have the energy not to," she added.

"To be honest, I have no idea what you're talking about, Johanne."

"He told us about five cases," she continued as if she hadn't heard him. "One was . . . It was about one of those eccentrics you only find in the States. A slightly twisted, intellectual type. With green fingers. He had a beautiful garden, which he protected, tooth and nail. I can't remember how he made a living, but he must have had money, because the garden was the jewel of the neighborhood. Then a neighbor sued him over a boundary dispute. The neighbor claimed that the fence was a few yards too far into his property, and the court ruled in his favor, after having put the case through several rounds in the judicial system. I don't remember all the details. The point is that . . ."

She froze, with the tip of her tongue on her lips and her head cocked.

"Did you hear something?"

"No. Can't you . . ."

She swallowed and sighed deeply before carrying on.

"The point is that the neighbor was found dead just after the final judgment. His tongue had been cut out and was lying in a folded envelope, made from the cover of *House & Garden*. A magazine. About—"

"Houses and gardens," said Adam, exasperated. "Can you please sit down? You're freezing. Come here."

"Are you listening?"

"Yes, but—"

"His tongue had been cut out! And beautifully wrapped! The most banal, vulgar symbol—"

"I am sure," he interjected in a quiet voice, "that there are examples of bodies that have been dismembered in that way all over the world, Johanne. Without it having anything to do with the death of Fiona Helle. You said it yourself, it was a long time ago and you don't remember all—"

"The worst thing is that I do remember," she burst out. "I remember everything now. Please try to understand, Adam! Don't you know how . . . hard it is to force yourself to remember something that you have desperately tried to forget? How . . . how much it hurts to—"

"It's difficult for me to understand something I don't know about," Adam retorted and immediately regretted it. "I mean . . . I can see that it's painful for you. That's not difficult to—"

"Don't push it," she almost screamed. "I will never, ever talk about what happened. I'm just trying to explain to you why this story got hidden. It's so painfully close to—"

He got up. He grabbed her by the wrists and felt how thin she had become. Her watch, which had been too tight to wear in the last months of pregnancy, was now in danger of slipping off her wrist. Without any resistance, she let him hold her. He stroked her back. He could feel the sharp vertebrae through her sweater.

"You need to start eating," he said with his face buried in her lifeless and matted hair. "You need to eat and sleep, Johanne."

"And you need to listen to me," she cried. "Can't you just listen to my story? Without asking what . . . Without mixing everything . . ."

With a sudden angry movement, she straightened up and put her hands on his chest.

"Can't you just stop asking about things that are my business, and my business alone? Can't you forget that and just listen to what I'm saying?"

"It's difficult. At some point you're going to have to—"

"Never. Okay? Never. You promised not—"

"We were getting married the next day, Johanne. I was scared that you'd cancel the whole wedding if I didn't go along with your demands. It's different now."

"Nothing is different."

"Yes it is. We're married. We've got children. You're about to . . . You're upset, Johanne. You're suffering because of something you refuse to let me in on. And I won't accept that."

"You have to."

He let go of her. They stood there for a while, close but not touching. He was nearly a head taller than her. Johanne lifted her face. There was a darkness in her eyes that he didn't recognize, and his heart started to race when for a moment he saw something that he thought might resemble . . . hate.

"Johanne," he whispered.

"I love you," she said quietly. "But you have to let it lie. Maybe one day I will be able to tell you about what happened between Warren and me. But not now. Not for a long time, Adam. I have spent the last few weeks trying to find my way back to that memory, and it's been a tough journey. I can't take any more. I want to leave it behind. To come back. To my life here. To you and the children. Us."

"Of course," he said in a hoarse voice. His heart was still pounding.

"But I took a story back with me that I really need to tell. I put a lid on the rest. And it will be there for a long time, maybe forever. But you must . . . you have to listen to what I have to say."

He swallowed and nodded.

"Shall we sit down?" he said, his voice still raw.

"Don't be like that," Johanne said and stroked his cropped head. "Can't you—"

"You frightened me," he said, keeping his eyes locked on hers.

They were normal again. Friendly. Johanne's own normal, friendly eyes.

"I didn't mean to."

"Can we sit down?"

"Can you please stop—"

"What?"

"I'm sorry that I frightened you. But you don't need to treat me as if I'm a casual guest."

For a moment her eyes were hostile. Not full of hate, as he had felt before, but aggressive and hostile.

"Bullshit," he said and smiled. "Okay, let's just drop you and . . . you and Warren. Now tell me the rest."

He got another cup and poured them both coffee, then sat down on the sofa and patted the cushion beside him.

"Come on," he said with strained cheerfulness.

"Are you sure?" she asked and took the fresh cup of coffee without sitting down.

"Absolutely."

His smile still hadn't reached his eyes.

"Okay," she said slowly. "The other case was a small-town murder in California. Or . . . yes, it was California. A local politician was literally suffocated with Bible quotations. Nailed to the wall with his mouth full of wet paper. Pages from the poor bastard's own Bible."

Johanne's eyes wandered around the room, as if she needed to find comfort in the security and familiarity it offered before she could continue. Darkness enveloped the house like an insulating cape. It was so quiet that Adam thought he could hear the whirring of his own thoughts. They were careening around in his head, confused and unstructured. What was this? What kind of absurd story was she telling him? How could three murders in Norway in 2004 be connected to a repressed and forgotten lecture in the States thirteen years ago?

Bible then, Koran now.

Beautifully wrapped tongues. Then and now.

"Why was he killed?" was all he could think to say.

"A pastor who had his own wacky following believed that this local councilman deserved to die because he had encouraged ungodly racism. He got one of his followers to carry out the murder. A simpleton. Who just grinned throughout the court case, told them everything . . . or so we were told."

"Racism," thought Adam.

Victoria Heinerback was not a racist. Victoria Heinerback

worked primarily with economics. They had hardly paid the issue any attention. They had looked for political motives: unpopular budget cuts and brutal power struggles. Racism was quickly dismissed as a motive, despite the Koran. The young party leader had avoided the issue and was smart enough to answer questions generally and harmlessly whenever forced into a corner by journalists who were not satisfied with platitudes about immigration costs and resource issues.

"But Victoria Heinerback did have several fellow party members," Adam hesitated, "who might be accused of not liking our new countrymen."

He hadn't touched the coffee. He leaned forward over the coffee table. His hand was shaking.

"That's two cases," he said and left the cup where it was. "You said there were five."

"A journalist was beaten to death," continued Johanne. "He had uncovered a financial mismanagement case in a company on the East Coast, I can't remember what it was about. The story cost him his life."

"But he wasn't killed by a . . . pen?"

"No."

She gave a wan smile.

"A typewriter. A Remington, a huge, old-fashioned . . ."

Adam wasn't listening anymore.

"A typewriter to the head," he thought. "A pen in the eye. Two journalists, then and now, killed by the tools of their trade. Two politicians, then and now, crucified and desecrated with religious scripts. Two tongues. Two people accused of lying.

"Jesus Christ," he whispered.

Johanne picked up a red rag doll from the shelf by the TV. It was missing an arm. Its face was dirty gray, and its red hair was as faded as its dress, almost pink after countless spins in the washing machine.

"I heard all this on a warm day in early summer many years ago," she said, and ran her fingers down the doll's absurdly long legs. "Each case individually is not that interesting. America's criminal history is full of far more spectacular stories than that."

All of a sudden, she threw the doll into the toy box.

"What's interesting for us is that someone in this country is trying to emulate the series again. But we shouldn't get bogged down in the past, we have to focus on . . . on Fiona Helle, Victoria Heinerback, and Vegard Krogh. On today. Our own murders. Don't we?" Johanne paused.

He wanted to nod. He really wanted to smile and agree. What she had told him was useful enough, sketchy and imprecise though it was. It was sufficient.

They both knew that it was impossible.

She had told him an important story and at the same time had driven a wedge between them. He would use the next few days to put the heavens in motion, to trace every detail of the cases. He would get international organizations involved. They needed transcripts, judgments, hearings. They needed names and dates.

They needed Warren's help.

"I think," he said and hesitated for a moment before continuing, "I think that's enough for this evening. Tomorrow's going to be a long day."

"I know," she said and hunkered down. Jack had woken up and was rubbing against her. "We can't do much good now. Go to bed."

"Come with me."

"There's no point, Adam. Go to bed."

"Not without you."

"I don't want to. Can't."

"Are you hungry?"

"I know that you're going to talk to Warren. I understand that you need to."

"Should I make an omelet?"

"You're just like Mother. You think that food solves everything."

She buried her nose in the warm, acrid smell of dirty dog and mumbled, "Don't act as if I'm stupid, Adam."

Again, he didn't know what to say.

"Of course I realize what you have to do with the information I've given you," she continued. "I'm not asking for fanfares for having dived back into a past I wanted to forget, but I would like some kind of respect. Just pretending that everything is fine and I've just told you a goodnight story, I think that's . . . unfair."

She lifted up the dog and hid her face in his fur.

"We should be happy," he said. "We should be delighted about Ragnhild. About Kristiane's progress. About each other. We get along well together, the two of us. The four of us. That morning, a month ago, feels like an age now, when Kristiane thought we'd gotten an heir to the throne, wasn't I happy then? Satisfied? The baby was healthy. You were a bit anxious and very happy. I want to turn back time and forget everything that is alien and secret, that opens up this chasm between us. Your eyes were hostile, and now you're slipping away from me."

"Just keep me out of it," Johanne said. "Do what you have to, but keep me out of it. Okay?"

He nodded.

Jack wriggled in her arms and wanted to get down.

"He doesn't like being held," Adam said.

"Is Mats Bohus definitely out of the question?"

"What?"

"Are you one hundred percent sure that Mats Bohus is not behind all the murders?"

"Yes."

The King of America made a leap for it and landed on the floor with a dull thud. He whimpered a bit and then shot off into a corner with his tail between his legs.

"What can it be?" Johanne said and sat down on the other sofa.

"You mean who, don't you?" he said in a flat voice.

"Well, both who and what."

"I can't bear this," he said.

"What?"

"Your coldness."

"I'm not cold."

"Yes, you are."

"You're hopeless. You want me to be happy and warm and close all the time. That's impossible. Grow up. We're two adults with adult problems. It doesn't mean something's wrong."

She said "doesn't mean something's wrong." He'd wanted to hear "nothing's wrong." He folded his hands and studied his knuckles, which were white now. In fourteen months he would be fifty. The signs of age were getting clearer, the dry, loose skin on the backs of his hands, even when he curled his fingers.

"Do you think someone might be setting this up?" she asked, doubtfully.

"Oh, come on," he mumbled and opened his right hand.

She looked at Jack, who was still turning in circles on his cushion, trying to settle down.

"Maybe there's someone else outside who's manipulating others to commit murder," she said, mostly to herself, as if she was thinking out loud. "Someone who knows about these old stories and who, for some reason, is trying to re-create . . ."

The dog finally lay down.

"I'm going crazy," she murmured.

"We're going to bed," Adam stated.

"Yes," she said.

"You mentioned five," he said.

"Five what?"

"Five murders. The lecture was about five murders. All examples of what Warren called . . . proportional revenge?"

"Retribution."

"What were the last two cases?" he asked without looking up from his hand. Johanne took off her glasses. The room became fuzzy, and she cleaned her glasses with half-closed eyes.

"Who was killed?" he asked. "And how?"

"An athlete."

"What happened to him?"

"He got a javelin through the heart."

"A javelin . . . like the ones you throw?"

"Yes."

"Why?"

"The killer was a competitor. He felt he'd been overlooked when one of the Ivy League schools awarded an athletic scholarship. Something like that. I can't remember exactly. I'm exhausted."

"So now all we can do is just sit tight," he started. "Completely helpless . . . and wait for an athlete to be brutally murdered."

She was still polishing and rubbing her glasses with the corner of her shirt, without purpose or reason.

"And the last one?" he asked almost inaudibly.

Johanne held her glasses up to the lamp and closed one eye. She squinted into the light through both lenses, several times. Then she slowly put the glasses back on. Shrugged her shoulders.

"You know what, I think I might actually try to get some sleep. It's been—"

"Johanne," Adam stopped her, then drank the rest of his coffee in one go.

The mug thumped down on the table.

A harsh light appeared on the ceiling. The beam wandered slowly from the kitchen to just above the door out to the south-facing balcony. The throb of an engine made the windowpanes vibrate.

"Garbagemen," Adam said quickly. "So?"

If he hadn't been so tired, he might have noticed that Johanne was holding her breath. If he had looked at her instead of going over to the window to check who was letting their engine idle in a residential area in the middle of the night, he might have noticed that her mouth was half open and her lips were pale. He would have seen that she was sitting tensely, with her eyes on the front door, then the children's room.

But Adam was at the window, with his back to Johanne.

"Teenagers partying," he said, peeved. "It's only February. They don't have their exams until May. They start earlier and earlier."

He hesitated for a moment before going back to sit on the sofa opposite Johanne.

"The last one," he insisted. "What happened in the last case?"

"He didn't succeed. Warren included the example because—"

"Who did he try to murder, Johanne?"

She reached out for both cups and got up. He caught her as she passed.

"It doesn't matter," she said. "He didn't succeed."

The movement with which she broke free was unnecessarily harsh.

"Johanne," he said, without following her. He heard the cups being put in the dishwasher. "You're just being difficult now."

"I'm sure."

"Who did he try to kill?" Adam repeated.

He was surprised to hear the noise of the dishwasher. He pulled up his sleeve and looked at his watch. It was nearly half past one. Johanne was rummaging around in the drawers and cabinets.

"What are you doing?" he muttered as he went into the kitchen.

"Cleaning," she replied tersely.

"Well," he said and pointed at the clock, "I see that you're getting used to living in a semidetached house."

The cutlery drawer fell to the floor with a crash. Johanne bent down on her knees and tried to gather up the knives and forks, spoons and other gadgets.

"It was a family man," she sobbed, "who was being investigated for insurance fraud in connection with a house fire. He . . . he set fire to the policeman's home. The investigator's home. While the whole family was sleeping."

"Come here."

He held her by the arms, firm and friendly, pulled her up. She resisted.

"No one is going to set this house on fire," Adam said. "No one is ever going to set our house on fire."

TWELVE

For hundreds of years, people had walked the narrow streets between the low, crooked houses that clung together. Steps wound up narrow passages. Feet had trodden on the stone steps, in the same place, year after year, leaving behind a smoothly polished path that she crouched down to touch several times. The shiny hollows were cold against her fingers. She put her fingers in her mouth and felt the sting of salt on the tip of her tongue.

She leaned over the wall to the south. A grayish blue mist fused sea and sky. There was no horizon out there, no perspective, only an endlessness that made her dizzy. There was no wind, not even up here on the hilltop. A dank humidity swathed the medieval town of Eze. She was alone.

In summer this place must be unbearable. Even with shuttered windows and unwelcoming shop doors, closed for the winter, the signs of the summer season were obvious. Souvenir shops stood wall to wall, and on the few small squares that opened out in the heart of the town, she saw the scars from scraping chairs and countless cigarettes that had been stubbed out on the cobbles. As she walked by herself along the wall facing the sea, she imagined the sound of the summer hordes—chirruping Japanese and loud, red-cheeked Germans.

She was a veritable wanderer now. She had gradually discovered the old paths and found ways to avoid the main roads that were dangerous, with no sidewalks and a steady flow of roaring traffic.

Her new duffel coat was warm without being completely windproof. She had bought it in Nice along with three pairs of pants, four sweaters, a handful of skirts, and a suit that she wasn't really sure she would dare to wear. When she came to France, just before Christmas, she only had two pairs of shoes with her. They were now in the trash can down on the street. Yesterday evening she had resolutely put them in a plastic bag and dropped them into the container, even though one pair was barely six months old. They were brown and solid. Sensible shoes, best suited for a middle-aged housewife.

The duffel coat was beige, and her Camper shoes were comfortable to walk in. The lady in the shop hadn't so much as raised an eyebrow when she asked to try them on. A young boy sat beside her on one of the bright yellow ottomans and tried on the same shoes. When he caught her eye, he gave a friendly smile. Nodded in appreciation. She bought two pairs. They were very comfortable.

She walked.

Walking made it easier to think. It was during her long, slow walks along the sea, in the mountains and across the steep hillsides between Nice and Cap d'Ail, that she felt most acutely that her life had been injected with new vigor. Sometimes, often when she came home at night, she felt a tiredness in her muscles that was a wonderful reminder of her strength. She would take off her clothes and wander naked around the house, her reflection in the windows confirming the changes she was going through. She drank wine, but never too much. She enjoyed food, whether she made it herself or went to a restaurant where she was recognized, always recognized now, by polite waiters who pulled out her chair and remembered that she liked to have a glass of champagne before her meal.

Over the past few days, she had been filled with a sense of gratitude.

She had driven directly from Copenhagen, where she had left her car in an anonymous parking lot before taking the ferry to Oslo and back. Ferry passenger lists between Denmark and Norway were a joke. She traveled as Eva Hansen and stayed in her cabin. Both ways. Then after one night in a hotel, she managed to sit behind the wheel for thirty-five hours without ever really getting tired. She did feel a stiffness in her muscles and joints whenever she took a short break, small detours from the main road to fill the tank or to eat in a roadside café in a German village or along the Rhône. But she never felt the need for sleep.

She delivered the car back to the Moroccan waiter at the Café de la Paix. He was well rewarded for the hassle of renting the car in his name. He might not have entirely believed her explanation that she really needed a car but because she had a bad cold she wanted to avoid an unnecessary trip into Nice. But as he was going back to Morocco and a newly opened restaurant owned by his father, he accepted the money with a smile and no questions.

Then she walked home. As soon as her head hit the pillow, she fell into a dreamless slumber that lasted for eleven hours.

She had derived no pleasure from all those years of meticulous planning, gathering detailed information and doing painstaking research, other than that it was her work. It was necessary if she was to do the job she was paid for. She was good and had never been found out. No one could say that she made mistakes, was sloppy, or took shortcuts whenever she could.

Despite everything, she was grateful for those lifeless years. They had given her knowledge and insight.

Even though the filing cabinet was in Norway, she could remember enough. The huge metal cabinet contained information about the people she had studied. Known and unknown. Famous people and celebrities, alongside the postman from Otta who always filled her mailbox with junk mail, despite the clear notice that it was not welcome. She registered people's weaknesses and routines, observed their desires and needs, stowed their love lives, secrets, and movements in files, and stored it all in a huge gray metal cabinet.

She wasn't sloppy. The secret of her trade was knowledge. Her memory never failed her.

All those living-dead years were not wasted. She was grateful for them now. She could assemble an AG-3 gun blindfolded and hotwire a car in thirty seconds. It would take her less than a week to get hold of a fake passport, and she had an overview of the Scandinavian heroin market that the police would envy. She knew people that no one else wanted to know; she knew them well—but none of them knew her.

It had gotten colder. An insidious wind blew down from the hills, dispersing the mist out at sea. The duffel coat was not protection enough, so she hurried down the mountain path. It was too cold to walk all the way back home. If the bus came when it was due, she would take it. If not, she could always treat herself to a taxi.

She had become more generous recently.

Suddenly a splash of color appeared in the sky to the north. A person swayed rhythmically from side to side under an orange paraglider. Another paraglider appeared over the top of the hill, red and yellow with green writing that was impossible to read. A sudden turbulence made the fabric flap. The glider lost its lift and dropped some fifty or sixty yards before the pilot managed to regain control and slowly cut down into the valley below her.

She followed him with her eyes and laughed softly.

They thought they were challenging fate.

Extreme sports had always provoked her, primarily because she thought the people who participated in them were pathetic. Of course, not everyone had been granted an exciting life. Quite the contrary. Most of the world's six billion people, the greater part of the inhabitants of Europe and probably all of the Norwegian population, lived uneventful lives. Their fight for survival consisted of getting enough food to live, taking care of their children, finding a better job, or having the newest car in the neighborhood. Human existence was and would always be a mere bagatelle. The fact that depraved, spoiled young people found it necessary to defy death by jumping and diving from sheer rock faces at great speed was an expression of Western decadence that she had always scorned.

Loathed.

They suffered from ennui because they believed they deserved something else, something better than what life in fact was to most: an insignificant period of time between life and death.

"They think they can escape from the meaninglessness of life," she thought to herself. "By throwing themselves over the edge of Trollveggen with a parachute made from unreliable fabric. Or crossing one of the poles. Climbing an unclimbable mountain. They want to go higher, further, and to more daring lengths. They don't notice the boredom that constantly shadows them, gray and sneering. They don't see it until they've landed, before they're safely at home. So they repeat the exercise, do something different, more dangerous, more daring, until they either understand that they can't outwit life or meet their death attempting to prove the opposite."

The paragliders were nearly down now; they were aiming to land on a slope with long rows of dwarf vines. She thought she could hear them laughing. Only imagination, obviously, as the wind was blowing in the wrong direction, and the bottom of the valley was far away. But she could see the two pilots slapping each other on the back and jumping up and down with excitement. Two women came running up the terraced slope. They waved happily.

She still was disgusted by the way they played arbitrarily with death.

The only thing they risked was their lives.

Dying was nothing more than a pleasant end to the boredom. And dying also enhanced your reputation, as obituaries were full of praise, not truth. If you died young, life had not yet aged you, made you ugly, fat, or skinny. A person who doesn't live to be old leaves behind a tragic memento: a glamorized, redeeming story where what was boring becomes exciting and what was ugly becomes beautiful.

She thought about Vegard Krogh and bit her tongue.

She didn't want to read about him anymore. The articles were all lies. Journalists and acquaintances, friends and family all contributed to the image that was drawn of Krogh, the artist. An uncompromising and upright champion of what was genuine and true. A colorful spirit, a fearless soldier in the service of that great and incorruptible force, culture.

She swore out loud and started to run down the road. The bus was just pulling out from the bus stop on the main road but stopped when the driver saw her. She paid and plopped down into an empty seat.

She would be going back to Norway for good soon.

She had to leave the house in Villefranche. The lease had been extended until March 1, but not longer. In just over a week she would be homeless, unless she went home.

She pictured her apartment, tastefully decorated and far too big for one person. Only the steel cabinet in the bedroom broke with the soft style she had copied from an interior decor magazine. She'd bought most of the stuff at IKEA but had also come across a couple of the more expensive items at sales.

She somehow didn't fit into her apartment in Norway.

She seldom had guests and didn't need the space. When she was at home, she generally sat in the messy study and therefore didn't really get much pleasure from the fact that the rest of the apartment was so tasteful. In fact, she had never really felt at home there. It was more like living in a hotel. On her many trips to Europe, she had always stayed in rooms that felt more personal, warmer and more comfortable than her own living room.

She didn't fit in in Norway at all. Norway was not for people like her. She felt suffocated by its grand egalitarian philosophy, excluded by the narrow-minded, exclusive elite. Norway was not big enough for someone like her; she was not recognized for what she was and had therefore chosen to protect herself with the cloak of anonymity. Aloof. Invisible. They didn't want to see her. So she wouldn't show herself to them.

The bus rolled westward. The suspension was French and not good enough. She had to close her eyes so as not to feel sick.

To risk dying was no great feat. The danger they exposed themselves to, these mountaineers and air acrobats, solitary rowers in fragile boats crossing the Atlantic and motorcyclists performing death-defying stunts in front of audiences charged with the hope that something might go terribly wrong, was limited to the journey they each took, whether it lasted three seconds or eight weeks, one minute or maybe one year.

She was taking a gamble on life itself. The suspense of never landing, of never achieving her goal, made her unique. The risk increased each day, as she hoped it would and wanted it to. It was constantly there, intense and invigorating, the danger of being caught and exposed.

She leaned her forehead against the window. Evening was falling. The lights had been lit along the promenade below. A light rain darkened the asphalt.

There was nothing to indicate that they were getting closer. Despite the clues she had left, the obvious invitation in the pattern she had chosen, the police were still at a loss. It was so annoying and made her more determined to continue. Of course, the fact that the woman had just had a baby did upset the equation a bit. The timing was not optimal, she had already known that when she started, but there were limits to what she could control.

Maybe it would be a good thing to go home. To get closer.

Run a greater risk.

The bus stopped, and she got off. It was pouring rain now, and she ran all the way home. It was the evening of February 24.

THIRTEEN

M aybe there's someone behind it all who's manipulating the situation," said Adam Stubo as he tucked into his chicken in yogurt sauce. "That's her latest theory. I'm not too sure."

He smiled with his mouth full of food.

"How do you mean?" asked Sigmund Berli. "That someone's getting other people to do the killing, or what? Duping them?"

He broke off a piece of naan bread, held it between his thumb and finger, and peered at it suspiciously.

"Is this some kind of bread?"

"Naan," Adam replied. "Try it. The theory isn't that stupid. I mean, it's pretty logical. In a way. If we accept that Mats Bohus actually killed Fiona Helle but none of the others, then it's plausible that someone is behind it all. Pulling the strings. An overriding motive, as it were. But at the same time . . ."

Sigmund chewed and chewed. Didn't manage to swallow.

"For Christ's sake," whispered Adam and leaned over the table. "Pull yourself together. There've been Indian restaurants in Norway for thirty years! You're behaving as if it's snake meat you're eating. It's bread, Sigmund. Just bread."

"That guy over there's not an Indian," his colleague muttered and nodded in the direction of the waiter, a middle-aged man with a trimmed mustache and a kind smile. "He's a Paki."

The handle of Adam's knife came crashing down onto the table.

"Cut it out," he hissed. "I owe you a lot, Sigmund, but not enough to accept that kind of crap. I've told you a thousand times, keep that goddamn—"

"I meant Pakistani. Sorry. But he is a Pakistani. Not an Indian. And my stomach can't cope with things that are too spicy."

He made an exaggerated face as he clutched his belly dramatically.

"You ordered mild food," Adam growled as he helped himself to more raita. "If you can't eat this, you can't eat sausage and mashed potatoes. Bon appétit."

Sigmund put a tiny bit on his fork. Hesitated. Cautiously put it in his mouth. Chewed.

"I just can't figure it out," Adam said. "It's somehow so . . . un-Norwegian. Un-European. That anyone would think of using some poor bastard as a pawn in a killing game."

"Now it's you who should cut it out," retorted Sigmund. He swallowed and took some more. "Nothing is un-Norwegian anymore. In terms of crime, I mean. The situation is no better here than anywhere else. And it hasn't been for years. It's all these"—he stopped himself, thought about it, and continued—"Russians," he ventured. "And those fucking bandits from the Balkans. Those boys know no shame, you know. You can see the evil in their eyes."

The expression on Adam's face made him raise a hand.

"Describing reality is not racism," he protested fervently. "Those people are just like us! Same race and all that. But you know yourself how—"

"Stop. There are no foreigners in this case. The victims are pure Norwegian. All of them fair, in fact. And the same is true of the poor bastard we've arrested on one count. Forget the Russians. Forget the Balkans. Forget"— he gave a sudden jerk and put his hand to his cheek, "sorry, bit my cheek," he mumbled. "Hurts."

Sigmund pulled his chair into the table. Put his napkin on his knee and picked up his knife and fork, as if he wanted to start the meal all over again.

"Have to admit, that lecture of Johanne's is pretty freaky," Sigmund said, unscathed by Adam's reprimand. "A bit *X-Files*. Time warps and the like. What do you think?"

"Not much," Adam admitted.

"So what, then?"

"It could just be a coincidence, of course."

"Coincidence," Sigmund snorted. "Right. Your wife sits over there on the other side of the world thirteen years ago and listens to a lecture about highly symbolic murders, and then the same method, exactly the same symbols, appear in Norway in 2004! Three times! Screw coincidence, I say. No way."

"Well, then maybe you've got an explanation! I mean, you watch *X-Files*."

"They've stopped making it. It got a bit too absurd toward the end."

Adam helped himself to some more from the small iron pot. The rice stuck to the serving spoon. He shook it lightly. The white, sticky mass fell into the sauce with a splash. Red spots appeared on his shirt.

"I think there's an evil bastard out there," Sigmund said calmly. "An evil bastard who's heard the same lecture. And enjoyed it. And toyed with the idea of playing with us."

Adam felt a chill run down his spine.

"Right," he said slowly and stopped eating. "Anything else?"

"The symbolism's too clear. In the original cases, the killers were a bit simple, at least from what you've said. Idiots choose obvious symbols. But our man's certainly not an idiot. Our man's"—Sigmund's smile was almost childish now; he saw a new and unfamiliar acknowledgment in Adam's narrowed eyes and slight nod of the head—"If we take it as given," Sigmund continued, "that Johanne is right, and that there's someone out there pulling the strings, getting other people to do the killing"—a furrow appeared between his heavy eyebrows—"and gets them to do it in a very particular way, then we're definitely not talking about someone of limited capacity. Quite the opposite."

There wasn't a sound. They were the only guests now. The waiter had disappeared into a back room. All that could be heard was the gentle Indian music coming from the speakers on the other side of the room. The loudspeakers vibrated on the higher notes.

"Hmm," Adam said eventually, lifting his mineral water in appreciation. "That's not bad. But if this Mr. X has heard the same lecture, it must be someone who . . . someone whom Johanne knows from—"

"No," Sigmund interjected and tried another piece of bread. "It's been a while now since I went to the police academy, but I do remember one thing. The lectures were the same, year after year. The teachers just turned over the pile. I borrowed some notes from a friend who was in the year above me. A blueprint. This bread is actually quite good."

"Try the tandoori," Adam suggested. "But you're forgetting that we're not talking about any old teacher. Warren Scifford is a legend. He would hardly—"

"As if good teachers are any better than bad ones when it

comes to that," Sigmund exclaimed, looking at his fork before cautiously putting the meat in his mouth. "The opposite, I'd say. If a series of lectures is successful, all the less reason to change it. Students come and go. Teachers stay. Have we managed to get ahold of the guy?"

"Warren?"

"Yes."

"No. If you don't want your food, I'll—"

"Help yourself."

Sigmund pushed his plate across the table.

"The FBI's mandate changed, to put it mildly, after 9/11," Adam said. "Now it's all antiterrorism and hush-hush. Finding Warren has proved to be harder than anticipated. Before I could just pick up the phone and have him on the other end of the line within thirty seconds. But now . . ." He shrugged. "My guess is Iraq," he said lightly.

"Iraq? But the FBI has limited jurisdiction! Aren't they supposed to stick to their own territory? To the U.S.?"

"In principle, yes. In reality, well . . ." Another slight shrug of the shoulders. "I think they could use Warren's expertise down there in that hellhole."

"What does he actually do?"

Adam guffawed and wiped his mouth with the starched napkin. "Easier to say what he doesn't do. First he got a PhD in sociology, then he trained as a lawyer. But most important, he's been connected to what's clearly the world's best police organization for more than thirty years. He's a star."

"And now he's in Iraq."

"I don't know that he's in Iraq," Adam corrected. "But looking at the way the Americans are doing down there, I wouldn't be surprised if they needed their best men there. Whether that's FBI folk or anyone else, I don't know. But I haven't given up trying to find him yet."

The waiter came back. He politely overlooked the fact that Adam had two plates in front of him.

"Would you like anything else to drink?"

"Water," Sigmund said gruffly and put his elbows on the table.

"Yes please," Adam smiled and praised the food. "A sparkling mineral water, please."

He poked the wound in his cheek with his tongue.

"Hurts," he mumbled.

"Do you believe in my theory?" Sigmund asked. "In Johanne's theory?"

Adam took his time.

"I can't quite . . . quite imagine how it's possible to manipulate people in that way. On the other hand . . ."

The waiter poured the water into their glasses, smiled, and withdrew again.

"It may be because I don't dare," Adam admitted and took a sip. "If you're right, it means that the investigations will be . . . even harder. Because among other things, it means that the real mastermind doesn't necessarily have any obvious connection with the victims. But the murderers do. And so far, we've only found one of them."

"A raving lunatic in a nuthouse," sighed Sigmund.

Adam raised his fork, and Sigmund quickly added, "I mean, someone with mental health issues who's in an institution. What do you think we should do? Should we pursue the . . . theory?"

"We should at least bear it in mind," Adam said. "As we have to keep looking for connections between the three victims, it won't make much extra work if Mats Bohus is included in the picture."

"Hmm? I don't understand. He hasn't been killed, he—"

"If you and Johanne really are onto something, he's the

only one we've got. So while we keep looking for links between Fiona Helle, Victoria Heinerback, and Vegard Krogh, we can also look to see if there are any hidden connections between Mats Bohus and the other two. Long shot, but why not. The problem is that we can't talk to Mats Bohus anymore. Completely lost it. The hearing last Saturday was obviously too much. Dr. Bonheur was right. And now we have to pay the price: the man's in a closed ward, so it won't be easy to find out whom he's had contact with."

He snatched up the last piece of bread and popped it in his mouth.

"I'm full," he mumbled. "Shall we go?"

"What about coffee?" Sigmund suggested.

"I'd advise against that. The coffee here isn't exactly—"

His phone started ringing. Adam got out his phone and signaled to the waiter that they'd like the bill.

"Stubo," he said curtly.

When he hung up about a minute and a half later, without having said more than yes and no, he looked very concerned. His eyes were narrower than ever, and his mouth was pursed with tiredness and worry.

"What's wrong?" asked Sigmund.

Adam paid and got up.

"What the hell is it?" Sigmund repeated impatiently as they came out onto Arendalsgate. A bus thundered past.

"Trond Arnesen was lying," Adam replied and started to walk toward Myrens Engineering Workshop, where the car was parked outside the old factory.

"What?" Sigmund bellowed, jogging along beside him.

A trailer was stopped at the stoplight, and the noise was deafening.

"Trond Arnesen is not as innocent as I thought," Adam yelled back. "He was having an affair on the side."

The lights turned to green, and the trailer accelerated and disappeared up to Torshov.

"What?"

"With a man," Adam said and ran over the road. "A young boy."

"Isn't that what I've always said?" Sigmund said, speeding up to keep pace with his partner. "You can't trust a faggot."

Adam couldn't be bothered to react.

He had been absolutely convinced of Trond Arnesen's innocence.

Johanne was woken up by someone coming up the stairs. Fear froze her limbs. Ragnhild was lying between her left arm and her body. She was fast asleep. It was still light outside. It must still be daytime. Sometime in the afternoon. How long had she been asleep? Someone came closer.

"Were you sleeping? That's good."

Her mother smiled and came over to the sofa.

"Mother," Johanne stammered. "You scared me! You can't just—"

"Yes, I can," her mother replied firmly. Johanne suddenly realized that she hadn't even taken off her coat. "I used the spare key you left with us. To be honest, I was afraid you wouldn't open the door if I rang the bell and you looked out and saw it was me."

"Of course I would've—"

Johanne struggled to sit up on the sofa without waking Ragnhild.

"No, dear. I don't think you would have opened the door. How long have you been asleep?"

Johanne looked at her watch.

"Twelve minutes," she yawned. "Why are you here?"

"Just relax," her mother said and disappeared into the kitchen.

She could hear drawers and cabinets being opened. The fridge door opened and closed. Johanne heard the clinking of bottles and the reluctant sucking noise of the freezer being opened. She managed to get up on her feet.

"What are you doing?" she muttered in irritation.

"I'm packing," her mother replied.

"Packing—"

"Good thing you've got so much of your milk in the freezer. There."

With a practiced hand, she wrapped each of the frozen bottles in newspaper.

"What are you doing, Mother?"

"Can't you just be a good girl and get out some clothes? Her pajamas. Some diapers. No, actually, your father has already bought some. Libero, that's the brand you use, isn't it? Just put a little bag together. And please remember to pack some extra pacifiers."

Johanne tried to move the baby over to her other arm; Ragnhild's eyes opened and she started to whimper.

"You're not taking Ragnhild, Mother."

"Yes, I most definitely am."

Her mother was already putting the well-insulated bottles into a soft thermal bag with a Coca-Cola logo on it.

"No way."

"Now listen to me, Johanne."

With an angry movement, her mother zipped the bag shut and put it on the island. Then she ran her fingers through her gray hair before catching her daughter's eye and saying, "I will decide that."

"You can't—"

"Be quiet."

Her voice was sharp but level. Ragnhild didn't react.

"I am fully aware that you think I'm generally pretty hopeless, Johanne. And that we haven't always been the best of friends. But I am your mother, and I'm not as stupid as you think. Not only could I see that you were absolutely exhausted during dinner on Sunday, but I also detected something that I can only interpret as . . . fear."

Johanne opened her mouth to protest.

"Don't say a word," her mother scolded. "I have no intention of asking you what it is you're frightened of. You never tell me anything anyway. But I can help with the tiredness. So now I'm going to take my grandchild home with me, and you are going to go to bed. The time is"—she looked over at the wall clock—"half past two. I've asked Isak to pick Kristiane up from school. Adam said he'd be working late tonight. He'll stay over at our house, so you're not disturbed. You"—her finger was shaking when she pointed it at Johanne—"go to bed and get some sleep. You're no fool, and you know perfectly well that Ragnhild is in the best hands. With me, with us. You can sleep for as long as you need. Or you can read books all night if that makes you any happier. But I think . . . oh, darling."

Johanne hid her face in the baby's blanket. It smelled of clean clothes, and she started to cry. Her mother stroked her hair and then gently loosened Ragnhild from her daughter's arms.

"You see," she clucked. "You're overtired. Go to bed, dear. I'll find what I need myself."

"I can . . . You can't . . ."

"I've raised two children. I passed my home economics exams. I've looked after a house and home for as long as I remember. I can look after a baby for a night or two."

Her mother's heels clicked on the parquet as she turned and

walked resolutely toward the children's room. Johanne wanted to follow but couldn't face it.

Sleep. Hours and hours of sleep.

She was almost ready to lie down on the floor. Instead she grabbed a half-full bottle of water from the counter and drank it. Then she went into the bedroom. She barely had the energy to take off her clothes. The sheets felt cool and good to touch. The room was cold. The duvet was warm. She heard her mother mumbling in the children's room for a few minutes. Footsteps moving around, into the bathroom, back to the kitchen, into Ragnhild's room.

"The cream," Johanne murmured. "Don't forget the diaper rash cream."

But she was already asleep and didn't wake up until sixteen hours later.

------------ ✳ ------------

"I'm not like that," Trond Arnesen said in desperation. "I'm not really inclined that way!"

Five elegant envelopes lay on the table between him and Detective Inspector Adam Stubo, tied together with an old elastic hairband. They were all addressed to Ulrik Gustavsen. The writing slanted to the left, just as it did in the Filofax that was lying beside them.

"Trond Arnesen," Adam Stubo read, tapping his finger on the page. "You've got very distinct handwriting. I think we can agree that there's no need to analyze the writing. Are you left-handed?"

"I'm not like that! You have to believe me!"

Adam tipped his chair back. He clasped his hands behind his neck, ran his thumbs over the folds of skin. His cropped hair brushed against his fingers. The back of the chair hit the wall rhythmically. He looked at the boy without saying a word.

His face was blank and neutral, as if he was bored and waiting for someone or something.

"You have to believe me," Trond insisted. "I've never been with . . . any other guys. I swear to you! And that night, that night, was the very last time. I was going to get married and . . ."

Big tears spilled down his cheeks. His nose was running. He used his sleeve to wipe his face but couldn't stop crying. His sobbing sounded like a small child. Adam rocked on his chair and kept on rocking. The back of the chair hit the wall. Thump. Thump. Thump.

"Will you stop that?" Trond pleaded. "Please!"

Adam kept on rocking. He still didn't say anything.

"I was so drunk," Trond said. "I was already wasted by nine. It had been a long time since I'd seen Ulrik, so . . . Then about half past ten I went out to get some air. I went outside to clear my head. And he didn't live that far away. Huitfeldtsgate. So I—"

Adam's chair slammed back down to the floor. The young man jumped. The plastic cup from which he had just drunk some water was knocked over. The policeman retrieved the letters. He pulled off the hairband and looked at the envelopes again without opening any of them. Then he put the hairband back around them and dropped the pile into a gray file. There was nothing to remind Trond of the friendly policeman from the crime reconstruction. It was impossible to read his eyes, and he said so little.

"It's been really hard," he whined and sobbed as he drew breath. "Ulrik has been . . . He said he . . . I meant to tell. I wanted to tell the truth, but when I realized that you thought I'd been at Smuget the whole evening, I'm not sure why . . . I thought . . ."

He suddenly put his head back.

"Can't you say something?" he appealed. He pulled his head back up and slammed his palms down on the table. "Can't you at least say something?"

"You're the one who's got something to say."

"But I've got nothing more to say! I'm really sorry that I didn't tell you immediately, but I . . . I loved Victoria! I miss her so much. We were going to get married, and I was so . . . You don't believe me!"

"Right now, it's not important whether I believe you or not," Adam said as he pulled on his earlobe. "But I am very interested in learning exactly how long you were away from the night-club."

"One and a half hours, I told you. From half past ten until twelve. Midnight. I swear. Just ask the others, just ask my brother."

"They obviously made a mistake the last time we questioned them. Or lied, all of them. They swore that you were there all night."

"They thought I was there! Jesus, it was chaos, and I was only away for a while. I should have told you immediately, but I was . . . embarrassed. I was about to get married."

"Yes, we know," Adam said, unrelenting. "So you keep saying."

"I should have told you," the young man moaned again. "It was just so . . . I thought—"

"You thought you could get away with it," Adam Stubo said. His voice had an unfamiliar edge to it. "Didn't you?"

He got up, put his hands behind his back, and walked slowly around the room. Trond shrunk, he lowered his head and hunched his shoulders, as if he was afraid of being hit.

"What's interesting . . ." Adam said. His voice now had an exaggerated, fatherly tone to it, both strict and friendly at the same time. "What's interesting is that you just told me something we didn't know."

The boy had stopped crying. He dried the snot and tears with a corner of his shirt and for a moment looked more confused than desperate.

"Don't know what you mean," he said, looking the policeman in the eye. "You've obviously spoken to Ulrik and that night—"

"You're wrong," Adam said. "Ulrik refused to talk to us. He's sitting in a cell in Grønland station and keeping quiet. And he has every right to. Not talk, that is. So we actually didn't know that you'd lied about your alibi. Not until now."

"In a cell? What's he done? Ulrik?"

Adam stopped about a yard away from the young man. He put his right elbow in his left hand and stroked his nose, thoughtfully.

"You're not that stupid, Trond."

"I—"

"You what?"

"I really don't know what it's about."

"Hmm. Fine. You want me to believe that you've had a relationship with Ulrik . . . you know him, well, intimately, as they say—"Adam nodded at the file. The letters were sticking out of the top. Trond's face blushed red—"without knowing that Ulrik was involved with illegal substances," Adam continued. "With all due respect, I find that very hard to believe."

Trond looked like he'd seen the devil himself, with horns on his forehead and a burning tail. His eyes were wide, his mouth agape, and he made no move to wipe his running nose. He made nonsensical noises. Adam chewed his knuckles but made no attempt to help.

"Drugs," Trond finally managed to say. "I knew nothing about that. I swear!"

"I have a little girl at home," Adam said and started to walk again, taking long, slow strides backward and forward across the small interview room. "She's nearly ten and has an enviable imagination."

He stopped and smiled.

"She lies all the time. You say 'I swear' more than she does. It doesn't exactly make you more believable."

"I give up," Trond muttered, and it looked like he really meant it. He leaned back in the chair and repeated, "I fucking give up."

His arms hung loose by his body. He head fell back. He closed his eyes. His legs were apart. He looked like an over-grown teenager.

"Then you didn't know, either, that Ulrik was a prostitute?" Adam asked calmly. His eyes did not leave the sprawling young man's face so that he could catch every emotion.

Nothing happened. Trond Arnesen just sat there, his mouth half open, his knees wide apart, his hands moving in rhythm.

"Of the more exclusive type," Adam added. "But of course you didn't know that. Because I'm sure you never paid."

The young man still didn't react. For a long time he didn't move at all. Even his hands were still. Just a twitch in his eye-lids showed that he had heard at all. The only noise in the stuffy interview room was of Adam's even breathing and the barely audible buzz of the air-conditioning.

"You shouldn't have written those letters," Adam said quietly and maliciously, though he didn't know why. "If you hadn't written those letters, everything would be fine now. You'd be sitting at home. In your house. You'd have everyone's sympathy. Life would have normalized again eventually. You're young. In six months or so the worst would be over, and you could move on. But you had to write those letters. Not very smart, Trond."

"Now I'm being mean," Adam thought to himself and pulled a big aluminum cigar case out of his breast pocket. "I'm punishing him for my own disappointment. What am I disappointed about? That he lied? That he had secrets? Everyone lies. Everyone has secrets. No one has a streamlined life without shame, without faults and stains. I'm not punishing him for being immoral, I've seen and understood too much for that. I'm disappointed that I've been duped. For once I chose to believe. My whole working life depends on other people's lies and deceit, cowardice and betrayal. There was something about this boy, this immature man. Something innocent. Genuine. But I was wrong, and I'm punishing him for it."

He could smell the cigar. Opened the case a little and inhaled.

Slowly, Trond straightened up in his chair. His eyes were full of tears. A fine dribble of spit hung from the left-hand corner of his mouth. He caught his breath in gasps.

"I never paid," he said and put his face in his hands. "I didn't know he took money from others. I didn't know that there were others . . . apart from me."

Then he was overcome by tears. He was inconsolable. He didn't stop crying when Adam gently put a hand on his shoulder, when his mother hugged him after she had been called in, agitated and terrified, half an hour later, nor when his brother gave him an awkward brotherly embrace in the parking lot before helping him into the back of the car.

"He's well over the age of consent," Adam replied to his mother's many questions. "You'll have to ask him what it's about."

"But . . . you must tell . . . is he . . . was it him who—"

"Trond didn't kill Victoria. You can be sure of that. But he's a troubled young man. Take good care of him."

Adam stayed in the parking lot long after the red taillights of Bård Arnesen's car had disappeared. The temperature fell a degree or two while he stood there, without a coat. It started to snow. He stood very still, without acknowledging the people who left the building and called out good-byes before getting into their cars, shivering, and driving home to their families and their own skewed lives.

It was times like these that he was reminded why the passion he once felt for his work was now no more than an occasional and subdued feeling of satisfaction. He still believed that what he was doing was important. His job still challenged him every day. He could draw on a wealth of experience and knew that it was valuable. His intuition had also become stronger and more precise over the years. Adam Stubo was a great old-fashioned champion of what is good and just, and he knew he could never be anything other than a policeman. But he no longer felt a sense of triumph or overwhelming joy when he solved a case, as he had when he was younger.

Over the years it had grown harder and harder to live with the destruction that every investigation involved. He turned other people's lives upside down, changed destinies. Revealed secrets. Hidden parts of people's lives were pulled out of drawers and forgotten cupboards.

Next summer, Adam Stubo would turn fifty. He had been a policeman for twenty-eight years, and he knew that Trond Arnesen was not guilty of murdering his fiancée. Adam had met many Trond Arnesens before, with all their weaknesses and foibles; ordinary people who unfortunately suddenly had floodlights trained on every dark corner of their lives.

Trond Arnesen had lied when he felt threatened and was deceptive when he thought it would help. He was just like everyone else.

The snow was getting thicker, and the temperature was falling steadily.

Adam stood there and enjoyed the feeling of being bare-headed and thinly clad in an open space in bad weather.

Enjoyed the sensation of being cold.

———————— 🌿 ————————

Kari Mundal, the party's former first lady, stood for a moment, as she usually did, and looked up at the façade before climbing the stone steps. She was proud of the party headquarters. Unlike her husband, who thought that he would be the stranger at the wedding if he didn't stay away, Mrs. Mundal popped in several times a week. Generally she didn't have any particular errand, and sometimes she just came in to drop off some bags on one of her frequent and extensive shopping trips in the center of town. And she always paused for a few seconds to relish the sight of the newly renovated façade. She got great pleasure from all the details, the corniced stringcourses at each level, the statues of saints in the niches above the windows. She was particularly fond of John the Baptist, who was closest to the door and looked down at her with a very realistic lamb in his arms. The steps were wide and dark, and she was out of breath when she put her hand on the door handle, opened the door, and went in.

"It's only me," she chirped. "I'm back."

The receptionist smiled. She stood up so she could look over the high reception desk and nodded approvingly.

"Beautiful," she said. "But should you be wearing them in this weather?"

Kari Mundal looked at her new boots, held her foot out provocatively in front of her, turned her ankle, and clicked her tongue.

"I'm sure I shouldn't," she said. "But they're so elegant. You're here late tonight, my dear. You should head home."

"There's lots of meetings this evening," the woman replied.

She was big and heavy with unflattering glasses. "I thought it would be best to stay a while longer, with people coming and going all the time. And not everyone is good at making sure the door is locked behind them. But if I'm here, it's not so much of a problem."

"You truly are a loyal trooper," Kari Mundal praised her. "But please don't wait for me. I may well be very late. I'll be in the Yellow Room, if you want anything."

She leaned conspiratorially over the desk and whispered, "I'd rather not be disturbed."

With her hands full of shopping bags, she tripped over the spiral pattern on the floor. As always, she cast a glance at the gold shield bearing the party's motto and smiled before heading for the elevator.

"Did you find everything I wanted?" she asked suddenly, turning back to the entrance.

"Yes," replied the stout lady behind the desk. "Everything should be there. Forms, vouchers, everything. Hege in accounting is working overtime today, so you just go to her if you need anything. I didn't mention it to anyone else."

"Thank you," said Kari Mundal. "You're an angel."

Rudolf Fjord paused for a few minutes on the broad landing on the second floor that looked down into the foyer, where the chandelier had been lit, casting a soft yellow glow on the room below. Then he drew back into the shadows by the wall, by the impressive palm next to the door to his office. The fear that he had managed to repress, the anxiety he had buried on the day he received the party's unconditional acceptance, flared up again, as he had known it would, even though he had prayed to God that it would never haunt him again.

"I really appreciate your discretion," he heard Kari Mundal call before a click and nearly inaudible rush of air told him that the elevator was on its way up.

———————— ☙ ————————

Vegard Krogh's widow opened the door and smiled half-heartedly. Adam Stubo had called in advance and found her voice unusually pleasant. He had pictured a dark woman. Tall, with a straight back, a large mouth, and languid movements. But she was in fact small and blonde. Her thick hair was tied up in two tired pigtails. Her sweater looked like it had been pulled from a seventies time capsule; it was brown with orange stripes and a drawstring at the neck.

"Thank you for letting me come," Adam said, giving her his coat.

She led him into the living room and gestured that he should sit down on a stained, light-colored sofa. Adam moved a cushion, lifted up a book, and sat down. He looked around the room. The shelves were crammed and chaotic. The newspaper rack was overflowing, and he noted two copies of the phone book and a torn copy of *Le Monde diplomatique*. The glass table, between the sofa and the two armchairs that didn't match, was dirty, and a wineglass with the remains of some red wine was standing unsteadily on a pile of magazines he didn't recognize.

"Sorry about the mess," said Elsbeth Davidsen. "I haven't exactly had the energy to clean recently."

Her voice didn't match her body. It was deep and melodious and made her pigtails look like a joke. She had no makeup on, and her eyes were the palest that Adam had ever seen. He smiled in understanding.

"I think it's homey," he said and meant it. "Who's that by?"

He nodded at a lithograph above the sofa.

"Inger Sitter," she mumbled. "Can I offer you anything? Haven't got much in the house, but . . . coffee? Tea?"

"Coffee would be nice," he said. "If it's not too much trouble."

"Not at all. I made some half an hour ago."

She pointed at an Alessi coffee pot and went to get a cup.

"Would you like milk or sugar?" he heard from the kitchen.

"Both, please," he laughed. "But my wife doesn't let me, so I'll just take it black."

When she came back, he noticed that she had a great figure under her shabby clothes. Her jeans needed to be washed and her slippers must have once belonged to Vegard. But her waist was small, and her neck was long and thin. Her movements, when she put down the mugs and poured the coffee, were graceful.

"I thought I was done with you guys," she said without sounding unfriendly. "So I wonder what you want. A friend of mine, he's a lawyer, said that it's unusual for you to visit people at home. He said . . ."

Her smile was unreadable. A thin finger brushed her left eyebrow. Her eyes, when they met his, were almost teasing.

". . . that the police call people in to make them feel insecure. You're at home in the police station, not me. But here I'm at home. Not you."

"I don't feel particularly threatened where I'm sitting," Adam said and tasted the coffee. "But your friend has a point. So you could draw the conclusion that I don't intend to make you feel insecure. It's more that I'm looking for—"

"To talk?" she observed. "You're at a bit of loss, and you're the kind of policeman who looks around, tries to get a better overall impression, a bigger picture. And then maybe you'll discover a new angle. Paths and evidence that you hadn't noticed before."

"Hmm," he said, astonished. "Not so far from the truth."

"My friend. He knows you. You're quite well known." She gave a short laugh.

Adam Stubo resisted the urge to ask who her friend was.

"I can't quite get a handle on your husband," he said.

"Don't call him my husband, please. We only married for one reason, and that was that if we wanted to have children, it looked like we'd have to adopt—which is much easier to do as a married couple. Please just say Vegard."

"Okay, I can't quite get a handle on Vegard."

Laughter again, deep and short.

"I don't think there were many who did."

"Not even you?"

"Certainly not me. Vegard was many people. We all are, I suppose, but he was worse than most. Or better. Depends on how you want to look at it."

The irony was obvious. Again, Adam was struck by her voice. Elsbeth Davidsen used a wide range of expressions. Small, telling movements in her hands and face, and careful but obvious changes in her voice.

"Do tell."

"Tell? Tell you about Vegard . . ."

She picked absentmindedly at her knee.

"Vegard wanted so much," she said. "At the same time. He wanted to be obscure, literary, and alternative. Innovative and provocative. Unique. But he also had a craving for recognition that was difficult to combine with writing essays and inaccessible novels."

Now it was Adam's turn to laugh. As he put down his mug and looked around the room again, he realized that he liked this woman.

"Vegard had a great talent," she continued thoughtfully. "Once upon a time. I wouldn't exactly say that he . . . wasted it, but he . . . he was an angry young man for too long. When he was younger, he was full of charm. Energy. I was fascinated by the uncompromising strength in everything he did. But then . . . he never grew out of it. He thought he was fighting against everyone and would never admit that as the years passed, he was only fighting against himself. He lashed out, not realizing that whoever it was he was trying to hit had long since left. It was . . ."

Adam hadn't reacted to the fact that the woman, up to now, appeared to be untouched by her husband's brutal death just over two weeks ago. A sensible strategy, he thought, given the situation. She was talking to an unknown policeman. But now he could see that her lower lip was quivering.

"It was actually quite pathetic," she said and swallowed. "And pretty damn horrible to watch."

"Who was he after the most?"

With a listless hand, she puffed up a dirty red cushion.

"Anyone who achieved the success that he felt he deserved," she explained. "Which he felt . . . robbed of, in a way. In that sense, Vegard was the classic cliché of an artist: he was misunderstood. The one who had been passed by. But at the same time . . . at the same time he tried to be one of them. More than anything, he wanted to be one of them."

She leaned forward and picked up a card that had fallen on the floor. She handed it to him.

"This came a day or two before he died," she said and pulled at one of her pigtails. "I've never seen Vegard so happy."

The card was cream-colored and adorned with a beautiful royal monogram. Adam tried to repress a smile and carefully put the card back down on the glass table.

"You may well laugh," she sighed sadly. "We had a terrible argument about that invitation. I couldn't understand why he felt it was so important to get in with that crowd. To be honest, I was worried. He seemed to be obsessed with the idea that he finally was going to 'be someone,' as he put it." She made finger quotes in the air.

"Did you often argue?"

"Yes. At least recently. When Vegard really started to get stuck and definitely couldn't be called young and promising anymore. We've been soooo"—she held her thumb and her forefinger an eighth of an inch apart—"close to splitting up. Several times."

"But you still wanted to have children?"

"Don't most people?"

He didn't answer. There was a sudden commotion outside on the stairs. Something heavy fell on the floor, and two angry voices bounced off the concrete walls. Adam thought they were speaking Urdu.

"Nice here in Grønland," she said dryly. "Sometimes it can be a bit too lively. At least for those of us who can't afford to buy an apartment in the new buildings."

The voices out in the stairwell died down and then trailed off. Only the monotone drone of the city forced its way in through the dilapidated windows and filled the silence between them.

"If you could choose one," Adam said finally, "one of Vegard's enemies . . . someone who really had a reason to wish him ill, who would that be?"

"That's impossible," she answered without hesitation. "Vegard had offended so many people and threw his shit around so liberally that it would be impossible to pick out one person. And in any case . . ."

She picked again at the hole on the knee of her jeans. The skin underneath was winter-white against the indigo blue.

"Like I said, I'm not really sure if he could cause that much damage anymore. Before, he was hard-hitting and on target with his criticism. Recently it's just been . . . shit, like I said."

"But would it be possible," Adam tried again, "to identify . . . one group, then . . . one group of people that has greater reason to feel they've been wronged? Tabloid journalists? TV celebrities? Politicians?"

"Crime writers!"

Finally, a broad and genuine smile. Her teeth were small and pearly white, with a slight gap between the upper front teeth. A dimple appeared on one of her cheeks, an oval shadow of forgotten laughter.

"What?"

"Some years ago, when all his antics still attracted attention, he wrote a parody of three of that year's best sellers. Nonsense, really, but very funny. He got a taste for it. And in many ways it was his trademark for years. Haranguing crime writers, that is. Also in situations where it was completely unjustified or inappropriate. A kind of personal version of Cato's 'Moreover, I advise that Carthage must be destroyed.'" Again she made finger quotes in the air.

A car backfired outside the living room window. Adam heard a dog barking in the backyard. His back was sore, and his shoulders ached. His eyes were dry, and he rubbed them with his knuckles, like a tired child.

"What are we doing?" he asked himself. "What am I doing? Searching for ghosts and shadows. Getting nowhere. There's no connection, no common features, nowhere to go. Not even an overgrown, invisible path. We're flailing around in the dark, getting nowhere, without seeing anything except more new, impenetrable scrub. Fiona Helle was popular. Victoria Heinerback had political opponents, but no enemies. Vegard Krogh was a ridiculous Don Quixote who waged war with popular fiction authors in a world full of despots, fanaticism, and threatening catastrophe. What a . . ."

"I have to go," he muttered. "It's late."

"So soon?" She seemed disappointed. "I mean . . . of course."

She went to get his coat and came back before he had managed to struggle out of the deep sofa.

"I'm terribly sorry, on your behalf," Adam said as he took his coat and put it on. "For what has happened, and for bothering you like this."

Elsbeth Davidsen didn't answer. She walked silently in front of him down the hall.

"Thank you for letting me come," Adam said.

"It is I who should thank you," said Elsbeth Davidsen seriously and held out her hand. "It's been a pleasure meeting you."

Adam felt her warmth, the dry, soft hand, and dropped it a second too late. Then he turned and left. The dog in the backyard had gotten company. The animals were making a din that followed him all the way to the car, which was parked a block away. Both side-view mirrors had been broken and a parting message from Oslo East had been scratched onto the curbside doors: *Fuck you, you fucker.*

At least it was spelled correctly.

FOURTEEN

If you don't mind me saying, Johanne, you look damn great tonight. You really do. Cheers!"

Sigmund Berli lifted his glass of cognac. It didn't seem to bother him that he was the only one drinking. A red flush spread around his eyes like a rash, and his smile was broad.

"Amazing what a good night's sleep can do," Adam said.

"More like eighteen hours," Johanne said under her breath. "Don't think I've slept that long since I was in my last year of school."

She was standing behind Sigmund's back, asking Adam silently, with gestures and facial expressions, why he had invited his colleague home with him on yet another weekday.

"Sigmund's a grass widower at the moment," Adam explained in a loud, cheerful voice. "And the man doesn't have enough sense to eat unless the food is put on the table in front of him."

"If only I got food like this every day," Sigmund said and swallowed a burp. "I've never tasted such a good pizza. We normally have Grandiosa. Is it hard to make it? Do you think I could get the recipe for the wife?"

He grabbed the last piece as Adam started to clear the table.

"Would you rather have a beer?" Johanne asked in desperation, looking at the cognac bottle on the windowsill. "If you're going to eat more, that is. Doesn't it, well . . . go better?"

"Cognac goes with most things," Sigmund said happily and launched into the last piece of pizza. "It's really nice to be here. Thanks for asking."

"You're welcome," Johanne said flatly. "Are you still hungry?"

"After this, I could only be hungry for life," grinned the guest, washing down the pizza with the rest of the cognac.

"Dear God," muttered Johanne and went to the bathroom.

Sigmund was right—the sleep had done her a world of good. The bags under her eyes were no longer so dark, even though they were more obvious than Johanne liked in the harsh light by the mirror. This morning she had taken the time to have a proper bath, wash her hair, and cut and polish her nails. Put on makeup. When she finally felt ready to collect Ragnhild, she had lain down and slept for another hour and a half. Her mother had demanded that she look after her grandchild again on the weekend. Johanne had shaken her head, but her mother's smile showed that she wasn't going to yield.

"What is it about mothers?" Johanne asked herself. "Will I be like that too? Will I be just as hopeless, project my feelings onto my daughters and annoy them, be equally good at reading their needs? She's the only person I can give my baby to without feeling worried or ashamed. She makes me feel like a child again. That's what I need, I need to have no responsibility, no demands every now and then. I don't want to be like her. I need her. What is it about mothers?"

She let the cold water run over her hands for a long, long time.

More than anything, she wanted to go to bed. It was as if the previous night's long sleep had reminded her body that it was possible to sleep, and now it was screaming for more. But it was only nine o'clock. She dried her hands thoroughly, put her glasses on, and reluctantly went back to the kitchen.

"Or what do you think, Johanne?"

Sigmund's moon face smiled expectantly at her.

"About what?" she asked, trying to muster a smile.

"I was saying that surely it must be easier to develop a profile of the killer now. If we take all your theories seriously, I mean."

"All my theories? I don't have many theories."

"Don't be a pedant," Adam said. "Sigmund's right, isn't he?"

Johanne picked up a bottle of mineral water and drank. Then she screwed the lid back on, thought about it, smiled fleetingly and said, "We've certainly got a lot more to go on than before, I agree."

"Come on, then!"

Sigmund pushed a pen and some paper in her direction. His eyes were bright, like an excited child. Johanne stared at the sheets of paper in irritation.

"Fiona Helle's the problem," she said slowly.

"Why?" asked Adam. "Isn't she the only one who's not a problem? We've got a murderer, a confession, and a perfect motive that underpins the murderer's confession."

"Exactly," Johanne agreed and sat down on the empty bar stool. "And for that reason, she doesn't fit in."

She took three pieces of paper and laid them side by side on the counter. She wrote FH in felt-tip pen on the first page and pushed it to one side. Then she took the second and wrote VH in big letters and left it in front of her. She chewed the pen for a while before she scribbled VK on the last piece of paper and put it in line with the others.

"Three murders. Two unsolved."

She was talking to herself. Biting the pen. Thinking. The men were quiet. Suddenly she wrote Tuesday, January 20, Friday, February 6, and Thursday, February 19, under the initials.

"Different days," she murmured. "No pattern to the intervals."

Adam's mouth moved as he calculated the days.

"Seventeen days between the first and second murders," he said. "And thirteen between the second and third. Thirty between the first and the last."

"At least it's a round number," Sigmund tried.

Johanne moved the FH sheet to one side. Then pulled it back.

"Something's not right," she said. "There's something that just doesn't fit."

"Can't we try to base our discussion on the assumption that someone is behind it all?" Adam suggested impatiently and pushed the sheet over. "Imagine that Mats Bohus has been influenced by someone. The same person who's manipulated someone to kill Victoria Heinerback and Vegard Krogh. Let's—"

Johanne wrinkled her nose.

"But that's completely crazy," she said. "I don't understand—"

"Let's just try," Adam insisted. "What does that conjure up? What sort of person could—"

"It has to be someone with an incredible insight into the human psyche," she started. Again, she seemed to be talking to herself. "A psychiatrist or a psychologist. Maybe an experienced policeman. An insane priest? No . . ."

Her fingers drummed on the sheet with Fiona Helle's initials. She bit her lip. Blinked and straightened her glasses.

"I'm afraid I just can't," she said in a whisper. "I can't see what the connection is. Not unless . . . what if . . ."

She stood up abruptly. A file of notes lay on the shelf by the TV. She flicked eagerly through it as she came back across the floor and found the photo of Fiona Helle. When she sat back down, she put the picture directly above the sheet of paper with the victim's initials on it.

"This case is actually completely clear-cut," she said. "Fiona Helle let down her son. She can hardly be blamed for what happened in 1978, when Mats was born and her mother made a decision that would affect the fate of three generations. But I'm sure that I'm not the only one who has some kind of understanding of Mats Bohus's extreme reaction to what happened. You can think what you like about some people's strange desire to discover their biological origins, but . . ."

Her eyes did not leave the photograph. Johanne took off her glasses, picked up the photo, and studied it.

"It's all about dreams and great expectations," she said in a quiet voice. "Often, at least. When things go wrong and life is difficult, it must be tempting to think that there's something else out there, your true self, your real life. A kind of comfort. A dream that can sometimes become an obsession. Mats Bohus has had a harder life than most. His mother's final and absolute rejection must have been . . . crushing. This time she had everything to offer, but nothing to give. Mats had a motive for killing her. He killed her."

Deep in thought, she put the photo on top of the sheet of paper and bound them together with a paper clip. She sat in silence as if the others were no longer there and stared at the photograph of the beautiful TV star with fascinating eyes, a straight nose, and a provocative, sensual mouth.

Sigmund stole a look at the bottle by the window. Adam nodded.

"What if," Johanne began again; they could hear the enthusiasm in her voice. "What if we assume that it's not three cases in a series?"

"Sorry?"

"Huh?" uttered Sigmund as he filled his glass.

"We should perhaps—" Adam started.

"Wait," Johanne said sharply.

She placed the sheets in a triangle, with her hand over Fiona Helle's face.

"This case has been solved," she said. "A murder. An investigation. A suspect. The suspect has a motive. He confesses. The confession is confirmed by other facts in the case. Case closed."

"I have no idea where you're going," Adam admitted. "Are we back to square one? Do you think it's just coincidence and that we're talking about three unconnected—"

"But what about the symbolism?" Sigmund interjected. "What about the lecture you heard thirteen years ago that—"

"Hang on a minute! Wait!"

Johanne stood up. She walked in circles around the floor. Every now and then she stopped by the window and looked aimlessly out at the street, as if she had no expectation of seeing anyone there.

"It's the tongue," she said. "The severed tongue is the key. The starting point."

She turned toward the two men. Two bright circles were growing on her cheeks, touching her glasses, which were steamed up. Adam and Sigmund sat still, in deep concentration, as if they were spectators about to watch a dangerous stunt.

"We had it already on day one," Johanne said, excited. "The very first day, when Fiona was found with her tongue cut off and all wrapped up. It was there. We said that it was so banal. Such simple, obvious symbolism that it could almost have been taken from a cheap book about Red Indians. You said it yourself, Adam, just the other day . . . you said that there must be countless examples of bodies with dismembered tongues throughout history. You were right. You're absolutely right. Fiona Helle's murder had nothing to do with the lecture I heard on that hot summer's day in an auditorium in Quantico. It's so"—she put her hands to her face and swayed slightly from side to side—"clear," she said, half stifled, "so obvious. Jesus."

Adam stared at her, bewildered.

"Don't touch me," Johanne warned. "Let me go on."

Sigmund didn't drink. He was staring, his moist pink lips slightly open. His eyes moved from Johanne to Adam and back. Jack, the King of America, had come in from the living room. Even the dog stood stock-still, with his mouth shut and a twitching nose.

"These three cases," Johanne finally said and dropped her hands, "have a number of common features. But rather than looking for more, perhaps we should ask ourselves, what are the differences? What makes them different from each other? What makes the Fiona Helle case so different from the others?"

Adam hadn't taken his eyes off her since she started to wander around the room. Only now did he dare reach out for the bottle of water. His hands were shaking slightly as he unscrewed the top.

"It's been solved," he quipped.

"Exactly!"

Johanne pointed at him with both hands.

"Exactly! It's been solved!"

Jack wagged his tail, and it hit her legs when he came close. She stepped on his paw by accident as she hurried back to the counter. The dog howled.

"You found the answer in the Fiona Helle case," she said,

picking up the photograph and paying no attention to the dog. "You struggled, fumbled around, and were lost for a while. But the answer was there. The postmortem revealed details that led back to an old, sad story, which in turn led to Mats Bohus. To the murderer. Motive and opportunity. Everything was there, Adam. And it normally is. Murders are usually solved in this country."

Sigmund grabbed his glass and took a drink.

"Hello, I'm here too," he complained.

"But now take the other two cases," Johanne continued and slid the photograph down to the end of the counter, before grasping the other two sheets marked with the big letters VH and VK. "Have you ever in all your working life come across cases so devoid of suspects? So chaotic and full of false leads and distractions? Trond Arnesen . . ."

She spat the name out over the counter.

"A boy. He certainly had things to hide, just like everyone else. But he obviously didn't kill her. His alibi is airtight, even with a one-and-a-half hour interlude for a lovers' tryst."

"Rudolf Fjord is a name that still interests me," objected Sigmund.

"Rudolf Fjord," she sighed. "God, I'm sure he's no angel, either. Angels don't exist. So overall . . ."

Adam put his hand on hers; she was leaning against the counter, clutching a sheet of paper in each hand. He stroked the taut skin.

"In these two cases," she said and pulled away, "you will never achieve anything, except upsetting people's lives, standing on their toes with spiked shoes. As the police never give up, you will turn people's lives upside down, in ever-increasing circles around the victims. And before you give up, before you finally admit that you will never find the murderer, you will have destroyed, derailed so many, so many lives . . ."

"Okay, calm down now, Johanne. Sit down. I assume you want us to understand what you're trying to say, so you'll have to take it slower around the corners."

She forced herself to sit down and unsuccessfully tried to tuck her hair back behind her ears. It kept falling forward because her bangs were far too long.

"You need a drink," Sigmund declared. "That's what you need."

"No thanks."

"Wine would be better," Adam said. "I'm definitely going to have a glass."

A car rattled past outside. Jack lifted his head and growled. Adam took a bottle out of the corner cabinet, held it at arm's length, and nodded in satisfaction. He calmly put three glasses on the table, without comment, and opened the bottle. Then he poured a glass for himself and one for Johanne.

"I agree with the distinction you're making," he said, nodding. "The Fiona Helle case is a more . . . normal case, you might say. Than the other two."

"Normal and normal," Sigmund said and filled his own glass to the brim. "There's nothing very normal about cutting tongues out of people's mouths."

Adam ignored him, took a sip, put down his glass, and crossed his arms.

"I just don't understand the connection you're making . . ."

He gave her a friendly smile, as if he was frightened he might annoy her. It annoyed her.

"Listen," she said in a voice that was higher than normal, with a mixture of fear, enthusiasm, and anger. "The first case triggered the other two. That's the only way it works."

"Triggered," Adam repeated the word.

"Triggered?" Sigmund was more alert now and pushed his glass away a touch.

"It doesn't make sense any other way," Johanne said. "As I see it, the first murder happened more or less as we think it did. Fiona Helle destroyed Mats Bohus's dreams. He killed her and cut out her tongue, split it in two as a symbol of how he felt. She had lied about the most important things in life. Outwardly, she appeared to be a fixer of dreams, a savior to those with difficulties. When her own son needed her, he discovered it was all a show. A huge lie. How could he feel otherwise?"

Jack barked. At the same time, as if he'd caused it, the kitchen window slid open. A cold draft blew out the candle. Adam swore and got up.

"We've got to get these windows replaced," he said and bashed the frame into place before taking a match and relighting the candle.

"So there has to be someone out there," Johanne said, as if nothing had happened. Her eyes were fixed somewhere on the wall. "Someone who's heard Warren's lecture on proportional retribution. And who then decides to copy it. And is doing just that."

An angel passed through the room.

The silence was prolonged.

The candle was still flickering in the draft. Jack had gone back to sleep. Sigmund was breathing through his mouth. The pleasant smell of cognac swathed the three people around the kitchen table.

"That has to be the case," Johanne thought to herself. "Someone was . . . inspired. Someone seized the moment when they read about a murder where the victim's tongue had been cut out and wrapped up. The first piece was in place. Mats Bohus was an ignorant, arbitrary trigger."

Still no one said a word.

"I've never heard anything like it," Adam was thinking. "In all my years on the job, with all my experience, and everything

I've studied and read, I've never, ever heard of a case like that. It can't be right. It just can't be true."

The silence continued.

"She's a fantastic lady," Sigmund thought. "But she's lost it this time."

"Okay," Adam said, finally. "And what would the motive be for doing something like that?"

"I don't know," replied Johanne.

"Try," Sigmund encouraged her.

"I don't know the motive."

"But what sort of—"

"He has to have above-average intelligence. With more knowledge than most. He has . . ." She moved imperceptibly nearer to the table, closer to the others. "It has to be someone who has unusual insight into police work. Investigations, both technical and tactical, procedures and routines. So far you haven't found a single biological trace of any significance. And my guess is that you won't. Tactically, you're at a loss. This is obviously a man with no . . ."

She had a faraway look in her eyes when she took off her glasses.

"A man with no empathy," she concluded. "A damaged person, in some way. Personality disorder. But probably well adjusted. He won't necessarily have a criminal record. But I can't help—"

The look she sent Adam, unclear and searching, was one of growing desperation.

"He has to be a policeman," she said in despair. "Or at least someone who . . . How can he know so much? He must have heard Warren's lecture. It can't be a coincidence that he's using the same symbolism."

She held her breath. Then slowly she let it out again through clamped teeth.

"We're looking for someone who works with crime professionally," she said without expression or tone. "A twisted, clever, and knowledgeable mind."

"So he hasn't influenced others, made them kill?" Sigmund ventured. "Have we dropped that theory now?"

"He's done it himself. Definitely."

Johanne held onto Adam's eyes.

"He doesn't trust anyone," she continued. "He despises other people. He probably lives what we would call a lonely life, but without being a loner. People don't interest him. His actions are in themselves grotesque, and copying the symbolism is so sick that . . ."

She ran her hand slowly over the counter and looked away.

"He doesn't necessarily have anything in particular against Victoria Heinerback or Vegard Krogh."

"That would make him the only one," muttered Adam, "regarding Vegard Krogh. If he has nothing against him, that is. But if you're right, what would the motive be? What the hell would the motive be for someone to—"

"Wait!"

Johanne gripped Adam's hand and crushed it.

"The motive doesn't need to have anything to do with Victoria or Vegard," she said with renewed enthusiasm and vigor, as if catching a thought that had slipped away. "They may have been chosen simply because they were famous. The killer wants the murders to attract attention, like the first one did, Fiona Helle's murder. This case has—"

"Vegard Krogh wasn't famous," Sigmund cut in. "I, for one, didn't have a clue who the guy was before he was killed."

Johanne let go of Adam's hand. She put her glasses on again, raised her wineglass, and took a sip.

"You're right," she said. "You're absolutely right. I don't quite know how—"

"He was pretty well known in certain circles," Adam said. "He'd been on TV and—"

"Sigmund has a point," Johanne insisted. "The fact that Vegard Krogh was not more famous weakens my theory. But on the other hand . . ."

She broke off with a thoughtful expression on her face, as if trying to grasp some vague and undefined feeling so she could share it with the others.

"But the motive," Adam repeated. "If the primary purpose was not to harm Victoria or Vegard per se, what was it? To play with us?"

"Hush! Shhh!" Johanne was completely awake and alert now. "Did you hear that? Is that coming from . . ."

"It's only Kristiane," Adam said and got up. "I'll go."

"No, let me."

Johanne tried to be quiet when she went into the hall. Ragnhild might still sleep for another hour before she needed food. Johanne heard sounds from Kristiane's room that she couldn't make out.

"What are you up to, sweetie?" she whispered as she opened the door.

Kristiane was sitting up in bed. She had put on some tights and a thick sweater. She had a felt hat on her head, a green Tyrol hat with a feather in it that Isak had once brought back from Munich. Four Barbie dolls lay strewn over the bed. The girl had a knife in her hand and was smiling at her mother.

"What . . . Kristiane! What are you . . . ?"

Johanne sat down on the bed and carefully loosened her daughter's hand and took the knife.

"You shouldn't . . . It's dangerous . . ."

Only then did she notice the dolls' heads. The Barbies had been decapitated. Their hair had been cut off and lay like old golden Christmas decorations on the duvet.

"What have you . . ." Johanne stammered. "Why have you ruined your dolls?"

Her voice was angrier than she intended. Kristiane burst out crying.

"Don't know, Mommy. I was bored."

Johanne put the knife down on the floor. She hugged her daughter to her, pulled her into her lap, pushed off the ridiculous hat, and held her tight. Rocked from side to side. Kissed her tousled hair.

"You shouldn't do things like that, sweetie. You should never do things like that."

"But I was so bored, Mommy."

The window was open, and the room was freezing. Johanne felt she was shivering all over. She threw the remains of the dolls into a corner, pushed the knife far under the bed, and lifted the duvet. She lay down beside her daughter, with her stomach to her daughter's back. Johanne lay like this, whispering tender words to her, until the crying child finally fell asleep.

Kari Mundal didn't know the ins and outs of accounting, but she did have a sharp mind and robust common sense and knew roughly what she was looking for. Not because anyone had told her, but because in the weeks since Victoria Heinerback's death she had used her long morning walks to think, from exactly ten past six until she returned to her husband and a freshly brewed pot of coffee fifty minutes later.

Victoria Heinerback had originally been Kari Mundal's project. It was the older woman who had discovered the girl's talent, when Victoria was only seventeen years old. Potential successors to the throne had come and gone over the past fifteen years, but none of them had delivered what they once promised. A couple of them had even stabbed the old king, Kristian

Mundal, in the back. Out they went. Others had fallen victim to extreme liberalism, which did not sit comfortably with the party's persistent efforts to become a new popular party, the people's party, with stringent state regulation in crucial areas of society. Such as immigration.

Out went the liberals as well, and behind them all stood Victoria Heinerback.

It was Kari Mundal who found her. The seventeen-year-old from the suburbs, from Grorud, who chewed bubble gum and tied her bleached hair up in a ridiculous ponytail. But her eyes were blue and alert, and she had a quick mind. And she was attractive once Kari Mundal persuaded her to get a new haircut and to ditch the pale pink wardrobe.

And she was loyal to Kristian, unstintingly loyal. Always.

It wasn't easy to get close to Victoria. Even though they had seen each other every day for years, Kari and Victoria had never really been close. Not on a personal level. Maybe it was the age difference that made it difficult. On the other hand, Victoria Heinerback was not open with anyone, as far as Kari Mundal knew. Not even with that show-off she was engaged to. Mrs. Mundal thought the boy had no integrity, but was wise enough not to say it. They certainly looked good together. And that was something.

Politically, however, it was a different matter. Victoria Heinerback was not forthcoming with her views about her own and the party's future, but when she did speak out, she always allied herself with Kristian and Kari Mundal. The three of them had long since laid down a long-term strategy for the party, aside from the manifesto and the other party members. The first milestone had been achieved when Victoria had been elected by acclamation to succeed Kristian Mundal as party leader. The next would come after the parliamentary elections in 2005, when the party would, for the first time in history, be in a position where the old king could make a comeback as a minister. Then by 2009, the country should be ready for another young female prime minister.

Rudolf Fjord might be a problem.

They had realized that already last summer during the leadership campaign, when the man was blessed with a wave of goodwill from the party apparatus. He was popular in the regions. He traveled a lot, and local government was his forte. It was easy to promise millions to local governments as long as the party was in opposition, and Rudolf was a master of the art. For a while it looked as though the race between the two leadership candidates might be closer than the Mundals cared for. But Kari knew what to do. She whispered a few well-chosen words in selected ears about Rudolf's relationships with women, and the desired results were achieved. The man seemed to be incapable of commitment. There was something suspicious about the way he always turned up at premieres and A-list parties with a new woman on his arm. It just wasn't appropriate for a man of his age.

Victoria felt that Rudolf was necessary for the party and seemed to be quite happy to have him as deputy leader. But Kari Mundal, with her sharp nose, well trained and finely tuned from working as Kristian's closest adviser for over a generation, knew that Victoria was hiding something. She became very alert whenever Rudolf was near. There was something in her eyes, a watchfulness that Kari never managed to grasp and that Victoria avoided explaining the few times Kari had mentioned it.

"Rudolf should be grateful that everyone is so happy about the new building that no one takes a closer look," Victoria had said the last time they spoke together. "He has done a good job as chairman of the works committee, but he should tread carefully!"

Victoria had been furious when she said it. Rudolf Fjord had taken part in a TV debate where he had openly broken a pact they had made. They had agreed to keep on good footing with the government for a while, as it wasn't long until the revised national budget was to be announced. They had a plan. An agreement. He broke it, and her eyes were dark when she repeated, "That man should be careful. I could crush him. Like a louse, if I wanted to. He's walking on thin ice. But he should watch out what's coming from above, literally."

And then she had to rush off to a meeting, and Kari never found out what she meant. They never saw each other again, as she was killed two weeks later. When she had confronted Rudolf about Victoria's outburst during the memorial service at the house on Snarøya, he had claimed that he didn't know what she was talking about. But the color in his cheeks intensified, and he had been very uncomfortable when they ran into that policeman in the hall.

It was only three days ago, when she had gone to Rudolf's apartment in Frogner to drop off some papers for Kristian, that she had finally discovered one possible explanation for Victoria's outburst. Rudolf was irritated by her being there, impatient for her to leave. She asked if she could use the bathroom. He looked angrily at the clock but couldn't say no. And it was there, as she let the warm water run over her thin, sinewy, and soapy hands, that she realized where she should look.

The accounting department was situated right above Rudolf Fjord's office. The name was a misnomer, as it wasn't really a department, just a nice small room with cream wallpaper and cherrywood filing cabinets. The light flooded in through a large window facing the back and over the desk where Hege Hansen sat alone and kept the accounts for the party and the operations company, Kvadraturen Building Ltd.

Victoria had said, "He's walking on thin ice, but he should watch out for what's coming from above."

It was late, and the building was almost empty. Kari Mundal had drunk a whole thermos of tea. She wasn't used to figures and columns. She didn't even do her own taxes. Kristian took care of things like that. But curiosity drove her on as she plowed through the accounts for the extensive renovation project, from cover to cover, from the ledger down to the smallest receipt. Every now and then she stopped, straightened the glasses that were perched on the end of her sharp nose, and squinted a bit longer at an invoice before shaking her head and carrying on.

Then she stopped.

Div plumbing
PStarck porcelain
Ft ++
Wk se ok 03
Tot NOK 342,293
VAT NOK 82,150.32
To pay NOK 424,443.32

She had been studying unclear and meaningless vouchers for five hours now, but this was by far the worst. The words "porcelain" and "plumbing" were easy enough, but it took a while before she realized that Ft had to mean "fittings" and that there were in fact spaces between se and ok and 03. Had someone inspected the work and said it was okay in 2003? What did PStarck mean? Postscript tarck? And why was there a PS at the top of the invoice?

The VAT had been invoiced and paid.

Se ok 03.

Se ok, pondered Kari Mundal.

September–October 2003, perhaps? Strange abbreviation.

She thought back to autumn last year, when it looked like everything was going wrong with the building. It was primarily the cellar, roof, and façade that were causing the problems. They had chosen the wrong kind of paint. The stone couldn't breathe, and they had to repaint the whole thing. And there was something wrong with the drainage. Following a torrential rain, the cellar flooded. The flooring on the first floor had to be pulled up and replaced due to water damage, which was an expensive and time-consuming operation that had nearly ruined all plans for a big opening Christmas party.

The bathrooms were already finished in June.

PStarck.

Philippe Starck.

When they were doing up the big house on Snarøya, their youngest daughter had deluged her with interior design magazines. "Think new, Mom," she nagged and pointed at jacuzzis that Kari couldn't bear and toilets that looked like eggs. She most certainly did not want to feel like a hen every time she went to the bathroom was how she dismissed her daughter's suggestion.

The big building in the Kvadraturen area of Oslo was renovated meticulously and with great care. The toilets were old-fashioned, with high-level tanks and porcelain hand pulls on gold chains.

But in Rudolf's apartment, in his newly refurbished bathroom, everything was of the moment. Philippe Starck. She had been there, she had seen it, and the realization of what she had just unearthed made her hands sweat. She resolutely drank what was left of the lukewarm tea.

Then she took the voucher out of the file and went to get the key to the photocopying room. When she opened the door, the silence in the corridor was like a dense wall. She hesitated for a moment, listening. She seemed to be alone.

Had Rudolf killed Victoria?

For making a fuss about a bill for 424,443.32 kroner? He couldn't have. Or could he?

Did he know that she knew? Had she threatened him? Was that why everything had suddenly gone so smoothly just before the election, when Rudolf unexpectedly withdrew his candidacy and asked his supporters to vote for Victoria?

Rudolf Fjord couldn't have killed Victoria. Could he?

Kari Mundal put the copy in a small brown handbag before tidying away all the papers and quietly letting herself out of the building.

The woman who had wintered on the Riviera was on her way back to Norway. She was looking forward to it, in a way. At first she didn't recognize the feeling. It reminded her of something rare from her childhood, something unspecific and vague, and she wasn't even sure that it was pleasant. She felt restless, she had an uncomfortable feeling that time was passing too slowly. Only when the plane climbed steeply into the sky and she watched the wide Baie des Anges disappear under steel gray clouds, did she smile. Then she understood that it was anticipation she was feeling.

It was Friday, February 27, and the plane was only half full. She had a whole row to herself, and when the flight attendant asked if she would like some wine, she replied "Yes, please." It was too cold. She put the bottle between her thighs and leaned back in her seat. Closed her eyes.

There was no way back.

Everything would be closer now. More intense.

More dangerous—and better.

Ulrik Gustavsen was petrified. The madman who had arrested him just under a week ago had come to get him from the prison cell. Ulrik had tried to protest. He would rather sit in his cell until he rotted than spend time with the oversized bald man who obviously didn't give a shit about anything or anyone. Particularly not Ulrik Gustavsen and his democratic legal rights.

"Jesus," he thought to himself as he was shoved into a spartan interview room in Oslo's main police station. "I only had some cocaine and a damned joint. A whole week! One week! When are they going to release me? Why hasn't my lawyer done anything? She promised I would be out of custody by the weekend. I need to get a new lawyer. I want one of the top ones. I want out. Now."

"I'm sure you're wondering why we've kept you in so long," the policeman said in an unexpectedly cheerful voice as he pointed to a chair. "I understand, believe me. But you see, we can generally get the judges to do what we want. When we're not happy with the trash we pick up. I once had"—he bellowed with laughter and closed the door behind him before sitting down on a chair that didn't look like it would take his weight—"a real little shit. Not that unlike you. Pulled him in with three grams of hash in his pocket. Three grams, mind you. He was in custody for fourteen days, he was. Down in the backyard. Wasn't even room for him in a proper prison cell. Fourteen days he was inside. For three grams! Just because he couldn't understand that"—suddenly he leaned forward and smiled. His teeth were even and surprisingly white—"that I'm really a good guy."

Ulrik swallowed.

"A good guy," the policeman repeated. "Right now, I'm the best friend you've got. So you see, I get disappointed when"—he brushed his hand over his scalp, with a hurt expression on his face—"when you just ignore me. Won't answer my questions or anything."

Ulrik fiddled with the sleeve of his sweater. A thread had come loose. He wound it around his fingers, tried to push it in between two loose stitches.

"I'm sure that your lawyer's made loads of promises," the policeman continued. "That's what they do, you know. But for her, you're just one of many. She's got better things to do than—"

"I want a new lawyer," Ulrik said loudly and pulled back closer to the wall. "I want the best, I want Tor Edvin Staff."

The policeman laughed again.

"Tor Erling Staff," he corrected him and grinned. "I'm sure he's got much more exciting things to do. But you just listen to me . . ."

He leaned so far over the table that Ulrik could feel his breath on his face. Garlic and stale tobacco. The detainee pressed his head back against the wall and gripped the edge of the table.

"You're probably wondering why I'm keeping you here," the man said, and again his tone was almost conciliatory, friendly. "I understand, I really do. You haven't exactly killed anyone, have you? But let me tell you something. It's what I call . . . the delicate ecology of crime."

He sat back and straightened up again, at last. He looked puzzled, as if he didn't really understand what he'd just said. Ulrik let the chair down to the floor again and dared to breathe out.

"Smart," the man said, pleased with himself. "The delicate ecology of crime. Not used that expression before. You know, everything's connected. Out there in the wild."

He waved one of his massive fists at the wall, as if nature were pressing in through the drywall.

"If there's lots of midges, there's plenty of food for the birds.

If there's food for the birds, they lay lots of eggs. Snakes and martens eat the eggs. If there are lots of martens, it's good for the fur trade . . . oh, hang on, they've got tame martens as well, don't they? Minks, isn't that what they're called?"

For a moment he looked thoughtfully at Ulrik. The blue eye nearly closed, the brown one squinting. Then he shrugged and gave a quick shake of the head.

"You get the point," he stated. "Everything's connected. It's the same with crime. The smallest junkie creep is connected with the worst bank robber, the most brutal killer. Or maybe it's better to say . . . their actions are connected. It's a web, you see. An incredibly intricate web of"—he hunched his back, lifted his elbows, and clawed his fingers, as if he was trying to frighten a child—"evil," he hissed. "You buy drugs. Someone has to smuggle them in. They get rich. They get greedy. They steal. Kill if they have to. Sell drugs. Kids get addicted. Attack old ladies on the street."

He was still pretending to be an enormous crab. His fingers were waving around in front of Ulrik's eyes. His nails were bitten to the quick.

"The man's a lunatic," Ulrik thought to himself. "Does anyone else know that I'm here? He locked the door. It's locked."

"And that takes us back," continued the policeman, who resumed his normal behavior, "to why I didn't just let a squirt like you back on the streets again, as soon as I'd gotten your details last Saturday. Do you see why now?"

Ulrik didn't dare to answer. It obviously made no difference.

"Because when the name Trond Arnesen popped up, it suddenly became more than just the white lines and a spliff," the policeman explained. "'Cause everything . . .'"

He paused and made an encouraging, rotating movement with his right hand.

". . . is connected," mumbled Ulrik.

"Well done! Exactly! Now we're getting somewhere, son! And I'll show you what I found at your place the other day. Had to take an extra look around, you see. Around your lovely, expensive apartment."

He slapped the seat of his pants. Then his face lit up, and he pulled a notebook out of his breast pocket.

"Here it is," he said, pleased with himself. "So, I'm guessing that these are your accounts."

Ulrik opened his mouth to protest.

"Shut it," the man snarled. "I've been banging up people like you since way before your dad got hairs on his dick. This is your book, and these are your customers." He tapped his finger on the initials in the margin of an open page. "Telephone numbers and everything, so I've managed to identify lots of them already. Strange, really, the secrets people carry around. But not a lot surprises me anymore."

He clicked his tongue and shook his head. He seemed to be completely engrossed in the little book.

"But not all of them," he said suddenly. "I'm missing three names. I want to know who AC is. And APL and RF. And Ulrik . . ."

He got up slowly. He scratched his mustache, stretched, pulled on his earlobe. Smiled and then was very serious. Both his palms smashed down onto the table. Ulrik jumped in his chair, quite literally.

"Now don't fuck me around," he snapped. "Don't you even try. They're your customers, and I want to know who they are, okay? We can sit here until the cows come home, but that would be damn uncomfortable. For both of us. But mainly for you. So start talking. Now."

His hand landed lightly on Ulrik's neck. And squeezed. Not

too hard. He loosened his grip but left his hand there. It was enormous and burning hot.

"Don't waste our time, son."

"Arne Christiansen and Arne-Petter Larsen," Ulrik forced out.

"RF," the man barked. "Who's RF?"

"Rudolf Fjord," Ulrik whispered. "But I haven't seen him for ages. A couple of years, at least."

The hand gently stroked the back of his head and then withdrew.

"Good boy," the policeman said. "Now what did I say?"

Ulrik looked at him, terrified, the blood was pounding in his ears, and he was sweating.

"What did I tell you?" the man asked again in a friendly voice. "Lost your tongue?"

"Everything's connected," Ulrik whispered quickly.

"Everything's connected," nodded the man. "Remember that. Next time."

"He'd get Mother Teresa to admit to triple homicide," Sigmund Berli said cynically as he tapped the report the policeman had written after questioning Ulrik Gustavsen. "Or Nelson Mandela to admit to genocide. Or Jesus to—"

"I get the picture, Sigmund. Got it immediately, in fact."

They were walking. Adam had insisted on going to Frogner Park first. Sigmund protested all the way. They didn't have much time. It was freezing cold. Sigmund was wearing the wrong shoes, and his wife was in a bad mood because of all the overtime he was putting in. He couldn't understand why they should waste twenty minutes in a park full of ugly statues and aggressive dogs on the loose.

"I need some air," Adam explained. "I need to think, okay?

And that's not easy with you chattering away like a five-year-old. So shut up. Enjoy the exercise. We need it, both of us."

He thought, "Johanne's wrong," and picked up pace. He felt an unfamiliar twinge under his rib cage. He'd never doubted her abilities before. He'd admired them. Needed them. He needed her, and he was losing her. Her instincts were wrong. Her intellect weakened by sleepless nights and a greedy baby. "The theory doesn't hold. If the murderer wanted to create an uproar, make a noise, get attention, he wouldn't have chosen Vegard Krogh. Victoria Heinerback, yes. Everyone knows her. But Vegard Krogh? A sham of an artist, a quasi-intellectual fool? Who practically no one had heard of? Johanne's wrong, and we're back to square one. We don't know what we're looking for. Where to look."

"Why don't we just call the guy in?" Sigmund was surly. He had short legs and had to jog to keep up with his colleague. "Why do we always have to visit people at home all the time? Damn it, Adam, we're wasting taxpayers' money by throwing away all this time."

"People's tax money is used for far worse things than us trying to find a way out of the mess we're in," Adam leveled. "Get over it. We're nearly there."

"I don't believe that Gustavsen boy. Rudolf Fjord's not a fag, you know. He doesn't look like one. Why the hell would he pay that runt for sex? Huh? A tall, good-looking guy whom the ladies love! My wife reads all those magazines, you know, with pictures from premieres and parties and all that, and he's definitely not a fag."

Adam stopped. He took a deep breath. The air was so cold that it caught in his throat.

"Sigmund," he said calmly. "Sometimes I get the impression that you're just plain stupid. But as I know that you're not, I must ask you to"—he warmed his ears with his hands. Took another deep breath and shouted, suddenly—"Shut up!"

Then he set off again.

They passed through the ornate gates onto Kirkeveien in silence. Two buses were parked diagonally outside. Adam pulled his scarf tighter around his neck. A flock of traditionally dressed Africans in wide, colorful garments were boarding one of the buses. It was hard to imagine why tourists came to Norway, Sigmund thought. And in February, when there was snow everywhere, and you got slush all the way up your legs, it was incomprehensible.

"You've got to admit that those dresses are silly," he muttered.

"You look pretty ridiculous too, with leather patches on your ass, a red bolero, and silver buckles on your shoes," Adam retorted, "but that doesn't seem to stop you from wearing your national costume. It's probably some sort of official thingamajig. What time is it?"

"Nearly six," Sigmund complained. "I'm cold as hell. And anyway, it's not a bol . . . bolero. It's a woolen jacket."

Eleven minutes later, Adam's finger ran up and down a list of names on a metal plate beside a gray door.

"Rudolf Fjord," he murmured and pushed the bell.

No one answered. Sigmund banged his feet together to keep warm and muttered under his breath. A young woman walked up with a bag over her shoulder. She fished out a bunch of keys and smiled at Adam.

"Hi', she said as if she knew him.

"Hi," he replied.

"Going in?"

She held the door open, and he caught it. The woman had red hair. She ran up the stairs, whistling like a girl, leaving behind a scent of fresh air and light perfume.

"Have a good evening," she called. They heard a door open and close again.

"So here we are," Sigmund said and looked up the stairs.

"Fourth floor," Adam said and went over to an ancient elevator with folding iron gates. "I'm not sure this will hold both of us."

"Max load 550 pounds," Sigmund read on an enamel sign. "We'll risk it, eh?"

It worked. Just. The elevator whined and groaned and stopped a foot before the fourth floor. Adam struggled to get the door open. The gates were jammed against the floor.

"I'll think I'll take the stairs on the way down," groaned Adam as he finally managed to get out.

It was an impressive building, even if the elevator was ancient. The stairwell was wide and carpeted. The windows out to the back had diamonds of red and blue glass that threw a play of colors on the walls. There were two front doors on the fourth floor. Between them hung a glass-framed painting of a golden brown landscape somewhere in southern Europe.

Adam hadn't even rung Rudolf Fjord's bell before the door opposite opened.

"Hello," said a woman in her seventies.

She was beautiful in a high-class way, Sigmund noted. Slim and very small. Groomed hair. Skirt and sweater and a pair of neat leather slippers. She was wringing her hands and seemed to be distressed.

"I'm terribly sorry to butt in, I know it's none of my business," she said. Adam noticed now that despite her old-fashioned, almost subservient appearance, her eyes were sharp. The two men had been weighed and measured up in a flash.

"Are you friends of Mr. Fjord? Or colleagues, perhaps?"

Her smile was sincere enough, and the worried furrow in her brow was genuine.

"I have to admit that I've been listening in case anyone came," she said before they had a chance to answer. "For once I was grateful to hear the noise of that thing."

A thin finger with a manicured nail pointed to the elevator.

"You see, Rudolf is such a boon to us here. He looks after us. Figures everything out. When I broke my leg just before Christmas"—she modestly lifted her left leg. It was beautiful, slim and whole—"he stopped by every day and did my shopping. We're good neighbors, Rudolf and I. But now I'm . . . oh, I do apologize."

With practiced hands, she undid the chain and came toward the two men.

"Eva Helleland," she said, offering her hand.

The two men mumbled their surnames.

"I am so worried," said the woman. "Rudolf came home about nine o'clock last night. I happened to come in at the same time. He had been to the theater with a lady friend. Rudolf and I always have a little chat when we bump into each other. Sometimes he even comes in for coffee. Or a glass of something. He is always so . . ."

"She's like a weasel," Adam thought to himself. "An energetic, curious weasel, with playful hands and darting eyes that see everything."

She patted her hair, coughed a little.

"Nice," she concluded.

"But not last night," Adam suggested, questioningly.

"No! He barely answered when I spoke to him. Looked pale. I asked if he was unwell, but he said he was fine. Be that as it may, when . . ." Eva Helleland's smile took ten years off her. There was a flash of gold from her beautiful teeth, and she had deep dimples. "He's a man in his prime, and I'm an old widow. I understand perfectly that he may not always have time for me. But . . ."

She hesitated.

"It was unusual behavior," Adam contributed. "He behaved very differently from normal."

"Exactly," said a grateful Mrs. Helleland. "And since then, I'm ashamed to say that I've been keeping my ears open."

She looked Adam straight in the eye.

"Not very nice, I admit, but sound does carry easily in this building, and I feel that we should all . . . look out for one another."

"I totally agree," Adam assured her. "And did you hear anything?"

"Nothing," she said in obvious distress. "That is the problem. I usually hear footsteps from the apartment. Music. Sometimes the TV. The only . . ." The furrow reappeared on her brow. "The telephone has rung," she said decisively. "Four times. Rung and rung."

"Maybe he went out again," Sigmund suggested.

Eva Helleland gave him a reproachful look, as if he had insinuated that she was asleep at her post. She pointed to two newspapers on the doormat.

"The morning and evening edition," she said meaningfully. "The man is newspaper obsessive. Unless he snuck out during the night when I was asleep, I say he's at home. And he hasn't even taken in the papers!"

"He may have done just that," Adam said. "He may have gone out last night."

"I'll call the police," the woman said with some force. "If you won't believe that I know Rudolf Fjord well enough to know that something is wrong, I will call the authorities."

She turned around and walked back toward her own door.

"Wait a minute," Adam said in a calm voice. "Mrs. Helleland, we are from the police."

She spun around.

"Excuse me?"

Her agile hands quickly brushed over her hair again before she smiled with relief and added, "Of course. It's that awful business with Victoria Heinerback. Terrible. It did so affect poor Rudolf. Of course, you're here to get more information. But then . . ."

She cocked her head to one side, then the other—small, quick movements. Now she really did look like a weasel, with a pointed noise and small, darting eyes.

"Then we should go in," she decided. "But first I must ask to see your ID. Just a moment, I'll go and get the keys."

Before the two policemen could say anything, she'd disappeared.

"I don't like the sound of that," Adam said.

"Of what?" Sigmund asked. "She's got the key! And you can say what you like, the woman talks a lot of sense."

"I don't want to think about what we might find."

Eva Helleland reappeared. She glanced at the ID cards that the two men held up and nodded.

"Rudolf had his bathroom renovated last autumn," she explained and put the key in the lock. "It looks super now. But with the workmen coming in and out, it seemed best that I had a set of keys. You never know who you can trust. And I've just kept them. There!"

The door was open.

Adam went in.

It was dark in the hallway. All the doors to the rooms were shut.

"The drawing room is this way," Mrs. Helleland said, meeker now.

She slipped under Adam's arm and walked to the end of the hall. Then she stopped in front of a double door.

"Perhaps it's best . . ." she started and nodded to Adam.

He opened the door.

A chandelier lay on the table. The crystals were tangled. One lonely crystal dangled over the edge of the table. Rudolf Fjord was hanging from a rope slung over a hook in the center of an enormous ceiling rose, to which the chandelier had obviously until recently been attached. His tongue was blue and swollen. His eyes were open. The body hung absolutely still.

"I think you should go back to your own apartment and wait there," Adam said. Mrs. Helleland had not dared to look into the drawing room yet.

Without asking, without even so much as glancing into the room, she obeyed. The front door was left open behind her. They heard her steps crossing the hall. Her door closing.

"Shit," said Sigmund Berli as he walked over to the body.

He pulled up Rudolf Fjord's pant leg and touched the white skin.

"Completely cold."

"Do you see a note?"

Adam didn't move. He just stood there, frozen, and watched the movement that Sigmund had set in motion. The body turned incredibly slowly around its own axis.

An overturned chair lay on the floor.

"Johanne was certainly right about one thing," Adam thought. "She was right about the price of this case. The cost is too high. We're stumbling around in the dark. Lifting up a corner of someone's life here, pulling a thread there. Then it all goes to pieces. We can't find what we're looking for, but we keep going. Obviously Rudolf Fjord couldn't. Who told him? Was it Ulrik? Was it Ulrik who called to warn an old customer, to say that his secret was out? That there was no point in parading around with women anymore, pretending to be a man of the world?"

"No letter, not here anyway."

"Keep looking."

"But I have—"

"Keep looking. And call the officer on duty. Immediately."

Rudolf Fjord had not killed Victoria Heinerback, Adam was sure of that. He couldn't bring himself to move. "He had dinner with some party colleagues in Bærum on the night she was murdered. His alibi was good. He was never a suspect. But we still couldn't let him be. We can never let anyone be," he thought to himself.

"There's no note here." Sigmund Berli sounded irritated. "He hanged himself because he was scared of being caught with his pants down. Not much to write home about, maybe."

"And that . . ." Adam said, and finally managed to walk over to the body, which had stopped turning. "The fact that Rudolf Fjord may have paid for sex with Trond Arnesen's lover is something that we will keep to ourselves. There are limits to how much damage we can do to other people's lives and"—he looked up at Rudolf Fjord's face. The broad, masculine chin seemed bigger now, and his eyes were bloodshot. He looked like a stranded deepwater fish—"reputation," Adam finished. "We'll keep that to ourselves. Okay?"

"Okay," Sigmund agreed. "Fine by me. Oslo police are on their way. Ten minutes, they said."

They got there in eight.

When Kari Mundal answered the phone four hours later, annoyed that someone should call at half past ten on a Friday night, it only took a minute before she sank down onto the chair by the little mahogany shelf in the hall. She listened to what the party secretary had to say and barely managed to answer his questions adequately. When the conversation finally ended, she stayed sitting where she was. The chair was uncomfortable, and it was dark and cold in the hall. But she couldn't get up.

She had called Rudolf yesterday. There was nothing else she could do. She had tossed and turned on Wednesday night, weighing the pros and cons of blowing the whistle, and by Thursday morning, she had made up her mind.

And it had been fatal, she realized that now.

Without having decided how she would pursue the matter, she had called him. Without having thought about how the party, and thereby Kristian Mundal, would cope with such a scandal, she had told him what she knew.

"I was so angry," she thought, hearing only her own breathing, shallow and fast. "I was so disappointed and angry. I wasn't thinking straight. I just wanted him to know that he wasn't out of the woods yet. He needed to know that his secret hadn't gone to the grave with Victoria. I was so angry. And so very disappointed."

"What's the matter, dear?"

Kristian Mundal emerged from the living room. Light flooded through the double door and nearly blinded her. Her husband was a dark figure in the doorway, with his pipe in one hand and a newspaper in the other.

"Rudolf is dead," she said.

"Rudolf?"

"Yes."

Her husband moved toward her. She could still hear only her own breathing, her own pulse. He turned on the light, and it hurt her eyes. She was crying.

"What are you talking about?" he asked and took her hand.

"Rudolf committed suicide," she whispered. "They're not sure when. Yesterday, possibly. They don't know. I don't know."

"Committed suicide? Taken his own life?" Kristian Mundal bellowed. "But why in the world would that idiot go and take his own life?"

The party secretary had told her that no note had been found. Not in the apartment, nor on his computer. They would, of course, keep searching, but for the moment, nothing had been found.

"No one knows," Kari Mundal said and let go of his hand. "No one knows anything yet."

"I hope you didn't leave a note, Rudolf," Kari Mundal thought. "I hope that your mother, poor soul, never finds out why you were so frightened that you had to take your own life."

"I need a drink," Kristian Mundal said and swore savagely. "And so do you."

She followed him without saying any more.

It was a busy evening, with telephone calls and lots of visitors. No one noticed that the normally vivacious woman was completely silent for the first time in her long life. Everyone talked at once. Some were desperate. Some cried. People came and went far into the night. Kari Mundal made coffee and tea, mixed strong drinks, and prepared sandwiches at midnight. But she said nothing.

As dawn approached, when Kristian had finally fallen asleep, she got up and went downstairs. In her handbag, in a compartment of her voluminous purse, was a copy of the incriminating invoice. She took it out and went over to the fireplace. There she lit a match. Only when the flames licked her fingers did she let go of the paper.

Two days later, she made up an excuse to look at the old accounts again. She immediately found what she was looking for. The original invoice was torn to shreds and flushed down the toilet on the third floor, an old-fashioned toilet with a high-level tank and a porcelain hand pull on a gold chain.

No suicide note was ever found. For a while, a couple of policemen in Oslo thought they knew why Rudolf Fjord had hanged himself in his own living room so soon after he'd been elected as the much-celebrated leader of one of the largest political parties in Norway. They never said anything. After some years, the episode faded and was forgotten.

An elderly lady on Snarøya, to the west of Oslo, was the only person who knew the reason he had committed suicide.

And she never forgot.

FIFTEEN

"Leap year," shouted Kristiane. "Leap bound bang bang!"

"No pretend guns in the house," Johanne reprimanded and took the plastic spatula she was brandishing out of her hand.

"Honestly, you can't seriously call that a pretend gun," Adam said, irritated.

"Bang, bang! What's a leap year?"

"It's a year that has a day like today," Adam explained as he hunkered down beside her. "The twenty-ninth of February. Days like this come only once every four years. Maybe they're shy."

"Shy," repeated Kristiane. "Leap year. Peep here. Bang!"

She stopped and put her hair behind her ears, like her mother had just done.

"But what's the scientific explanation?" She was serious. "I want to understand, not just be told something funny."

The adults exchanged looks; Johanne's was anxious, and Adam's was proud.

"Well, the Earth takes a bit longer than 365 days to . . ."

He stroked his head and looked over at Johanne for help.

"To go around its own axis?"

"That takes twenty-four hours, Adam."

"To go around the sun?"

Johanne just smiled and wrung out a cloth.

"To go right around the sun," he said with conviction to Kristiane. "That's what we call a year, but it's a tiny bit longer. So, every now and then, we have to gather together all the extra bits that add up to make a full day. Every fourth year. And then there was something about Gregory and Julius, but I can't remember that."

"You're smart," Kristiane said. "Julius is a chimpanzee in the zoo, Adam. I'm going to play leap years with Leonard, and today Daddy is coming to get me. You're not my daddy."

"No, but I love you very much."

Then she shot off, with Jack at her heels. The small feet clattered down the stairs, and the door slammed behind them. Adam snorted and got up with pride.

"I wonder how many times we'll have to go through that whole rigmarole that I'm not her father," he said. "We'll have to get the custody agreement figured out soon. It's been chaotic this winter. Wasn't she supposed to stay at Isak's on Friday?"

"What's the matter with you?" Johanne asked and stroked his hair. "Is it just the Rudolf Fjord case, or is it—"

"Just? *Just?*" He pulled his head away, a bit too abruptly. "It's fucking not 'just' when your job forces people to commit suicide."

"You haven't driven anyone to suicide, Adam. You know that."

He sat down on the nearest bar stool. A half-eaten celery stick was lying on a dirty plate. He picked it up and took a bite.

"No, actually, I don't know that," he said and took another bite.

"My love," she said, and he had to smile.

She kissed him on the ear, on the neck.

"You haven't killed anyone," she whispered. "You catch spiders and then let them out into the garden. Rudolf Fjord took his own life. He chose to die. By his own volition. Of course it's"—she stood up and looked him in the eye—"of course it's not your fault. You know that."

"I miss you," he said, chewing on the celery.

"Miss me? I'm here, you fool."

"Not quite," he answered. "None of us are all here. Not like before."

"It will get better," she thought. "Soon. I've finally started to sleep now. Not a lot, but a lot more. Spring will soon be here. Ragnhild is growing. Getting stronger. Everything will get better. If only this case were over and you—"

"Have you considered taking some time off?" she asked lightly as she started to stack the dirty plates in the dishwasher.

"Time off?"

"Yes, take your paternity leave. For real."

"As if we can afford that . . ."

He chewed and chewed and stared at the green, half-eaten stick.

"I could start working again," she said. "Wouldn't it be good to have this case off your hands? To forget it? Let someone else take over, someone else take—"

"No way."

He scratched his groin.

"Isn't it strange," he said with his eyes narrowed. "Isn't it strange to choose death rather than—"

"Don't change the subject. Have you actually considered it?"

"You're entitled to more leave, Johanne. Which is only fair

and reasonable. You've just given birth, you're breast-feeding. It's good for Ragnhild. So it's good for us."

He threw the remains of the celery at the garbage can in the cabinet under the sink, as if to underscore that the conversation was over. He missed.

"But isn't it peculiar," he continued and opened out his hands, "that a person should choose to take his life because he risks being outed as a homosexual? In 2004? For Christ's sake, they're everywhere! We've got hordes of lesbians at work, and they don't seem to feel persecuted or bothered, and we—"

"Actually, strictly speaking, you don't know much about that," she said as she picked up the celery. "You barely know them."

"Come on, the finance minister of Norway is gay, for Christ's sake. And no one seems to be too bothered about that!"

Johanne smiled, and it annoyed him.

"The finance minister is a . . . soigné gentleman from the west end," she said. "Discreet, professional, and according to what little we know of him, an excellent cook. He's lived with the same man for centuries. That's a *bit*"—she held her index finger and thumb together in an exaggerated gesture—"different," she continued, "from someone who buys sex from young boys while parading around with blondes on his arm whenever there's a camera nearby."

Adam said nothing. He put his head down on his arms.

"Why don't you get a little sleep?" she said quietly and stroked his back. "You were up all night."

"I'm not tired," he said into his sleeve.

"What are you then?"

"Depressed."

"Can I do anything for you?"

"No."

"Adam—"

"The worst thing is that Rudolf was cleared as a suspect so early on in the case," he said angrily and sat up. "His alibi was fine. There was nothing to indicate that he was behind it. Quite the opposite—according to his colleagues in the Storting, he was devastated. So why couldn't we just leave the man in peace? What the hell does it matter to us who he's fucking?"

"Adam," she tried again and held his neck between her hands.

"Listen to me," he said and pushed her away.

"I'm listening. It's just a bit difficult to answer when what you're saying isn't very sensible. You had every reason to investigate Rudolf Fjord in more detail. Especially after the argument you heard between him and Kari Mundal. At the memorial service out at—"

"I remember it well enough," he cut her off, cross. "But it can't be more than five days since you sat here and drew a profile of a killer that was nothing like Rudolf Fjord. Why did I then have to pursue—"

"You never believed in that profile," she said curtly and got out the dish soap. "Not then and not now. And to be honest, I think you should stop moping."

"Moping? Moping!"

"Yes, you're moping. Feeling sorry for yourself. You can just stop it now."

She slammed the dishwasher shut, put the box of detergent back on the shelf in the cabinet, and turned to face him, with her right hand on her hip. And grinned.

"Meanie," he mumbled and smiled reluctantly back. "Anyway, you said yourself that the profile had a number of weak points. Vegard Krogh didn't fit. He wasn't well-known enough."

Johanne picked up Sulamit the fire engine, which had been abandoned on the floor. The eyes on the radiator grill had lost their pupils and stared blindly at her. She fidgeted with the broken ladder.

"I've been doing some more thinking," she said.

"And?"

"Do you remember . . . do you remember when we were sitting here with Sigmund? Not last Tuesday, but a few weeks ago?"

"Of course."

"He asked me what would be the worst imaginable murder."

"Yes."

"And I answered that it would have to be something like a killer without a motive."

"Yes."

"They don't exist."

"Right. So what did you mean then?"

"I meant . . . I still think my reasoning stands, by the way. A killer who chooses his victims completely arbitrarily, without a motive for the individual murders, would be extremely difficult to catch. Assuming that a number of other factors are in place, of course. Such as the killer doing a good job, to put it simply."

"Aha . . ."

He nodded and put his hand on his stomach.

She put Sulamit down with a thump.

"You can't actually be hungry again. You ate less than an hour ago. Now listen."

"I'm all ears," Adam said.

"The problem is that it's difficult to imagine a completely random series of victims," Johanne said and sat down on the stool beside him. "People never function in a vacuum! We're never unbiased, we all have our likes and dislikes, we . . ."

She pressed her fingers together so that her hands looked like a tent, and then she put her nose in the opening.

"Let's imagine," she continued, in full concentration. Her voice sounded nasal when she sat like that. ". . . a murderer who decides to kill. For whatever reason. We'll come back to that. But he decides to kill, not because he wants to take someone's life, but because he—"

"It's difficult to imagine that anyone can be murdered in cold blood, unless the murderer actually wants them dead."

"Try to imagine it all the same," she said impatiently. She folded her hands and clasped them together until the knuckles turned white. "The murderer would possibly choose the first victim fairly randomly. Like when we were children and spun the globe. Then, wherever your finger hit—"

"You would go in twenty-five years' time," he finished. "I even read a children's book about something like that. *The Kept Promise*."

"Do you remember what tended to happen the second time you tried?"

"I cheated," he said and smiled. "Opened my eyes ever so slightly to make sure I got somewhere more exciting than my friend."

"In the end I would stand there with open eyes and aim," Johanne admitted. "I wanted to go to Hawaii."

"And your point is . . ."

"I've read in the papers," she said, letting him stroke the back of her hand, "that they're calling these cases the perfect crime. Not so strange, really, considering how helpless the police seem to be. But I think perhaps we should shift focus and instead say that we're in fact talking about the perfect murderer. But"—she chewed her lip and reached for a caper in one of the bowls—"the point is that there is no such thing," she said, studying the stalk. "The perfect murderer is completely

free of any context. The perfect murderer feels nothing—no
fear, no horror, no hate, and certainly no love. People have a
tendency to think that insane murderers have no feelings and
are completely incapable of relating to other human beings.
They forget that even Marc Dutroux, the epitome of a pedo-
phile monster, was married. Hitler inflicted terrible suffering
on the Jews and sent six million to their deaths, but it's said
that he was very fond of his dog. And presumably he was even
kind to it."

"Did he have a dog?"

She shrugged her shoulders.

"Think so. But you get my point, at least."

"No."

She got up slowly, still chewing on the stubborn caper. She
looked around the room and then went over to Kristiane's toy
box.

"I am a person who has decided to kill," she said and swallowed before stalling his objection. "Just forget why for the
moment."

She picked up a red ball and held it out in front of her in
her right hand, in a dramatic pose, like Hamlet and the skull.
Adam chuckled.

"Don't laugh," she said in a level voice. "This is my world.
I know a lot about crime. It's my subject. I know there's a connection between the motive and how a case is solved. I know
that I'm more likely to get away with murder if no one can
find a connection between me and the victim. So, I spin the
globe."

She closed her eyes and blindly pressed her finger into the
red rubber.

"I have chosen a completely random victim," she said. "And
I kill that person. Everything works out. No one suspects me. I
get a taste for more."

She looked up.

"But in some way, I've changed. All our actions, everything that happens, affects us. I feel . . . successful. I want to do it again. I feel . . . alive."

She froze. Adam opened his mouth.

"Shh," she said sharply. "Shh!"

They could hear the children running from room to room downstairs. Jack was barking angrily. Then they heard a muffled, cross grown-up voice through the floor.

"Maybe I should go down and get her," Adam said. "Sounds like—"

"Shh," she said again. She had a distant look in her eyes, and she had frozen in a theatrical comedy pose, with one leg tantalizingly in front of the other. The ball was still in her right hand.

"Alive," she repeated, as if she was tasting the word.

Suddenly, she grabbed the ball with both hands and threw it to the floor. It bounced against the fireplace and knocked over a plant that was standing on the floor, without Johanne seeming to notice.

"Alive," she said for the third time. "These murders are a form of . . . extreme sport."

"What?"

Adam stared at Johanne. He tried to see beyond the unfamiliar, frightened expression, beyond her unfamiliar behavior; he tried to see inside her mind. She stood as if in a trance.

"Extreme sport," she repeated without paying him any attention, "a way of feeling alive. That's how people describe it. The adrenaline kick. The rush. The feeling of defying death and succeeding, time and again. Nearly dying is the most intense way of feeling alive. Actually feeling life. Understanding it better. The rest of us just ask why. Why push yourself to get to the top of Mount Everest when the journey is, in every sense, paved with dead bodies? What would drive someone to throw themselves from a high cliff in Mexico when the slightest misjudgment could mean that the waves below hurled them straight back into the cliff face?"

"Johanne," Adam tried and put up his hand.

"They say it gives them the feeling of being alive." She answered her own questions.

She still didn't look at him. Instead she grabbed Kristiane's rag doll from the windowsill. She pulled to it to her by the leg and then hugged it, long and hard.

"Johanne," he tried again.

"I just don't understand it," she whispered, "but that's the explanation they give. That's what they say when it's all over and they're smiling at the camera, at their friends. They stick their middle fingers up at life. And laugh. And then they go and do it all over again. And again. And again . . ."

This time he got up and went over to her. Pulled the doll from her hands and put his arms around her. He didn't know if she was crying, so he kept still.

"As if life isn't valuable enough in itself," she mumbled into his chest. "As if human triviality is not bad enough. As if loving someone, having children, getting old isn't frightening enough."

She pushed him away. He didn't want to let go, but she was determined and forced him to. But she did look him straight in the eye when she continued.

"We can see it everywhere, Adam. More and more, new variations all the time. Jackass stunts for young people. They set themselves alight, dive from a roof on a bike. People are bored. *People are bored to death!*"

She was nearly screaming and slapped him on the chest. Her voice trembled.

"Did you know that some people play a kind of Russian roulette with HIV? Others heighten their orgasm through strangulation? And sometimes they die before they come. Die!"

She was laughing now, hysterically. She went over to the island and managed to perch on a stool. She covered her face with her hands.

"Death is the only real news for people today," she said. "I can't remember who said that, but it's true. Death is extremely titillating, as it is the only thing we will never understand. It's the only thing we know nothing about."

"So what you're saying," Adam tried to bring her back to day-to-day reality, "is that we're talking about a killer who's . . . bored?"

"Yes. His motive has nothing to do with whom he kills but rather that they are killed."

"Johanne . . ."

"It has to be," she insisted. "Killing someone is the most extreme of all extreme actions you can take. The murderer . . . It fits, Adam. It fits with the theory that he didn't kill Fiona Helle. He was just sitting there. Somewhere. Bored. Then Mats Bohus killed his mother, in a grotesque way, and everyone went crazy. The murder had all the right ingredients: a famous victim, the characteristics of ritual, strong symbolism. The reaction was deafening. I can hardly imagine anything more stimulating, a more exciting trigger than that murder. Especially as it had so many similarities to the first murder in another series, in another story about—"

"Now listen to what you're saying," Adam insisted. He had raised his voice now. "If we summarize your profile, we've got the following. A"—with his right index finger, he pointed to his left thumb—"The murderer knows everything that's worth knowing about crime. B: At some point or another, he heard Warren's lecture about proportional retribution."

"Or heard about it," corrected Johanne.

"Which means that he may not necessarily be Norwegian," Adam added and grimaced. "Third: Killing for this person is a kind of hobby, a way to relieve a boring, humdrum life. He chooses—"

"his victims by apparently random criteria," Johanne concluded. Her cheeks were flushed, and her eyes were shiny. "At least to begin with. He has only one criterion. The person has to be famous. He wants maximum effect. It's the thrill he's after. He's playing, Adam."

"And then we're back to square one," he said and rubbed his cheek in resignation. "Vegard Krogh was not famous."

"He was famous enough," she corrected him with great intensity. "There was enough commotion about his death, for goodness sake! Especially as he was number three in a series of celebrity murders. The murderer knew that. He knew that Vegard Krogh was sufficiently well known, and that was why he decided to forgo . . . randomization!"

"What?"

"Only a computer can achieve a completely random selection, Adam. We humans, we let ourselves be swayed, consciously or subconsciously. Vegard Krogh was chosen because he . . ."

Once again the look in her eyes became distant and dark. She pulled at a tangle of hair and chewed it. The commotion downstairs had died down a while ago. The children had been sent out to play in the rain. Adam could hear them in the garden.

"The murderer wanted him dead," she said slowly. "The motive was first and foremost the game. The challenge of killing someone and getting away with it. But the murderer gave in to temptation this time. By choosing someone he wanted to get even with."

"Everyone wanted to get even with Vegard," Adam groaned. "And your profile doesn't match any of the people we've come across, spoken to, or in any way suspected in connection with this case. And do you have any idea how many people that is? Do you know how many statements we've taken?"

"A lot, I guess."

"Several hundred! Nearly a thousand statements. And not one of them, not a single witness, matches your description of . . . What shall we do? Where is he, what needs to be—"

"He won't stop. Not yet. I guess we just have to wait."

"Wait for what?"

"For—"

"The world's best mommy," shouted Kristiane.

She had her raincoat on, and her boots were soaking. They squelched as she ran over the floor and threw herself into her mother's lap. Jack was in hot pursuit. He stopped in the middle of the floor, between the living room and open kitchen, and shook himself. A shower of water sprayed around him. Sand and fine gravel pattered down on to the parquet.

"The best dog in the world," Kristiane said. "The best Kristiane. And Daddy. And Adam. And house. And—"

"Afternoon all! The door was open, so I just came up. Is her bag ready?"

Isak laughed and patted the eager, happy dog.

"I've been sailing," he said, "so I'm just as wet as Kristiane. Great weather for sailing though! Cold as hell. Good wind. But then it started to rain. Shame. Come on then, princess! We're going go-carting today! Won't that be fun!"

He tracked his dirty shoes across the floor. Picked up the fire engine, gave a big smile, and put it in his pocket.

"Bye, Mommy! Bye, Adam!"

The girl danced after her father. Adam and Johanne sat in silence and listened to them rummaging around in her room. He put his hand on her thigh when she wanted to go in and

·help. Five minutes later, they heard Isak's Audi TT accelerate powerfully down Haugesvei.

"I bet he forgot her pajamas and toothbrush," Johanne said and tried to ignore Adam's exasperated sigh when he answered.

"He can buy a toothbrush at any gas station, Johanne. And she can sleep in a T-shirt. Isak remembered Sulamit, and that's what's most important. Don't make such—"

She got up suddenly and went to the bathroom.

"I'm boring," she thought to herself and started to load the washing machine. "I'm unexciting and unsophisticated. I know. I'm responsible and very rarely spontaneous. I'm boring. But I certainly never get *bored*."

The man sitting in the chair with a target pinned to his breast pocket with a safety pin was an unpopular star. His long hair was tied back in a ponytail. He had a widow's peak that gave him a diabolical look. There was something primitive about the way his brows jutted out over his eyes; his eyebrows met in the middle, looking like a fat, hairy caterpillar was crawling across his face. His nose was straight, narrow, and sophisticated. His lips were full. An unbecoming goatee sprouted on his chin below his mouth. His tongue was just visible between his eye teeth, which had been filed into points. The corners of his mouth turned down in an unattractive grimace. Above his head, a zinc bucket was attached to the wall with a nail.

Håvard Stefansen was a professional biathlete. His greatest achievement as an adult to date was two individual silver medals in the world championships. He had won three world cup titles last season. And as he was only twenty-four, he was one of Norway's great hopes for the Winter Olympics in Turin in 2006.

As long as he could control himself, the national team coach had publicly warned him only six weeks ago.

During the course of his first two seasons in the senior national team, Håvard Stefansen had been sent home from meets and competitions four times. He was an arrogant winner and an appalling loser. He usually openly slandered his competitors when he lost a race. He accused them of taking drugs. They cheated. He treated foreigners and his own teammates with contempt. Håvard Stefansen was rude and egocentric, and no one wanted to share a room with him. Which didn't seem to bother him.

The public didn't like him either, and he had never had personal sponsors. In his chosen sport, boasting and menacing tattoos were not common. When he raced, he was often met with boos or silence, and in some weird way, he seemed to get a kick out of that. His speed increased, and his shooting improved every month, yet he did nothing to change his terrible reputation.

Now it was too late.

It was the night of March 2, and the bull's-eye on the target over his heart had been hit. His eyes were glassy. When Adam Stubo leaned over the body, he thought he saw slight bruising on the eyelids, as if someone had forced them open.

"He wasn't killed in here," said an officer from the Oslo police. His red hair was poking out from under the paper cap. "That seems fairly clear. He was stabbed in the back with a knife. While he was asleep, we assume. No indications of a struggle, but the bed is full of blood. The footprints are obvious out here. It looks like his clothes were just thrown on. We think he was killed in his sleep and then dragged out here, dressed, and arranged on the chair."

"The bullet hole," Adam muttered. He felt queasy.

"Lead pellet, sir," the other replied. "He was shot with an air rifle. This is some kind of indoor shooting range." He pointed to the target covering the top of the bucket. "For air guns only, of course. The pellets are caught in the bucket. Air rifles only make a 'pff' sound, which explains why no one heard anything. If the guy was alive when he was shot, it would presumably have hurt like hell, but nothing more. That, on the other hand . . ."

The policeman, who had just introduced himself as Erik Henriksen, pointed to Håvard Stefansen's right hand. It was half open and resting on his groin. His index finger was missing. Only a ragged stump remained.

"His trigger finger," Henriksen said. "And if you look over here . . ."

He went to the other end of the corridor, his paper overalls rustling as he moved. An air rifle was attached to a sawhorse with tape and rope. The barrel of the gun was balanced on a slanting broom handle. Håvard Stefansen's finger was on the trigger of the gun, which was aimed at his heart. The finger was blue, and the nail was slightly too long.

"I have to leave," Adam said. "I'm sorry, I just have to . . ."

"Even if this is our case," Erik Henriksen said, "I thought it would be best if you guys had a look. It's suspiciously like—"

"A sports celebrity," Adam thought desperately. "That's what we were waiting for. And I couldn't do anything. Couldn't guard every sports celebrity in the country. Couldn't raise the alarm. It would only have caused panic. And I couldn't know anything for certain. Johanne believed and thought and felt, but we couldn't be sure. What could I have done? What should I do?"

"How did the killer get in?" Adam forced himself to ask, determined to stick it out. "Break in? Window?"

"We're on the fifth floor," Henriksen pointed out with a hint of irritation. This NCIS guy was certainly not living up to his reputation. "But take a look at this."

Although the apartment was in an old building, the front door looked new and had a solid, modern lock. Henriksen used his pen as a pointer.

"Old trick, really. A small piece of wood has been pushed into the keyhole and here . . ."

The pen moved over the spring bolt.

"It's stuck," he said. "Matches, presumably."

"God," Adam mumbled. "A simple old con trick."

"At the moment, we're assuming that the door was open when Håvard Stefansen was at home and awake. Somebody has tampered with the lock. The apartment is big enough for someone to go about their business out here while he was eating, for example. And as this is the top floor, there's less risk of being seen."

He put his pen back in the breast pocket of the white overalls.

"It's uncertain whether Håvard Stefansen even tried to lock the door before he went to bed. A tough guy like him, with all these weapons in the house, maybe he wasn't that bothered. But if he tried, it would have been difficult."

"He's getting bolder," Adam managed to think to himself through his thumping headache. He narrowed his eyes. "He's more and more daring. Has to have more. Like climbers who always have to go higher, steeper, to live dangerously. He's getting there now. This victim must have been physically more powerful than him. But he knew that and took precautions. Killed Håvard Stefansen when he was asleep. A simple ambush. No sophisticated tricks. It didn't matter to him. It's us who are supposed to get the message. The outside world. Not the victim. He wants us to be shocked by this tableau: the marksman aiming at his own heart of steel. It's us he wants to provoke. Us. Me?"

"The guy slept with a ponytail?" Adam asked, just to have something to say.

"Looks cool, dunnit!" Detective Sergeant Henriksen shrugged and added, "Maybe the killer put his hair in a ponytail to make him look . . . more like himself, kind of thing. Make the illusion stronger. And he succeeded, didn't he? Fu—"

He stopped swearing just in time. Perhaps out of respect to the dead. A colleague stuck his head around the door from the stairs.

"Hi," he whispered. "Erik, the woman's here. The one who called us. She found the body."

Erik Henriksen nodded and raised his hand to signal that he would be there in a minute.

"Have you seen enough?" he asked.

"More than enough," Adam nodded and followed him out of the apartment.

A woman was standing on the landing. She was solid, with dark hair that fell in big, untidy curls. Her skin looked healthy and weatherworn. It was difficult to determine her age. She was wearing jeans and a chunky green sweater. The stair lighting reflected in her small glasses, which made it hard to see her eyes. Adam thought there was something familiar about her.

"This is Wencke Berger," said the policeman who had just called them. "She lives downstairs. Was going up into the loft to put away some suitcases. The door was open, so she—"

"I rang the bell," she took over. "When there was no answer, I took the liberty of going in. I guess you know already what I found. I called the police immediately."

"Wencke Berger," Erik Henriksen said and took off his comical paper cap. "Wencke Berger, the crime writer?"

She gave an inscrutable smile and nodded.

Not to Henriksen, who had asked the question. Nor was the smile intended for the uniformed policeman, who looked as if he was about to pull out a piece of paper and ask for an autograph.

It was Adam she was looking at. It was him she turned to, held out her hand, and said, "Adam Stubo, isn't it? A pleasure to meet you, finally."

Her handshake was firm, almost hard. Her hand was big and broad, and the skin was unusually warm. He let go quickly, as if he had burned himself.

SIXTEEN

***

The celebrity killer was a monster.

The press had calmed down when Fiona Helle's murderer turned out to be a patient in a psychiatric hospital with a motive that most people could understand. For a while it seemed that the journalists had caught on to the idea that these might be copycat murders. That it perhaps wasn't the work of a serial murderer, but rather a frightening constellation of individual, gruesome murders. When Rudolf Fjord chose to take his own life, the press had been surprisingly subdued, giving the tragic death sober coverage.

When Håvard Stefansen was found dead, sitting on a chair as a target in his own improvised shooting range, people in Norway went crazy.

Psychologists were pulled back into the picture. Along with private detectives and foreign police chiefs, researchers and crime analysts. Experts discussed and explained in column after column and on all the channels. Within twenty-four hours, the serial murderer was back on everyone's lips. He was a monster. A twisted psychopath. Over the course of a few days, the celebrity murderer took on mythical proportions, with features akin to those found only in dark, gothic tales.

The royal family went abroad, and the palace couldn't say when they were likely to return. Rumor had it that security at the Storting had been reinforced, but the head of security, tense and serious, refused to comment. Opening nights at the theater were cancelled. Planned concerts were shelved. A high-profile marriage between a well-known politician and a business tycoon was stopped three days before the wedding. It was postponed until the autumn, explained the somber bridegroom as he assured everyone that he and the bride were still madly in love.

Even ordinary people, most of whom had never had their name in the papers or their photo printed in a glossy magazine, threw away movie tickets and decided not to go out that weekend after all. A mixture of shock and curiosity, fear and tension, malice and genuine despair made people stick to those they knew.

It was safest.

Johanne Vik and Adam Stubo were also at home. It was now Thursday, March 4, and nearly half past eight in the evening. Ragnhild was asleep. The TV was on, with the sound turned down. Neither of them was watching.

They had barely spoken to each other for two days. Both of them carried a fear that was too great to share with the other. The murderer had chosen an athlete this time. Only one case remained from Warren Scifford's lecture on proportional retribution, and Johanne and Adam conversed with a stiff and false friendliness. Life in the semidetached house in Tåsen was hectic, as everyday activities helped to disguise the fear.

For a while, at least.

Adam was putting up shelves in the bathroom. They had been stored in the cabinet for six months now. Johanne expected to hear Ragnhild crying at any minute; his hammering could wake the dead. But she couldn't face talking to him. She sat on the sofa and turned the pages of a book. It was impossible to read.

"Tonight's evening news has been extended by an hour," said a very faint voice on the TV.

Johanne found the remote control. The voice got louder. The opening music and graphics rolled.

The host was dressed in black, as if he was going to a funeral. He didn't smile as he usually did at the start of the program. Johanne couldn't remember ever having seen the long-serving anchorman wear a tie.

The chief of police was also dressed for the occasion. The already slim woman had lost a lot of weight over the past few weeks, and her uniform hung off her. She sat straight and tense in her chair, as if on duty. For once she had problems giving a clear answer to the questions she was asked.

"Adam," Johanne called. "You should come and see this."

Angry hammering from the bathroom.

"Adam!"

She went to get him. He was down on all fours, trying to separate two shelves.

"God damn it," he said tersely. "These damned instructions are all wrong."

"There's a special program about your case," Johanne told him.

"It's not my case. I don't own it."

"Don't be silly. Come on. Come and watch it. The shelves won't run away."

He put the hammer down.

"Look," he said, ashamed, and pointed at the floor. "I smashed one of the tiles. Sorry. I didn't think—"

"Come on," she said curtly and went back into the living room.

". . . we do of course have a number of leads in this case," said the chief of police on the screen. "Or cases, I should perhaps say. However, they are not explicit, and it will take some time to figure this out. We're looking at a complex web of events."

"Leads," Adam muttered. He had followed Johanne into the living room and slumped down on the other sofa. "Show me them, then. Show me your leads!"

He wiped his face with a corner of his shirt and grabbed a lukewarm can of beer from the table.

"Can you understand that people are worried?" asked the anchorman as he leaned forward and opened his arms in despair. "Terrified! Following four horrific murders? And the investigation seems to have come to a complete standstill?"

"I must correct you there," the chief of police said and then coughed into her hand. "We're talking about three cases. The murder of Fiona Helle has been solved, according to the police and the authorities. Some investigation still needs to be carried out, but a charge will be made shortly—"

"Three cases," the anchorman interrupted. "Okay. And what leads do you have for those three cases?"

"I'm sure you understand that I can't give out any more details about an ongoing investigation. The only thing I can say this evening is that we are drawing on considerable resources—"

"Understand!" the host exclaimed. "You ask for our understanding when you seem to have no answers at all. People are barricading themselves in their homes, and . . ."

"He's frightened," Adam said and drank the dregs of the flat beer. "He never gets angry. Isn't it more his style to wheedle and entice? To smile and let people make a fool of themselves?"

Johanne responded by turning up the volume even more.

"He's terrified," Adam muttered. "Him and a couple of thousand other Norwegians who live vicariously through that box." He pointed at the TV with the empty can.

"Shh."

"Come over here."

"What?"

"Can't you come over here and sit next me?"

"I . . ."

"Please."

The chief of police was finally allowed to go. While they swapped interviewees in the studio, they tried to run a report from the building where Håvard Stefansen had been murdered two days earlier. The film got stuck. The panning shot from the entrance to a window on the fifth floor froze in midswing and became an unfocused still of a woman peering out from behind a curtain on the third floor with a shocked expression. The sound was fuzzy. Something beeped. Suddenly the anchorman was back on the screen.

"We apologize for the technical problems," he coughed. "But now I think we're—"

"We'll always be lovers," murmured Adam as he smelled her hair; she had curled up beside him and pulled a blanket over them both.

"Maybe," she said and stroked his arm. "As long as you promise never to do anymore DIY."

"Welcome to the program, Wencke Berger."

"What?" Adam sat up.

"Shh!"

"Thank you," said Wencke Berger without a flicker of a smile.

"You are the author of no less than seventeen crime novels," the anchorman introduced her. "All of which are about serial killers. You are considered to be something of an expert in the field and have gained widespread recognition for your thorough preparation and extensive research. Even within the police, as we found out today. Now, you were originally a lawyer, right?"

"Yes, that's right," she replied, still serious. "But there's not much of the lawyer left in me now. I've been writing novels since 1985."

"We are particularly pleased to welcome you to the program tonight, as it has actually been twelve years since you gave an interview here in Norway. But it is, of course, the current tragic circumstances that have brought you here. All the same, I would like to start by asking a somewhat lighthearted question: how many people have you killed over the years?"

He leaned forward in anticipation, as if he expected her to share a huge secret.

"I don't know anymore," she said and smiled. Her teeth were unusually white and even for a woman who must be in her midforties. "I've lost count. After all, quality is more important than quantity, even in my field. I concentrate on the details, not the numbers. I get my . . . pleasure from finding original twists, if you like."

She pushed her bangs away from her forehead, but they fell back immediately.

Johanne managed to free herself from Adam's arms. He was about to strangle her. He had just grabbed the *Dagbladet* paper that was lying on the table. He looked at something and then dropped it on the floor. She turned around toward him and asked,

"What is it?"

. . . *and you found the most recent victim,* the TV droned, . . . *who was your nearest neighbor. In your view, as an expert, what might lie behind . . .*

"What's wrong, darling?"

. . . *the wish to be seen as something other than . . .*

"Adam!"

His skin was sweaty. Gray.

"Adam," she screamed and fell off the sofa. "What's wrong with you?"

. . . more like cases from other countries. Not just the United States, but also the United Kingdom and in Germany we know . . .

Johanne lifted her hand. Smacked him. The sound of her palm against his cheek made him look up at last.

"It's her," he said.

. . . be cautious about jumping to conclusions about . . .

"It's her," he repeated. "That woman."

"What's wrong, Adam?" Johanne screamed. "I thought you were having a heart attack! I've told you a thousand times that you need to lose weight and cut out sugar and—"

. . . bearing in mind that I've been abroad for the past few months and only followed the case on the Internet and in the occasional newspaper, I would say that . . .

"Have you gone insane?" Johanne exclaimed. "Have you gone stark raving mad? Why would—"

He was still pointing at the TV screen. The color was returning to his face. His breathing had slowed. Johanne turned slowly back to the TV.

Wencke Berger wore frameless glasses. The reflection of the sharp lights in the studio made it hard to see her eyes. Her suit was a touch too tight, as if she had bought it in the hope of losing some weight. There was a small brooch on the collar. A thin gold chain shone around her neck, and she had good color for the time of year.

"I don't hold out much hope of that," she answered to a question that Johanne had not heard. "The police don't seem to have a clue, so I find it hard to imagine that the likelihood of the murders being solved is anything but slim."

"Do you really believe that?" the anchorman asked with a gesture that invited a full reply.

"I don't understand," Johanne said and turned around again to try to get Adam's attention.

"Be quiet," he said. "Let me hear what she has to say!"

"Well, I'm afraid that's about all we have time for," the anchorman said. "But in the light of the recent tragic events, I must ask in closing whether you ever get tired of it. Of thinking up murders and crimes for entertainment."

Wencke Berger straightened her glasses. Her nose seemed too small for her broad face, and her glasses kept threatening to fall off.

"Yes," she admitted. "I do get tired of it. Sick and tired of it, sometimes. But writing crime is the only thing I can do. I'm getting older and"—she waved a stubby finger and looked into the camera. Suddenly her eyes were visible. They were brown and sparkled with a smile that made her cheeks split into two deep dimples—"obviously the pay is fantastic, which helps."

"Wencke Berger, thank you very much—"

Click.

Johanne put down the remote control.

"What do you mean?" she whispered. "You scared me so badly, Adam. I thought you were about to die."

"It's Wencke Berger. She killed Victoria Heinerback," he said, squeezing the beer can with both hands. "She killed Vegard Krogh. And she killed her neighbor, Håvard Stefansen. She's the celebrity killer. She has to be."

Johanne sank down onto the coffee table. The house was quiet. Not a sound could be heard from outside. The neighbors downstairs were away. Johanne and Adam were alone, and a light was turned off in the house across the road.

Suddenly a sound could be heard from the children's room: the piercing, vulnerable cry of a six-week-old baby.

Wencke Berger walked slowly through the swinging doors at the NRK TV studio. It was a chilly March evening with a cutting wind. When she looked up, she saw Venus twinkling against a patch of deep blue sky between moving dark clouds. She smiled at the journalists and let the photographers take yet more pictures before getting into the taxi and telling the driver her address.

Everything was different now. The difference was greater than she had ever hoped for. She'd noticed it at Gardemoen Airport the previous Friday, when she, with a broad smile, thanked the flight attendant for a pleasant trip. Whereas before she used to walk with a hunched back and heavy steps, she now stood up straight. She sauntered down the endless corridors with a duty-free bag swinging from her hand. She looked up and out. Noticed all the details of the beautiful building, the enormous lime wood beams and the color play of the artwork by the stairs down to the arrival hall. She waited patiently for her luggage and chatted with a red-haired child who poked her laptop with curiosity. She smiled at the child's father and straightened the lapel of the new Armani coat she had bought at Galeries Lafayette in Nice, which made her look as new as she actually felt.

She was strong.

And supremely confident.

She had made a decision many years ago when she delivered her first manuscript and discovered that this was something she could do. She would become an expert in crime. A specialist in murder. Literary critics were an unreliable tribe. The reasoning of the media was predictable and petty: they would build you up only to pull you down. Her editor had warned her about it, way back then. Looked at her with indescribably sad eyes, as if by making her debut as a crime writer, Wencke Berger had stepped into purgatory. And so she decided then and there, she would never read a review.

And she would never, ever make a mistake.

She would devise perfect plots. She would never misjudge the effect of a weapon. She would learn all there was to know about human anatomy, about stab wounds and punches, about bullet wounds and poison. Investigations and tactics. Chemistry, biology, psychology. She would build up an understanding of the business of crime, from the big, powerful organizations down to the pathetic junkies who sat at the very bottom of the ladder, holding out a hand: *Can you spare any change?*

She hadn't managed to keep the first promise.

She read the reviews as soon as they came out.

But no one could say that Wencke Berger didn't know what she was talking about.

And no one did.

She had studied and read constantly since 1985. Done field studies. Traveled. Observed and researched. And eventually she realized that theory could never surpass practice. She had to look to real life. The fictional universe wasn't concrete enough. Real life was full of details and unexpected turns. Just sitting at a desk, it was hard to imagine the multitude of seemingly insignificant, trivial events that could in fact be decisive in a murder case.

She started to catalog real people.

Her archive dated back to 1995. She had needed a principal of a children's home and a policeman with a threadbare reputation for a book she was going to write. She was shocked at how easy it was to find them. Surveillance was boring, naturally, with hours of waiting and unimportant observations. Her notes were dry and dispassionate.

But it was easier to write.

The reviews were positive. Book number eight was received with considerable enthusiasm, as her first book had been. A couple of critics remarked that Wencke Berger was fresher than she had been for a long time, almost revitalized.

They were wrong.

She was more bored than ever. She lived in a parallel world. She cataloged other people's lives without ever taking part in them. Her archive grew. She bought a steel cabinet, a fireproof device that was installed in the bedroom.

Sometimes she would sit in bed at night and read through a file. Often she got irritated. People led such similar lives. Work and children, infidelity and drink. There were renovation projects and divorces, financial problems and tag sales for the football team. Whether they were politicians or dentists, rich or on welfare, men or women, the people she observed were all so damn similar.

"I am unique," she thought to herself and settled back in the comfortable taxi seat. "And now they can see me. Finally I'm being seen for what I am. An extraordinary expert. Not someone who publishes a book like handing in an exam every autumn, for bitchy comments. I can. I know. I do.

"He saw me. He was frightened. I could tell, the way he withdrew his hand and looked away. They see me now, but not like I see them. Not the way I see her. Her file is fat. It's the biggest file I have. I have watched her for a long time, and I know her.

"They see me now, and there's nothing they can do."

"Take a look at this."

Adam held up page five of that day's edition of *Dagbladet* for her to see. He was still pale, but he didn't look fatally ill anymore.

"Wencke Berger," said Johanne. She was walking around the room with Ragnhild over her shoulder. "And?"

"Look at the pin. On her lapel."

She carefully passed the baby over to him, took the newspaper, and went a few steps closer to the lamp.

"It all fits," he said, rocking Ragnhild. "Too much of your profile fits. Wencke Berger really does have crime as her profession. An internationally acclaimed crime writer! Superior to most when it comes to serial killers. Eccentric and difficult, if we're to believe the portraits they've managed to put together, even though she doesn't speak to Norwegian journalists. Until now, that is. Something must have changed. She's been a loner for a long time. Just like you said. Just how you put it in your profile."

Ragnhild's eyes were heavy. He stroked her forehead and said, "Look at her pin."

The picture in *Dagbladet* was not particularly flattering. Wencke Berger was just about to say something: her mouth was open, and her eyes were wide behind her glasses, which were perched on the end of her snub nose. But the outlines were sharp. The pin on the author's left lapel was clear.

"She knew who I was," he said to no one in particular. "It was me she was interested in."

"This is worse than you think."

"Worse—"

"Yes."

"What do you mean?"

She went into the bedroom without answering. He heard her rummaging around in the big chest of drawers. A cabinet door banged. The steps went further, into the closet, he guessed.

"Look."

She had found what she was looking for. She took Ragnhild from him and put her down on her back under a baby gym on the floor. She gurgled and reached for the colorful figures. Johanne handed him the binder she'd been looking for. It was white, with a big circular logo on the front.

"The FBI logo," he said and wrinkled his brow. "Of course I recognize it. I've got a poster of it in my office. That's my point, that's why I . . ."

He pointed to the photograph in *Dagbladet*.

"Yes," she said, "but that's why it's worse than you think."

She sat down beside him on the edge of the sofa.

"Americans love their symbols," she said and straightened her glasses. "The flag. The Pledge of Allegiance. Their monuments. Nothing is arbitrary. This blue"—she pointed to the emblem's background color—"symbolizes justice, along with the scales in the top center of the emblem. The circle contains thirteen stars to represent the thirteen original American states. The red and white stripes here are from the flag. Red stands for courage and strength. White for purity, light, truth, and peace."

"They obviously think that courage and strength are more important than truth and peace," Adam observed. "I think there are more red stripes than white."

Johanne couldn't bring herself to smile.

"It's the same in the Star-Spangled Banner," she said. "One red stripe more than white. The toothed edge around the emblem symbolizes the challenges the FBI faces and the organization's strength."

Ragnhild wriggled and kicked. The wooden figures banged against each other. Adam scratched his neck and mumbled, "Impressive, but I don't see what you're getting at."

"You see these two branches?"

She ran her finger along some branches on each side of the innermost red and white shield.

"Laurels," she told him. "With a magnifying glass, you can

count exactly forty-six leaves, the number of states in the U.S. in 1908, when the FBI was founded."

"I'm still very impressed," Adam said. "But—"

"Now look at this."

She held the newspaper photograph of Wencke Berger up to the light.

"Her pin. The laurels. You see?"

"They're not laurels." He narrowed his eyes.

"No," she confirmed.

"Are they feathers?" he asked.

"Yes."

"Feathers instead of laurels. Why?"

"They're eagle feathers," she told him.

"Eagle feathers?"

"Who used eagle feathers?"

"The native Indians."

"Chieftains."

"Chieftains," he repeated lamely, confused.

Johanne walked over to Ragnhild. She gently lifted her up and put her across her shoulder. She breathed in the scent of soap and poo. A sludgy brown stain was spreading over the baby's romper leg. She held her tight.

"The Chief," she said. "Warren Scifford. A group of students got those pins made. A hundred or so. All hell broke loose when it was discovered. You don't mess with the FBI heraldry. The pins became quite valuable after a while. People wore them on the inside of their jacket collars. A sort of membership badge, a sign that you were in the inner circle. One of Warren's disciples. He . . . he loved it, of course. Didn't want to get involved with it, but . . . loved it."

"So that means that —"

"That means that Wencke Berger knows Warren in some

way or another. She has either met him, heard him, or spoken to someone who knows him."

"Which in turn means—"

"That she wants us to see her," Johanne said.

"What?"

"She's giving us an invitation. She's challenging us. She pops up on TV after being silent for twelve years. She lets herself be photographed. She talks. She kills her neighbor and calls the police. She doesn't want to hide anymore. She's been hiding for years and found it unbearable. She wants to be in the limelight, not out of it. And she's wearing that pin in the hope that she'll be recognized. By us. In the hope that we'll understand. She's playing with us."

"Us? The two of us?"

Johanne didn't answer. She made a face at the increasingly pungent smell and disappeared into the bathroom. He followed.

"What do you mean?" he asked in a subdued voice.

She still didn't want to answer. She turned on the water and bent down to pick up a cloth, keeping one hand on Ragnhild's stomach where she lay on the changing table. Her poo was green and runny, and Adam held his nose.

"Wasn't there a book that disappeared?" she asked.

"A book?"

"Don't hold your nose, Adam, it's your daughter."

She let the water run over Ragnhild's bottom and continued, "Yes, Trond Arnesen. He said a book was missing. And a watch. The watch was found, but was the book found? Pass me the cream."

He rummaged around in the basket by the sink.

"There was a book," he said slowly and stopped. He had a tube of zinc cream in one hand and a clean diaper in the other. "That's right. I was preoccupied with the watch for a while. I'd forgotten about the book. Completely. Especially once Trond found his damned watch. The book seemed pointless. It was a crime novel, I think, a book that Trond claimed had been lying on his bedside table, but—"

"Wencke Berger," she said. "Wencke Berger's latest novel."

Her hands were unusually swift, almost impatient as she slid the diaper under the baby and then taped it on.

"It was her first murder," she said just as fast. "She was careful. Victoria Heinerback's house was isolated, and she was on her own that night. Anyone who visited her Web site knew that. Not a dangerous murder. Almost risk-free, if you knew what you were doing. Wencke Berger knows what she's doing. So she took the book. It was a clever signature, but no one got it. No one understood what it meant. And the next time . . ."

The baby resisted. Johanne couldn't get her right arm into her sleeve, and Ragnhild started to cry.

"Here, let me do it," Adam murmured and took over.

Johanne sat down on the toilet seat with her elbows on her knees and her chin cupped in her hands.

"The next time she pushed it a bit more. Went further."

Johanne seemed to be afraid of her own reasoning. Her voice was low, and she was speaking more slowly. She sat up straight and chewed her thumb. Adam dressed Ragnhild in clean pajamas. She made contented noises when he laid her on her stomach over his lower arm and held her to his body.

"The second time," Johanne continued without making any sign of getting up. "The second time she chose Vegard Krogh. Whom she hated. Presumably she was mad at him. He had mocked her for years. Ridiculed everything she stood for. Wencke Berger knew that Vegard Krogh's"—she hit her forehead with her hand—"ridiculous campaign," she groaned, "would give a tiny nudge in her direction. Not too obvious. Definitely not. He had lots of enemies. But still . . ."

Finally she got up. A fleeting smile crossed her face as she kissed the baby's head.

"Then she went the whole way. Killed her neighbor, called the police. Was pulled into the investigation. She's in the spotlight, Adam. She is standing there, floodlit. In the center of attention. And she's loving it. She's thumbing her nose at us, and she knows she's won."

"Won? She hasn't won yet! Now that we know what—"

She put her finger to her mouth and hushed him. Then she gently stroked Ragnhild's neck.

"She's asleep," she whispered. "Can you put her down?"

She went back into the living room. She took a bottle of wine out from the corner cabinet and opened it. Took the most beautiful glass she owned, a crystal glass from her grandparents' summer house. She'd had four of them originally, big glasses with fine chased metal rings and thin gold leaf around the rims. Three had been broken. And this one was never used. She took it out a couple of times a month. Dusted it, looked at the pattern in the light from the lamp. It reminded her of long summers and saltwater, of her grandfather on the terrace with a glass of white wine, his nose red from sun and happiness, with cake crumbs in his beard. He used to let her have a taste. She wet her tongue and made a face, then spat it out. He always laughed and gave her some Fanta instead, even if it wasn't Saturday.

She poured out the wine and watched it swirl around the glass.

"What do you mean, she's won?" Adam asked.

"Is she asleep?"

He nodded and looked surprised when he saw which glass she had chosen. He went out into the kitchen to get another glass and helped himself.

"What do you mean?" he repeated. "Now we know it's her. Now we know where to look. In a way—"

"You won't manage it," she said and took a drink.

"What do you mean?"

His glass stood untouched on the dining table. Johanne turned to face the window. The garden looked sad, with some patches of snow left on the yellow, sodden lawn. The streetlights in Haugesvei had finally gotten new bulbs. A man in a yellow raincoat was out walking his dog. It wasn't on a leash and rushed from side to side on the road, sniffing the ground. It stopped by Johanne's old Golf and cocked its leg. It stood there for a long time before following its master, tail wagging.

"She was in France," she said, "when Victoria Heinerback was killed. And when Vegard Krogh was murdered in the small forest in Asker. You seem to have forgotten that."

"Of course I haven't," he said, a touch irritated. "But both you and I know that she can't have been there. Unless she has an accomplice, a—"

"Wencke Berger doesn't have an accomplice. She's a loner. She kills in order to feel alive, to prove her strength. To . . . grow. To show how smart . . . how superior she is."

"Make up your mind," he said. "If she was in France, she can't have killed them. What do you actually mean?"

"Of course she wasn't there. Not all the time, at least. She must have traveled up and down in some way or another. We can speculate about how she succeeded. We can make up theories and reconstructions. But the only thing that is certain is that we will never find out."

"I don't know how you can say that," he said and put his arm around her. "What makes you so sure? How can you—"

"Adam," she interrupted, and looked up into his face.

His eyes were so clear. His eyebrows were growing long and looked like an old man's pointy, optimistic brows. His skin was clear and smooth. His broad mouth was half open, and she could feel his breath on hers; wine and a taint of garlic. She put her finger on the deep cleft in his chin.

"I've never said this before," she whispered. "And I hope I will never have reason to say it again. I am a profiler. Warren used to say that I was profiler by nature. That it was something I could never run away from."

She laughed quietly and stroked her finger over his lips.

"For years I've tried to forget it. Do you remember how reluctant I was that spring four years ago? When all those children were abducted and you wanted . . ."

She wasn't whispering anymore. He bit her fingertip gently.

"I was working on my research. Digging deeper. I had more than enough with Kristiane and . . . then you came along. Our life here and Ragnhild. I don't want anything else. Why do you think I've sat here night after night, working on a murder case that, strictly speaking, has nothing to do with me?"

"Because you're compelled to," he said, his eyes not leaving hers.

"Because I'm compelled to," she nodded. "And I'm telling you this because I have to: Wencke Berger has won. In all these weeks, you haven't found one, not one piece of evidence that is linked to her. Nothing. She doesn't want to be caught. She wants to be seen but not caught."

"But I still have to try," Adam said. It sounded more like a question, as if he needed her blessing.

"Yes, you still have to try," she confirmed. "And the only hope you have is to find a way of proving that she was at the scene of the crime. Prove that she wasn't in France."

"But you will never manage it," she thought to herself again, but she didn't repeat it out loud. Instead she drank the rest of her wine and said, "The children can't stay here. Wencke Berger still has one case left. We have to move the children."

And with that, she went to call her mother, even though it was nearly midnight.

"So what you're saying," the head of the NCIS said as he scratched his ear with his pinkie, "is that the whole investigation should be reorganized on the basis of a missing crime novel and a brooch? A goddamn brooch?"

"A pin," corrected Adam. "It's a pin."

The head of the NCIS was seriously overweight. His stomach bulged over his belt like a sack of potatoes. His shirt was stretched over his navel. He had stayed silent while Lars Kirkeland and Adam Stubo gave their reports. Even when the rest of the small gathering had discussed the case for more than half an hour, the boss had not said a word. Only his small, plump fingers had given him away as they rapped impatiently on the table whenever anyone spoke for more than twenty seconds.

His double chin was quivering in anger. He got up with great difficulty and went to the flip chart, where the name Wencke Berger was written in red letters under a timeline with three dates. He stopped and snorted three times. Adam was unsure whether it was with scorn or whether he had breathing difficulties. He smoothed down his comb-over with his right hand before tearing off the sheet and scrunching it up.

"Let me put it this way," he said and turned his small, beady eyes on Adam. "You are one of my most valued colleagues. That is why I've sat here for more than an hour listening to this"—he pulled at his mustache, which curled cheerfully at the corners of his mouth and normally made him look like a fat, friendly uncle—"crap," he concluded. "With all due respect."

No one said anything. Adam looked at his colleagues. Six of

the most experienced investigators in Norway sat around the table and did not look up, instead playing with a cup or fiddling with eyeglasses. Lars Kirkeland appeared to be deeply engrossed in his doodles. Only Sigmund Berli looked up. His face was red and distressed, and he looked as if he was about to stand up. Instead, he put up his hand, as if he was asking permission to speak.

"Is it not worth a try? I mean, we're in deadlock as it is! If you ask me, this is—"

"No one is asking you," the boss said. "Enough has been said. Lars has given a detailed report of the investigation so far. Everyone here knows that there is no . . . hocus-pocus in police work. Meticulousness, people. Patience. No one knows better than we do that hard work and the systematic processing of all new evidence is the only way to go. We are a modern organization, but not so modern that we would throw weeks of intensive, good police work out the window because some woman feels and thinks and believes that maybe she knows."

"That's my wife you're talking about," Adam said in a level voice. "And I will not allow you to call her 'some woman.'"

"Johanne is just some other woman," the boss said, equally calm. "In this context, that is what she is. I apologize if my choice of words offends you. I have the greatest respect for your wife, and I am fully aware of how useful she was in that kidnapping case a few years ago. And that is one of the reasons why I have"—he passed his hand over his scalp again. The thin strands of hair looked like they'd been drawn on his head—"been tolerant," he said, "of your somewhat dubious handling of case documents. But the case is very different now."

"Different!" Sigmund spluttered. "We know nothing. Not a damn thing! What Lars just presented was actually an endless string of technical findings that lead absolutely nowhere and tactical analyses that basically mean only one thing: we have no idea where to look! Jesus, we—"

He stopped himself.

"Sorry," he said feebly. "But listen—"

The boss raised his hand.

"No," he said. "The last thing we need now is more criticism in the press. If we go after this Wencke Berger . . ."

He peered into the wastepaper basket as if the crime writer was in there, together with her name written in red felt-tip pen.

"If we even look in her direction, all hell will break loose. She's becoming extremely popular, as far as I can see. I saw her on TV twice yesterday, and according to NRK's previews, she's the main guest on *First and Last* tonight."

He sucked in through his teeth. The sound was annoying. Then he smacked his tongue and twirled his mustache with his thumb and forefinger.

"And if, God forbid, there is any truth in this hypothesis of yours," he added, looking at Adam, "in this absurd, spaced-out theory based on old lectures and boredom, then the woman's a hard nut to crack."

"Therefore, it's better not to try," Adam said and looked straight back at him.

"Spare me your sarcasm."

"But you'd rather have three unsolved murders than a fuss in the press," Adam said and shrugged his shoulders. "Fine by me."

The head of NCIS stroked his immense belly. Stuck his thumb in under his tight belt. Sucked through his teeth again. Hoisted up his pants, which immediately slipped back down to the crevice below his gut.

"Okay," he said eventually. "I'll give you two weeks. Three. For three weeks, you are absolved from doing anything other than finding out Wencke Berger's movements around the times of the murders. And only that. Do you hear?"

Adam nodded.

"No other capers. No digging around in other parts of her life. I don't want any trouble. Okay? Find out if her alibi does have any cracks. And my tip is, start with the last murder. With Hå-vard Stefansen. She was certainly close by when he was killed."

Adam nodded again.

"If I hear *one* word that that woman is being investigated"— his face was beet red now, and the sweat was shining on his fore-head—"from anyone other than the people around this table, who"—his fat little hand slammed down onto the table—"are damn well going to keep their mouths shut about this"—he took a deep breath and let it out between clenched teeth—"I will be very angry," he concluded at last. "And you know what that means."

They all nodded like eager schoolboys.

"And you," the boss pointed at Sigmund, "if you absolutely must be Adam's squire, that's fine by me. Three weeks. And not a day more. Otherwise, the investigation continues as before, Lars. The meeting is closed."

The chairs scraped on the floor. Someone opened a window. Someone else laughed. Sigmund grinned and gestured that he had to go to his office to make a phone call.

"Adam," the boss said and pulled him to one side as the room emptied.

"Yes?"

"I don't like that last case," he said quietly.

"Håvard Stefansen?"

"No, the last case in that old lecture. The one that hasn't happened yet. The fire. The policeman's house getting burned down."

Adam didn't answer. He just blinked and looked out the window, distracted.

"I've asked Oslo police to do a few extra rounds," the boss continued. "At night. To Haugesvei."

"Thank you," Adam said and held out his hand. "Thank you. We've moved the kids to their grandparents'."

"Good," muttered the boss and made as if to leave.

But for a short second he hesitated, with Adam's hand in his.

"And that's not because I believe in this profile of yours," he said. "It's just a precaution. Okay?"

"Okay," Adam said in earnest.

"And," the boss continued and whipped the cigar case from Adam's breast pocket. "I'll take this. Please stop smoking in your office. I get such a chewing out from Health and Safety."

"Okay," Adam said again, but this time with a broad smile.

He had imagined that it would be more glamorous. Maybe not quite Hollywood, with the stars' names glittering on their doors, but an aura of something special. There was nothing special about the puce-colored room at the top of a long staircase, with tepid coffee in a thermos and tea bags in a paper cup. There were two benchlike sofas along one wall, where five people sat waiting for something. Adam had no idea what function they had. They weren't famous, and they did nothing. Sat there in sloppy clothes drinking coffee while they looked at the clock, constantly. Just below the ceiling in the corner was a monitor in which he could see the studio. People with headsets wandered backward and forward as if they had all the time in the world.

"Hi," he mumbled to two uniformed policemen who were standing by the stairs, looking out for whoever approached.

As security had been stepped up in connection with all NRK's activities, it had been easy to gain access to the studio. He only needed to show his ID to the young man down in reception, and he was pointed in the right direction. He nodded and smiled, but no one seemed to notice. Some of them were talking, while the others ran in and out of the room. The chair opposite the monitor was empty. Adam sat down and grabbed a paper so that he wouldn't look completely lost.

"Adam Stubo," said a voice, and someone touched his shoulder.

He turned toward the voice and then got up.

"Wencke Berger," he said.

"I get the impression you're following me," she said and smiled.

"Not at all. Just tighter security measures."

He waved his hand in the direction of the two policemen.

"Well, that certainly is tight security measures," she said and straightened her glasses. "Using an experienced and respected homicide investigator as security during the recording of a light entertainment program is impressive. But perhaps not the best use of resources?"

She was still smiling. Her voice was friendly, almost teasing. But he caught a look behind her glasses that made him straighten up.

"We have to use what we've got, you know."

He was sweating, so he took off his coat.

"These days," he added.

He threw his coat over the back of the chair he had just gotten up from.

"These days," she repeated. "What sort of days are they?"

"A murderer on the loose," he said.

"Or several," she smiled. "As far as I can tell, you aren't even sure if it's one and the same man."

"I'm sure," he answered. "One man. Or woman for that matter. Not to be sexist. These days."

Her cheeks split into dimples, from her eyes to her jaw.

"Better to be on the safe side," she nodded.

She didn't want to go. The anchorman came up the stairs, greeted everyone, had his nose powdered again by a sprightly young girl, then disappeared into the studio. Wencke Berger didn't move. Her eyes were locked onto Adam's face.

"Nice pin you've got there," he said with deliberation.

"This one?" She patted her lapel without looking at it. "Bought it in a secondhand shop in New York."

"It's got a special history," he said.

"Yes," she nodded. "That's why I bought it."

"So you know . . . you know why the laurels have been replaced with—"

"Eagle feathers? The Chief, of course!"

Her laughter was soft and dark. The chatter in the room had died down, as if their conversation fascinated more than just the two of them.

"The Chief?" Adam asked. "Do you know him?"

"Warren Scifford? No. That would be an exaggeration. I know of him, naturally. Have probably read everything he's written. I once had the pleasure of meeting him. At St. Olaf College. In Minnesota. I followed a series of lectures there. I'm sure he wouldn't remember me. But it's impossible to forget Warren Scifford."

She looked down at the pin at last. Stroked it with a stubby finger.

"Ask your wife," she said lightly without looking up. "Warren is a man you never forget."

Everything was spinning for Adam. His head felt light, he put his hand to his throat, and tried to swallow.

"But . . . know?" he stuttered incoherently.

She looked at the ceiling as if she was savoring her last words.

"No," she replied.

Then she leaned toward him. Her face was barely a hand's breadth from his.

"What are you doing here, Stubo? Truthfully, I mean?"

It was uncomfortably quiet. The makeup girls' chat from the adjoining room filled the stillness with a slight hum. Her eyes were darker now, almost black behind the clear lenses of her glasses. He noticed that she had a fleck on her iris, a white patch that was eating into her left eye; he couldn't see anything but the yellowish-white defect in Wencke Berger's staring eye.

"We have to go in now," whispered a woman wearing big headphones and holding a timetable under her arm. "We're going on air."

Wencke Berger straightened up and pushed her bangs away from her face; they fell down again.

"Are you coming?" asked the production assistant and pulled her by the arm.

"There are lots of Norwegians at St. Olaf," said Wencke Berger without showing any sign of moving. "And people of Norwegian descent. Maybe that's why—"

"I'm sorry, but we really must—"

The production assistant put her hand on her arm. Wencke took three slow steps backward.

"Perhaps that's why Warren always ends his lectures by saying—"

"Come," said the woman with the headphones, obviously annoyed now.

"That Johanne Vik is the best profiler he's ever met. Or maybe it's just true."

Then she disappeared into the studio. The heavy steel door swung slowly shut behind her.

"Is everything okay, sir?" the younger policeman asked. He seemed worried and offered Adam a glass of water. "Detective Inspector? Is everything . . ."

But the detective inspector was glued to the monitor. The titles were rolling, a hare and a tortoise danced around in a psychedelic labyrinth and forced Adam to lean against a chair for support. The host appeared on the floor to enthusiastic applause from the carefully primed studio audience.

Wencke Berger sat down.

Her suit was deep red.

The host laughed at something she said. Adam wasn't listening. He was staring at a small pin that was nearly invisible on the screen. Only every now and then the metal would flash in the studio lights when the author moved, when she leaned forward as the host did. They exchanged confidences in front of a million viewers, and Adam heard nothing until the fair-haired man asked, "And what did you do down there? On the Riviera, I mean, in the middle of winter."

"I've been writing," she said. "I'm working on a novel about a crime writer who starts killing people because she's bored."

Everyone laughed. They laughed in the studio, a vibration, a rumbling over the floor. They laughed in the small room where Adam was standing, laughed long and loud, and the host laughed longest and loudest.

"You can say what you like," Wencke Berger concluded when things quieted down. She put her hand on the man's thigh, soft and maternal. "If there's anyone who knows what there is to know about murder, it's us. And what's more"—she smiled and finished—"we know how to get away with it."

"God damn it, Adam. That's some story."

In a house in Sagveien, just behind the old mills by the Aker River, a good fire was burning in the brick fireplace. It was late at night. Adam was leaning back in a deep wing chair. When he closed his eyes, he could hear the waterfall at Mølla, where the river roared toward the fjord some miles further south, swollen by the spring thaw. Outside the windows, it was dark and wet. Inside it was warm and sleepy.

Adam had told the story that he wasn't supposed to tell.

"Yes," he said. "It's quite a tale."

The other man got up and came back with two glasses from the kitchen. Adam could hear the ice cubes clinking.

"Here," said Bjørn Busk as he handed him a generous glass of whiskey before putting another log on the fire and sitting down in the other chair. "Is Johanne at home alone?"

"No, she's staying with her parents. But only for one night. She has this idea that Wencke Berger knows where we are at any given time, so she doesn't want to stay in the same place as the kids. It's the two of us the woman is after. Not the children. We'll stay at home. Kristiane will stay with Isak for a while, and Johanne's mother will look after Ragnhild, at night that is. God knows how long we can stand it."

Bjørn Busk put his feet on an ottoman and took a sip of whiskey.

"You're absolutely convinced," he said thoughtfully.

"That she's out to get us? No. But I am one hundred percent certain that she killed Victoria Heinerback, Vegard Krogh, and Håvard Stefansen. And I've never actually"—he stopped and stared at the light playing in the amber drink—"said that before," he finished. "That I'm certain that she's guilty. In a case that is chemically cleansed of evidence."

"I'm glad you said that yourself," Bjørn Busk smiled. "Because as far as I can tell, there's nothing to give reasonable cause for suspicion."

"Which is why I've come to you. In the middle of the night. Without calling."

"No problem. After Sara moved out—"

"I'm so sorry, Bjørn. I should've gotten in touch when I heard. I should've—"

"Forget it. That's life. We all run around. Are busy. Have enough with our lives without having to get involved in other people's problems. I'm fine, Adam. In a way . . . I've gotten over it. And I really appreciate your coming here tonight."

Bjørn Busk smiled and put down his glass on the small table between them. He was a big man, the same age as Adam. They had been friends ever since they went into their first classroom together in 1962, with short hair and blue bags slung over their narrow, suntanned shoulders.

"It could be said," he mused, "that our criminal justice system doesn't really take account of motiveless murders. If there is no real evidence or it's weak, we tend to build on the motive. I've never quite seen it like that before, but"—he took a drink. A deep furrow appeared in his brow—"as normal citizens have to be protected from arbitrary interference by the authorities, by setting standards for reasonable doubt before an actual investigation can be instigated—"

"Enough, that's all a bit legal, Bjørn. The point is that if we can't find a motive, we can't do a damn thing. Unless of course the murderer is caught with a knife dripping with blood, his pants down, or by three witnesses with cameras."

"Perhaps a bit extreme, the way you put it. But yes, that's roughly what I meant."

They chuckled. Then it was quiet.

"You're asking me to do something that's actually illegal," Bjørn said.

Adam opened his mouth to protest.

"Not illegal," ran through his mind. "I'm just asking you to stretch the limits a bit. To look through your fingers. Take a chance, that's all. In the name of justice."

"Yes," he said instead. "I guess I am."

"There are no grounds for compulsory disclosure. Absolutely none whatsoever. Or for disclosure at all, for that matter."

"Without a court order, I won't have a chance of checking her account," Adam said. He could feel the heat from the whiskey burning his cheeks. "And without checking her account, I haven't got a chance in hell of finding out where she was when the murders took place."

"Couldn't you just ask her?"

Bjørn peered at him over the top of his glasses.

"Ask her . . . hah!"

"If you can check her account, I mean. Not about where she was. From your description of her, it wouldn't surprise me if she said yes. Your story is about a woman who wants to be seen. Who wants you to get a glimpse of her, out of reach, but still . . . there. Present. Like a fairy in the woods. If you've seen one, you'll swear on your life that they exist. But you can never prove it."

The wood crackled on the fire. Every now and then the flames flared up with blue tongues. The hint of burnt resin mingled with the smell of the malt whiskey—tar and burnt bark. Bjørn reached for a wooden box on the shelf and opened the lid.

"Take one," he said, and Adam felt his eyes go moist.

"Thank you," he said. "Thank you."

They prepared their cigars in silence. Adam struck a match and had to hold back a sigh of sleepy pleasure.

"You should know that Wencke Berger," he said and then blew a smoke ring up toward the ceiling, "has thought of everything. I don't know whether we could get anything from her account statements. Probably not. Judging by what she's managed so far, she will have thought about that. She's sharp, and she knows her stuff. It would be unbelievable if she hadn't covered all her tracks, even the electronic ones. But if she hasn't . . ."

He put the cigar in his mouth. The dry, fine tobacco stuck to his lips. The smoke was mild and almost felt cool against his palate.

"If, contrary to expectation, she has overlooked such an important thing, it will only be because she hasn't overlooked it."

He laughed and looked at the short, fat cigar.

"Then it would be part of the game. She is so sure, so utterly convinced that we will never find anything to nail her with, that she feels safe. She knows that we can't get access without her permission. Or get a court order on the basis of reasonable doubt. We have neither. And she knows it."

Bjørn pushed the ashtray over to him.

"I have to have that order," Adam said and knocked his cigar on the edge of the ashtray. "I know it's a lot to ask. But you have to understand that . . ."

The wind had changed. It was a westerly now. The rain had been replaced by sleet. A flash of lightning illuminated the garden. The naked trees were visible for a moment, sharp with flat shadows, like an unsuccessful photograph. The thunder followed a few seconds later.

"Thunder and lightning at this time of year," muttered Bjørn. "A bit early, isn't it? And when it's so cold?"

"You're a judge," Adam said and puffed on his cigar. "You've been in the judicial system for . . . how long?"

"Eighteen years. Plus two as an associate lawyer. That's twenty years."

"Twenty years. And have you ever, in all those years, come face to face with . . . evil? I don't mean situational madness, a kind of materially determined opportunism. I don't mean wretchedness, character disorders, or egoism. I mean pure, genuine evil. Have you ever come across it?"

"Does it exist?"

"Yes."

They drank in silence. The smoke lay like a comfortable, scented blanket under the ceiling.

"Do you have anyone who can submit a request?" Bjørn asked.

"What else do we have young, easily manipulated lawyers for . . ."

They smiled without looking at each other.

"Make sure it gets to the courts on Wednesday," Bjørn Busk said. "Not before and not after. Then it will be certain to end up on my desk. But I'm not promising anything."

"Thank you," Adam said and made a move to get up.

"Can't you stay for a while?" Bjørn asked. "Sit down. We've got whiskey in our glasses, and this box is full."

He tapped the wooden lid with his fingers. Adam leaned back in the chair. He put his feet on the ottoman in between them.

"If you insist," he said and shut his eyes. "If you dare to have me here."

"It's pouring rain," Bjørn Busk replied. "The house won't burn down tonight."

SEVENTEEN

There was some satisfaction in the fact that they were frightened.

She had seen their fear, even though she no longer bothered to check that often. Every evening about seven, they carried the youngest child to the car and drove a couple of miles to Johanne's childhood home. The strange one, who always carried a fire engine around with her that she should have outgrown years ago, was staying with her father. She often came to visit them in Haugesvei, but as far as Wencke Berger could make out, she never slept there.

Not that it really mattered.

Things had changed.

Everything.

It was Sunday, March 21, and she was puttering about in the apartment, cleaning. She had been busy recently. Not only was she working hard on her manuscript, but the interviews and TV appearances took time. She had barely been home in the last couple of days, except to change clothes. And they were now strewn over chairs in the living room and on the bedroom floor.

Old friends had suddenly reappeared. Not that they were any more interesting, but they had at least changed their attitude, which basically meant very little. She couldn't be bothered with everyone who came back to knock on her door, enthused by all the attention Wencke Berger was now getting.

The most important thing was that she was being taken seriously at last. She was an expert. Not on fiction, but on reality. She was no longer the epitome of commercialism and an easy read, the trademark of culture in decline. Now she was in the opposition, a skeptic, someone who was critical of the authorities and an eloquent debater.

She was barely recognizable. Even to herself.

She stopped in the bathroom. Looked at herself in the mirror. She looked older. That must be the weight loss. She no longer had crow's-feet only when she smiled; the wrinkles now followed her cheekbones as if the skin on her face was slightly too heavy.

It didn't matter. Age instilled her analyses with authority, gave substance to all the comments she was now asked to give and gave happily. No longer just about the serial killings, but also the disappearance in Vestlandet, a nasty rape case in Trondheim, and a sensational bank robbery in Stavanger. Wencke Berger was the expert that everyone wanted to hear from.

And it was Fiona Helle's murder that had started it all.

Wencke Berger opened the drawer of new makeup. She wasn't used to it. She tried to put mascara on her short lashes.

She missed.

The thought of Fiona Helle always made her hands shaky. She tried to breathe normally and turned on the faucet. Cold water running over her wrists helped to clear her head.

She hadn't really felt any pleasure when she read about the murder, what now seemed like a lifetime ago. At the time, her feeling was closer to rage, a liberating rage, against the victim. She remembered the evening remarkably well. It was a Wednesday evening in January. The smell of asphalt hung in the air, as the road above the house had been repaired. She was restless but couldn't do anything other than move from chair to chair in front of the panorama window with a view of the bay and Cap Ferrat.

The appalling Internet connection had nearly prevented her from surfing the day's papers in Norway. When she finally did log on, she stayed up all night.

Something happened.

Whereas previously she had been irritated and on occasion provoked, this time she was overwhelmed by rage.

Fiona Helle sold other people's lives for her own fame and fortune. The show was an affront to her, Wencke Berger, with all its life lies and biology. It was she who Fiona Helle spat on every time she entertained the viewers with vulnerable people's dreams in her one-hour, lightweight program; the dreams that were once Wencke Berger's dreams, though she had never dared to admit it.

"I must learn how to do this," Wencke Berger thought as she pulled the mascara brush from the sticky black contents of the silver cylinder. "I'm not old yet. I still have a lot to do, and I'm changing. I'm no longer just an observer, I am being observed. I must learn to look good."

Ten years ago, when her true history had come to light on an aging document, she was already paralyzed. She was on the verge of becoming invisible. She didn't belong anywhere. No one wanted to know her. She wrote books that everyone read but no one admitted to reading. Her father was a parasite, he wanted money, money, money. Her false mother barely spoke to her and couldn't understand what she called "Wencke's horrible scribblings."

Her real mother, the woman who gave birth to her in pain

and then died, would have been proud of her. She would have loved her in spite of her heavy body, her unattractive face, and her increasingly closed nature.

Her mother would have kept all her novels in the bookshelves in the living room, and maybe had a scrapbook with press clippings.

She couldn't face finding out more. Wencke Berger knew nothing about the woman who had died twenty minutes after her daughter was born. Instead, she started to catalog other people's lives. She became a better author.

And grew more and more invisible.

She didn't care about the world, just as the world obviously did not care about her.

But that was then. Not now.

It was a waste of time trying to put on makeup. Her hands felt too big; she wasn't used to the tiny brush in the eyeshadow compact. The lipstick was too brazen, too red.

It smelled of asphalt, she remembered, that evening in Villefranche. Wet, soft tar mixed with the brine of the sea and rain. She went to bed at dawn but couldn't sleep. Somewhere in her head was a thought that kept evading her. It took a week before she grasped it. All these years, she had thought, all these years of futile work that had given her nothing but money and dissatisfaction. Then there it was, right in front of her, a shining new opportunity. All the preparations were made. She could just begin. Fiona Helle's tongue had been cut out and beautifully wrapped. Wencke Berger smiled coldly when she read that; she laughed furiously and remembered another case, from another world, six years ago. She remembered a man with intense eyes, extreme energy, and fascinating stories, remembered how she had moved closer and closer to the front with every lecture, with questions and observant comments. He gave her a fleeting smile and then bent down over an elegant brunette, quoting Longfellow, and winked. Wencke Berger gave him a book with a respectful dedication in the front. He left it behind on the desk. In the evenings she followed him; he went to the pub where he was boisterous and told stories, surrounded by women who took turns taking him home.

She was already too old then. She was invisible, and he bragged about Johanne Vik.

All this came back to her, and she realized what she should do. She would no longer wait for something that would never happen. She would be the one who made it happen.

And she had succeeded.

And now she had to learn to put makeup on, to display her new self. She just had to stop thinking about the past so much, getting so emotional.

Forget Fiona Helle!

Wencke Berger closed the drawer in the bathroom and went into the bedroom. She picked up clothes on the way. Her wardrobe was steadily expanding. She shopped regularly, nearly every week; she was no longer afraid of asking sales clerks for advice.

More than a hundred people's lives were stored in the filing cabinet by the wall. She stroked the ice-cold door handle. Put her finger on the lock. Leaned against the solid weight of steel.

People's good and bad habits, rhythms, desires, and needs had been noted, analyzed and cataloged. Wencke Berger knew them better than they knew themselves; she was clinically neutral, the cold observer. She knew enough about over a hundred people to be able to disguise them lightly and then kill them with pen and paper. She knew their lives inside out. When she woke up that sunny January morning in Villefranche and decided to make fiction real, she had plenty to choose from.

She knew, both then and now, that she should select ran-

domly. Arbitrary victims were the safest. But the temptation
was too great. Victoria Heinerback had always irritated her,
though she never really knew why. The most important thing
was that she could be taken for a racist. Everything had to fit.
Johanne Vik had to have a chance of understanding. If not after
the first murder, then later.

And Rudolf Fjord would tumble in any case.

He was pathetic.

Wencke Berger opened the metal cabinet. Found a file.
Read. She smiled at how good her memory was, how easy it
was to recall all she had seen and written down.

Rudolf Fjord was despicable. He wouldn't survive if the police turned a searchlight on his life. If he didn't fall on one
count, there were plenty of others that would nail him. His file
was almost as extensive as Johanne Vik's. For a while she considered choosing him as her first victim. But then she decided
against it. That would be too easy. Rudolf Fjord would self-
destruct on his own.

She was right. He couldn't ride out a storm.

Wencke Berger closed the file. She pulled out another, much
thinner, studied the name but didn't open it. A moment later
she put it back and locked the cabinet.

Vegard Krogh deserved to die. She could hardly bear the
thought of him. Now he was gone.

Wencke Berger went into the living room. It was neater
now. Some flowers had been standing for a few days too many
and were giving off a potent smell; she had been given them by
the committee of the Students' Association for taking part in a
debate on chemical castration.

She opened the balcony door. The cold air caressed her face;
it felt like it was wiping away all the wrinkles she had just been
examining in the mirror.

For some reason, she couldn't quite come to terms with having sacrificed that whore in Stockholm. One prostitute more or less on Brunkebergs Torg was, of course, neither here nor there. But there had been a kind of bond between them. Maybe it was the physical likeness. It hadn't taken long to find her; whores come in most colors and shapes. The woman was large despite her obviously meager diet. Her hair was curly and dry. Even her glasses, which were so exclusive that they must have been stolen, were like hers.

And the woman fell for it.

She hadn't run away with the credit card. She could have spent as much as she liked before the card was cancelled, then disappeared. But she had believed the promise that she would get lots of cash in return for doing what she was asked: to eat a good meal. Take a taxi. Buy something in a kiosk or two and be back at the hotel just before midnight. Be seen, but not say a word.

When they met again the next morning, the prostitute was almost happy. She was clean. She had eaten well. Had a good night's sleep in a warm bed, with no customers.

Of course she didn't get the money.

As expected she threatened to go to the police; she was smart enough to realize there was something suspicious about the offer she'd been made. As expected, she didn't do anything before injecting the heroin that Wencke Berger had given her, a gesture of goodwill in return for her work well done.

As expected, she died of an overdose.

Now she was dead, cremated and no doubt laid to rest in an unmarked grave.

Wencke Berger stood on the balcony and frowned at the thought of the dead whore. Then she lifted her face to the sky and decided never to give her another thought.

A light rain started to fall. It smelled of spring in Oslo, exhaust fumes and rotting garbage.

Håvard Stefansen's death was simply a necessity. Johanne Vik had disappointed her; she didn't understand the pattern. She had to make it clearer, and Wencke Berger finally stepped into the spotlight.

And she stayed there.

People recognized her on the street now. They smiled at her, and some people asked for her autograph. One of the tabloids had run a three-page profile of the crime expert and international best seller writer in its Saturday magazine: Wencke Berger, photographed at her computer in her chaotic study, in front of a large, beautifully set dining table with a raised glass, on her balcony with a view over the town, smiling at the photographer. She'd had help from a stylist with the makeup.

She hadn't let them into the bedroom.

She went back into the living room. The smell of the flowers was nauseating. She took the vase into the kitchen. Emptied out the water and put the flowers in a plastic bag.

The book would soon be finished.

At the bottom of her cabinet, where it wouldn't be found until she died, lay the most important file. On the cover, in big, regular capital letters, she had written ALIBIS.

For seventeen years, she had studied and researched. A good alibi was a prerequisite for a successful crime, the very foundation of a good thriller. She created and constructed, considered and discarded. The file grew slowly. Before she went to France, she had counted. Thirty-four documents. Thirty-four plausible alibis. She had already used some of them; others lay waiting for a new book, a more suitable story. None of them were perfect, because there was no such thing as a perfect alibi.

But her constructions were very, very good.

Three of them could never be used in a book.

They had been put to better use.

As they were not perfect, they kept her alive and on her toes.

Every morning she felt that thrilling fear. When the doorbell rang, when the phone rang, when a stranger stopped on the other side of the street, looked twice, and then crossed the road toward her, she felt the fear; she was reminded of how valuable life had become.

On the way out to throw the flowers down the garbage chute, she stopped and hesitated. The book she had taken from Victoria Heinerback's bedroom was in the shoe closet in the hall. She had looked at it only last night. Felt the pages, felt the excitement of touching the paper that the young politician had taken to bed with her, read on the bus; maybe she had even sneaked a few pages during boring plenary sessions and the endless waiting around in the Storting.

It was Rudolf Fjord's copy.

She wanted to throw it away. She snatched it up and dropped it down the chute with the flowers. She stood there listening to the sound of the heavy book banging on metal, duller and duller until it ended in a muffled, nearly inaudible thump.

Someone might find it. Someone might wonder what a book belonging to Rudolf Fjord was doing in the garbage room of the apartment house where Wencke Berger lived and wrote. She hadn't destroyed it, hadn't torn out the page with the owner's name on it. She could have burned the book or thrown it away somewhere else.

But there wouldn't be any excitement in that.

Wencke Berger lived on a continuous high. She had thrown herself off the highest cliff.

"Three weeks," Sigmund Berli said. "Our three weeks are up."

"Yes," Adam Stubo replied. "And we've got nothing. Nothing at all."

On the desk in front of him, there were two piles of printouts. One contained statements from Wencke Berger's three accounts from the period from January 1 to March 2, when Håvard Stefansen was murdered. The other was an itemized log from the phone company.

"When Victoria Heinerback was killed," Adam said, "Wencke Berger was in Stockholm. Just as she's said in several of these"—he kicked a pile of newspapers and magazines on the floor—"stupid interviews. About how shocked she was when she read about the murder, how . . . She's so damned cunning."

For three weeks, Sigmund and Adam had worked alone. They had gotten a court order for compulsory disclosure on the basis of a creatively modified and in part false petition. And since then, they had worked day and night, looked at Wencke Berger's every move under a magnifying glass, only going home to change and get a few hours of unsettled sleep before returning to the painstaking work of reconstructing the woman's life by studying her money withdrawals, phone calls, and where she had surfed the Internet.

Wencke Berger was well off but spent surprisingly little money. She had renewed her wardrobe just before coming home, but even around Christmas, her spending was absurdly low. She seldom called anyone and was hardly ever contacted by anyone other than her various publishers in Europe. She hadn't spoken to her father since before Christmas.

She told the papers that she'd had a meeting with her publishers in Stockholm, a quick trip to plan the autumn's book launch and a tour. Sigmund called and pretended to be a journalist; he fished for confirmation of the meeting. He was disturbingly unaffected by the growing number of lies they had to tell. Adam, on the other hand, was deeply affected. Not only were they pushing the limits of what was permissible, they were doing the opposite of everything he had learned and stood for in his years with the police.

Wencke Berger had become an obsession.

They had spent a week trying to work out the different ways in which she could have gotten from Stockholm to Oslo on February 6. They had juggled with possible times, studied maps, and combed the passenger lists that Sigmund had managed to extract from the various carriers using charm, threats, and lies. At night they tramped around in the corridors, sticking yellow Post-it notes on the walls, with times on them. Tried moving them closer together. Tried to find holes and weak points, a tiny opening in the solid wall of impossible times in Wencke Berger's bank statements.

"Just can't get it to work," Sigmund had concluded at around four o'clock every morning. "I just can't get it to work."

She had checked in at the hotel at three in the afternoon. Bought something in a kiosk at seventeen minutes past five. She took a taxi just before seven in the evening. At twenty-five to twelve, roughly the time that Victoria Heinerback was murdered in her home in Lørenskog, Wencke Berger had paid a substantial amount for a meal at a restaurant near the Dramaten theater in the center of Stockholm.

One morning, after working for sixteen hours with no results, Sigmund got on a plane to Stockholm in a rage. He came back that afternoon defeated; the night porter was absolutely certain that he had seen Wencke Berger returning to the hotel at around midnight on the night in question. He had nodded at the picture Sigmund showed him. No, they hadn't spoken, but he seemed to remember that the woman in room 237 had gotten some ice from the machine in the reception area. It had something wrong with it, so he had to mop up the water on the floor after she'd gone. She had also dropped some clothes into the laundry that afternoon, and when he left them outside her door first thing the next morning, he heard loud music coming from the room.

She had checked out at around ten o'clock.

The only thing that was odd about Wencke Berger's trip to Stockholm was that she'd splurged on herself, which was very unusual.

Otherwise, everything was just as it should be. Adam and Sigmund had given their all and gotten nothing in return. The deadline had passed.

"What do we do now?" Sigmund asked quietly.

"Yes, what do we . . ."

Adam played with the statements. When Vegard Krogh was killed, Wencke Berger was apparently in France. Two days earlier, she'd withdrawn a substantial amount from her account and then didn't touch it for four days. The next transaction was in a fishmonger's in the Old Town in Nice.

Sigmund and Adam had been encouraged by this unaccounted-for period and spent several days investigating it. Theoretically it was possible for her to have gotten to and from Norway using the cash. But her name did not appear on any of the passenger lists, nor was it registered with any of the car rental firms in Nice.

It was harder to get hold of the lists from Stockholm. She could easily have stolen a car. After three weeks' intensive work in the office, the only thing the two investigators knew was what they had been convinced of to begin with: Wencke Berger had been in Oslo when the murders happened.

But they didn't know how she'd managed it.

They could keep on looking, investigating further.

That's what they should do. That's what they both wanted to do.

But to do that, it could not be official.

Their deadline was already past, and their colleagues had

begun to make fun of them. They grinned when Adam and Sigmund came to lunch, pale and drawn. They sat by themselves and ate in silence.

When Håvard Stefansen was killed, Wencke Berger had been sitting at her computer, working, one floor below. She had given her witness statement, and a very detailed one at that. Hadn't seen or heard anything unusual, she was so engrossed in her work. She had been on the Internet for several hours, trying to find out more about South American spiders. It was only when she went to take her suitcases up to the loft, after her prolonged stay abroad, that she noticed the open door, stuck her head into the foyer of the apartment, and discovered the body. Then she called the police. The story was consistent with the phone company's log. It could hardly be called an alibi, but it didn't give them anything to go on, either.

And Wencke Berger blossomed. She was everywhere, and there was great anticipation about her new novel coming out in the fall.

Adam stood up abruptly. He gathered all the papers and stacked them together as one great document.

"We've lost," he declared and threw the pile into a box for shredding.

He stroked his hand over his head and added, "Wencke Berger has won. The only thing we have, after all these weeks of hard work, is proof that . . ." He laughed, quietly and reluctantly; he didn't want to finish the sentence.

"That the woman is innocent," Sigmund concluded slowly. "We've worked day and night for three weeks without proving anything other than that . . . the woman's innocent. We have proven Wencke Berger's innocence!"

"That is precisely what we have done," Adam said and gave a long yawn. "And that's exactly what she intended. She knew this would happen. And you . . ."

He came around the desk. For a moment he stood looking hard at Sigmund, who had lost weight. His face was still round. His chin was still chubby, but his clothes were too loose. The lines around his nose were clearer and deeper than before. His eyes were bloodshot, and he smelled of stale sweat when Adam gave him his hand, pulling him out of the chair.

"You are my best friend," he said and gave him a hug. "You are truly my Sancho Panza."

THURSDAY, JUNE 4, 2004

─────────────── ⚘ ───────────────

Summer was just around the corner.

April and May had been and gone, and the weather had been unusually warm and sunny. The leaves on the trees and flowers had sprung early this year, making spring hell on earth for people with allergies. The crown princes of Denmark and Spain had both gotten married. Preparations were under way in Portugal for the European Cup, and the Athenians were working against the clock to get ready for the Olympic Games in August. The world had been shocked by the abuse of prisoners in Abu Ghraib, but only enough for a few photographs to make the front pages of newspapers in Norway. The historical expansion of the European Union to the east didn't cause much of a stir either in the small, rich country on the periphery of the Continent. People were more interested in the prolonged transportation strike, which had resulted in empty shelves in stores and fights over toilet paper and diapers. Rosenborg won match after match in the football league series, and the revised national budget was passed without any political drama. If you looked carefully, you could still sometimes find the odd article about the unsolved murders of Victoria Heinerback, Vegard Krogh, and the biathlete Håvard Stefansen. But not often. Nothing had been written about the cases for a couple of weeks now.

A woman was sitting on a bench by the Aker River, reading the paper.

Johanne Vik had also used the spring to try to forget. She was well trained in the art. As the weeks and months passed, and nothing more happened, it became impossible to keep the children in hiding. The house in Haugesvei had been under police surveillance, but that too seemed unnecessary after a while, certainly to those responsible for the Oslo police's already strained budget. Patrol cars no longer included Haugesvei on their nightly rounds.

And no one had tried to set fire to the box-shaped, white, semidetached house where the Vik-Stubo family lived with their children and a dog and friendly neighbors.

She had just started to sleep again too. She had gotten into a daily rhythm. She went for walks.

The carriage was standing beside her. The baby was asleep, covered by a light cotton blanket. Johanne glanced up at the sky every now and then; it looked as if the good weather might be coming to an end.

She enjoyed sitting like this. She came here every day. She bought the papers at the gas station on Maridalsveien. Before she reached the bench under the willow tree, where the river took a swing between Sandaker and Bjølsen, the baby was asleep, and she had an hour to herself.

Another woman walked toward her, down the path. She was probably in her midforties. Her hair was curling in the light breeze, and she had sunglasses on.

"Johanne is so damned predictable," the woman thought to herself. "Hasn't she learned anything? She sits here every day, unless it's raining. She doesn't seem to be frightened anymore.

The children are at home again. It annoys me that I overestimated her."

"Hello," the woman said as she walked up to Johanne. "It is Johanne Vik, isn't it?"

Johanne stared at her. Wencke Berger smiled when the other woman put her arm over the carriage, her fingers splayed over the crocheted blanket.

"I've met your husband on a couple of occasions," said the author. "Is it okay if I sit down?"

Johanne didn't answer. She didn't move.

"Wencke Berger, pleased to meet you. We've got mutual acquaintances, in fact. In addition to your husband, that is."

She sat down. Her upper arm brushed Johanne's arm as she made herself comfortable, sitting confidently with her legs crossed. She bounced her upper foot.

"Terrible thing," she said and shook her head. "All those celebrity murders. I was a witness in one of the cases. Perhaps you remember. It looks as if the poor victims are forgotten already, sadly."

She nodded at the pile of papers between them.

"That's the way it goes. As long as there are no real suspects, the papers run out of things to write. And with those cases . . ."

She nodded at the papers again. Johanne sat poker-straight and paralyzed on the far end of the bench.

". . . they seem to have come to a dead end. The police, I mean. Strange. Apparently there's no leads. They simply have nothing to go on."

Johanne Vik had finally managed to pull herself together. She tried to get to her feet while clinging onto the carriage and picking up a bag full of baby stuff.

"Wait," Wencke Berger said in a friendly voice and gripped her arm. "Can't you stay for a while? Just a few minutes. We have so much in common. There's so much I'd like to tell you."

"Is it curiosity that keeps her sitting here," she wondered, "or won't her legs carry her?"

Johanne sat still, with the bag on her lap and her arm protecting her daughter.

Wencke Berger sat up straight on the bench and turned her head toward the younger woman.

"Have you ever suspected anyone other than me?" she asked, still friendly.

"She's not answering. She has no idea what to say. She's not curious anymore. She's frightened. Why doesn't she scream? What would she scream?"

"I received this letter."

Wencke Berger pulled out a folded sheet from her back pocket. She unfolded it and flattened it over her knee.

"Notification of compulsory disclosure," she explained. "From the court. As prescribed by law, there's also information about how to proceed if I want to complain about your husband sticking his nose in my business."

She held the letter up for a moment. Then she shook her head and put it back into her pocket.

"But I can't be bothered to. In fact, it's good for me that I've already been cleared, in the event of any later accusations. The job's done, you might say."

Her laughter was dark. She tried to tuck her hair behind her ear.

"The Stockholm trip must have puzzled you," she said before getting the letter out of her pocket again.

She took it in her right hand and scrunched it up. Then she stood up and barred the way for the carriage.

"Lovely little girl," she said and bent down over Ragnhild. "She'll have a cleft in her chin."

"Get away. Get away!"

Wencke Berger took a step back.

"I'm not going to harm her," she smiled. "I'm not going to harm anyone!"

"I have to go," Johanne Vik said and struggled with the brakes on the carriage. "I don't want to talk to you."

"Of course. I won't force you. I certainly didn't intend to distress you so. I just wanted to talk. About our shared interests and mutual . . ."

The brakes had gotten stuck. Johanne pulled the carriage down the path. The rubber wheels screeched on the asphalt. Ragnhild woke up and started to howl. Wencke Berger smiled and took off her sunglasses. Her eyes were lightly made up. They looked bigger and darker.

"She'll never go away," thought Johanne. "She'll never disappear. Not until she dies. Not until I manage to . . ."

"I've finished the book, by the way," Wencke Berger said as she sauntered along behind the carriage. "It's good. I'll send you a copy when it's printed."

Johanne stopped suddenly and opened her mouth to scream.

"Of course," Wencke Berger said, as she lifted her hands, as if to stop her. "You don't need to give me your address. I know perfectly well where you live."

Then she gave a slight nod, turned her back, and walked away down the path in the opposite direction.

POSTSCRIPT

This book opens with a quotation by Walter Benjamin. The quotation was used in Lars Fr. H. Svendsen's book *Kjedsomhetens filosofi* (*A Philosophy of Boredom*) (Universitetsforlaget 1999), which has been a great source of inspiration and help in writing *What Never Happens*.

On page 193, there is a quotation from an unnamed source: "And you're dying so slowly that you think you're alive." I am obliged to say that this is taken from the title poem in a collection of poems, *Og du dør så langsomt at du tror du lever*, by Bertrand Besigye (Gyldendal 1993).

I would like to thank Alexander Elgurén for his irrepressible enthusiasm and Randi Krogsveen for her invaluable help.

This book is for you, Tine, as all my books are.

Anne Holt

Oslo, June 18, 2004

ABOUT THE AUTHOR

ANNE HOLT is a best-selling thriller writer, with three million books sold worldwide—and a former minister of justice, lawyer, journalist, and TV editor and anchor. *What Is Mine* was her English-language debut and the first of a three-book series featuring ex-FBI profiler Vik and police detective Stubo. A former resident of the United States, Anne Holt currently resides in Norway and France.